A SUMMER WEDDING
AT THE CORNISH MANOR

A SUMMER WEDDING AT THE CORNISH MANOR

Linn B. Halton

An Aria Book

First published in the UK in 2023 by Head of Zeus Ltd,
part of Bloomsbury Publishing Plc

9 7 5 3 1 2 4 6 8

A catalogue record for this book is available from the British Library.

ISBN (PB): 9781804546468
ISBN (E): 9781804546444

Cover design: Head of Zeus

Typeset by Siliconchips Services Ltd UK

Printed and bound in Great Britain by
CPI Group (UK) Ltd, Croydon CR0 4YY

Head of Zeus Ltd
First Floor East
5–8 Hardwick Street
London EC1R 4RG

WWW.HEADOFZEUS.COM

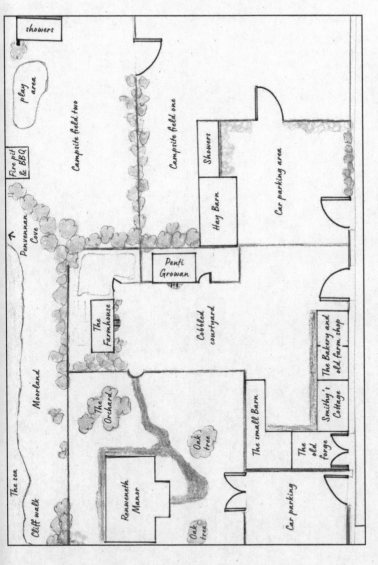

Renweneth Farm, Cornwall

showers

play area

Fire pit & BBQ

Penvennan Cove

Campsite field two

Campsite field one

Showers

Hay Barn

Car parking area

Penti Growan

The Farmhouse

Cobbled courtyard

Moorland

The Orchard

Oak tree

The Bakery and old farm shop

Smithy's Cottage

The small Barn

The old Forge

The sea

Cliff walk

Renweneth Manor

Oak tree

Car parking

'Living is easy with your eyes closed. That was me, until the day I woke up and realised it was time to spread my wings and make my dreams come true.'

The character of Jess Griffiths (née Newman)

Prologue

An intimate, get-to-know-you, real-life interview
with Jess Griffiths, who runs Renweneth Farm

By Susan Penhaligon from *A Cornish View* magazine

Susan: Thank you for taking part in our newest feature,
Jess. Everyone's journey is unique and yours is particularly
inspirational. I hear on the grapevine that from the very
first day you arrived at the farm, you embraced the
community spirit. What inspired the move from Stroud, in
Gloucestershire, to an isolated moor in Cornwall?
Jess: An age-old story many will connect with, Susan. My
world literally imploded when the man I loved broke
my heart.
Susan: I'm terribly sorry to hear that. They do say that
the range of emotions you go through is on a par with a
bereavement; there is no quick fix, and everyone's experience
is different.
Jess: Well, I can attest to that. It took nigh on eighteen
months, and involved me, and our daughter, Lola, leaving
family and friends behind to start over again. It was a huge
upheaval and I freely admit that it was a struggle at first, but
it made me reinvent myself.

Susan: They do say that every cloud has a silver lining... Have you found yours?

Jess: I like to think so (*followed by gentle laughter*). I swapped the stress of wondering why my husband fell out of love with me, for the challenge of becoming caretaker of my grandparents' farm. In that bewildering first year of sweat and toil, I not only learnt some new skills, but I also discovered a lot about who I was; my strengths and my weaknesses.

Susan: All good, I hope!

Jess: Mostly. My husband realised our relationship was over long before I could admit it to myself. Once I faced up to the truth, I felt free, and even more determined to turn Renweneth Farm into a hub for the community. I think it's important to show my daughter, Lola, that life is what you make it. Change is something to be embraced, even though it can be daunting at times.

Susan: You've certainly succeeded in putting Renweneth Farm on the map, Jess, in tandem with making a wonderful new life for you and your daughter.

Jess: We've made a good start, Susan, but it's an ongoing journey into the unknown. Every time a challenge is conquered, the next one is already waiting in the wings. I'm lucky that as our team here has grown, it's attracted hard-working, like-minded people who are totally invested in what they do.

Susan: It was an inspired idea turning an old barn into the Renweneth Farm Hub. It's been a lifeline for a wide variety of local businesses who have now found a home there. But this is a family operation still, as I hear that your granddad – Cappy – is back lending a hand.

Jess: Yes. The weekly market days have proved to be very popular too. So much so, that we're extending our car parking facilities and he's going to be managing that project. And my lifelong friend, Ivy, recently took over The Farmhouse Bakery. Opening the self-service café has turned the bakery into the beating heart of Renweneth Farm. It's a place for people to sit and chat over coffee and cake, after a leisurely browse around the wonderful stalls in The Courtyard Hub.

Susan: It's safe to say that last year ended on a high, then?

Jess: It did indeed. Family and friends – old and new – joined us for a fabulous Christmas Day celebration at Renweneth Farm Bakery. Ivy, and her husband – Adam – supported us from day one and now this is their home too.

Susan: With the worst behind you, is it time to relax a little and take some time out to enjoy your new lifestyle?

Jess: (*after a hearty chuckle*) I'm afraid not. A new year dawns and the to-do list seems endless... but do you know what? I wouldn't change a single thing because I'm an eternal optimist. Maybe you should come back in August, though, and ask me that question again.

Susan: Why August?

Jess: This is the summer that I hope everything in my life will suddenly fall into place. If we really do have the power to manifest our wildest dreams, I won't just be rolling up my sleeves as I have done, but I'll be leaving the universe in no doubt at all about what I want.

Susan: And if it doesn't turn out quite as expected?

Jess: (*there's a short pause*) I'm aiming for the moon, but I'm a realist. I guess the stars will do for now.

JANUARY

JESS

I

The Big Day is Finally Here

It's Monday the ninth of January and my granddad, Cappy, gives his great-granddaughter, Lola, a wink across the breakfast table before insisting he does the school runs today.

'That's great, Cappy.' My daughter's eyes light up. 'Don't forget we're giving Daisy a lift, too.'

A loud 'miaow' makes us all turn in the direction of the doorway, as Misty – our feline princess – announces her arrival.

'You don't like school days, do you, girl?' Lola puts her hand out and Misty eagerly trots over for an ear rub and, no doubt, a treat.

She knows exactly how gorgeous she is, with her beautiful grey and white markings and those citrine-coloured eyes, but she is a little minx. I smile to myself. If it weren't for the bell on her collar, she'd be proudly carrying in presents several times a day. She's Lola's devoted companion when she's at home and fills the empty hours when Lola's not here honing her hunting skills.

'Will there be lots of people working on Renweneth Manor today?' Lola asks, as she tucks into a plate of scrambled eggs.

'Riley, three other builders and me.'

'It's exciting, Jess,' Cappy joins in.

'I know but—'

He flashes me one of his sobering looks, raising an eyebrow. 'Don't you go worrying about the unknowns. It's an old house and we know most of the timbers are rotten. Riley intends to replace everything, and he's a man who knows what he's doing. The roofing work I had done a couple of years ago means it's watertight, so once the interior is all stripped out it's just a case of putting in new services and fitting it out again.'

Cappy makes it sound easy, but I know from poring over the plans with Riley that there's a huge amount of work to get through. Fortunately, I have the best builder in the whole wide world on board.

When Riley Warren breezed into my life last summer, I wasn't expecting him to steal my heart. As autumn approached, an easy friendship had become so much more than either of us expected. Unfortunately, his situation isn't clear-cut. Riley has an eight-year-old son he lost contact with until recently. Ollie asked his mum to reach out to his dad, but the situation is rather delicate and, for now, Riley is a part of our daily lives here but returns each night to Wind Rush Cottage, a short drive away.

I've given my handsome and caring builder-man a deadline of the beginning of August for the manor to be partially habitable. Enough for Riley, Lola and me to start our life together properly. Lola can't wait, but our happiness won't be complete until Ollie is able to join us for visits and Riley is still working on that.

The plan is to celebrate our union with a civil ceremony for our small, inner circle, to be held at Renweneth Village Hall. It will be followed by a party for friends and family here in the grounds of Renweneth Manor. There won't be a honeymoon until the manor is complete, which could take a year. Then, we hope to fly off with Lola and Ollie to travel around Italy and, as our blended family bonds, make some forever memories.

I'm hoping that before the year is out, I will have convinced Cappy to return to the farm to live for good. He left because he couldn't cope with his grief after losing Grandma. Having moved close to my parents in Stroud, it's been obvious to Mum, and me, that he's been struggling to occupy his time. It's been affecting him both mentally and physically.

The recent passing of another of his long-time friends hasn't helped, either. But as with all losses, time is a natural healer and he's the sort of man who thrives when he's active and feels needed. So, he's staying at the farmhouse for six months, taking over the role of site manager, while I'm tied up with the next round of building works.

He thinks I'll be letting out The Farmhouse once Lola and I move out, but how can I? Grandma was all about family and friends, and I can't bear to think of strangers living here. And while it took Cappy a while to walk back through the front door, when he's here, he's his old self again. Our lives are better with him in it and even if one of us is in a grump, every single day is precious.

In the meantime, I need to stay focused to drive the project forward. My intricate plan has a lot of moving parts and to say it's ambitious is an understatement. 'Only you, Jess', as my best friend Ivy often says. Sadly, life has taught me not to take anything for granted. So, I plough forward with gritted teeth, determined nothing is going to prevent my dream for us all from coming true.

'Look at the time!' I glance up at the clock. 'We'd better get a move on. Finish your breakfast, Lola, then grab your school bag and coat. Your lunch box and drink are on the island.'

'Don't worry about us – you get off, Jess.' Cappy ruffles Lola's hair as he walks past her. 'We'll sort the dishes, won't we, my sparkly girl?'

Lola nods her head enthusiastically.

'Thanks, you two. I'm off to wield a sledgehammer.'

I give them both a quick kiss on the cheek and hurry out into the hallway to grab a beanie hat, my work gloves, and pull on a hi-vis vest over my padded jacket. Bending to tie the laces on my steel-toe-capped boots, I reflect that building work isn't glamorous, but a little fizz of excitement still courses through me. It's time to turn the plan into reality.

As Lola and Cappy come to give me a good luck hug, everything in my world feels right. The thought of all those happy years Granddad spent at the farmhouse with Grandma, before the spark in her began to fade, warms my heart. At the very end of her life, we could all see that she was at peace. But the truth is that we weren't ready to face a future without her. She instinctively knew that and this is where she wanted us all to be: together at Renweneth Farm. It wouldn't be the same without his presence and it's simply a case of waiting until he realises that for himself.

After a long and tiring day, Riley and I give our hard-working team a grateful wave, as the guys all head for home. We walk back inside Renweneth Manor feeling content and I pull off my beanie hat, shaking out my hair to make me feel a bit more human. At least the dust in the air is settling a little and it's nice not wearing a mask. Riley comes closer, wrapping his arms around me and hugging me tightly.

'You certainly held your own today, Jess.' He steps back, grabbing my gloved hand. 'Come on, let's inspect our handiwork.'

We traipse up the stairs to the first floor, which is now almost entirely open plan. The outer walls are all exposed stone, but the internal walls were ripped out many years ago and replaced with panelling. Some of the wood is salvageable, but a lot is water-damaged from the leaks that went unchecked for several years.

'Don't worry, Jess. I know what you're thinking. We're smashing everything up and you feel there won't be many original features left. But we'll probably have enough usable panelling to create an updated but period feel in the sitting room and maybe even the hallway.'

I gaze around, my arm muscles still trembling from the constant reverberation of swinging the sledgehammer against the splintering wood. I'm aching all over and I can't wait to sink into a hot bubble bath.

'I'm glad we've made a start, Riley, but August seems like an eternity away. Every single day that we're not living together as a family is a day wasted… one we'll never get back again.'

Now he looks as downcast as I feel, but that wasn't my intention. We rarely acknowledge that ache that doesn't go away, because at the end of a long, hard day, we simply want to lie in each other's arms. Like any new relationship, even though we work side by side most days, it's still a journey of discovery. Past hurts, present worries and future hopes are things we're still diving into. To do that, we need alone time in a relaxing environment and the chaos of The Farmhouse isn't it.

So, late at night, we lie in our separate beds chatting on the phone, discussing our dreams for the future. And, occasionally, he spirits me away to his beautifully renovated cottage for some time together; it's enough to keep us going for now.

I'm not one for dwelling on the past because I simply don't have the time. Day to day, my biggest headache is keeping an eye on the cash flow. The business is growing fast; a lot of people are now dependent upon the farm for their livelihoods. General overheads and taxes mount up as we expand, and it's a balancing act when it's all about reinvesting the profit to secure the future.

'I know,' he replies, softly. 'Hopefully, by then Fiona will be more receptive and agree to us having some sort of regular access to Ollie. Then we'll really be a family, Jess.'

It's hard not to sigh. Riley has a lot more faith in his ex than I have. Just before Christmas last year, Ollie came to stay with Riley at his cottage for the first time. It was supposed to be a chance for the two of them to bond. It didn't turn out quite as expected when Fiona invited herself along, too. She was supposed to be dropping her son off on the Friday evening, staying overnight and returning home the next morning. She ended up staying all weekend, even though that wasn't the arrangement they'd made. Hearing about what happened after the fact did unsettle me at the time. Having had my heart broken once, I'm understandably wary. It's not that I doubt Riley's love for me, but if I had to choose between a man and my daughter... well, I just hope it doesn't come down to that for Riley and his son.

He's a good man and he has a big heart. Being a mum in a similar situation to Fiona, now that my ex-husband Ben has a significant other in his life, I totally understand her wanting to satisfy herself that Ollie was in safe hands for that first visit. Fiona didn't really know much about Riley's new life after their acrimonious split four years ago. I get that she wanted to see for herself where her son was staying.

However, it threw Riley into a bit of a panic when she invited herself to stay the second night and at breakfast, started planning out their day. What sort of signal was that sending Ollie? I can't help wondering. Riley should have put his foot down at the time, but he didn't and that threw me a little.

The following Monday, when Riley sat me down to tell me how the weekend turned out, he was clearly uncomfortable about it. It was then that I pushed him to tell Fiona about us and it's something I've come to regret. Ever since, it's either been total silence from her end, or when he has reached out hoping to at least talk to Ollie, he's received hurtful text messages suggesting that he's not putting his son's interests first.

'I do hope so, Riley. Renweneth Manor is made for family gatherings, and it'll only be special if we can all spend time there together.'

The sadness I see reflected in his eyes pulls on my heartstrings and I give Riley the biggest smile I can muster. 'Come on. Let's head back to The Farmhouse for a shower. Cappy assumed you'll be staying for dinner tonight.'

My lovely, warm-hearted man gives me one of his artful grins.

'Great, I'm starving. I'll just get some clean clothes from the van.'

Will there ever come a day when Riley can hang his clothes up here? I sigh, as we make our way downstairs. How wonderful that would be. Looking at it now, it's going to involve nothing less than a miracle to get this place into any sort of shape. There's a lot more demolition work to come before we can even begin to think about putting the manor back together again. From where I'm standing, it's not a hill we have to climb; it's a flipping mountain.

Wednesday is yoga class at The Hub Studio, and I have knots in my back and shoulders that I'm hoping will benefit from some gentle stretching. The mid-week slump I'm feeling is down to a real fear that I'll run out of steam before Friday is here. Being surrounded by four burly men working like well-oiled machines, I'm pushing myself as hard as I can.

My bestie, Ivy, is in a downward-facing dog pose and glances across at me from beneath her arm, making me laugh. I wince and it's all I can do not to groan out loud, as my tired muscles are screaming at me.

'*Are you okay?*' she mouths at me.

'*Sorry, everything hurts,*' I mouth back.

Our teacher, Flo, talks us through the final movements before we finally get to lie prostrate on the floor. Thankfully, the winding-down stretches seem to even out a few kinks. The only problem is that everyone else is now up on their feet, and I'm simply lying here, staring up at the ceiling considering whether it's natural for parts of me to feel numb.

Ivy stares down at me. 'Do you need a hand to get up?'

'No. I'm in heaven. If I stay completely still, nothing hurts, nothing at all – it's total bliss!'

Flo wraps up the session with a few motivational words and as everyone begins clapping, I reluctantly ease myself into an upright position to join in.

As we filter out of the studio, I give Flo a warm smile. 'Sorry I lagged behind a bit tonight,' I admit.

Ivy and Flo make eye contact and they both start laughing.

'What?'

'We were all suffering with you at every groan,' Flo replies.

I stare at them apologetically. 'I thought that was just in my head and when I did let slip, I hoped your voice helped to mask it, Flo.' I laugh.

'Don't you worry about that, Jess. We're all eager to see some life breathed back into Renweneth Manor. It's a shame to see a beautiful old building like that standing empty for such a long time and everyone is in awe of what you're doing.'

'That's kind of you to say so. How are things going with…' I glance around, checking the three of us are now alone. '…Prudie?' She's an old friend of my late grandma Maggie's, and by association, Cappy. Although I think he usually disappeared whenever the two ladies got together for their little chats.

Flo rolls her eyes. 'You won't believe this, but the man who rents out the village hall where I used to hold my classes gave me a call yesterday. He offered me a discount if I move back there. I declined and told him that the studio at Renweneth Farm is perfect for me. Then he mentioned that our esteemed local artist has been bending his ear.'

My jaw drops and I don't quite know what to say.

'Prudie not only exhibits for free in the bakery café, but she still wants the studio all to herself for her art classes?' Ivy sounds scandalised.

'That's about the long and the short of it,' Flo confirms. 'I moved away from the village hall because the ambience isn't quite right there. So many clubs use it for different things and the noticeboards are cluttered. The studio here is all clean lines with no distractions and it feels like a sanctuary. Adding this mezzanine floor to the old barn was an inspired idea, Jess. I'm not giving in to Prudie Carne just because she thinks she's superior and her art classes have more to offer the community than my yoga classes.'

I can see that Ivy is just as shocked as I am. Flo is usually such a relaxed and quiet person; admittedly, she's put up with a lot from Prudie and clearly this latest upset is the final straw.

'Oh, Flo, she's just annoyed with herself for missing out on the opportunity to take the studio on, that's all. If she doesn't respond to her emails that's her fault, because she had the chance.'

'Well, whatever, but I've bent over backwards to accommodate her classes and have rearranged my own itinerary to keep her happy. If she keeps this up, I'll be less amenable in future when she wants to add extra dates. I know she's an old friend of Cappy's and your late grandma, and while I don't want to cause offence, my patience is wearing thin.'

I think it's time I sorted this out once and for all, and this time, it's not my aching muscles that make me groan; it's the thought of confronting Cappy.

2

Treading on Eggshells

It's a frosty start to the day but at least it's dry. Riley's team of ground workers are due to begin work, digging out the hole for the new septic tank to the rear of the manor.

When I return from the school run, a lorry is in the process of dropping off the biggest skip I've ever seen. Riley walks up to greet me sporting a broad smile.

'I'm going to get two of the guys to start loading it up. The aim is to fill it by lunchtime and get another one delivered this afternoon. What I'd like you to do is to start sorting through the attic.' He gives me a pointed look. 'You know there's stuff up there that won't get used, Jess. It's in the way and putting it off will cost you money. The skip is here, so let's fill it.'

I'm in agreement but even so my stomach dips. 'Okay.'

'That'll leave two of us to strip out the ground floor and the aim is to get shot of the debris by the end of tomorrow. All I need you to do is put this tape on anything that can go.'

He hands me a role of white tape with the word *fragile* written over it in large red letters and I glance at him, askance.

'It's not reverse psychology.' He grins at me. 'These guys need a clear marker and anything with fragile tape is bin fodder. They don't always appreciate the difference between a family heirloom and…'

'Something that's fit for the tip, but that a sentimentalist like me can't bear to throw away?' Admittedly, some of the furniture

I'm keeping isn't in prime condition, but each piece means something to me, or Cappy, and will be repurposed.

Riley quickly scans around to check no one is watching us and he steps forward to plant a kiss firmly on my lips before pulling away. 'Sorry, I know it's tough letting things go. Anyway, the attic floor is perfectly safe now. It was only that large area in the far corner where the main leak was that needed replacing. The guys have put down some sheets of marine ply as a temporary measure and we're hoping to get some reclaimed boards to patch in the floor. A lot of that furniture is water-damaged, Jess, and you know it's not salvageable.'

'It's time to suck it up, isn't it?'

He looks away and I watch as he pushes back on his hard hat to capture some of the dark curls that have escaped.

Seemingly out of nowhere, a random voice makes us both turn. 'Hey, mate. I'm dropping off a mini digger. You got any boards to lay over those cobbles, so I can drive it in?'

I reach out to touch Riley's arm, giving him a fleeting smile. 'You sort out the lorry driver and I'll make a start.'

As I turn and hurry back inside, I have the strongest feeling that Grandma is walking alongside me. Instead of recoiling at the devastation as two men rip the ground-floor walls apart, I'm starting to see a wonderful blank canvas and I give them a thumbs-up. I tell myself that I'm realising her dream, too, as I climb the stairs to the attic. She'd be the first one to say *Oh, that awful display cabinet should have gone a long time ago*, which makes me smile to myself. It's not *things* that are important, it's memories, and those you carry in your heart forever.

The awkward, and twisty backstairs will soon be gone, to be replaced with a new staircase off the main one. Anything I decide to keep will be put into the shed behind the manor; I suspect the rest will be broken up in situ to make carrying it downstairs a little easier.

I enter what I refer to as the storeroom, but it's the scent of autumn filtering through from the room ahead that makes me keep going. The narrow aisle between my stored treasure leads into the second of the three attic rooms. Many years ago, when this was a sheep farm and times were hard, these rooms were filled with bunk beds to house casual labour. With no direct access to the main house, they had to mount the creaky backstairs and tiptoe past the housekeeper's quarters on the second floor. I imagine a stern, older woman whose eyes were everywhere, keeping them in line.

Harvest time was always busy, as what is now the campsite was originally a huge orchard. I draw in a deep breath, the sweet scent leading me into the last of the rooms. This is where the apples were stored; last autumn, for the first time in goodness knows how many years, that's just what Lola and I did, aided by her best friend Daisy. Now, the pantry in The Farmhouse is full of jars of jam, apple chutney and mason jars filled to the brim with apple slices. Daisy's mum, Erica, took home boxes and boxes of fruit, enough to keep her stall loaded with tarts throughout the winter.

Instinctively, I walk over to the single window to the rear, mindful not to crack my head on the beam above it. This is the room that Grandma promised Lola, the one she said always smelt of autumn bounty and it does, even though the apple crates are all empty now. In the second phase of the work, Riley's team will be installing three large dormer windows in a line, which will look directly out to sea. Despite having to bend to stare out of the small panes of glass, the view is mesmerising.

'Right,' I murmur, turning on my heels. Progress calls for a clear head, not one muddled by misplaced sentimentality. Some of this stuff is only fit for the fire, as it has more wormholes than wood. I've got this!

Over lunch, Riley, Cappy and I catch up with the morning's progress.

'You did well filling that skip in such a short time,' Cappy remarks. 'How's the attic looking, Jess?'

A little wave of unease washes over me. They're not my things I'm trawling through. When Cappy moved out of The Farmhouse, he took very little with him, using the excuse that his new house is much smaller and most of the furniture here was dark and bulky. He was happy for me to use what I wanted and give away the rest. While I've already upcycled a few pieces, there isn't much of what remains that is earmarked to stay. 'By late afternoon, it should be clear, bar a few special items.' I give him a wistful smile and he gives me a wink.

'It's not an easy job, but there's no point hanging on to things for the sake of it. That shed won't take much to fill it. Did the… uh… old armoire make the cut?'

I was just about to pop a forkful of pasty into my mouth. I pause, horrified that he should think that I'd throw away an heirloom. 'Of course, it did! You bought it for Grandma to celebrate your twenty-fifth wedding anniversary. I have big plans for that!'

His smile touches my heart. 'Ah, I'm glad you could find a use for it.'

Riley joins in. 'When Jess says that, she means it, Cappy. She's even drawn me a sketch, as it involves a little carpentry work, but I think you'll be delighted with the end result when it's in situ.'

Cappy chuckles. 'I can't wait to see what you do with it. From the sounds drifting over to the campsite, I hear the digger has been put to work this morning. It'll be good to get that septic tank in and the hole backfilled in case the snow returns.'

Riley frowns. 'It's been on my mind, too. The forecast is that we're in for some heavy frosts and that could make groundworks difficult.'

'I'm just as concerned as you. Tomorrow, we'll have ground workers on site over in the first field. We're hoping to take out some of the hedging that runs along the front of the campsite, ready to install the second entrance. I'm still waiting for a date from the highways team about when they're going to lower the pavement, but I want to get ahead before we start digging out the trench for the new shower and toilet block.'

They've both finished eating but I continue, listening intently. Their concerns are my concerns, too. Both Cappy and Riley have work schedules and having booked in the relevant trades, it means everything must run smoothly. If it doesn't, delays cost money and we can't afford to have people hanging around doing nothing.

There's a sharp rap on the front door and Riley goes to investigate. He comes back a couple of minutes later with his coat in his hand. 'I'm needed on site. Thanks for lunch, Jess. I'll see you later, Cappy.'

With that, he disappears, and I start clearing the plates.

'Do you have time for a quick coffee, Jess, or do you want it in a thermal cup to go?' Cappy asks, as he walks over to the counter and flicks the switch on the kettle.

This is my chance to have a word with him while we're on our own, and as that doesn't happen very often these days, I'd better grab it.

'Why not? The guys all take an hour's break and I think it sets the wrong example if we don't do the same.' I'm frantically trying to come up with the right words to launch into what is a potentially sensitive conversation about Prudie.

'I'll have some updated figures for you with regard to the upgrade to the parking facilities and the campsite, by the end of tomorrow, Jess. When are you due to sit down with the accountant next?'

'Michael and I are meeting up on Friday afternoon to go through everything in detail.'

Midway through stirring the coffee, Cappy half-turns to look directly at me. 'Are you expecting any problems?'

'The only unknown will be the size of the tax bill, as our

profits have significantly increased with the new income streams. I just need to make sure I'm putting enough aside so we don't get any nasty shocks once the accounts go in for the current financial year.'

He nods his head, seemingly satisfied. 'It'll be easier once you can move into the manor and get an income from this place. I bet Vyvyan can't wait to put it up on the website and you should get twice what you're getting for letting out Penti Growan.'

Cappy's right, of course. It's mostly couples who rent out our little two-bed cottage. But that's not a part of my action plan for The Farmhouse; he's just not ready for me to broach the subject yet.

As marketing manager, Vyvyan is delighted about the thought of adding it to our portfolio. However, I've warned her not to take it for granted that will be the case.

What I'm banking on is that Ivy and Adam won't be renting out Smithy's Cottage for much longer. As soon as they can get a mortgage sorted to buy it, that will be a welcome cash injection, which could solve all my problems in one go.

Cappy carries the mugs over to the table and I grab the cake tin and two small plates.

'Fresh from The Farmhouse Bakery this morning,' I inform him, as I slip off the lid. 'Ivy's latest addition – kiwi parfait slices. They look, and smell, amazing. Help yourself.'

'She never fails to amaze me, does Ivy. And not a doughnut in sight!'

I laugh. 'She doesn't do deep-fried, or refined white sugar, but her cakes taste heavenly, don't they?'

There are a few moments of silence as we take our first, then second bites.

'Definitely moreish,' Cappy declares, polishing his off and licking his fingers before wiping them on a paper napkin.

'Cappy, this problem between Prudie and Flo has raised its head again. Flo's patience is wearing thin and the informal agreement between the two of them might not be viable for much longer.'

He looks at me shiftily. 'Oh. I thought that had all settled down.'

'Me, too.' When I tell him exactly what Flo told Ivy and me last night, I get the feeling it doesn't come as a complete surprise and that's disconcerting.

'Most artists struggle to cover their costs, Jess, and that's a fact. It took Prudie more than thirty years to get people to take her seriously and her watercolour paintings have done a lot to promote Cornwall. She spent the next twenty years on a mission to raise the profile of as many Cornish artists as possible. Now she's back here at a time in her life when she's committed herself to mentoring those with talent who are on the brink of giving up. It's not only a worthy cause, but she attracts a lot of publicity.'

Inwardly I sigh. This isn't some random speech; he knew this talk was coming and Prudie prepared him for it.

'I'm well aware of that, Cappy. But Flo is the one who signed the lease and both she, and Ivy for that matter, are bending over backwards to support Prudie. I don't see what more we can do.'

Cappy shrugs his shoulders. 'Look, Jess. I told you I wouldn't interfere when I handed the farm over to you. I know I broke my word on Prudie's behalf when she lost out on getting the studio—'

Lost out? Vyvyan, offered Prudie first refusal. I put up my hand to stop him there. 'No, she didn't lose out, Cappy. Vyvyan emailed her and asked if she was still interested in renting the space. Prudie didn't respond.'

He sits back in his chair, emitting a drawn-out sigh. 'I know... and that was very unfortunate indeed, but it was a misunderstanding. As Vyvyan later discovered, Prudie was in London at the time, organising an exhibition, and her focus was elsewhere.' Cappy is making excuses for his old friend, but it's all academic now.

'I understand that, but business is business, and it was all about getting The Courtyard Hub fully signed up before we opened.'

Another sigh. 'Yes, but I really do think you're missing a trick here, Jess. Prudie requires a studio of her own to rent and she'd bring a lot of attention, and business, to Renweneth Farm if she had more of a presence here.'

I drain the last of my coffee and stand. Quite frankly, I'm done talking about Prudie Carne. 'Well, you tell me how we can accommodate her, and I'll think about it. In the meantime, as she's exhibiting in Ivy's café for free, and Flo has come to an arrangement with her for access to the studio two days a week, I think we've done all we can. Now, I must go. There's an empty skip that needs filling before the end of the day.'

It's not easy for me to shut Cappy down like that, but I'd have nipped this in the bud at the start if it weren't for the fact that Prudie's an old friend of his and Grandma's. As I tidy the table, he flashes me a rather guilty look.

'I'll have a quiet word with her, Jess. I promise. After all, none of this is Flo's fault.'

No, it isn't and it's not mine, either.

3

Expect the Unexpected

The guys have already left by the time the lorry turns up to collect the second skip, which is so full that Riley helps the driver to tie a tarpaulin over the top. He walks back to me looking tired but happy.

'Are you staying for dinner tonight?' I check, as I pull the door closed and turn the heavy cast-iron key in the lock.

'No, I'd better not. I had a text from my brother, Tom, this morning. He's going to give me a call tonight.'

I stare back at him in surprise. He's only ever mentioned his brother once, when he told me the full story of how he ended up leaving everything behind and settling in Cornwall. 'There's nothing wrong, is there?'

Riley shrugs his shoulders. 'He just asked if I was around to have a chat this evening.'

Even though I've not seen a lot of Riley today, I sensed he had something on his mind, and I wasn't wrong.

'Anyway, I'd better get off. I'll see you in the morning.'

He cradles me in his arms, a huge smile on his face as he gazes down into my eyes. 'I missed you today. It's not the same when we're not working side by side, is it?'

'You're always so focused on the task in hand that I'm surprised you even notice when I am working next to you.' I laugh.

'For me, it's enough just knowing you're around,' he half-whispers, before placing his lips on mine.

Instinctively, I close my eyes. His kiss is warm, loving and sincere – all the qualities I love about Riley and as we reluctantly pull away from each other, I let out a gentle sigh.

'Hey.' His arms tighten around me. 'We're on countdown now the work's in full swing. At some point, I'll need to ask your dad's permission for your hand in marriage and formally pop the question to you, of course.'

I pull a wry face. 'Really? Can't we skip that bit? I think everyone – including me – is rather taking that for granted.'

'No. In case you haven't noticed, in many ways, I'm a rather formal type of guy and I love the old traditions. I want to do it properly. You know, get down on one knee and slip a ring on your finger.'

Butterflies begin to flutter in my stomach, as I put my gloved hand up to his cheek. 'I don't feel comfortable being the centre of attention – you know that by now.'

'And I'm a romantic at heart, so I'm hoping you'll forgive me when I surprise you.'

I groan. 'Proposals don't require witnesses, remember. And romantic means a quiet, candlelit dinner for two – just saying.'

Riley rolls his eyes. 'Okay. I'll take that into consideration. If I don't call you to say goodnight later, it'll be because I'm still on the phone with Tom. It's been a while and no doubt we've a lot to catch up on.'

I follow Riley down the path and through the archway into the main courtyard. When his car pulls away, I give him a wave and remind myself it won't be like this forever. As I turn towards The Farmhouse, Ivy calls out to me.

'Jess! Fancy a quick coffee?'

I saunter over to the bakery; it's all lit up and looking inviting. 'You're working late; it's just gone six.'

'I know. Prudie's assistant, Karl, dropped by – you just missed him. They've sold two more paintings. One of the replacements would look perfect on the breast wall in the sitting room in Smithy's Cottage. I'm sorely tempted, but it's a bit pricey. Are you in a rush?'

'No and I'd love a coffee. Let me text Cappy to let him know Riley's not joining us for dinner.'

I step inside and Jess puts up the closed sign, then locks the door.

Standing at the counter, I send the text while she makes our drinks.

'Is Riley all right?' she enquires over her shoulder.

'He's excited now that most of the demo work has been completed. Once the floors have been made good, it really will be little more than a shell, but hopefully a sound one.'

Ivy carries the tray through to the café area and I follow her. 'It's been what, ten days since I last wandered in here to browse, but you have several new paintings on display.' I pull out two chairs and we settle ourselves down.

'Yes. Prudie must be pleased but I haven't seen her, only Karl.'

I raise my eyebrows to the heavens. 'Hmm… you'd think she'd pop in every now and again to cast her eye over the collection, even if it's on her way to one of the art classes.' And, as the paintings are selling, a brief "thank you" every now and again would be a nice touch.

Ivy brushes it off. 'It's great for our customers to have something interesting to look at and for the community, so I'm fine with it. Flo came in this morning for her usual herbal tea. She looked a bit down in the mouth, but I didn't have time to stop for a chat.'

'I told Cappy about the village hall incident and asked him to have a word with Prudie.'

Ivy looks at me rather apprehensively. 'Was he receptive?'

'I think he got the message that he'll be a lot more diplomatic than I will. What annoys me is that he keeps making excuses for Prudie. Now he's saying we're missing out on a business opportunity.' I grab the coffee mug and take a sip, savouring the smell that wafts around me. Nothing beats freshly ground coffee.

'For what?'

'I think he knew about Prudie's underhanded tactic trying to get Flo to go back to the village hall. It's as if he had an answer prepared, in case I tackled him about it. Anyway, I left the ball in his court.'

'You did the right thing. It'll be better coming from him, especially as Prudie was the one who dragged him into it in the first place. She knows you run Renweneth Farm now and that was out of order. Anyway,' Ivy diplomatically changes the subject, 'I don't suppose Riley has heard anything from Fiona?'

'No. It's only the fact that he can throw himself into the new project that's keeping him upbeat. But... um...' For some reason, I find myself frowning, as I stare down into my coffee mug and Ivy fills the silence.

'It's good he's got something else to focus on, though, isn't it? Fiona needs time to get her head around the fact that he's found someone he wants to settle down with.'

'And that's my fault,' I concede. 'Riley wasn't ready to tell her. So much has happened between him and me in such a short space of time; six months ago, we were strangers.' At the Renweneth Farm End of Summer Party in late September, we outed ourselves as a couple and I don't think anyone was really surprised. 'Riley has eased his way into being not just a part of the decision-making team because I want him by my side, but also a part of the family. Lola has accepted him without question, because he's always taken time to talk to her; in fact, she knew he had a son before I did.'

'Oh, Jess.' Ivy reaches out to touch my arm and give it a squeeze. 'No one was happier than me that day when you admitted it wasn't just a casual fling and that you wanted Riley in your life forever. I also knew how blindsided you felt on another level. After almost ten years as a married woman and then having your heart broken, it was never going to be easy to trust someone again, but you surprised us all.'

I guess I did, but most of all I surprised myself. 'Neither of us wants a big fuss, just a simple civil ceremony at our wonderful village hall, then back here for a big party in the garden. But now Riley is talking about a formal proposal and putting an engagement ring on my finger.'

Ivy looks at me, clearly puzzled. 'And what's wrong with that?'

How can I explain it without sounding ungrateful, or worse – weird? 'Ben and I did all that the first time around and look how it ended. I love Riley from the bottom of my heart, and I don't need him to impress me with a sparkly ring. I've lived the fairy tale and it didn't have a happy ending. I don't want to jinx what we have. Is Riley feeling pressured to do what's expected because he thinks that's what I want? I'd happily just live together because a marriage certificate is simply a piece of paper. It's what's in your heart that counts.' Now I'm feeling tearful.

'Talk to him, Jess. Explain how you feel.'

If only it were that simple, but it's not just about Riley and me. My parents, Lola, Cappy and our friends will all have their own expectations. And when two children are involved, it's not solely about what the adults want, but what's best for everyone. To be seen to make a commitment to someone, in front of those you love, is special and I know that this time around it will be forever.

'His brother is phoning him tonight. As far as I'm aware, Tom is the only one from his past who kept in contact with Riley. Talking about his old life is difficult for him and I get that. I no longer dwell upon the life I had with Ben before I came to live at Renweneth Farm. This is my future now. But he's still got one foot in the past because Fiona won't set him free, free to see his son and be a part of his life going forward. What if that's why his brother wants to talk to him?'

'Jess, this isn't like you. Riley is equally in love with you, as you are with him, and everyone can see that. There is nothing his brother can say that could possibly upset your plans.'

What is truly heart-breaking is that I needed to hear someone say that. Why, after all this time, do I still feel vulnerable? Fear is an awful thing. It eats away at you when you lie in bed in the early hours of the morning, your thoughts churning. 'Maybe his family are hoping at some point he'll go back to Fiona,' I reply.

'Don't let the past colour your future with Riley. You're a different woman now, Jess, to the one you were when you were married to Ben. It's like you've broken free, and the real you refuses to be held back. The truth is, Riley stole your heart even though you weren't ready to trust again. The fact that two people still smarting from old wounds fell for each other, is a sure sign if ever I saw one. You are soul mates and, despite the problems, you'll work through them together.'

My head is saying the same thing, but my heart is wary, as if it's expecting something to go wrong. It's time to change the subject. 'Thanks for being my listening ear, Ivy. So, you're drinking coffee again, I see.'

It's an innocuous comment but Ivy looks uncomfortable, shifting uneasily in her seat. 'Yes,' she replies, brightly.

But as I study her face, I know something isn't right. I drain the last dregs from my mug and go to stand, when she starts talking.

'You'd better sit down for this one, Jess.' Her tone is serious, and I look at her, puzzled, wondering what's coming. 'We weren't going to tell anyone until I've had the scan but—'

'You're pregnant?' I squeal, excitedly.

Her expression is a mix of bewilderment and joy. 'It seems I am. I'm having an ultrasound on the thirtieth of January.'

'Congratulations, Ivy. I'm super thrilled for both you and Adam.' I jump up and hold out my arms as she eases herself to her feet in a bit of a daze. 'When's the baby due?'

'The doctor thinks I'm about ten weeks, so sometime in August. You won't breathe a word of this to anyone, will you?

Adam wanted to tell our parents at Christmas, but I'd been doing some online research and—'

And she's reading all sorts of scary things about what can go wrong in the first trimester. 'Of course I won't! I'm guessing the problem with drinking coffee in the mornings is the nausea?'

She nods her head. 'It comes and goes. I'm fine from lunchtime onwards. Thankfully, no one has really noticed, although sometimes the smells in the kitchen get a bit overwhelming. In which case I take a break and help serve.'

'But you were drinking at Christmas, weren't you?'

She laughs. 'People assume if you have a wine glass in your hand, it's something alcoholic.'

I lean in again to give her a second hug. 'Oh, this is wonderful news. Your dream is about to come true!'

'It's still sinking in, to be honest. At least Tillie will finally have a little cousin and my sister, and our parents, are going to be overjoyed when we break the news. Thank goodness we converted the office above the bakery into a spare guest room, as they'll all want to come visit.'

A part of me wonders how Ivy's mum, Sarah, will feel. She's a part of her granddaughter Tillie's life on a daily basis and Ivy's sister couldn't have coped without her. With Ivy's child, it's going to be a little different and they're all still adjusting to Ivy and Adam no longer living on their doorstep in Stroud.

I give her an encouraging smile. 'It's going to be a wonderful August,' I remark, happily. 'A wedding and a new baby at Renweneth Farm!'

I'm just about to put down the book I'm reading and turn out the light when my phone starts buzzing. It's Riley.

'Good, you aren't asleep. I didn't know whether to ring, or not.' He sounds edgy, which is very unlike him.

'I'm glad you did,' I reply, softly.

'Tom rang to let me know his fiancée, Helen, is about to send out the wedding invitations for the twentieth of May. He wanted to know if my plus-one has a name.'

Last summer when Riley started working for me, I vaguely recall him mentioning that his brother was getting married this year. However, he seems rather subdued about it now. 'Did you tell him... about us?'

'Naturally. I've nothing to hide and he was genuinely delighted. He said he can't wait to meet you.'

Oh, so we are going to the wedding. 'Great, I'll mark that on the calendar then.'

'The trouble is...' He clears his throat and I close my eyes, wondering what's coming. 'I think I mentioned the fact that he loaned me some money when I first came to Cornwall. I've already paid him back a large chunk of it and he said he wasn't in a hurry for the rest. He's not strapped for cash, but with the wedding coming up, I feel honour-bound to settle up with him. Unfortunately, it's going to wipe out my savings.' The line goes quiet for a second. 'I feel bad about that, Jess, because it means the ring shopping will have to wait a while.'

'Without that loan you wouldn't have the cottage, would you? The fact that your brother was the only one to help you out at a time when you had nothing, just a derelict cottage to renovate and a tent to live in, is a truly wonderful thing. It's absolutely the right thing to do. I don't need a ring on my finger, Riley. I'm not the type of woman who is bothered about glittery things.'

'But it's what you deserve, because what's on the outside should match what's on the inside. Lola, too, exudes that same vibrant energy; it's why Cappy calls her his sparkly girl. The sparkle comes from the heart, of course, but both of you light up a room when you enter.'

I smile to myself. 'I'm not sure everyone would agree with you but life's too short to be maudlin, isn't it?'

'I guess it is. Anyway, are you up for going to the wedding?'

'Of course!'

He lapses into silence again for a few seconds. 'I'll be honest with you, I'm not sure how I feel about it. Oh, it'll be great to catch up with Tom and finally get a chance to meet Helen, but on the day, the rest of my family may well turn their backs on us.'

It must be coming up to almost five years since Riley left to start over again. Surely enough time has passed for them to want to heal the rift. Even though, from what he told me, at the time they all thought he was out of control. A disagreement with his business partner turned nasty when a fight broke out, and Riley left under a shadow. To avoid charges being pressed, he walked away from the business with less than he was due, but enough to be able to hand the marital home over to Fiona.

'Don't overthink this,' I beg. 'Go into it with no expectations and a positive attitude. If we're not made welcome, at least we will have shown our faces and that's all that will matter to your brother and his fiancée.'

He draws in a deep breath. 'You're right. And it got me thinking about the cottage. We don't really talk about money, do we? But what happens after we're married?'

It's a subject we've avoided but everything is speeding up now, and this conversation is way overdue. However, I'm not sure what his reaction is going to be. 'After Grandma died, Cappy set up the farm as a trust.'

'I have no idea what that means. I was rather hoping I could sell the cottage, put some money aside for Ollie's future and then chip in with the renovation costs for Renweneth Manor.'

This is the tricky bit. 'It's not quite as straightforward as that, I'm afraid. The trust owns the farm. As a trustee, I manage all the money, property, and assets that Cappy placed within it. As it stands, both Lola and I are the only two beneficiaries. I'm not sure what impact getting married will—'

Riley interrupts me. 'Look, Jess, that's a huge relief for me. The farm is your family's inheritance. It's nice to know that Cappy, together with your parents' blessing, has an eye to the long-term future. There's no need to change a thing. However, I do feel that I should be contributing in some way, considering that Renweneth Manor is going to be our future home. It seems wrong, like I'll be living there rent-free.'

I burst out laughing. 'Considering how hard you work, Riley, I'm pretty sure I'm not paying you enough. As the saying goes, there's no such thing as a free lunch.'

I really don't want this to become a thing between us and that's why I've been avoiding the subject. Now I'm cross with myself for not taking Cappy to one side when Riley and I told him at the garden party that the two of us were planning a future together. Riley is already an integral part of the running of the farm and going forward, I want to do right by him. But it's Grandma and Cappy's wish that, ultimately, the farm ends up in Lola's hands.

'It's nice to know I'm appreciated,' he replies, softly.

'Look, the cottage is your legacy for Ollie down the line,' I state firmly. 'You could rent it out and if we continue as we are, together with your salary from the farm—'

He gives a disparaging laugh. 'Me, a landlord?'

'Why not?'

'Managing big financial decisions isn't one of my strengths.'

'That's what accountants are for. Let's talk about this once we've both had time to think it through. There's no need to decide now.'

'Except that the pressure is on you to keep the bills paid,' he replies, adamantly. 'Don't think that it doesn't weigh heavily on me knowing that you don't just get hands on, but the other part of your job is vitally important too. You keep everything running smoothly by keeping a constant eye on the cash flow. If there's anything I can do to help, I pick things up quickly and I'm a stickler for detail.'

My bottom lip begins to waver, and I draw in a deep breath to stop myself from getting tearful. Riley's only concern is that I don't sink under the pressure of trying to keep on top of everything. He doesn't care about who owns what, only being a part of something that is so much bigger than just the two of us.

'I never refuse an offer of help,' I respond with enthusiasm. 'Builder, project manager and now budget holder.'

He gasps. 'You're giving me a budget to manage?'

'I am. You can monitor the pot of money I've set aside for the contractors' invoices.'

There's a brief pause. 'Guess I'm going to be cracking the whip in future then,' he muses.

'Exactly!'

I know he's careful about every penny he spends on behalf of Renweneth Farm, but this is about showing him how much I respect and value what he does.

Thinking back, Ben never really supported me; it was all about him: his problems at work, his stress levels, his lack of sleep if I was up all night with Lola whenever she was poorly and upset. In contrast, Riley appreciates every little thing anyone does for him because he doesn't take anything for granted. Having reached rock bottom once, it changes a person's outlook on life forever. And that makes me love him even more.

As we say goodnight and the line goes dead, I think about Ivy's news. Another thing Riley and I haven't discussed is the possibility of having a child together. Lola is nine on the twenty-ninth of January and I think Ollie is only a couple of months younger. With a new baby putting in an appearance at the farm in August, who knows what yearnings that might stir up? If it does, I'm not sure how I feel about it.

4

Unwelcome Truths

Friday dawns and the sound of a car pulling into the courtyard announces the arrival of my good friend Erica, and her daughter, Daisy. Erica offered to do the school runs today as Cappy is tied up on site. As for me, my laptop is already set up and waiting on the kitchen table even before I wave them off, as I'm meeting with Michael this afternoon to go through the figures and check that we're on target.

Cappy was up and out early this morning. The ground workers are here to dig the trenches ready to install a third shower block on the far side of the first field. That will allow us to turn the second shower block, which backs onto the car park, into a bespoke toilet block to accommodate visitors on market days. Together with Vyvyan's husband, Keith, who is our campsite manager and his assistant, Len, they all have a fraught day ahead of them. Cappy wasn't in the best of moods, although I did wonder whether it was because he'd called Prudie and the conversation didn't go well. I guess I'll find out when he's ready to give me an update.

Two hours in and my head is full of figures, when my phone rings and it's Mum.

'Hey, Mum. How are you and Dad doing?' In truth, it's a welcome interruption.

'Good, my darling, thank you. I know you're probably busy, but I had to call to see how the work is progressing on the manor.'

I sit back in my chair, smiling to myself. 'Oh, Mum... if only Grandma were here. She'd be delighted. I mean, it looks a total wreck inside, but the rotten wood is being replaced and all the rubbish has now been cleared out. I can finally picture how it's going to look and I'm so excited.'

Mum gives a little laugh. 'That's wonderful, Jess. And how are the plans for the wedding coming along?'

Having just taken a quick slurp of my coffee, I almost choke as it goes down the wrong way. It would be a lie to say everything is under control when a lot of the details haven't exactly been thrashed out. 'I've booked the village hall. Their wedding package covers everything. From decorations, to arranging the ceremony,' I begin, positively. 'And Ivy and her team are doing the wedding buffet, with the help of Erica, so it's all good.' I leave out the bit about Ivy badgering me for a headcount.

'And the flowers? Have you thought about the style of dress you want to wear? Is Lola being a bridesmaid, or a flower girl?'

I gingerly put down my coffee mug, realising that there's no fooling Mum. 'Isn't it a bit early to think about outfits? I mean, August is a long way off.'

'These days, you don't just buy a wedding dress off the hanger, Jess. You try on a sample and then they place an order for it. That can take several months at least and then when it comes in, you go for a fitting so it can be tailored to suit.'

'I wasn't thinking of wearing anything too fancy,' I admit.

'Yes, but you'll want something special. Is Riley hiring a suit, or will he be buying one?'

Now my head is starting to ache. 'I don't know, Mum.'

'I appreciate that you want a low-key affair and, given how busy you all are at the farm, it makes perfect sense. But a wedding is a memory you'll hopefully treasure forever. Dad asked me last night whether he's escorting you into the venue. He was a bit surprised that I was as much in the dark about what's happening as he is. Do you even have a guest list yet?'

I gulp, feeling like I've been caught out. 'Yes, I'd love Dad to walk me into the ceremony and no, to the second…'

There's a disapproving 'Hmm,' followed by a gentle sigh. 'Nowadays, it seems most brides have a wedding planner. Someone who fusses over the details once the bride and groom have decided what they want.'

I begin to chuckle. 'Maybe if it's a big do, but the cost would probably wipe out my entire budget in one go.'

'I wasn't suggesting you hire someone when I have time on my hands, and I can always draft in your dad to lend a hand.'

'Doing what?'

'Depending on who you invite, some of your guests might appreciate someone organising group transport to travel down to Cornwall and then there's the accommodation to sort. And what about Riley's family?'

My hands are now getting clammy. 'It's just a handful of close friends and family at the ceremony, and then we're hiring a marquee for the buffet in the manor's garden for our wider circle. The summer party didn't take that much arranging, did it?'

Mum gasps. 'Jess, you can't compare the two events! I know you and Riley are concentrating on getting the manor ready, but it's your *wedding day*. I'm worried that a little further down the line, you'll look back and regret doing everything in such a rush.'

'Mum, the second time around changes the emphasis. Trust me, I'm not going to have a meltdown if every little thing isn't perfect. It's what… seven months away. There's plenty of time to work out the fine-tuning.'

'Believe me, the time will fly. At least get an invite list sorted, as you can't spring this on people last-minute just because your focus is elsewhere right now.'

Mum's right, I suppose. 'The whole family aren't expecting an invite… are they?'

'I've told them all it'll be a small gathering, but your aunt asked me last weekend if cousins will be invited. I said I wasn't sure. Cappy mentioned you've been a bit snappy lately and it's no wonder with your to-do list.'

'Really? What exactly did he say?'

'Something about your patience wearing thin, which is so unlike you.' Mum trails off. 'Um... the two of you haven't had a disagreement, have you?'

Oh, this is about The Hub Studio. 'No, Mum. Everything is fine. Do you remember a woman named Prudie Carne?'

'The name rings a bell... It's not that artist lady, is it? She was quite a good friend of your grandma's. Why?'

'Just between you and me, she's been causing a few problems here at the farm. Unfortunately, she's been trying to get Cappy on her side. If I've been short with him, it's because she wants the impossible and now it's down to him to tell her precisely that.'

'So... it's nothing to do with falling behind on the wedding arrangements?' Mum asks, hesitantly, sounding a tad relieved.

As for me, maybe I should be panicking. Riley's brother's wedding is in May and they're about to send out the actual invitations.

'No, but I'd love to take you up on that offer, if you're sure you have the time. Perhaps we could get our heads together and I can hand over what I have so far?'

'Oh, that would be lovely!' Mum sounds delighted. 'As for Prudie, your grandma often invited her to The Farmhouse for afternoon tea. They'd chatter away quite happily, putting the world to rights but Cappy always made himself scarce.'

'Well, I can understand why. Prudie is a woman who doesn't give up easily. Anyway, consider yourself our official wedding planner. I'll email you everything in my wedding folder so far, although I will warn you it's rather scant, and we can take it from there. And I'll talk to Riley about who he wants to invite.'

'Big isn't always best, my darling.' Mum pauses for a moment, and I know we're both thinking about my first time around.

'I know. Remember how I burst into tears and started

hyperventilating when the limousine didn't appear dead on the dot of two o'clock?'

'And I told you that brides are supposed to be late – it's the custom. Then, as you dried your tears and we repaired your make-up, the chauffeur rang the doorbell.'

'It's easy to get it out of perspective and worry about the things that don't matter,' I reflect. All that money wasted on a marriage that ended up falling apart, but it gave Ben and me our beautiful daughter. I guess every cloud really does have a silver lining.

'Even an intimate and cosy celebration requires a fair bit of planning. I simply want you and Riley to remember your wedding day for all the right reasons – that's all.'

'I'll send that email over this evening. Give Dad my love and tell him I can't wait to have him walk me into Renweneth Village Hall. I know it's the second time around, but it's definitely the last!'

'That's a lot more than I've planned on setting aside for future tax bills,' I bemoan, as I look at the sheet of figures my accountant, Michael, hands me. 'It's quite a leap on our liability compared to last year's account.' His projections will certainly put a dent in my budget for round two of the work on Renweneth Manor.

His expression doesn't waver. 'I did warn you a sudden uplift in profits would result in a large tax hit by the time we reach the end of the next tax year, in April. You've had a number of new income streams kick in over the last six months, Jess, and those figures only include the first quarter's earnings from The Courtyard Hub. It also impacts the amount of tax you pay on account for the following year, so it is a bit of a double hit. The following year, you'll have a similar problem, taking into account a full year's income from The Courtyard Hub, but after that, I should imagine your income will remain pretty consistent.'

It's bad news, though, as it's not something I'd factored in.

'Have you been able to run the forecasts through to the start of April to come up with an estimated bottom-line net surplus after tax?'

My brow lifts significantly as he slides another A4 sheet my way. 'On paper it looks promising.'

'The cash flow is good and this time next year, you'll see a significant increase yet again. Now that you're holding two market days a week, renting out the bakery and the two cottages, and the income from The Courtyard Hub is kicking in, it more than makes up for the fact that the campsite is quieter at this time of the year. Obviously, if Adam and Ivy do buy Smithy's Cottage instead of renting it, the farm will get a sudden influx of cash. However, when you move out of The Farmhouse, it will boost your rental income yet again. Overall, you should be pleased, Jess. There are lots of business owners who'd be sitting there giving themselves a mental pat on the back glancing over those figures.'

Michael is right, and I push my shoulders back and lift my head, acknowledging his comment with a smile. 'It's good to see and it makes the hard work worthwhile.' Even so, our overheads have increased too, and it means there'll be less to draw down after tax to cover both Riley's and Cappy's budgets for the works in progress.

'It is good news,' I reflect soberly, 'but from now until August, our outgoings will skyrocket. Cappy has costed out the programme for the new showers and toilet block and extending the car park at around thirty thousand pounds. As we know, the profit I've managed to set aside from last year will only fund about three-quarters of the cost of implementing stage one of the works on the manor.'

Michael's natural expression is always serious, so it's hard to gauge what he's thinking. 'It's highly unlikely there will be no overspends, Jess, and you'll need to add that figure onto the shortfall. Do you have it covered?'

There's no point sugar-coating it and that's why I employ

Michael. 'I have personal savings I can draw on to loan the business until it has the cash to pay me back, but that's strictly between you and me. However, if Ivy and Adam manage to get a mortgage on Smithy's Cottage, all my problems will be solved in one go.'

Worryingly, he raises an eyebrow at me. 'And you're sure that taking a short-term gain, over the prospect of a longer-term income, is the best option?'

I shrug my shoulders. 'I regard Ivy and Adam as family; if things don't work out business-wise for them here, I'll have first refusal to buy the cottage back. It's not just to help ease the finances; it's as much about them being an asset to our little community. It's important everyone works as a team, and I know I can count on them. Ultimately, they don't want a rental property, but a forever home.'

He gives a pragmatic nod of his head. 'I get it. Growing the empire is one thing; keeping the wheels oiled and everyone going in the right direction is something else entirely. With family as the nucleus and a common goal driving you all forward, I suppose it makes sense.'

It's obvious he has his doubts. 'The bakery, with its café and art gallery, is a bigger draw than The Courtyard Hub right now. Together with market days, it keeps the footfall up on a regular basis and from a growing catchment area. Come summer, that emphasis could change slightly; when we're crowded with campers, The Courtyard Hub will be holding pottery and jewellery-making sessions, so it's all going in the right direction. I'm hoping for some bumper profits when the peak season hits, just in time for round two of the renovation work.'

'Well, the figures certainly show a sharp uptick already, and you're no longer having to use the profits from the peak season to help you cover overheads throughout the winter period. That's a first for Renweneth Farm.'

I laugh. 'Cappy is complaining that with one field being used as overwinter storage for camper vans and caravans, and Vyvyan's marketing initiative to attract groups at off-peak discounted rates about to kick off, trying to dig trenches is going to be a nightmare. However, Vyvyan doesn't intend on it being such a quiet winter in future.'

Michael's eyes widen. 'Go Vyvyan and fair play to Cappy. I know he's got Keith and Len to help things run smoothly, but he's always up for a challenge. Just like his granddaughter. Fearless.'

I stare at Michael and a hint of a smile plays around his lips. My goodness, I do believe he's teasing me.

'Ha! Ha! The apple doesn't fall far from the tree I guess.' There's a lot to be said for having a stubborn streak, I admit. 'The focus is on increasing the number of visitors all year round, as word spreads about what we have to offer.'

'Renweneth Farm is fast becoming a family, fun day out attraction. You certainly have a great team, Jess. But, as usual, I'll wrap up this meeting with a word of caution not to be tempted to overextend yourself.'

'And I really appreciate that, Michael. I love my spreadsheets and I'm constantly adjusting the budgets and forecasts, but you're the one who keeps me grounded. I'm well aware that just because our income is growing, if I plough too much back in too quickly, it could leave us in a vulnerable position.'

This time, I get a big smile from him. 'As Cappy himself would say, belt *and* braces, just in case!'

That makes me giggle. 'Ironically, I've never known anyone who wears braces, including him.'

'Thankfully, nine times out of ten, just a sturdy old belt will do!' Michael banters, but he's making sure I understand that you can't factor in all the unknowns. If I cut it too fine, I could live to regret it.

After the meeting with Michael, I grab a quick sandwich then start packing up my paperwork. When there's a sharp rap on the door knocker, I wonder if Cappy has forgotten his key. I thought he might have already popped back to grab something to eat. So, when I swing open the door to see Prudie standing there, my heart sinks in my chest.

'Is now a good time to talk? There's somethin' that needs sayin' and I want to get it off my chest.' Cornish women are strong, determined, but Prudie is also feisty.

Why is it that every time we speak, I feel as if she's spoiling for a fight? How about *Hi, Jess. I'm not interrupting your lunch, am I?*

'It's fine, Prudie, do come in.' I've been brought up to be polite no matter what, but this woman has a cheek. She obviously didn't get the answer she wanted from Cappy, so it's time for a showdown.

'Can I offer you a tea, or a coffee?'

'No. I won't take up more of your time than necessary.'

Necessary for what? I wonder.

'Please, head on through to the sitting room on your left and take a seat.'

Now would be an opportune time for Cappy to make his entrance and I pop my head outside to see if he's about. I'm a little surprised when I find myself sitting opposite Prudie and there's still no sign of him. As the minutes pass, I can only assume that she's here under her own steam.

'You've done a good job with The Farmhouse; Maggie would have approved,' Prudie remarks, which throws me.

Why would I care whether she thinks Grandma would have approved, or not? I knew her better than she did. I give Prudie a fleeting smile but say nothing.

'You know, of course, that Maggie and I weren't just friends, but she was one of my many benefactors.'

Now that's something I wasn't aware of but, for some reason I can't explain, I don't care to admit it. 'Grandma loved watercolour paintings, especially of the sea, and she always felt a special connection to Cornwall. Her granddad on her mother's side was born in Penzance.'

Prudie gazes around the room, as if looking for something. 'Just before she died, I gave her one of my early paintings, one she'd always admired.'

Does she think I got rid of it? 'I remember it, but it wasn't signed. I had no idea you were the artist. I do believe that Cappy has it hanging on the wall in the hallway of his house back in Stroud.'

'As I said,' she continues, 'it was one of my first pieces of work and it was signed on the back. It was a special piece and when I had it framed, I placed the original sketch that inspired it behind the canvas. Anyway, that aside, I owe you an apology.'

I glance at her, rather surprised. 'For what, exactly?' She owes Flo an apology, but not me.

Much to my surprise, her expression softens, and I notice that she clasps her hands together nervously in her lap. 'I'm old-school. In my opinion, this preoccupation everyone has with bein' available 24/7 is somethin' that shouldn't be encouraged. People are slaves to their phones as if their world will fall apart if they don't instantly respond. Except that I did miss a crucial email from Vyvyan, which I have since come to bitterly regret.'

Me, too. A quick response and The Hub Studio would have been hers. What can I say? I remain silent and still there's no sign of Cappy.

'I let Cappy down, as we both know that Maggie would have been thrilled for me to have a proper home here. She knew all about my years of struggle and how hard I fought to encourage other talented local artists not to give up. It meant somethin' to her.' That Cornish lilt, which often sounds hard coming from her lips, is now more colloquial.

Whatever she has to say won't change the fact that Flo has signed a twelve-month contract for the studio, with every intention of renewing it annually.

'Prudie, I don't wish to be rude, but you do have a home here. Exhibiting at the café, which I think is the best place to showcase the artwork – not least because it's on the ground floor – was an inspired idea of Ivy's. The bakery is growing in popularity, and with Flo graciously coming to an arrangement with you to accommodate your classes, you really do have the best of both worlds.' It's tempting to throw in that Ivy isn't charging her to display the artwork, but this isn't about scoring points.

She shifts uneasily in her seat. 'You, of all people, might understand when I say I have a vision for the future, Jess. As I advance in years, I'm not about to give up on what I set out to achieve. I want to leave behind a legacy. I owe it to the people who supported me in my work and to the wider Cornish community of artists and patrons who continue to spread the word. But it was time for me to come home and without being a part of that prestigious gallery in Bristol, I need a new base for my art school.'

Art school?

'That's uh… a wonderful aim, Prudie.'

'It breaks my heart to see talented but penniless artists fall by the wayside. My assistant, Karl, isn't a painter himself, but he instinctively knows deep down inside when he sees raw talent. In him I've found someone who has the soul of an artist, with the ability to identify those who have the right skills to ensure The Carne School of Painting will survive me. And, yes, I do appreciate what Ivy has done for me, and I agree that the café is the best place to display the artwork to gain much-needed sales. I'm sorry if I haven't made it crystal clear how grateful my artists are, but I intend to do somethin' about that.'

Well, that would be a start. 'That's good to hear, Prudie.'

'But what I need, Jess, is a bespoke studio to set up a centre of excellence and not a shared space. Somewhere artists, who mostly work at home in isolation, can come to be guided and have their spirits lifted. A pop-in studio, open seven days a week, where visitors and artists alike can interact, to spark not only an appreciation for art, but also a place to nurture new and emergin' talent. And I truly believe that the general public would love to see those artists at work. The farm is exactly the right sort of environment for that.'

The silence is almost ear-shattering, as I scrabble to formulate a response to her unexpected and impassioned plea. 'Even if a bay in The Courtyard Hub were to become vacant, Prudie, the problem is that you're talking about way more floor space than I can offer you.'

'As one businesswoman to another, all I ask is that if an opportunity arises, you give it some serious consideration,' she replies. 'You'd be lookin' at a guaranteed, long-term rental and another thing I can say with my hand on my heart is that it would attract a lot of interest from far and wide.'

This woman knows how to get what she wants and now I understand why Cappy decided to make himself scarce. I bet he's taken himself off to the pub for fish and chips!

'As I said, Prudie, the chances of Renweneth Farm being able to offer you what you need are slim, if not impossible. It might be wise to look elsewhere rather than risk being disappointed that all of a sudden, the right type of space will become available.'

There, the deed is done.

CAPPY

5

Caught in the Middle

Having spent all morning with Keith and Len clearing the debris as a mini digger rips out a part of the hedge abutting the main road, the cold is beginning to get to us all.

Len straightens, stamping his boots on the ground in quick succession. 'It's funny – even when I break out into a sweat, my feet are still like blocks of ice.'

'At least it's dry,' Keith remarks.

'The frost overnight wasn't as bad as I feared but the ground is still hard underfoot. The sun's put in an appearance, so maybe we should take an early lunch and hope it'll continue to thaw out a bit.' The guys all nod their heads in agreement. 'I hope that digger of yours has sharp teeth,' I banter with the operator. 'It's going to be a lot harder this afternoon when you start digging the trench between the two fields.'

'We'll soon cut a swathe through it, don't you worry, but some hot food would go down well right now. I'll see you in an hour.'

As he walks off, Keith turns to me, arching an eyebrow. 'It's goin' to take a bit of settin' up, Cappy. Vyvyan reminded me at breakfast that we have eighteen camper vans arriving mid-afternoon. It's to do with this weekend's antiques fayre they're holdin' at the village hall. I've been thinkin' about where best to let them park up. They won't appreciate bein' next to a mound of dirt and a hole in the ground.'

'It's not the best timing, but Vyvyan has worked hard to

attract various clubs and groups here during the winter and we can't let her down,' I reply, reaching up to pull my beanie hat further down over my ears. 'We'd better take a wander and see how we're going to make this work. If we didn't have market day tomorrow, they could have used the parking overspill area to the right, which would have been well away from the trench.'

The two men look at each other, weighing up the options, and Len speaks up. 'The ground workers have some heavy-duty metal sheets to lay over the trenches but it's going to make a bit of a mess, as the comings and goings will track the soil back and forth.'

'I think we're best keepin' our visitors this side of the works, Cappy,' Keith states, firmly.

The middle of the campsite is going to end up looking a mess no matter what we do. Even though it's temporary, it's not the image we want visitors to remember and neither Jess, nor Vyvyan, will be happy if we don't come up with a workable solution.

'If it warms up a bit, and we get some rain over the next couple of days, we could end up with a mud pit,' I agree. 'I've got another idea, but I'll need to have a word with Clem at the farm opposite. As long as the overwintering folk have access to their campers and caravans if needed, maybe it's wise to restrict access to the lower field.'

Keith, Len, and I walk back to the campsite entrance.

'We'll do whatever we can to make our campers feel welcome and minimise the disruption to the facilities,' Keith replies, adamantly. 'If we cordon off half of the overspill section and build a temporary fire pit up this end, it will save our newcomers the long walk down to the barbecue area. It's unlikely they'll want to use the grills in this weather anyway, but they might appreciate a late-night gatherin' around a campfire. That leaves plenty of space for the dozen or so other bookings on the schedule and a few last-minute drop-ins.'

'Great idea, Keith. When the main party arrive, offer them the use of one of the gazebos this evening if the wind doesn't pick up. Riley and I will be around to put it up for them. Right, guys, if I can leave you to sort that out after lunch, I'll catch up with you a bit later.'

'Here 'ee is then! I heard you was back.' Clem Pengali walks towards me proffering his hand and we shake as he looks at me pointedly. 'Is it for good this time?'

I give him a rueful smile. 'If it were up to Jess and Lola it would be, but Renweneth Farm has a new man joining Jess at the helm. Riley is settling in well and by August, they'll be living as a family in Renweneth Manor.'

'That's really happenin', then?'

'It is. They won't have the whole place fixed up by then, but enough to make it cosy. I'm content knowing the farm is in good hands; Riley and Jess make a good team.'

Clem nods his head. 'It's certainly goin' from strength to strength. You must miss it though, when you're not here. I know I would. There's no goin' back when the sea's been a big part of your life.'

It's the reason Maggie and I came here: my love for the sea. A career in the Royal Navy is like living two lives at once: there's life at home and life on the waves. 'The dream was that one day, I'd buy a boat in need of a bit of attention and get it seaworthy. Just good enough to venture out in her now and again and do a bit of fishing. It didn't quite turn out that way.'

Both Clem and I lost our wives within a year of each other and the eye contact between us is one of mutual understanding.

'It's only family that keeps us goin', isn't it? I still think back fondly of my days on the trawler. When the sea is ragin', I like to walk along the coastal path and thank my lucky stars the old girl made it through some of those storms. It reminds me that each day is a gift not to be wasted. And now here we both are, too stubborn to retire, yet needin' to keep ourselves busy.'

'Isn't that the truth. Retirement isn't all it's cracked up to be,' I reflect sadly.

'It's not too late to think about buyin' that boat. And if you need a hand, you know where to come. Anyway, you got some major work goin' on over at Renweneth Farm again, by the looks of it.'

'That's why I'm here. We've begun work on improving the car parking facilities and aside from market day tomorrow, we've a busy weekend at the campsite, too. Digging holes and vehicles going back and forth don't mix. It makes a lot of sense to use our overspill car park to avoid any potential problems.'

'I meant what I said, Cappy. You can have access to our storage container field whenever you want. I'm in the process of doin' a bit of tidyin' up over there. I refer to it as rusty gold because I never had time to go through it all, but now me son is runnin' things, I've no excuse. Some of that old equipment is fallin' apart. I keep tellin' him it's the story of his grandfather's and his father's lives...' Clem chuckles '...but, like most folk, he's got too much on his plate to be nostalgic about what he sees as junk.'

'Hmm... the pace of life these days is getting out of hand. Jess is the same – it's non-stop. Anyway, that's kind of you, Clem, and appreciated. We're happy to pay.'

He gives a disparaging laugh. 'Your guys helped us out at Christmas when that huge oak tree blocked the crossroads. A couple of weeks' access is nothin'. It's what folk do in a small community like this, isn't it? We're there for each other when the goin' gets tough. Kindness doesn't come with a price tag but it's good to return a favour.'

'And remember what I said if you decide to buy a boat. It's the dream all right. I can't think of a better way to spend a Sunday than tinkerin' with motors and doin' a bit of paintin', to be frank with you.'

His comments are food for thought; back in Stroud, I struggled to fill my days and what I discovered is that if a man ends up with too much thinking time on his hands, it's not a good thing.

Charlie Godden glances up, grinning at me as I hurry over and ease myself down gratefully into the seat opposite him at The Lark and Lantern. I have no doubt that I look like I'm in need of the pint he has waiting for me.

'What's up? You do know this is breakfast for me, as I worked a shift last night? If it weren't for the bin men making a racket, I wouldn't have been awake to answer my phone.'

Charlie is Erica's husband and he's a paramedic. After my chat with Clem, when I walked into the courtyard at Renweneth Farm and saw Prudie striding towards The Farmhouse, I panicked. I immediately turned around and made for the car park. Out of sight, I dialled Charlie in the hopes it was his day off.

'It was sheer desperation but I'm glad I wasn't the one to wake you. I'm in need of some advice,' I state, lifting the pint mug to my mouth. Seconds later, I let out a contented sigh. 'That hit the spot and some.'

'You look like you've had a shock, Cappy. I took the liberty of ordering two plates of the catch of the day. I'm guessing, for whatever reason, you're not in a hurry to get back?'

I nod my head in agreement. 'There's trouble brewing and I'm trying to stay clear of it.'

Charlie's eyes widen. 'Not with Jess and Riley?'

'No, no. They're doing just fine. He's still finding his feet now his role has expanded and it's my job to make sure it's clear that I won't be in the picture for much longer.'

I couldn't be happier that Jess and Riley are wrapped up in each other, when I really didn't think she was ready to commit again. I know Riley's overloaded workwise and I'm here to take some of that pressure off him, but the timing isn't good. The poor chap needs to get his feet firmly under the table without feeling I'm watching his every move, which I'm not, actually.

'Loneliness is an awful thing, Charlie, and I can say that with my hand on my heart, so I'm delighted with the way things have turned out. There's stuff the two of them still need to iron out, but in typical Jess fashion, she's set the date for the wedding and that means moving into the manor, too. I think August is an ambitious target, but you know what she's like when she's made her mind up.'

Charlie frowns at me. 'You don't think it's doable?'

'Well, if things aren't ready, it won't be for the lack of trying but once this little parking project is completed, it's my job to ease myself out of their lives again.'

'It doesn't sound little to me, Cappy, and Erica says that Renweneth Farm is a hive of activity. Riley's going to have a lot on his hands. Are you sure that leaving them to it is the right thing to do?'

'Yes, I don't want to cramp his style going forward. Who knows how long I'm going to be around. I'll be seventy-three this year.'

'And as long as you keep doing, you'll keep going. Besides, you look fit and healthy enough to me. I know men twenty years your junior who would blanch at some of the jobs you tackle.'

'I hope that's true. I'm feeling a bit redundant, Charlie; that's the truth of it.'

Our meals arrive and while the food looks great, a feeling of guilt washes over me for what might be happening as we speak. 'There's trouble brewing between Prudie and Jess,' I continue between bites. 'Having lunch with you is my excuse for making myself absent.'

'Oh… oh, right.' He pulls a long face.

When I explain how the situation arose, he agrees that I need to stay out of it. 'I fear I've already put my foot in it, mate. As you know, Prudie is an old friend; Maggie had a lot of time for her and what she's trying to achieve.'

I continue tucking into the cod and chips on the plate in front of me.

'At least it hasn't affected your appetite.' He laughs.

I grimace. 'It's been a hard morning but I'm dreading what I'm going to be walking back into. Jess will be suspicious, as she was expecting me home for lunch.'

'Having ducked out, Cappy, you need to explain yourself. Tell her you thought it was best that the two of them have a face-to-face chat without an audience.'

'That's a good one, Charlie, but Jess will see through it. I swore I'd never put pressure on her, but Prudie's cause is a good one and, I'll admit, she has my ear. Maggie would have backed her every inch of the way. The trouble is, Prudie has unwittingly rubbed Jess, and a few others at the farm, up the wrong way.'

'Look, if it's something you feel strongly about, then don't beat around the bush. Explain that to Jess; she'll understand that you and Prudie have history and it's a bit of a sensitive issue.'

It's tempting to scoff at his suggestion. 'And end up being the one in the middle every time there's a little misunderstanding between the two of them in the future?'

Charlie puts down his knife and fork to look at me. 'What's the alternative? Slink back to Stroud feeling you've let them both down?'

The man has a good point there. 'Jess calls the shots at the farm now and I can understand why I've annoyed her by what she sees as me *meddling*. And I suppose I walked into that one but Prudie, well, she's one of the few people around me who understands what it's like growing old. It's good to reminisce with her about the past, memories of Maggie, and happy times. What I admire about Prudie is that even given what she's already achieved in life, she's not done yet. That woman makes things happen and in some ways, she's so like Jess. I think that's the root of the problem. Prudie won't take no for an answer and, if their situations were reversed, Jess wouldn't either.'

'If only there was a way of finding a solution without upsetting either of them.'

'Well, it better be one that doesn't add to Jess's workload and shows Prudie in a good light. That woman does have a bit of a sharp tongue on her at times, but she also has a big heart.'

I raise my beer glass to him. 'If I can find a way to solve this little dilemma, maybe Riley won't be the only Mr Fix-It at Renweneth Farm.'

He puts his head back and gives a deep, belly laugh. 'You do know it's only the women around here who call him that? And they're all a bit put out that Jess has snagged him because he's sorely missed. My Erica can attest to that. I'm having to sort out leaking taps and hang shelves for her now. Somehow, it's never quite right and the missus doesn't hesitate to point that out.'

I give a chuckle. I bet tongues are really wagging as word gets out about a summer wedding at the farm.

To my surprise, Charlie goes off in another direction entirely. 'Did you know that Ivan is thinking of putting that old boat of his up for sale? The shed housing it needs demolishing before it collapses, and his wife has given him an ultimatum.'

My eyes widen. 'Is it worth selling?'

'I don't know. It's been in storage for what... the best part of ten years since he hurt his back.'

'If it was seaworthy when he bought it, it probably isn't anymore,' I remark.

'No, maybe not. I thought I'd take a quick look, though.'

'Really?'

Charlie shrugs his shoulders. 'It can't do any harm. If he's going to sell it off cheap, why not?'

Glancing at the clock, I think that an hour is about all I can justify. However, there's time for Charlie and me to make a firm commitment that this is the year we'll get some fishing in, before I head back to Stroud, and we shake on it.

On the drive back to the farm, Prudie rings and when her voice fills the car, it does put a smile on my face.

'Where are you?' I ask.

'At home. You're not at the farm – I've just got back from there.'

'Ah, I had lunch with Charlie.'

'It's nice that you were able to catch up. Besides, it does you good to have a bit of a break. I had a long chat with Jess about my vision.'

I swallow, hard. 'And?'

There's a gentle sigh. 'We seem to have got off on the wrong foot and I made it clear I regret that. Jess pointed out that the sort of space I'm looking for would be hard to accommodate at the farm and she's right. I need that studio, Cappy, to make it work. Even though I persuaded Neil, over at the village hall, to get in touch with Flo to make her an offer she couldn't refuse to return, she rejected it out of hand.'

I knew when Prudie told me of her plan that it was a bad idea and I remain silent, as she sounds a bit put out.

'Oh, Cappy. The village hall is perfect for a yoga studio but not for art classes. People don't understand...' She tails off, sounding dejected.

'Prudie, you've just hit the nail on the head. They *don't* understand.'

'It was good of Flo to allow me to hold some classes at the studio and I'm payin' her a fair rate. But all I can offer the students is watercolour and line drawin'; usin' oil paint in that closed environment is impossible. Her students wouldn't appreciate lyin' on their mats, relaxin' and stretchin' while breathin' in all the pungent smells of a real artist's studio. That's why I just can't set up anywhere. That sort of restriction doesn't apply to Flo.'

She has a passion that has never dimmed; it only grows and that's special. 'But she's the one with the contract, Prudie, and she's happy there.'

A gasp of exasperation from her makes my heart sink in my chest.

'How about I take you out to dinner tonight?'

'That would be lovely, thank you, Cappy. You're the only

person who listens to me when I witter on and I know that makes life difficult for you, but I can't give up – not now. There are some extremely talented people out there feeling isolated and alone, doubting their abilities. If I don't act soon, who knows what will be lost?'

There's a catch in her voice and, no doubt, tears in her eyes.

'Tonight, I'll book a table for two somewhere nice. I'll pick you up at seven and we can sit quietly, have a relaxing meal, and put the world to rights.'

'Cappy, my dear, you spoil me. Thank you.'

She's a lady well worth spoiling. Prudie works tirelessly to encourage and promote others; people forget that she's a mature lady who could so easily be spending her days enjoying coffee mornings and leisurely lunches, but that would bore her to tears.

JESS

6

A Spring in His Step

I have no idea where Cappy has been, but when he strides into the kitchen late afternoon, he's humming softly to himself.

'Our new campers are happy,' he informs me with a satisfied smile. 'Keith and Len have done us proud. And I've made a standing arrangement with Clem, at Pengali Farm, for us to use their container field as overspill parking until all the groundworks are completed here. It's been a productive day all round.'

'When you didn't turn up at lunchtime, I came looking for you. Keith said you'd popped over the road. I assume the two of you sloped off to the pub for lunch?' Now I feel bad for thinking Cappy was avoiding me, when he seems oblivious to the fact that Prudie has been here.

'Actually, I had lunch with Charlie.'

'Oh, that's nice. How is he?'

'Cheerful as usual. How was your day?'

Do I spoil his mood, or let things lie for now? I decide to put the subject of Prudie to one side for the moment. 'The session with Michael brought me up to speed on where we're at in terms of what I'll be able to draw down at the end of the financial year in April.'

He frowns. 'You're not smiling.'

'Our tax bill will eat into the profit because there's been a hefty jump in earnings, but this time next year, things should even out a bit.'

'Oh, the dreaded payment on account for the following year. It's unfortunate, as it only affects you if there's a sudden spike in the annual profit. It's good on one hand, but a bit unfair on the other. That's the price of success, for you.' He shakes his head, disapprovingly.

'Yes, and stupidly I didn't factor that in.'

'How is the budget for the renovation work looking?' I can see that Cappy is concerned and I don't want him to worry.

'I can cover the shortfall,' I reply, confidently.

'Jess, I don't want you using your nest egg from the sale of your old house. That's your cushion. If you need money, you only have to say as you might as well have it now rather than wait until—'

'Cappy! That's enough of that. You're here and you're working for free, which I so appreciate. I couldn't focus on the manor if you weren't around to bail me out. If I put any of my savings in to cover the shortfall, it'll be a short-term thing.'

'Well, the offer stands if you need it. By the way... I'm out this evening.'

I look at him quizzically. 'Again?'

'Might as well make the most of catching up with folk while I'm here.' He gives me a wink and a broad smile, which warms my heart.

'We love having you here, Cappy. It's not the same without you,' I confess.

'Get on with you. You'll soon establish a new normal once Riley's situation is sorted. And I don't intend on being a stranger.'

Hmm... it's obvious he's enjoying meeting up with old friends and happy to re-establish his social life. This could work in my favour.

'No doubt you'll be planning on digging out your fishing rods.' I grin at him, knowingly.

'The subject did crop up.' He chuckles, glancing at the clock. 'Make that coffee to go and I'll do the school run. When I get back, Riley said he'd give me a hand digging out a gazebo for our campers. Keith and Len built them a fire pit as they're planning a bit of an outdoor get-together this evening.'

'Oh, right. What a lovely idea. I must remember to drop by the village hall tomorrow with Lola to wander around the antiques fayre. It was an inspired idea of Vyvyan's and fingers crossed there's a good turnout, because she's been advertising it everywhere.'

'I never could see the point in buying someone else's junk,' Cappy replies, shaking his head and shrugging his shoulders.

'It's not junk, it's history. From a time when craftsmen and craftswomen made items that weren't just functional, but also beautiful and designed to stand the test of time.'

'Well, if you ask me, it's simply more stuff to gather dust. But I hope it all goes well, as you'll no doubt be delighted to welcome them back again next year.' He beams at me.

'I will. I'm also looking forward to the wedding fayre at the village hall at Easter.'

'And how are your wedding plans coming along?'

I raise my eyes to the heavens. 'Slowly, but Mum has offered to take on the role as my wedding planner.' I pass Cappy a thermos mug and he stares at me, narrowing his eyes.

'It's not going to be a fussy affair… bow ties and rented suits, is it?' he asks.

Cappy takes his mug, stopping to plant a kiss on my cheek before turning and heading for the door.

'No, I don't think that's Riley's style, but we haven't discussed it yet.'

'Thank goodness for that,' he calls out, as I hear the latch on the front door click open. 'See you in a bit.'

Whatever was pulling Cappy down earlier this morning has clearly passed and it's good to hear him sounding more like his old, cheerful self. If all it takes is a pub lunch with an old mate, then so be it!

'You're not in bed already, are you?' Riley quizzes me.

'How can you tell?' I question.

'Your voice is different when you're lying down.'

It's just gone nine o'clock and it's warmer working from my bed.

'In fairness, I do have a mass of paperwork scattered around me, but my eyes are beginning to droop. Lola is sound asleep, and Cappy won't be back for a while.'

'He's out and about again, eh? That's a good sign. Did he mention Prudie's visit?'

'No... I don't think he's even aware she came to see me.'

'So where do you go from here?'

'If I suddenly get a mass exodus from The Courtyard Hub and I can offer her a large enough space to do something with, we'll talk but the chances are slim to none. I told her to look elsewhere to avoid disappointment. A single bay becoming free wouldn't be any use and, besides, Vyvyan already has a waiting list.'

'Let's hope that's the end of it, Jess. Cappy seems to have perked up, so he must be content that you've done all you can. You didn't mention how your meeting with Michael went,' Riley enquires, trying his best to sound casual.

'It was fine. Pretty much as I expected. I'd already upped the contingency for the renovation work given your advice, although I assumed you were joking when you said to double the original budget.' I groan, and he laughs.

'Maybe that was a bit of an exaggeration, but I've seen how costs can spiral out of control. As long as you keep a tight rein on where we are expenditure-wise when the invoices start flooding in, it'll be fine. If you need me to cut a few man hours here and there, I can always pick up the slack at weekends.'

'You don't have to do that, Riley.'

'I know but it keeps me out of mischief. I'll be there bright and early tomorrow as I want to have a bit of a tidy-up ready for when the guys arrive on Monday morning. I like to run a clean site, and it's best to lead by example. Adam said he'd give me a hand in the morning for a couple of hours; he can't wait to see what progress we've made.'

That makes me smile. 'Honestly, builders never stop, do they? You'd think after running his own site all week he'd steer clear of the manor.'

'He's offered to take two weeks off in the spring to work alongside me. Just to show his appreciation for what *we've* done for him and Ivy. I told him I haven't done anything – it's all down to you, honey.'

I let out an involuntary gasp. 'Riley, don't do that!'

'Do what?'

'Act as if your hard work hasn't made a real difference. We're a team and, let's face it, it's been that way since the day you joined us. You've worked tirelessly and we wouldn't be where we are now if it weren't for that.'

He clears his throat and when he begins speaking again, his voice is a little uneven. 'I was captivated by you, Jess, from the very start. The way you rolled up your sleeves and never complained no matter what job I gave you. Whether you were clearing out smelly old wood and shrieking every two minutes as the mice scattered, or wading around ankle-deep in concrete, you just got on with it. How could I not work my socks off faced with that level of commitment?' Now he's laughing at me.

'I had no idea it was a competition,' I splutter. 'What I loved most was that even though it was obvious you prefer to work alone, you still kept a discreet eye on me. It's true to say I messed up on a few occasions, but I think you enjoyed coming to my rescue.'

He gives a happy little sigh. 'You're right, I did. But I never, for one minute, thought that we'd end up being a couple, Jess. Let alone that you'd consider marrying me.'

'So… when we started sleeping together, you thought I was just taking advantage of you?' I ask, trying my best to sound totally scandalised.

'You know that wasn't the case,' he chides. 'That spark

between us was there from the start, but I didn't think I was good enough. Not for someone like you.'

'What?' I'm appalled to hear Riley say that.

'My life was, and still is in some ways, a bit of a mess. If I'd handled things better, we wouldn't have this situation with Fiona hanging over us.'

'Riley, it takes two to make a *situation* as you call it, so you can only shoulder half of the responsibility. Is that why you tread so warily around Cappy now he's back? He senses it, you know, and he's a little uneasy because he doesn't want to step on your toes.'

Riley lets out a gentle moan. 'Has it occurred to you that I might not be the sort of person he hoped would capture his granddaughter's heart the second time around?'

'That's an utterly ridiculous thing to say. Trust me, Cappy wouldn't hold back if he felt we weren't right for each other. Why are you even thinking like this?'

There's a pause and I hold my breath for a few seconds before he begins speaking again. 'Fiona sent some fiery texts, you know, when I first told her about us.'

'What do you mean by *fiery*?'

'Just hurtful things harking back to the past, basically saying that she couldn't count on me. She said I haven't changed, and you'd soon suss that out.'

I sit bolt upright, anger beginning to fester in the pit of my stomach. 'You listen to me, Riley. I've known you for just over six months now and never once did you ever let me down in any way whatsoever. Quite the reverse. At times when I was stressed, tired and doubting we'd get everything done in time, you were my rock. You *are* still my rock. Have you ever stopped to consider that maybe the problem didn't lie with you in the first place?'

When he doesn't respond, I can only assume it's because he's trying to process that thought. 'Some people want everything their own way,' I continue. 'It's almost impossible to keep them happy unless you constantly give in to them. It was a little like that with Ben at times. With you and me, it always felt so natural, no matter what we're doing. There's no drama, no fuss just...'

I find myself smiling. '...setting ourselves impossible targets and getting on with it.'

'Ah, Jess. But what happens when the work on Renweneth Manor is finished? How will I fit in?'

My breath catches in my throat. 'Naturally, you'll be the site manager and we both know it'll be more than enough to keep you occupied.'

'But you want Cappy to stay, and he won't unless he feels he has a role to play.'

Now I'm beginning to understand. 'He's not getting any younger, Riley, and as Cappy settles back in, I think he's beginning to enjoy having more time to do the things he loves now that you're stepping up. Like meeting with old friends, doing the school runs, and pottering. Let's face it, there'll always be a long list of jobs on our to-do list. He will be needed, but he loves fishing and I'm going to try to encourage him to take it up again. That's what retirement is all about; the difficulty is in getting the balance right.'

'He doesn't feel that I'm... replacing him?'

'No. He only came back on the understanding that it was for six months. If he'd wanted the job permanently, he'd have said so. You'll be taking away the responsibility and in return, Cappy will be more than happy to lend a hand. I know him well enough to say that without hesitation but because you feel a little awkward around him still, he thinks you won't relax until he returns to Stroud. And that's the little problem we need to address at some point when things have settled down into some sort of routine. I don't want him to stay to work, but to enjoy his well-earned retirement.'

'I've always been a bit of a loner, Jess. I'm making a huge effort, but it isn't easy and the last person I want to upset is Cappy.'

'I know, Riley, but Cappy is on your side. As time goes on, you'll find that middle ground and you do that by asking his advice but making your own decisions. In the meantime, whatever you do, don't let Fiona undermine *us*. That's my only concern going forward.'

'Got it,' he replies, resolutely. 'I won't let you down, Jess. Thanks for the pep talk. Love you.'

'Love you, too. More than you know.'

It saddens me that Fiona still has the power to make Riley doubt himself. To me, that's the definition of someone who isn't happy with their own life. It's a huge relief to realise that it's not Riley who can't move on, it's Fiona. Sadly, that doesn't help the situation with regard to Ollie, but suddenly that ominous and unsettling feeling of uncertainty that has been hovering around me lifts.

Mum calls shortly after breakfast and after a quick chat, I hand the phone over to Lola so I can go and get ready. Cappy, Keith and Len are on car parking duty today, so Cappy was up and out at six this morning. The Saturday market starts early and the poor traders are up with the lark.

When she comes to find me, Lola is suddenly really excited about going to the antiques fayre. I don't know why exactly, but she thinks Riley should accompany us. I know he's at the manor and I'm pretty sure he's busy, but we head over to check.

'Riley, Riley—' Lola calls out, as I swing open the door to Renweneth Manor and she ventures into the hallway. She turns to look at me, lowering her voice as we hear footsteps on the landing above and two people talking as they hurry downstairs. 'What happened to the walls, Mum?'

'The water damage over the years meant some of the wood was rotten, Lola. We'll soon have new plasterboard ones and Riley is going to recycle some of the beautiful old oak panelling.'

'Hey, ladies,' Adam greets us as he descends the stairs, closely followed by Riley. 'Have you come to lend a hand?'

'No,' she retorts, doing a twirl as she's wearing her new, cherry-red coat. 'We've dressed up because we're off to look at the antiques. We thought Riley might want to come.'

Riley sits on one of the stairs so he's eye level with Lola. 'I'm in my work clothes and rather dusty I'm afraid. Adam has very kindly offered to help me carry some heavy bits of wood downstairs and it'll probably take us a couple of hours.' He pulls a long face and then breaks out into a grin. 'But don't you both look nice today and that colour really suits you, Lola. You look very grown up indeed.'

Her face lights up. 'Well, I am nearly nine, Riley,' she informs him, although he's probably tired of hearing about the plans for her birthday party at the end of the month. 'It's a pity you're busy, though.'

'I know,' he replies, sadly. 'We want our home to be cosy when we move in, don't we? It's going to take a lot of work so I'm going to have to pass today.'

'Okay, I understand. It is exciting, even though this is the boring bit.'

He raises an eyebrow. 'The boring bit?'

'It just looks messy to me,' she says, rather soberly. 'Mum and I like it when we're choosing paint colours and furniture, don't we, Mum?'

I try not to laugh but she's right.

'Adam and I had better get on with it, then,' Riley replies with all seriousness. 'And is this a shopping trip, or are you just going to check out the fayre?'

Lola turns to look at me. 'Grandma Celia said we need some pretty things to go on the wedding buffet table, didn't she, Mum?'

'She did. How do you feel about cut-glass crystal, Riley?' I muse and his eyes widen.

'It's funny, but no one has ever asked me that question before. I might need to think about it. Ask me later.'

I shake my head at him. If I end up buying anything, I'm guessing the answer will be that he loves it.

'Right, we'd better leave you guys to it. Thanks for lending a hand, Adam. Are you both off to the gym later?'

'It's my pleasure, Jess, and yes. Ivy's running one of her icing workshops so I'm best out of the way.'

Riley comes over to give me a quick kiss on the cheek. 'I'll catch up with you girls a bit later.'

Lola grabs my hand, encouraging me to turn in the direction of the door. 'Come on, Mum, we don't want to disappoint Grandma Celia, because she's given us a shopping list.'

I guess my little girl really is growing up faster than I give her credit. It seems I now have an assistant wedding planner, too.

7

Feeling the Good Karma Flowing

'Oh, Mum... isn't this adorable!' Lola exclaims, as she points at a heavy glass crystal jug.

The lady behind the counter gives Lola a little smile. 'You have good taste, young lady.'

The price is on the reverse of the label hanging from the handle, but it looks expensive to me. Under the guise of feeling the weight of it, I rather gingerly lift it up. 'Goodness, it's heavier than I expected.'

I lower it a little so Lola can get a better look, while hoping to catch a glimpse of the price. 'Oh, Mum, it's perfect.' She turns to look at the lady. 'My mum is getting married in August and we're looking for vases and jugs to go on the buffet table.'

'I see. Hmm... you're probably going to need a few, then. Let's look at the price.' The woman puts on her glasses and rubs her hand along her chin. 'I think I can do that for twenty pounds if you're interested.'

'Deal!' Lola says before I have a chance to even open my mouth. It's priced at thirty-five, so that's our first bargain snagged.

The woman carefully places it in bubble wrap and a recycled carrier bag, handing it to Lola as I dig out my purse. 'Thank you, we'll treasure it!' Lola says, with a beaming smile on her face and then she hurries off to the next stall.

It's busier than I thought it would be and as we're about to leave, mainly because we can't carry anything else, we bump into Vyvyan.

'My goodness, I hope you left a few treasures for me,' she remarks.

'Sorry, Vyvyan, but we got all the best vases. They're for the wedding,' Lola explains, in her serious voice.

Vyvyan raises her eyebrows. 'Ah, right. Well, thankfully, I'm looking for old books so I might still be in luck.' She gazes down at my daughter's sweet little face and then flashes me a heartfelt smile.

'It's a good turnout, Vyvyan. Well done you.'

Lola is getting fidgety and spots a school friend, so I take one of the carrier bags from her, indicating that she can go and have a chat.

'I'm simply relieved it's attracted so much attention,' Vyvyan admits. 'I wandered over to talk to our campers first thing this morning and it seems they had a bit of a party last night. They wanted to express their thanks to Cappy, Keith and Len for building the fire pit and for the use of the gazebo.'

'Well, that quells my concerns over the ugly trench and that pile of dirt. The guys wanted them to feel at home and I thought they did a pretty good job of it, all things considered.'

'They did that, all right, and it was a late one, by all accounts. Anyway, what a result all round! Like Renweneth Farm, the village hall needs to attract new sources of income to keep it running. I did feel a bit awkward when Flo moved her business to The Hub Studio, but Neil understands, and he's delighted with our new collaboration.'

'It was a great idea. I'm really looking forward to some of the future events you have lined up.'

'The wedding fayre in particular.' She laughs. 'Oh, before I forget, I… um… bumped into Flo when I popped into the bakery earlier on. Did you know that Cappy and Prudie had dinner together at Rivendale Country House last night? Flo was there and she spotted them together.'

'No. He just said he was going out but didn't mention who he was meeting up with.'

'The only reason Flo mentioned it was because it looked like they were having a business meeting. Prudie was talking and Cappy was making notes.'

'Really? Hmm. I didn't tell Cappy, but Prudie turned up, unannounced, at my door late yesterday morning. She began with an apology and then launched into a pretty intense speech about her vision for the future of her art school.'

Vyvyan's eyes widen. 'She still hasn't given up trying to get The Hub Studio? Flo wouldn't walk away, even if Prudie resorted to bribery to get her to move back to the village hall.'

'I know. Prudie laboured the fact that Grandma was one of her patrons and I know they were great friends. I told her straight that if a space comes up in The Courtyard Hub, it won't really be of any use to her, unless there's a mass exodus, as she'd need at least half of the ground-floor space. I advised her to start looking elsewhere.'

'Maybe that's the end of this little saga, then.'

I hope so. 'It might have been a smart move on Cappy's part wining and dining her, as I'm sure she was disappointed. Hopefully, they were brainstorming alternatives.'

'Anyway, Flo asked me to mention it to you. She used the word *plotting* but Prudie isn't her favourite person right now.'

'Hmm…' The sound of laughter makes me turn around. Lola and two friends are getting a little noisy. 'It would be nice if Cappy and Prudie could come up with a good solution for her. Right, I'd best reclaim my daughter and whisk her off home before that little gathering raises the roof with their noise. Have a good weekend, and well done again!'

'You too, Jess, and thanks.'

Lying in Riley's arms in the bedroom of his cottage, I reflect on the fact that this has become our little sanctuary. Cappy insisted the two of us head off for the night as he, Lola and Misty *had plans* for the evening. I'm pretty sure it involved watching back-to-back films, interspersed with making popcorn and probably ice cream sundaes. I did notice he'd bought Misty some new treats, so I threw a few things into an overnight bag, and Riley and I headed off.

'I thought you were asleep. What are you thinking about now?' Riley asks, sleepily, as he draws me a little closer.

'Popcorn and ice cream.'

That makes him chuckle. 'Are you hungry?'

'Always, at two in the morning.'

Riley eases away from me, then without warning leaps out of bed, immediately reaching for his dressing gown as the chill in the air is enough to give you goosebumps.

'Come back to bed; I was being indulgent and it's too cold to be faffing around grabbing snacks at this time of night.'

'Your word is my command,' he jokes. Seconds later, I hear faint sounds coming from the kitchen below.

Riley's decorating style is quite plain with a contemporary country feel. He's done an amazing job of rescuing what was once a derelict building and he's furnished it with pieces of furniture that are the new classics. Solid oak will always be in style, but people prefer the simplified look to the fussy carved panels of older pieces. And yes, you can tell that a woman doesn't live here.

As I'm wondering how we'll blend our styles in Renweneth Manor, he walks through the door, and even in the gloom I can see that's a rather heavily laden tray he's carrying in his hands.

'What on earth?'

'It's a picnic,' he informs me.

I sit up and he lays the tray down gently on my lap, yanking off his dressing gown and gingerly easing himself into bed next to me with a shiver.

'This is more like a feast,' I declare, with surprise. There's cold pizza, a dish of corn chips with a pot of creamy dip, some cheesy twists and two slices of melon. 'But I'm not complaining.'

'Get used to it – when we're living at the manor, I'll be whipping you up more than a cold platter if you can't sleep. I do the most amazing omelettes.'

Riley leans over to switch on the small salt lamp on the bedside table and it gives out enough of a glow to make the room feel cosy. He picks up a slice of pizza and begins munching as I follow suit.

'Mmm...' I groan, savouring my first bite. 'Nothing hits the spot better than cold pizza when you have the munchies.'

'Especially when the man you love has risked hypothermia to prepare it for you,' he jests before grabbing a few cheesy twists. 'That was a bit of a spur-of-the-moment suggestion tonight, but well done Cappy for thinking of it. I'm very grateful to him as it's a real bonus coming out of the blue like that.'

'Guilty conscience,' I mumble, as I finish off my pizza slice and start on the corn chips.

'Really?'

'He took Prudie out to dinner on Friday night, but he doesn't know I'm aware of it. In fact, he's even pretending he doesn't know that she turned up at The Farmhouse Friday lunchtime. Coincidentally, he didn't come home for lunch. I think she was hoping to put me on a guilt trip about The Hub Studio and if he caught sight of her, he didn't intend getting caught up in the conversation.'

Riley lets out a soft whistle. 'He's playing with fire there. I wouldn't want to be in the middle of you and Prudie.'

'She said she'd come to apologise but ending up making a sales pitch. And, yes, if I could accommodate her, I'd do just that. She played the friendship card with Grandma, which was out of order because my hands are tied.'

'It was a clever move on her part.'

'Not really. She's not just looking for a home for her classes, but for her art school. I told her she needs to consider other options because the amount of space she wants is way more than I'm ever likely to be able to offer her.'

Riley turns to look at me. 'So why did Cappy take her to dinner?'

'It was Flo who saw them, and she said it looked like they were plotting. Cappy was making notes.'

Riley lets out a sigh of relief. 'Then you're off the hook. She's accepted the situation and they were probably brainstorming.'

'Then why didn't he tell me that? He must know her visit unsettled me.'

'Ask him.'

I cough, starting to choke on some flaky crumbs and, as if by magic, Riley passes me a bottle of chilled water. I take a hefty slug and stare at him.

'You have a mini fridge in your beside cabinet?' I thought the low humming sound was coming from the bedside clock.

'I do.'

'You don't have any ornaments, but you have a fridge in the bedroom?' I challenge him.

His brow furrows. 'I hate dusting, so I like to keep all the surfaces clear. A fridge in the bedroom is like a TV; it's an essential.'

'Where's the TV?'

He tilts his body slightly as he reaches over to grab something, and I see it's a remote control. Riley aims it at the slim wall cupboard facing the bed. At the press of a button, the two doors effortlessly slide back to reveal a screen and I'm dumbfounded.

'You weren't expecting that, were you?'

I shake my head at him, starting to laugh and his frown deepens.

'What?'

'My bedroom essentials don't include a TV. It's a place to relax, recharge your batteries and have a little fun. Maybe read a book, but absolutely no electronics. I can see that we're going to have a bit of negotiating to do when it comes to setting up our new home together, Mr Warren.'

'I'm in trouble, aren't I?'

I lean in to plant a kiss firmly on his cheek before tucking into even more corn chips. 'No, of course not. But there's a reason why a lot of people's sleep is disturbed; they just don't research the reasons why. And if Lola saw this, she'd want a TV and a fridge in her bedroom too. What if you turn one of the rooms at the manor into a family entertainment room?'

Riley's frown turns into a grin. 'Seriously?'

'It's going to be *our* home, Riley. It has to work for us both. If you're prepared to keep the bedrooms as tranquil zones to please me, then you can have the biggest TV you can find, surround sound and whatever else will make you happy. And you can be honest with me; if you didn't like those jugs and vases that Lola and I picked up at the antiques fayre, you only have to say.'

He gazes into my eyes. 'They're perfect, Jess. I'm not good with the finer elements of design but you and Lola clearly have an eye for that. With regard to the wedding, it's over to you. So… we can have a fridge in the entertainment room?'

My body starts to shake as I begin laughing. 'You can have whatever you want. As for the rest of the house, we'll design it together, you and me. If I propose something you don't like, you only have to say. Lola and Ollie will want to design their own bedrooms, of course, but it would mean a lot to me if you supported my TV and Wi-Fi free policy in their little sanctuaries.'

'You really have a thing about it, don't you?'

'Don't take my word for it, just jump online tomorrow. Look up electric and magnetic fields – EMF – and health. A happy home environment means a healthy home environment and these days, it's not just about filling it with love and nurturing.'

'You never fail to surprise me, Jess. Now, how big a TV can I have?'

He's making a joke of it, but I can tell he's taking my concerns seriously, as I knew he would. 'That's entirely up to you. Why not go for a projector and use one wall as a screen?'

'Like being at the cinema? The kids would love that, but it's not in the budget.'

'Get me some figures and it will be. As long as we have a sitting room, a kitchen we can eat in, three bedrooms and at least one working bathroom, in addition to your entertainment room by August, I'll be a happy bunny.'

'You do know that I'm too excited to sleep now, don't you?'

I think we're both done eating.

'I was counting on it,' I reply, in my best sultry voice. I might keep surprising Riley, but he never disappoints me, no matter what I throw at him. And it's Ivy I have to thank for opening my eyes to the secret of a good night's sleep, although tonight I'm prepared to make an exception, but not because of the TV.

8

And Just Like That…

The last week has flown by and today, Sunday the twenty-ninth of January, is Lola's ninth birthday. To give Ivy and me a couple of hours to get the bakery café ready for this afternoon's tea party, Cappy and Riley are taking her to brunch at The Beachside Pantry. It's a bit of drive, as it's twenty miles away, but they do the most amazing pancakes – those fluffy, American-style ones – and the birthday girl is in for a real treat.

'Sorry, Misty,' I murmur as she sits halfway up the stairs watching me place a huge box on the doorstep. 'You're home alone for a while today. I've left you some treats and, when Lola gets back, she'll play with you before she puts on her party frock.'

Slamming the door behind me, I do feel a tad guilty as those citrine eyes of Misty's look so soulful at times, but a party takes a lot of organising.

Ivy spots me walking towards the bakery and swings open the door so I can gingerly negotiate the box through without hitting anything.

'It's not heavy,' I confirm, 'just awkward. It's full of bunting, balloons, paper napkins and plates and… argh… all sorts. And party favours.'

'Well, the cake is in pride of place, and I hope Lola loves it,' Ivy replies as she helps to steer me on into the café area, to place the box on the floor.

When I straighten, she beams at me. 'Can you believe that Lola is nine? I mean... nine? How did that happen?'

I lean in to give her a hug. 'And can you believe that you're having your scan tomorrow?'

'I know, it's all going to start feeling very real, isn't it? Adam's taking the morning off, but now I wish he'd booked the entire day.'

'It's funny,' I reply, as I cast my mind back to when I found out I was pregnant with Lola. 'Ben didn't come to the hospital with me for the scan. He attended the parenting classes, but that was all.'

'Do you think it's different... I mean having a baby when you're only twenty-two?'

I pause to consider it. 'Looking back, I just seemed to take everything in my stride. I do think that, as we get older, we worry more and that's not necessarily a good thing.'

'Tell me about it. I'm online whenever I get a chance.'

I shake my head, sadly. 'That has to stop, Ivy. It's time to tune in to your body and what it's telling you. I know you research everything, but having a baby is a natural thing. If you're anxious, the baby feels that. It changes the chemistry of your body.'

'It's funny you should say that, Jess, because I've started meditating each morning. Just in that time between opening my eyes and forcing myself to get up and into the shower.' She grins. 'But what a difference it's made to that queasy start to my day. I seem to be coping with it a whole lot better. Anyway, that box isn't going to empty itself.'

We make a start, and it isn't long before Adam appears. He hurries over, his face beaming. 'Morning, Jess. It's a big day for Lola. Ivy, you should have woken me up,' he complains, as he leans in to plant a kiss on her cheek.

She stops what she's doing, turning to face him. 'You were sound asleep and in need of a lie-in. Did you grab some breakfast?'

He nods his head. 'Yep. Three rounds of toast and a cup of tea. Right, what can I do to help?'

'We're almost done laying up the party table. There's a lot of bunting to hang but we haven't quite figured out how best to tackle it,' Ivy replies.

Adam stands back, scratching his head. 'Hmm… What if we run it from each corner of the room across into the central light fitting? I can make up a ring of some sort to sit on top of the light shade. It would simply mean drilling four small holes, one in each corner, as the width of the span would require a hook rather than a drawing pin. I can either take the hooks out afterwards and fill them in, or we can leave them up in case you get any more party bookings.'

'What do you mean *in case*,' I banter. 'Ivy will be taking photos to put on the website. Lola's unicorn party is going to be every little girl's dream.'

Ivy's lips are twitching. 'That's the plan, anyway.'

Adam wraps his arms around her waist. 'The two of you are unstoppable,' he declares. 'So, apart from putting up the bunting, what else can I do?'

'We have a large piñata unicorn that will need hanging outside, somewhere the kids can all have a go at swinging a bat without doing any damage. Any suggestions?'

'Don't worry, I'll think of something. Right, I'll go grab a few tools and some bits and pieces, and I'll be back.'

When I hear the tinkle of the bakery door shutting, Ivy and I look at each other, smiling.

'He's excited about tomorrow,' she says.

'And you are, too,' I retort.

'Excited and nervous in equal measure. Everything seems to be happening so quickly. I always assumed, like Ursula, I'd have Mum to rely on once the baby is here if I have a panic.'

'You won't panic, Ivy, and I'm just across the courtyard if you need a little support. You'll be a natural – I can tell from the way you were with Lola.' She doesn't look convinced. 'Try not to get too bogged down by what you read and see on the internet. Each new mum finds her own way through it. The biggest battle is the tiredness, but you might be one of the lucky ones whose baby is a good sleeper. Lola was colicky and the first few months, I can't lie, were a bit of a challenge.'

Ivy pulls a grimace. 'I remember calling in and taking it in turns with you to walk up and down with her over our shoulders while rubbing her back. She could burp for England.'

The pair of us start giggling as the memories come flooding back. 'Good times – and look at her now. She thinks that at the grand old age of nine she's all grown up and asking if she can have her ears pierced. I said maybe next year.'

'Is she having a separate birthday celebration with Ben and Naomi?'

'Yes, but a belated one. She's spending the week of half-term in February with them. It's going to be a joint party, as they're getting engaged.' I glance at Ivy and she gives a gentle sigh. I felt the same way when Ben told me; they should have separated the two celebrations. 'It's weird that increasingly, I'll have little to do with the life she has with Ben. Lola seems fine with it now, so I didn't make a thing of it. I know that if there are any problems, Naomi would call me immediately.'

'Is there a mention of a wedding date?'

I shake my head. 'No. I think Naomi just needed some sort of commitment from Ben. Given the age difference between them, I understand that. But she needn't worry because he wouldn't have let her move in with him if he weren't serious about their future.'

'You're okay with it, then?'

'I want him to be happy and it's stability for Lola. The worst-case scenario for me would have been if Ben had gone through a string of girlfriends. I'm not sure how she would have coped with that, and it would have made contact difficult. Now I can relax, even though it's tough not really knowing about the life she has when she spends time with her dad. I make a point of never questioning her when they video-call, or after visits. Sometimes she'll mention something, but I tend to keep my opinions to myself. I like to think Ben does the same when Lola talks about me.'

We both stand back to gaze at the table.

'Eighteen noisy nine-year-olds are going to love this!' I exclaim.

'Are we ready to start putting together the cake table? A mountain of unicorn cupcakes is going to require a lot of patience to assemble.'

'You'd better set aside a few for Adam,' I warn her.

'Already done,' she says with a laugh as we head up to the storeroom to start carrying down the boxes. 'Oh… I nearly forgot. Prudie popped in yesterday and said that as a *thank you* for giving the gallery a home, they'd like me to choose one of the pieces of artwork. She said that the artists are going to club together to gift me a painting of my choice from those on display.'

My jaw drops. 'Really?'

'I didn't quite know what to say, as it caught me off guard. Prudie had two new paintings with her to hang and asked me to give her a call when I've made my decision. Her group would like to gather together in the café to do a formal presentation.'

It is a lovely gesture, although I can't help feeling that the timing of it is suspect given my conversation with Prudie the other day. But I'm pleased for Ivy to have her generosity acknowledged.

It's chaos… but organised chaos. I'm not sure the guys fully understood exactly what they were volunteering for, but no one's complaining as they rush back and forth with various trays of party food. Cappy's in charge of drinks and seems to finally have the hang of how to make the fruit-based slushies.

The noise level in the café is off the charts, but it's mainly raucous laughter interspersed with high-pitched squeals. For some reason, the girls do that a lot when boys are around. I smile to myself. Everyone here is from Lola's class, and with eleven girls and seven boys, it's a pretty good mix.

'It'll soon be time to light the candles,' Ivy prompts me, as we stop briefly to pass each other on the stairs.

'Let me just refill this tray then I'll warn Lola. Oh, Ivy, this really is her dream party. I can't thank you enough for all your hard work.'

'Aww… it's been a total pleasure, Jess. She's brought so much love and laughter into all our lives!'

'That's what children do. Yes, they're hard work at times but they're a blessing, too.'

We head off in opposite directions, and I find myself wondering about the future with Riley. With Lola, and hopefully very soon, Ollie, in our lives will our family feel complete? Somehow, I can't see myself with a baby now and yet… oh well, who knows what might happen?

I quickly load up with mini hot dogs, which seem to be going down very well, and head back downstairs.

The buzz is wonderful to witness. Adam and Riley are bantering with two of the boys and Cappy is now clearing some plates.

'Anyone still hungry?' I call out and eager hands go up. 'It's almost time for cake.'

There's a flurry around the table but I think most of the children have eaten their fill. It's funny how kids always leave room for dessert, though.

I beckon to Riley and Adam. 'Can you guys do the honours with the ice cream? There are eighteen small bowls lined up in the kitchen and they need to be handed out with the cupcakes. I'm just going to get Lola moving ready to light the candles and sing happy birthday. Say, five minutes?'

'We're on it,' Adam confirms and off they stride.

I walk over to Cappy. 'How are you doing?'

'I haven't had as much fun as this in ages, Jess. Can't believe our girl is nine – the years have flown by. I've taken some photos to send to your mum and dad. They're gutted to miss the party, but I think they were both in need of a blast of sunshine. Winters in the UK can be draining at times.'

'I was surprised you didn't head off with them to Italy for a break. Don't you feel it, too, that winter slump?' This time last year, I know for a fact that he was feeling it. His spirits were low, and we were all worried about him.

'Not when there's so much going on. I spent my working life experiencing the very worst winters at sea, so with my two feet planted firmly on land, I'm not complaining. You look happy.'

'I am. I feel that things are finally beginning to fall into place, Cappy. You do know that you're a big part of that?'

He pauses for a moment, before responding.

'Never mind about me.' He laughs, heartily. 'You're just starting out on a whole new journey. Grandma was right; she said that Renweneth Farm was the future for our family. I thought she meant when the time came to sell it off.' I look at him aghast, but he puts up a finger to stop me. 'What she meant was a forever home for you and Lola. And now you have Riley, I'm a very happy man indeed.'

'But what if Riley feels overwhelmed by it all, Cappy?'

He frowns. 'What do you mean?'

'It's complicated. Fiona, well… she's trying to undermine him and seems to know what buttons to press. He sees you as a mentor, Cappy, a safety net.'

Ivy suddenly appears at my side. 'It's time!'

I can see that Cappy is a little caught off guard by what I said, but he turns to smile at Ivy. 'Let's see how long it takes for them to demolish the biggest display of cupcakes I've ever seen!'

We all make our way over to the cake table and I indicate for Lola to join us. Cappy ceremoniously lifts down the top tier of the Perspex pyramid. It's a ten-inch square cake with a forest scene and in the middle is a sparkly clear resin unicorn. It's something I know Lola will treasure forever.

Ivy passes me the rechargeable arc lighter. Suddenly, I'm

feeling tearful. With each candle I light, the memories of earlier birthdays come flooding back. It's overwhelming and when Riley sees that my hand is shaking, he steps forward to take over.

'I think the birthday girl should light the last two candles. What do you think, Lola?'

'Ooh... yes!'

Her face lights up as Riley passes her the lighter and I can tell that she's feeling very grown up indeed. When the last candle is lit, Ivy kicks off the chorus of 'Happy Birthday'. My eyes are brimming with tears. It's like my life is flashing before my eyes and it brings me back into *the now*. Me, Lola and Riley, here at Renweneth Farm. I can't let Cappy return to Stroud, simply because he thinks he'll no longer be needed because that isn't true.

Happy birthday, dear Lola, happy birthday to you!

As a cacophony of voices fills the air, my daughter's eyes are gleaming.

'After cake and ice cream, it's coat time and everyone outside as we have an enormous unicorn piñata with presents for everyone!' Ivy announces.

Instead of sweets, it's filled with fun things... packets of collectors' cards the kids are going wild about right now as it's linked to an online game, fun pens with superheroes on them and finger skateboards... I know, crazy... but the kids love them.

One thing I know for sure is that we're *all* going to sleep well tonight!

This morning, I ferry one very happy girl to school with a boxed cake to share with her classmates. With her best friend, Daisy, sitting next to her in the back seat of the car, they spent the entire car journey talking about the party. By the time I get back to The Farmhouse, wash up the breakfast dishes and change ready to get hands-on at the manor, it's almost ten o'clock. As I'm about to leave, my phone kicks into life.

'Ivy?'

'Oh, Jess… Adam's just left for work. It's all good but…'

She sounds in shock and my stomach turns over. 'But?'

'We're having twins – a boy and a girl.'

'Oh my, that's unexpected but wonderful news!'

Without warning, Ivy suddenly bursts out into floods of tears. 'Yes… it is wonderful, and we've been truly blessed, but what if motherhood doesn't come naturally to me? And what if I can't cope with two babies at once?'

I try to clear my head and think of something calming to say. 'You're going to take a few deep breaths and relax your shoulders. Where are you?'

'Walking towards The Farmhouse as we speak.'

'Good. I'll get the kettle on.'

I immediately text Riley.

I'm going to be a bit late joining you. Sorry, but something has come up and I'll be over as soon as I can. x

The moment I open the front door and see the pallor on Ivy's face, I can tell she's in shock. 'Go on through to the kitchen and sit yourself down. I know it wasn't what either of you were expecting to hear, but everything else is fine?'

She stands there nodding her head and I throw my arms around her shoulders. 'Then it's all good; you're not alone in this, Ivy. There are plenty of people you can call on to help.'

'Adam said that it will all be fine, but he won't be here most of the time. It's scary, Jess.'

My heart constricts in my chest. 'That's a natural feeling no matter how many babies you're having, Ivy. I felt like that when I found out I was expecting Lola. But the day I gave birth and held her in my arms for the first time, she looked up at me and I knew that somehow I'd get through it.' I'm not even sure she's listening to me, as I carry the coffee mugs over to the table to join her.

'Adam went very quiet when we saw two beating hearts on

the screen.' She swipes her eyes with the sleeve of her jumper and then reaches into her handbag. 'It's just... unbelievable. They're not identical twins, of course, since they're a boy and a girl, but fraternal. The obstetrician explained that each baby has its own sac and placenta.'

She hands me the black and white print and it's quite something to see. 'Oh, Ivy... in one way it's a miracle but naturally you're both reeling. It's a lot to take in.'

'We're going to call our parents this evening when Adam gets home from work. He said I shouldn't worry, that we'd draw up a plan of action. What does that even mean?'

I encourage her to take a sip of her drink. 'He wants to reassure you that you're in this together. Adam realises you'll need some extra support to begin with. It's a case of getting everything organised in advance, that's all.'

In truth, I hope I'm saying the right things, because as the news begins to sink in even I'm feeling overwhelmed for her.

'I was panicking about having one baby but two... it's unreal, Jess. How do you even manage if they both want feeding at the same time?'

I reach out to place my hand on her arm and give it a comforting squeeze. 'Just try to clear your head for a moment and take a few deep breaths. This is exactly why Adam said you'll need to make a plan. Babies do sleep a lot you know, and once they settle into a routine, you'll be able to plan your day around that.'

'Yes, a routine,' she repeats, sounding dazed.

'The best thing to do, is not to overthink this and allow yourself to get swamped by *what-ifs*. Now drink your coffee and give yourself a little time to get used to the idea. You are one of the most organised people I know. Without a shadow of a doubt, you'll have everything set up for the babies well in advance of the day. And I'm sure that both your mum, and Adam's mum too, will be on call if you need any help during those early weeks. Don't forget that I'm here as well, and I certainly won't see you struggle. It's nothing for me to take a couple of hours off to step in if you need me.'

I'm heartened to see the colour beginning to return to her cheeks and she gives me a watery smile. 'All we'll need is a dog and a cat, and my dream will have come true!'

With that, we both laugh until tears run down our cheeks. I know that if I were in Ivy's shoes, I'd be feeling the exact same way. Overjoyed on the one hand but scared on the other. Ivy and Adam are only just settling down after a series of major upheavals in their lives and now they're facing the biggest challenge so far. Even so, it's exciting.

MARCH

RILEY

9

Double Trouble

February seems to have flown by. With Lola away, spending half-term with her dad, Jess worked flat-out. If she wasn't at the manor sanding and painting, she was holed up with Vyvyan, looking at ways to increase the income at the farm.

Fiona is still ignoring my texts and I have no idea when I'll see Ollie next. He and Fiona are bound to be at my brother Tom's wedding, though. For now, I'm choosing not to dwell on the situation and have decided to back right off. I choose instead to live in the hope that, before too long, Ollie will press her to get in touch again. We had a great time when they came for the weekend, but the problem is that I think Fiona enjoyed it, too. What she must accept is that Jess is the person I'm destined to spend the rest of my life with. For me, there is no going back.

The first of March kicks off with a beautiful blue sky but a windchill factor that makes my toes curl. Even so, it's a slow start to the day.

'Steve, it's Riley. None of the plumbers have turned up this morning at Renweneth Farm and no one is answering their phones.'

He breathes out heavily and it's such a depressing sound that it makes my blood run cold. 'I can't believe I'm saying this, Riley, but we're shutting our doors. We had the guys in first thing to break the news that the bank is cutting off our credit. They're calling in our overdraft and business loan. It means it's the end of the line for us.'

'Just like that?' I can hardly believe what I'm hearing.

'It's been touch and go for a while, mate, but we really thought we could get the company back on an even keel. We're overrun with work but with rising fuel costs and interest rates on our debt going up and up, they decided to pull the plug. I'm just about to start contacting our clients to explain and tell them how gutted we are to find ourselves in this position. We've been going for nigh on twenty-five years now and our guys are some of the best in the trade. The loss of jobs is going to affect a lot of young families, as well as people who've stuck with us over the years.'

The poor guy sounds like the bottom has fallen out his world and I can't imagine how devastated he's feeling. He's a good man and well respected in the community.

'I don't know what to say, Steve. You've put your heart and soul into building that company.'

There's a slight pause. 'I really appreciate you saying that, Riley, but some people are going to be angry, and rightly so.' There's a low groan before he continues. 'It's like being on a speeding train. At what point do you pull the emergency lever? Now I see that I was kidding myself we could claw our way back to solvency. I'm going to lose everything, as I'd even remortgaged the house to keep us ticking over. And we're leaving you with a job half-finished.'

'It's been taken out of your hands, Steve, so don't feel bad about that.'

'The big corporations seem to get all the tax breaks and benefits, and yet hard-working companies like ours get hammered every year with higher taxes and costly changes in rules and regulations. I might sound paranoid, Riley, but it's like the system is stacked against us.'

I can only agree with him. 'In the building game, it's hard to keep up with the constant changes. To be frank, some of the new rules have me scratching my head. I'm pretty sure someone somewhere is making money off it, but it's not small and medium-sized companies, that's for sure.'

'It's the end of an era for Arnott Plumbing and a day I thought I'd never see. Please tell Jess and Cappy how gutted I am to let you all down.'

'They'll know that, Steve. Our thoughts are with you and your family. You know where I am, mate, if you need a listening ear.'

'Appreciated, Riley.'

As the line disconnects, I find myself standing here shaking my head in disbelief, as Jess hurries towards me.

'What's up?'

'The plumbers haven't turned up. That was Steve Arnott. They've gone bust.'

'No!' Jess looks understandably shaken.

'Yep. That was one of the worst conversations I've ever had with anyone. He's a broken man.'

'Oh, Riley. Poor Steve. He's one of the good guys and that's devastating to hear.'

'The bank has pulled the plug and I don't know how big his debts are but I'm guessing not enough to repay his creditors.'

Jess's eyes widen. 'So, we've lost the money we've already paid on account?'

'It's not that bad. The second payment was due in four weeks' time, so we'll maybe lose two grand, tops. But it's not going to be easy to find replacement plumbers. However, having laid off his guys this morning, I'll do a ring-around because they'll all be looking for work. If I can talk two of them into finishing off the job, we'll probably have to buy the materials and pay them a fixed day rate.'

'Right, you get onto that, and I'll let Cappy know; I'd hate him to hear this from someone else. It's such a shock, isn't it?'

I can see Jess is as taken aback as I am. 'Steve said he'll lose everything, Jess, including his house.'

A frown creases her brow, and she steps forward to throw her arms around me, hugging me fiercely. 'It's a reminder that it can happen to anyone, Riley, but I promise I won't let it happen to us. What impact will it have on the schedule?'

'If I can get at least two guys back on the job, then we'll probably lose seven or eight working days. Steve sent over anyone who was spare to lend a hand at odd times, as he was well aware of how tight our schedule is. It'll mean making a few changes and renegotiating start dates with some of the other trades.' It's hard not to sound deflated.

As I watch Jess set off back to The Farmhouse, her shoulders slumped, my phone pings, and it's a text from Adam.

Hey, mate, I've just had a chat with the planning officer and it's bad news. If you get a chance to talk any time after one o'clock, I'll be on my lunch break. I'd appreciate a few minutes of your time.

I did warn him that he was asking for the impossible and I'm pretty sure Cappy did, too. But this is going to cause a big upset and not just for Ivy and Adam. With their mortgage offer imminent, I'm not sure how much Jess was relying on that influx of cash from the sale of Smithy's Cottage. Can this day possibly get any worse?

With two plumbers back on site working out what they'll need to finish installing the basic plumbing system and central heating, I leave them to it and head off to phone Adam.

'Hey, is it a good time to talk?'

'Yes, I'm in the office grabbing a quick sandwich. You were right, the planning officer cited the fact that as it's an area of outstanding beauty, we can't install dormer windows on the roadside. That means there is no way we can convert the attic of Smithy's Cottage into a third bedroom without that extra headroom. Ivy is going to go into meltdown when I tell her. The truth is, as it stands, the cottage just isn't going to be big enough for our needs in the future. The babies will share a room to begin with but at some point, a third bedroom will be a necessity.'

My heart sinks in my chest. Just when everything was settling down nicely, this could throw everything into flux.

'The first round of plans that Cappy submitted included installing dormer windows in both The Farmhouse Bakery and Smithy's Cottage, but it got rejected for the same reason. Fortunately, because Renweneth Manor looks out over the moor, we can install them on the back of the property, although not on the front.' Rules, eh? 'It was a long shot, Adam, but worth a try. Sometimes they tinker with the guidelines, but areas of outstanding beauty come with a whole host of restrictions.'

Adam sighs. 'Then we're stuffed. I'm not even sure the amount of space we have on the ground floor will allow us to accommodate all the kit we're going to need. We've been looking at double buggies and they take up a huge amount of space. I doubt we'd fit one into the hallway and with the cloakroom being sited under the stairs, it'd have to be housed in the kitchen/diner. I can't see Ivy putting up with that.'

'It's time to look at other options, Adam.' I can't believe I'm saying that, but I can't see any other way out of this.

'I know, but we can only afford to buy something the size of Smithy's Cottage and Ivy needs to be close to work. If we start looking for a three-bed cottage further away, she'll be stressing about the problems that will throw up. I've been thinking outside the box and wondered if you, me and Cappy could get together this evening? Preferably just the three of us. I don't want to go back to Ivy until I know there's nothing I've missed. Obviously, it's going to impact Jess as well, so I think it's best we keep this between ourselves for the time being.'

Given the news I've had today, I think so too. 'No problem. I'll say we're going for a pint. How are you coping?'

'I'm trying to remain focused and get a handle on what we're going to need to make life as easy as possible once the babies are here. But I'm way outside my comfort zone and winging it just to keep Ivy calm. Her hormones are all over the place and the last thing I want is for her to look up and say she wants to move back to Stroud. If she does that, she'll have family close by, but I'll only get to see her and the babies at weekends. She won't want that and neither do I. We're realising a dream we had from more or less the day we exchanged our wedding vows and, somehow, I'll figure out a way to make it work.'

That thought had already crossed my mind, but I dismissed it very quickly as it doesn't bear thinking about. Things are going so well here at the farm and if Ivy and Adam leave, it would be like ripping our team apart. They're happy here and it's in everyone's interests to find a solution.

'I'll tell Cappy and we'll meet up in the car park at say, seven-thirty?'

'Perfect.'

'Don't worry, with three heads on the case, we'll think of something.'

'Thanks, mate. You have no idea how desperate I am.'

By mid-afternoon, the plumbers are hard at work, and I have a list of items to order. Making my way across to The Farmhouse, I spot Cappy coming out of the bakery and I head over to him. He looks at me rather guiltily, clutching a carrier bag in his hands.

'It's not for me,' he blurts out. 'It's for Prudie. She's invited me over for a cup of tea, but don't let on to Jess. There's still a bit of an atmosphere between the two of them.'

I roll my eyes. 'Don't worry, I'm keeping well out of it. Do you fancy a pint in the pub with Adam tonight? I'll drive.'

His eyes light up. 'Sounds good to me. Mid-week slump?' he asks.

'Hmm… sort of. The planning officer confirmed that the dormer windows aren't an option, and he was banking on that to solve his and Ivy's problem.'

Cappy frowns. 'What next? Let me give it some thought. I'm still reeling over Arnott Plumbing. It's unbelievable. Anyway, I'd best get off. See you later. Are you eating at The Farmhouse tonight?'

'I think I will, given that we're socialising later.' I grin at him.

'Good chap. Jess is in the kitchen poring over the budgets. I'm going to do the school run on my way back from Prudie's.'

'Enjoy!'

I know Jess thinks that Prudie is a bit of a troublemaker, but she's good for Cappy. It's true to say Prudie does have an agenda and she's like a dog with a bone: she doesn't give up. Unfortunately, she's met her match with Jess and I'm glad I'm not in Cappy's shoes.

As I unlock the door and step over the threshold, I call out: 'It's only me. I have some figures for the plumbing materials.'

'Good timing,' Jess replies. 'I'm in the kitchen.'

Jess is surrounded by little piles of paperwork and is trawling through a stack of invoices.

'The guys reckon it will take two of them another ten days to finish off this stage. They won't be able to hang the radiators until we've plaster-boarded the framework and have solid walls.'

Jess looks at me wearily. 'More delays. Great!'

'The good news is that the electricians are doing well. They've almost finished running their cables.'

Jess's eyes sparkle. 'Walls mean light switches and sockets! I'm just relieved you managed to get some plumbers back on site, though. Running water is a necessity, not a luxury.'

I grin at her, because for now, the only access to water we have is a single pipe with a brass tap on it coming up out the floor in a totally stripped-back kitchen.

'Anyway, is it okay for me to go ahead and place this order?'

I pass the list to Jess and watch as she scrutinises it. 'Do you have a ballpark figure of how much it's going to cost?'

'Three grand maybe. I don't know what's left in the budget but when the rooms are ready, the radiators and the boiler will probably come to around another six thousand, plus another 50 per cent on top for labour costs. You get me for the usual rate, of course!'

Jess starts laughing and then taps away at her calculator, but I can't read her expression. 'That's fine, Riley. Go ahead and place the order and thanks for being so careful about keeping costs down. I don't know what I'd do without you keeping tabs on everything.'

We both know that without the basic services in place, the building isn't going to be habitable any time soon. But doing the maths in my head, I'm pretty sure we'll be over budget. I warned Jess at the start to take the budget and double it. I like to think that she took me seriously and I know she did rework the original estimates.

'Oh, before I forget. Cappy, Adam and I are thinking of heading out for a pint this evening. Is it okay if I stay for dinner? I'm the designated driver.'

'We always cater for you anyway,' she declares, shaking her head at me. 'You should realise that by now. It's handy that you're going for a drink, though, because Ivy and I are well overdue a girls' night in. It's obvious she's still feeling in limbo, and I am concerned about her. So is her mum.'

'You've been talking to Sarah?'

'Yes, she rang me for an off-the-record chat. Sarah and Paul want to come for a visit, but Ivy keeps putting them off. She asked if everything was okay.'

Ooh, that's awkward but understandable given the situation. 'What did you tell her?'

Jess looks a tad uneasy. 'That Ivy's busy at the bakery and every spare minute she gets, she's doing what she calls *baby prep*. I told Sarah that I've been giving Ivy some space and when she's ready, she'll reach out to us all, I'm sure.'

Ivy was the same when she took over the bakery. She quickly pulled together her grand plan and from the moment she arrived, she didn't stop until everything was set up as she wanted it.

'I can barely remember Ollie as a baby now… just fleeting memories that pop into my head,' I reflect. 'I remember he cried a lot at times. Fiona and I would take turns pacing up and down with him until he settled. No two days were ever the same. Ivy is aware of that, isn't she?'

'She ought to be, as she gave me a hand with Lola after she was born but, as you say, memories dim and it was a long time ago. Ivy spends hours online researching and reading parenting books,' Jess admits. 'It's her coping mechanism, although I fear it's also information overload. But she'll gradually settle down and going into it feeling organised will stop her from panicking.'

I let out a deep breath. 'Adam's trying his best to act calm and collected, but I don't think he knows what to worry about first.'

'When the babies are here, the plan will go out the window and Ivy will just do what most new mums do.'

'Which is?' I query.

'Get through it one day at a time. We worry about our offspring when they're crying, and we worry about them when they're sleeping. I was constantly checking Lola was still breathing, poor little thing. The number of times I inadvertently woke her up when I put my hand on her chest because I couldn't see it moving, was ridiculous.' Jess laughs softly to herself. 'And I was constantly on the phone to my mum, asking her advice as what did I know? I was young and it was scary at times.'

As Jess is talking, her face seems to light up. 'Happy times, though,' I remark, and she nods her head in agreement.

'Nothing can prepare you for that feeling of joy; or for the roller coaster of emotions that follow when you realise you've brought a new life into the world and they're totally reliant upon you.'

Is Jess trying to tell me in a roundabout way that with Lola and Ollie, she feels our family is complete? Having a baby is a huge commitment, I get that, but it would have been wonderful to experience it with Jess. Oh, well – we've more than enough on our plate to cope with as it is and I've not exactly proven myself to be a role model when it comes to being a dad, have I?

Cappy isn't at all surprised when Adam reports back on what the planning officer told him. 'What I don't understand,' Adam continues, sounding perplexed, 'is that you got permission to install dormer windows to the rear of Renweneth Manor.'

'It's not listed, Adam, and the deciding factor was that the rear elevation can't be seen from the road, or another property. The cluster of cottages in the courtyard are even older than the manor itself and are a landmark around here. The outer shell has to remain unchanged and, even with the barn, we had to ensure the exterior was in keeping with the existing buildings. Cladding at ground level would have been so much cheaper than stonework, but the end result is pleasing to the eye; it just cost a heck of a lot more.'

I'm not sure the explanation helps, as Adam is looking crestfallen. 'There's no way we're going to be able to make Smithy's Cottage work for us when the babies are here, and Ivy is going to freak out. I could put up a shed in the garden and insulate it, so that it's suitable to store a double buggy and toys. But without a third bedroom, the cottage just isn't a long-term solution for us as a family.'

We're all aware of the impact of that. Cappy half-turns to reach into his backpack and pulls out a cardboard tube. 'I was looking at the architect's plans earlier, trying to figure out what options there might be.'

I help him to unroll the drawing, as Adam clears the table and casts around for four anchors to hold it flat.

'In theory, there are two options to create an extra room on the first-floor level. It might muddy the waters in terms of you and Ivy buying the cottage, Adam. It can be harder to get a mortgage when a part of the property would be what they refer to in legal terms, as *a flying freehold*.'

It's unusual but being in the trade Adam has probably come across this before.

Cappy stabs his finger at Smithy's Cottage on the plan. 'On one side you have The Farmhouse Bakery, on the other The Courtyard Hub, formerly the small barn.' We all lean forward in a huddle. 'I'm not saying either of the options are easy and I have no idea about cost, but let's set that to one side for now.'

Cappy begins tapping his finger on what is now The Courtyard Hub. 'When we did the conversion and created the mezzanine, the decision to extend it across approximately 50 per cent of the total area was to increase the amount of light on the ground floor. It might be possible to knock through from the second bedroom in Smithy's Cottage and extend the mezzanine. Admittedly, it would be a bedroom off a bedroom, but it would be a big room. We're talking at least the entire width of the cottage, maybe a bit more, so it could also accommodate a lot of storage space.'

It's not a bad idea, but I know what Jess's first question will be. 'What about getting light into the ground floor of The Courtyard Hub?'

Cappy points to the side wall of the barn, which abuts the large car parking area in the grounds of Renweneth Manor. 'It's more daylight, not visibility we're after. If we installed a whole run of windows the entire length of the room as high up as we can, every bay would benefit from natural daylight.'

'The extra room would be a part of the cottage but the ground beneath it would still belong to Renweneth Farm.' Adam frowns, as he gives it some serious thought.

'Exactly. Now, the other option is to knock through on the other side into The Farmhouse Bakery. It would mean moving the kitchen into the former office, which you're currently using as a spare guest room, Adam. I have no idea how that would affect the running of the bakery, as the stockroom would probably need moving, too. It would be a major upheaval, though, and would mean the kitchen would be out of operation for at least a few days.'

'Either way, both are flying freeholds,' I point out.

'Yes and this is just between us for now. I thought it might be worth considering. If it solves your problem, then we can delve into it a bit deeper.' Cappy sits back, picking up his pint as Adam continues to stare down at the drawings.

'What do you think, Riley? I mean, it's got to work for Jess, too.'

'The last thing Ivy is going to want is anything that upsets the running of the bakery. I think it would add yet another challenge into the mix. From the farm's point of view, I think it would be a mistake for The Farmhouse Bakery not to be a standalone property. However, the option to extend the mezzanine might work. It would just come down to cost and minimising the disruption to the businesses on the ground floor.'

Cappy runs his hand along his chin. 'Do you think that getting in the new joists and laying the floor above could be done in a day if we pulled together a small team, Riley?'

'It would take a bit of planning, but I don't see why not. That way the knocking-through bit, which is going to be dusty, wouldn't affect the businesses in The Courtyard Hub at all.'

'Well.' Cappy looks at Adam questioningly. 'Where do we go from here? Do you want me to pop into the council offices and check we wouldn't need to submit a planning application before we give this any further consideration? If we're lucky, it might just involve building regs, which would mean we could make it happen pretty darn quickly if Ivy and Jess like the idea.'

Adam sighs. 'Ivy's very sensitive right now so, yes, if you don't mind, that seems like a sensible next step. Look, I haven't told her that the dormer windows aren't an option yet. She's going to be gutted. Can I mention there might possibly be another solution we haven't considered?'

Cappy and I glance at each other rather uncomfortably and I suspect we're thinking the same thing. 'In that case, why don't we head back to The Farmhouse and put our cards on the table. Worst case is we get our hopes up and planning throw a spanner in the works, but it's better than nothing.'

He raises his glass and Adam and I join him. 'Here's to solutions, not problems!' Cappy states, robustly.

As for me, I think the cost and the disruption involved aren't worth it. The truth is, they need a bigger property.

JESS

IO

A Major Headache

After a late-night chat with Cappy, Riley, Adam and Ivy at The Farmhouse, I'm feeling as if our carefully made plans are beginning to unravel. We all want to come up with a workable solution, but at what point do we stand back and accept the inevitable?

This morning, Riley joins Cappy and me for breakfast and the three of us linger around the kitchen table for a second coffee while Lola gets ready for school.

'Last night, I felt there was an air of desperation around the table,' I conclude. The two men stare at me without saying a word. I swallow hard before I continue. 'At some point, Ivy is going to ask for my opinion and no one is going to like what I have to say.'

Now they're both frowning.

'Smithy's Cottage is perfect for a young couple with maybe one child, but not two. I understand that it's a huge comfort for Ivy, being able to walk from her front door to her business in seconds. If a problem arises at the bakery, she's on hand to sort it out. And, if she can find a good babysitter, she can maybe even consider working a couple of hours a day. But in the long term, even with a third bedroom, it won't work.'

'Why?' Cappy queries, his frown intensifying.

It's hard not to sound dismissive. 'Because a growing family needs space. Bedrooms are one thing, but the living areas are important, too. They'll soon outgrow the space they have. It'll drive Ivy mad when every inch is filled with all the things that come with not one, but two children. Refusing to address the problem now is just delaying the inevitable.'

'Is it because you're against the idea of extending the mezzanine in The Courtyard Hub?' Riley questions.

'No. If Smithy's Cottage were gaining a two-storey addition, then it would be the perfect solution. But I know what it's like at the end of the day to have to blitz the house because it feels like every inch is covered with toys, shoes, coats... you name it. And I only had one child to contend with.

'Let's face it, the sitting room and kitchen/diner are what you expect from a cottage: compact and cosy living. Adam and Ivy need to look at bigger properties, as close to the farm as possible. My fear is that if they don't, Ivy will end up finding it all too much and talk Adam into returning to Stroud. I genuinely think they'd regret it. Being pregnant and preparing for the babies is going to be a testing time for Ivy; add building work into the mix and it's going to make their lives a misery.'

They both nod their heads in agreement.

Cappy turns to face me. 'You need to have a heart-to-heart with Ivy. It's obvious the pair of you have been avoiding each other.'

There's no point in denying it. Even at our get-together last night before the guys returned, all we talked about was the growing list of baby clothes and various kit she thought she was going to need.

'I intend to. Adam is so desperate to find a quick and easy solution that he's not standing back to think about the bigger picture. Ivy is totally caught up with how she's going to manage to keep the business running while caring for two little ones and is doing much the same thing. It's better to face the fact that living on site isn't a viable option for them long term. In the short term, though, it's probably the only way for Ivy to cope.'

'So, you think they'll rent the cottage for a while until life has settled down enough to look at finding something affordable?' Riley asks.

'If I were in their situation, it's what I'd do, and it'll give them some breathing space. It will be a little while before they need to think about putting the children into separate bedrooms, unless they're constantly waking each other up. While the babies are small, they'll probably cope with the space they have but it's time to face facts. Smithy's Cottage isn't their forever home.'

However, it does leave me with a problem. Swapping a hefty influx of cash for a monthly rental income isn't what I need right now. But I must do the right thing by Ivy and Adam; I can't stand back and see them invest their savings in a place they'll soon outgrow.

It's a dent in the dream I had and in theirs, too. Oh, how wonderful it would be to have them living here and see their children growing up, day by day. I know that Lola would love it, too, but it's a decision that must be made with the head and not the heart. What Ivy needs now is practical advice and, as her best friend, it's about what's right for her, Adam and the twins.

Riley has put me on sanding duty in the manor, to bring some of the original wall panelling back to life. Layers and layers of old varnish obscure the beautiful moulding and while it's hard work, it's also a satisfying job. It's too windy to work outside today, so I'm in what was the original dining room. Only one of the internal walls is still in situ but the suction hose attached to the belt sander is doing a decent job of drawing in most of the dust, so it doesn't spread far and wide. It's also noisy, but with two plumbers drilling holes, and Riley on the first floor making a start on plaster boarding what will be the family bathroom, we're all wearing ear defenders.

My mind is on other things, though. Cappy really pulled out the stops trying to solve Ivy and Adam's problem. He meant well and I could see he was disappointed when I spoke my mind earlier on. But it also made me feel a tad guilty. He believes in Prudie's cause and maybe I've been quick to judge her, simply because her forthright style grates with me. She's spent her entire working life fighting for something she's passionate about and I admire her for that. If Grandma and Cappy supported her, then who am I to turn her away? I have an idea I think might work but I want to keep it up my sleeve for now. It could be another reason for Cappy to return to the farm for good, but it would change the dynamic of the courtyard. And until I know for sure whether Ivy and Adam are staying, I think it's wise to keep the status quo. If they decide to go back to Stroud, then I'll probably look to rent out the cottage on a twelve-month tenancy and I'll be back to square one with the bakery.

Some of my best thinking time is when I'm doing repetitive jobs, like restoring the panelling. Riley says I have what he calls *stickability*. I guess I've always been an ardent starter/finisher. There's something so satisfying about taking something that many people would throw away and discovering what will make it beautiful again. A carpenter laboured over the detail, making sure the mitred joints were perfect. Here we are, all these years later, and the quality of the workmanship still stands out. If it weren't for the water ingress, we could have saved all of it.

But I'm happy. I want the entrance hallway to be welcoming and cosy, and when I've finished sanding, undercoating and top coating these panels, the colour is going to create that warm welcome I want for our future home. Ivy isn't the only one who's nesting, and I get how important it is. When your life is about to be turned upside down, home becomes a sanctuary, and it would be wrong of me not to point out the obvious.

'Jess, have you sorted out the guest list yet?' Mum's patience is beginning to wear thin. 'You know that until we have a firm idea of numbers, nothing can be finalised.'

'It's top of my to-do list, I promise.' It wasn't, but it is now.

'I was wondering whether you and Dad fancied coming down for Easter weekend. There's a wedding fayre being held in the village hall. It's the weekend of the eighth and ninth of April.'

Vyvyan is one of the coordinators and there's quite a buzz about it. It's attracting vendors from all around the country and there's going to be a huge, heated marquee behind the village hall. Inside, there will be floral demonstrations and they'll even be holding two fashion shows. The campsite will be full, and Cappy has promised that there won't be a digger in sight by then.

'Oh, that would be lovely!'

'I'll sort out some accommodation for you.'

It's difficult not having any spare guest rooms at The Farmhouse. Life will be so much easier once we've moved into Renweneth Manor and have all those extra bedrooms. Then reality hits as I realise that given Ivy and Adam's likely plans, there's going to be a bit of a long pause between phase one and phase two, that's for sure.

Without a big injection of cash, and with an increasing tax liability to cover next year, there won't be as much net profit going into the capital expenditure account as I'd envisaged. Phase two could be delayed for a year, maybe longer.

Just getting the essential rooms up and running to allow us to move in is going to be a big stretch. We're already running 15 per cent over budget and that's with Riley keeping a tight rein on everything.

'How is everyone?' Mum enquires.

'Good. Ben's going to have Lola to stay for the weekend when Riley and I go to his brother Tom's wedding in May.'

'Oh, is it one of those do's where children aren't invited? I can never understand that. It's the kids that make a wedding – all that boisterous excitement is a joy to watch.'

'No, it's not that. Riley's not sure what sort of welcome he's going to get from his family. If it isn't a positive one, then to avoid any unpleasantness, we may well end up heading for home earlier than expected. That wouldn't be fair on Lola. Tom has also confirmed that Fiona and Ollie will be there and that, too, is going to be a little awkward if she's still not speaking to Riley. The last thing we want to do is cause a scene that could potentially spoil Tom and Helen's special day.'

'That's so unfortunate, Jess. You never know, it might not be quite as bad as he fears. Anyway, you're not just shopping for your wedding dress at the fayre then, but also for something nice to wear when you meet your future in-laws for the first time,' Mum points out.

In truth, I don't even know what to expect. My main concern is to be there to support Riley, no matter what happens. Will his parents even want to acknowledge me, I wonder, given that they've had no contact with their son?

'I will admit that my stomach churns at the thought of how badly wrong it could go on the day. Ollie will obviously want to talk to his dad, but will Fiona stop him? And if Riley's parents block him too, it could be devastating. Poor Tom and Helen, they mean well inviting us to their wedding, but let's hope they don't live to regret it. Riley said his brother Tom was the only one who kept in touch; and the only one who offered him help when he first moved to Cornwall. Helen says she's looking forward to meeting us both, which bodes well.'

'Ah, I was thinking the same thing.' Mum sighs. 'Is it worth talking to Riley and suggest he reaches out to his parents beforehand? Just to break the ice. Inviting them to your wedding is the perfect excuse, isn't it?'

It's hard not to smile to myself. It's what a good Mum does, isn't it, trying to smooth things over when they see a huge bump in the road coming. 'You're right. Gosh… that's two awkward conversations to look forward to now.'

'Two?'

'Yes, I need to have a talk with Ivy as well. The planners won't approve the installation of dormer windows at Smithy's Cottage because it will change the overall look of the rank of cottages. Cappy did warn them, but we've all been grasping at straws to make it work. It's never going to be big enough for a family of four and it's time Ivy and Adam faced that fact.'

'Poor dears. Just when their life was beginning to fall into place. I mean… twins! It's a blessing, but a lot to cope with given the upheaval they went through last year. I bet they're reeling.'

'Yes. Me, too. I just don't want to lose them, Mum. Life is better here with them being a part of it. If they can find somewhere suitable to live, I'll even offer to babysit for a few hours each day. By then, if I can convince Cappy to return for good, and with Riley here to finish off the building work, I can't think of a more delightful way to while away some time.'

'Are you getting broody?' Mum asks, sounding surprised.

'No… I don't think so.' I make light of it. 'Just returning the favours Ivy did for me in those early years when I was a new mum myself. Ben couldn't cope with my hormonal swings and, like you, Ivy knew when I needed someone to say, "Give Lola to me and take yourself off to bed to get a couple of hours' sleep." It made all the difference and now I want to be there for her.'

'You two have always had each other's backs. Ivy and Adam will find a solution and between you all, you'll make it work. Now, I'm banking on getting that guest list within the next week,' she says, adamantly.

'Okay, leave it with me. I guess you can only duck and dive for so long before you have to face the inevitable.'

'And how is Cappy?'

'A little stressed about the landscaping work over at the campsite. They've only just finished building the new toilet and shower block.'

'And the situation with Prudie?'

'She's gone very quiet. The artists all chipped in, to *gift* Ivy one of the paintings and the one she chose just happened to be painted by Gryff, Wenna's husband! Ivy didn't know that when she chose it, but it's a big deal for him, as it's the first painting he's sold.'

'Is Flo happy sharing the studio with Prudie?'

'I think Prudie realised anything is better than nothing, thank goodness. And Cappy is doing a lot more socialising. The Lark and Lantern at Polreweek has become his second home. He, Clem Pengali from the farm opposite, and Erica's husband, Charlie, have resurrected the Beer and Bait Club.'

'They can't do any fishing though. It's a bit too early in the year, isn't it?'

'Yes, but they can sit around chatting and supping a pint. He's in his element, Mum.'

Mum gives a little laugh. 'I know. He just doesn't want you, or Riley, to feel constrained. He was more than happy to hand the trust over to you to take it forward and with Riley by your side, he feels he should step back.'

'But he's so much more like his old self now – you won't recognise him when you see him next. He's been trying so hard to get the work on the campsite done before the spring rush. Honestly, there are people thirty years younger than him who would have struggled to pull it off. Riley and I want him to stay, Mum, not to work but to enjoy what he and Grandma started.'

'He might take some convincing of that, Jess, but it's good to hear he's taking time out to spend with his old mates. Anyway, Lola sent me photos of the vases for the buffet table, and she was so excited. Hopefully, when your dad and I pop down for the wedding fayre, we'll be able to firm up quite a few of the outstanding items on the list. The key one is whether there's a central theme and a particular colour you have in mind to bring everything together. Anyway, I know you're busy, so I won't hold you up any longer. We're sending our love to you all and roll on Easter!'

Riley didn't end up eating at The Farmhouse this evening as he worked late helping the plumbers. One of them has found a job starting on Monday and the pressure is on, because we're already falling behind. Riley has no choice other than to step in until a replacement can be found. It means employing someone else to do the work he was scheduled to do and that involved a couple of hours on the phone trying to find a person who could step in at short notice.

When any company closes, it affects the community around it, but never more so than in Cornwall. It has the ripple effect and small villages are feeling it already. Here at the farm, the plasterers were due to come in last week and having put them off once already, I know Riley is worried that they'll sideline us. Which means that instead of their full team coming in to blitz the job when it's ready, we'll just get whoever hasn't been assigned to another project. It could double, or even treble, the amount of time to complete the work on the manor.

It's gone nine by the time I can ring him.

'How are you doing?'

'Tired,' Riley declares.

'When you said to take my budget and double it, I thought you were exaggerating,' I reply, sounding a little jaded. 'Now I'm beginning to think you weren't far off.'

'Sometimes, things go well; other times, they don't, Jess. It's luck of the draw, and you can't predict when and where the delays will occur. If Steve hadn't shut his doors, two-thirds of the plumbing work would be done by now and he'd be hassling us to put pressure on the plasterers. He'd want to get his guys back in to install the boiler and finish off the bathrooms.'

Every day we're not working at full capacity, we're slipping further and further behind. 'If you need to hire extra help to get us back on track, then go for it.'

Riley groans. I assume he's in bed and he's just rolled over. He's working twelve-hour days and it's beginning to take a toll.

'Let's not panic, Jess,' he says with conviction. 'Throwing money at a problem is fine if you have an unlimited budget but that's not the case and we both know it. As long as we have the basics in time for the wedding, nothing will stop us moving in.'

Now's my chance. 'Talking of the wedding, Mum needs the guest list.'

There's another groan but this time, it sounds more intense. 'I don't know, Jess. Maybe it's safer to leave my family out of it.'

'Riley, that's avoiding the issue and you're not thinking straight. You're assuming your parents still want nothing to do with you, but what if they're disappointed that you haven't included them in your new life?' The silence is awful, but I can't quit now. 'What if… they're hurt and their perception is that you cut them off, not the other way around?'

'What are you asking, Jess?'

'Talk to your brother, Tom. He kept in touch and supported you when you needed help. Ask his advice. You're suggesting we leave your family out of it, even though you have no idea how they would feel about that.'

'They're close to Fiona and Ollie, and it's easy to see why they think I abandoned my family.'

'As an outsider, I understand why they might have thought that in the heat of the moment, Riley. And yet I know that you were only trying to save them the embarrassment of your partner pressing charges against you for assault. You weren't the only one who was out of control; you were simply doing your best to limit the damage afterwards. But has it ever occurred to you in doing that, you were the one cutting them off?'

'They… they didn't make any attempt… I mean… they were there for Fiona and Ollie; I know that for a fact. I remember Tom telling me that my parents went straight to the house when she rang to say I'd left, and I didn't intend returning.' The line goes silent for a few tense seconds and the wait is agonising. I can almost visualise the pain reflected on Riley's face as the memories return.

'My dad was angry and I suppose I was rambling as my adrenaline was off the charts. It was an argument that simply got out of hand. I didn't intend to break my ex-business partner's nose, but it was Will who threw the first punch. When I realised Dad wasn't really listening to my version of what happened, I turned my back on him. As I walked away, he called out something about no son of his would ever lash out in anger.'

'But they didn't know at that stage you were going home to pack your bags and leave forever, did they? Everyone was in shock,' I reply, gently. I'm hoping it will make him think about it from their point of view.

'No. I just knew that the best thing I could do for them all was to get out of their lives. Paying Will off by settling for less than what I was due for my share of the company when I left at least ensured they didn't have to endure the shame of seeing me in court.' His voice wavers and while it's like a dagger to my heart, this conversation is long overdue.

'Riley, don't you think it's time to forgive yourself and see that it could so easily have been the other way around? It could have been *you* pressing charges against Will, as he was the one who started the fight.'

'But I was the one who turned it into a bloody mess.'

'Or did you fall into a trap?'

'What do you mean?'

'You told me that the business was doing well, and Will convinced you to branch out into making and installing home offices.'

'Yes, we took on two men and suddenly, the pressure was on to make it all work. The orders were flooding in, but Fiona soon tired of hardly seeing me. It's what caused the split.' There's a sudden sharp intake of breath. 'Will set me up… He wanted me to walk away, and the timing couldn't have been more perfect. Having a third employee instead of a fifty-fifty partner. What a fool I've been.'

We chat until just after midnight, and I think he's gradually coming around to the idea that it's time to reach out to his family. It doesn't change anything retrospectively, but when he realised Will might have had a reason for escalating the argument, it was a light-bulb moment. Some people are prepared to do anything for money. Thankfully, Riley isn't one of them.

II

A Heart-to-Heart

'You didn't bring me out here under a false pretext... did you? It's not like you to suddenly want to talk about the wedding buffet and the cake when you've been avoiding the topic for a couple of weeks now.'

As Ivy and I saunter along the cliff path, it's pretty obvious there's something else on my mind. 'What gave me away?'

She turns to face me, cocking an eyebrow. 'There aren't many things that would pull you away from working on the manor and something tells me that includes your wedding plans.'

We stop for a while to lean on the guard rail and stare out across the bay. Relatively warm and sunny days this early in March are few and far between. It's a wonderful reminder that spring is around the corner and everywhere we look, nature is waking up. But today, it's the sea that steals the show.

'While we're on the subject... I just want to reassure you that I hope to have a guest list very soon.'

'Wonderful! It does help to know how many I'm catering for.' She grins at me. 'So, what's up?'

We stand here mesmerised by the movement of the sea; the gentle waves driven by the undercurrent are calming to watch. I decide just to go for it. 'I'm worried that you and Adam are so desperate to make Smithy's Cottage work, that you're in danger of making the wrong decision.'

When I turn my gaze back to Ivy, I see the concern reflected in her eyes. 'You don't like Cappy's idea of knocking through into The Courtyard Hub?'

'I think we both know it only solves a part of the problem. If you already had twins, there's no way you'd buy Smithy's Cottage. It's time to get real and oh, how it pains me to say that, Ivy. I think you could talk Adam into anything, and I know that for you, living next door to the bakery simplifies things. But it's not a permanent solution. A family needs a home with enough space for them to grow into it.'

The sound that escapes from between Ivy's lips is one of pure frustration. 'It's the one thing we couldn't have foreseen, isn't it? As if getting pregnant wasn't a huge surprise, how on earth am I going to cope with two babies at the same time? Everyone is reaching out to us, offering help. Adam is going to take two weeks off as paternity leave, and after that, his mum and my mum have been talking about taking it in turns to come and stay alternate weeks.'

'How do you feel about that?'

'Like everyone is assuming I won't be able to cope,' she exclaims. 'And maybe that's the case, but I won't know until after they're here. I think Mum wishes we were still living close by in Stroud, but what a life it's going to be for us as a family down here in Cornwall!'

Once Ivy has pulled a plan together, it grounds her and she's off and running. I have nothing to worry about. She'll steer Adam in the right direction.

'I just wish… I know the timing of this is awful for you, Jess. I'm glad we're finally able to have a good chat; this has been weighing heavily on my heart. Adam and I renting both the bakery and the cottage doesn't really help you, does it?'

Her tone is apologetic, and my eyes begin to smart. 'Oh, Ivy… this isn't about me; it's about the long-term future for your little family. The cottage is yours to rent for as long as you want. And there are lots of pretty cottages dotted here and there, within a stone's throw. They don't come onto the market very often, but time is on your side. You can rent Smithy's Cottage for as long as you want and when the right thing comes up, no one will be more delighted for you than me.'

She looks relieved. 'Having some breathing space to get myself sorted will make all the difference.'

'Will they let you go into labour? I read somewhere that, with multiple babies, they often induce you before the due date.'

'I have my heart set on a natural birth, if at all possible. The obstetrician has warned us that twins tend to come a little early anyway. However, they will induce me at thirty-eight weeks if I haven't already gone into labour by then. It all depends on how the babies are lying at that stage, anyway. If either of them are breach, for instance, it changes everything, but he's not ruling out a natural birth as a possibility. He says that either way, I'll need an epidural, just in case they end up having to do an emergency Caesarean section. I hope not, as that would mean spending a few days in hospital.'

'It makes sense.' I think she's being very brave indeed and she sounds determined. Her due date is so close to the wedding, and I know she'd be disappointed to miss it, but there are some things you simply can't control. Thankfully, the bakery will run as usual and her team, and Erica, are gearing up for the party of all parties.

'I don't know how long it will take after the babies are here to suss out how I'm going to juggle work and home life, but by then, there will be more money in the pot. Even if it means we can only get a fixer-upper, all that matters is that it's close to the farm.'

'It's good to hear you've thought it through, but a part of me can't help feeling a tinge of sadness that I won't get to see the twins every single day.'

She nods her head, pulling a long face. 'I know. Even as youngsters, we couldn't have imagined at some point we'd be living within a few paces of each other, could we? It's like the impossible dream.'

With that, we start laughing. 'By the time you have a routine going, I'll be able to make myself available for a couple of hours each day to look after the little ones. Once the first lot of work is done on Renweneth Manor, there will be a bit of a pause anyway. With Riley and Cappy here, they won't even miss me.'

Her eyes widen. 'I didn't realise it was a serious offer. You're not getting broody, are you?'

Not Ivy, too. That's just what Mum said. 'No. I just like the thought of all those cuddles and fun playtimes, then being able to hand them back.'

'Oh, rub it in, why don't you?' She giggles. 'Seriously, I'm probably the least confident mum-to-be ever to find herself expecting double the joy. I can't even visualise what life is going to be like once they're here. I'm glued to blogs and videos sharing tips on how to survive those early months. It still all feels a little surreal though, as if it can't really be happening. Whenever I share the news, there's either a gasp, or a momentary hesitation followed by "congratulations", and I know they're all thinking the same thing.'

'I'm glad it's not me?'

That makes her laugh out loud.

'But think of the upside. If you're stopping at two, then your family will be complete and you only have one pregnancy to contend with.' I grin at her. 'I will admit that there were times I wished Lola had a sibling to play with. Hopefully, very soon Ollie will become a part of our lives and I think they'll be good company for each other. The age difference between them is negligible and I think that will really help them to bond.'

Ivy's hand instinctively goes to her tummy. 'I talk to them all the time,' she muses.

At around sixteen weeks pregnant, Ivy still looks trim, just a little more rounded in the middle. But she's glowing and today, I can see that she's back in control.

'It's a wonderful feeling being pregnant, isn't it? It is a miracle. And don't worry, no one is going to let you struggle. As for your forever home... well, something will turn up when the time is right.'

'Just like the bakery did, to entice us here,' she reflects. 'Even so, we didn't intend on starting a family just yet. Maybe in a year's time, maybe two. If I had found a new location in Stroud, having committed to that level of financial pressure, I'd be frantic right now.'

I grimace. 'It doesn't bear thinking about.'

'With The Farmhouse Bakery, in the early months, I know that as long as I can pop in and out for an hour here and an hour there, everything will be just fine. I want to spend as much time as I can with the babies in those early years, as you did with Lola. I saw how quickly she changed and how time seemed to fly.'

'Even when you move, you'll all still spend a lot of time here at the farm. Imagine what it will be like in the school holidays. We'll be able to take it in turns keeping the kids occupied. Even Cappy could lend a hand and he'd certainly keep them out of mischief. He'd enjoy taking them for walks, teaching them all about nature and telling them stories about the sea.'

We both let out a contented sigh at the same time, turning to face each other and hug. 'We can get through anything, can't we? We've proven that already,' I quip.

'And some. But solving my problem leaves you with another. Riley mentioned something to Adam about the schedule at the manor running behind and being over budget already.'

I don't want Ivy to feel guilty because my financial pressures are of my own making. 'I never banked on receiving a lump sum as that was never a part of the original plan. There's enough to draw down to get the majority of phase one completed... Well, there will be by the time we reach the start of April, which is only what... four weeks away. As for any overspend, that's what my savings are for.'

Ivy shakes her head at me. 'Does Cappy know that you're going to be putting in some of your own money?'

'No, and I don't intend making a big deal out of it. Michael is going to treat it as a loan to the trust, so I can't see the harm in not making it common knowledge.'

Her frown tells me she doesn't agree. 'Cappy would be horrified if he knew what you were doing.'

'I'll get it back at some point in the not-too-distant future. The money is doing nothing sitting in the bank and making use of it means Renweneth Manor will come to life quicker. Come on, it's time to head back, or tongues will start wagging when people realise we sloped off together for a private chat.'

My attempt at changing the subject fails. '*But*,' she questions, labouring the word. 'Is it really worth the risk and the worry? Why not simply delay the wedding?'

'Because every day that Riley and I aren't living together as a family is a day we won't get back, Ivy. The wedding is the turning point.'

'Which will bring everything to a head?'

'Yes.' I scuff the toe of my boot against a pad of stubbly grass that has taken root on the stone pathway.

'That's either very brave, or foolhardy… I can't fathom which.'

I tilt my head back and let out an anguished sigh. 'Ahh! Nothing will change unless Riley and I make it happen. This time next year, I have no doubt at all that Fiona would still be messing Riley around, if it weren't for the fact that he'll be moving into the manor in August. Whether he sells his cottage, or rents it out, is his choice entirely but the message is loud and clear. For him, there is no turning back. If she stops Ollie seeing his father, she'll risk alienating her son. A loving mother couldn't bring herself to do that, no matter how big a grudge she has against her ex.' Tears of frustration are beginning to well up inside of me and we walk on in silence until the rear of Renweneth Farm is in sight.

'You're fighting for the man you love and a young boy who has a right to get to know his dad. I was wrong. That's brave, Jess, not foolhardy, and in your position, I'd probably do the exact same thing.'

'Really? There are times I feel as if I'm going to run out of steam and if that happens, I fear everything will suddenly implode,' I admit.

Ivy draws to a halt, reaching out to place her hand on my arm. 'Riley is worth fighting for because the two of you are perfect together. He's a good man, and if Fiona really loved him, she would have seen through all the drama that caused him to walk away from his family. She gained everyone's sympathy by painting him as a bad husband, but now it's backfiring on her. That's her problem, not Riley's, or yours.'

Just to hear someone else echo exactly how I feel about what's happening means more than Ivy could possibly know. I think it's obvious to Riley that he's being manipulated; he just doesn't know how to handle it. If you spend long enough telling someone they've failed you, it eventually becomes so ingrained, they no longer stop to question it. Riley has never let me down once since the day we first met.

Even at the beginning when he was doing odd jobs for me, he arrived early and worked late, and he was always respectful and kind to Lola. It was the way that he made time to listen to her chattering away that impressed me. Her curiosity knows no bounds, but he always answered her honestly and never brushed her off when he was busy. That told me he has a good heart.

'I can't imagine my future without Riley in it,' I admit. 'Even if it means putting in every penny of my share of the equity in the house Ben and I sold; to me, it's simply a means to an end. You can't put a price on happiness, can you?'

APRIL

JESS

12

Flowers, Frocks and Feeling
Totally Overwhelmed

Easter weekend at Renweneth Farm is a three-day event filled with a whole range of activities. The morning of Saturday the eighth of April brings with it a dusky, pale-blue sky and Riley, Cappy and Keith decide to erect the gazebos ready for some of the outdoor hands-on sessions as a sunshade, and not to shelter people from the rain. It feels like a bit of a miracle because this time last week, we had a downpour that lasted three straight days without stopping.

'Nice bit of sun today,' Len calls out. He's directing cars into vacant spaces but from what I can see, it won't be long before he'll be shutting off the car park and sending traffic to the overflow field opposite.

'I ordered it especially,' I reply, giving him a wave and a good-natured smile.

As I make my way past the Saturday stalls in the old hay barn on the way to the campsite, I spot Keith handing out leaflets to new arrivals. With the wedding fayre a short walk away, and a full programme here for the weekend, the place is buzzing.

Cappy is head down, hammering in a wooden stake to anchor one of the new cherry trees that they planted last week over by the new facilities block.

'This should do the trick,' he says, standing back to admire his handiwork.

'The new borders are looking tidy and will be wonderful once the shrubs get their spring growth. No one would know the turf has only been down a little over a month.'

'That rain last week did us a big favour. Fingers crossed, with a couple of days of sunshine, this lot will soon give us a blast of colour.' He gives me a wink.

'How's the new exit working? I was shocked to see Len on his own working the entrance. It used to take three of us to keep it under control.'

'It works sweet as a nut now that we have one way in and one way out, Jess. I don't suppose you've had time to check out the job they did lowering the pavement?'

'No. Give me the tour.'

Together with the work going on at the campsite, it was a big job and at one point, Cappy was stressing over whether the landscaping would be finished in time, but he got there. As we walk together over to the new car park exit in the far corner, it's a bit of a thrill to see children chasing around and having fun, and groups of adults sitting in between their camper vans and caravans, chatting. And I can even hear the buzz from the market stalls in the background.

'You did an excellent job as usual, Cappy. I know it wasn't the easiest of projects to manage, but I do hope that you can relax now and enjoy yourself for a bit.'

'And I brought it in under budget,' he reminds me with a great deal of satisfaction. 'I don't intend sitting around twiddling my thumbs, though. I hope to get in a bit of fishing with the guys. We're planning a trip around the bay at some point.'

'We?'

'Me, Charlie and Clem. Ivan's considering selling *The Silver Wave* and the two of them are thinking about chipping in to buy it.'

'Is it seaworthy?' I question, as every time it's been mentioned in the past, the words *rust bucket* usually follow.

He chuckles. 'He bought it on a whim, but it's been on a trailer in that hangar of a shed of his since the day it was brought here from Southampton. His wife's putting her foot down and it has to go. We think the boat itself won't be too bad, assuming Ivan manages to pull her out of there before the shed topples over.'

It's good news, as now that his work here is finished, this is something he'll want to be around for. An old boat that'll need some TLC is right up his street and I can't see him leaving his two best friends to get on with it without offering to roll up his sleeves too.

'We thought we'd invite Adam and Riley out for the test run to check the old girl out. What do you think?'

'I think they'd get a buzz from it.'

'Hmm... and they might appreciate getting a glimpse of the farm and the coastline from the water. It's as spectacular looking back at the land as it is looking out to sea. Anyway, with the hedge greening up from the brutal cut to accommodate the new gate, it's not looking too bad here, is it?'

We do a quick inspection and it's not as ugly as I'd feared. When the mini digger started ripping out this section, I had to keep well away. But now that the pavement has been lowered and the tarmac laid, another couple of weeks and everything will blend in quite nicely.

'I know it wasn't an expense you'd factored in, Jess, but it's one hit and what a difference it makes to market day. No more chaos, and long lines of cars queuing out on the road, or people getting impatient and parking up on the grass verges. It generates a nice, steady little income and it only really needs two people now to control it. Are you off to this wedding fayre thing?'

'Yes, shortly. I just wanted to check whether you needed me to do anything.'

'No. It's all good. I'm just pottering and keeping an eye out, as we've another four caravans due around lunchtime. Lola mentioned you're off to a fashion show a bit later.'

I roll my eyes. 'Yes, I was going to give it a miss and just walk around the various stands, but Mum insisted.'

When he smiles, there's a glint in his eye. 'I know your main focus is getting the manor ready to move into, but it's your wedding day we're all looking forward to, Jess. It changes everything.' He pauses, scanning around to check that no one is within earshot. 'It's not easy getting through life without having someone there by your side to share the highs and lows with. Life can become rather mechanical.'

Mechanical? My heart misses a beat. Is that how Cappy feels every morning when he wakes up? Simply get through the day as best he can and repeat it all over again tomorrow? Grandma would be as horrified as I am to hear him talking like that.

'That's why it's important to surround yourself with family and friends, Cappy,' I remind him gently. I cast around for the right words to lighten what could become quite a dark conversation. 'Having you here is a great comfort when things go wrong because you are the voice of experience. But as I said, now things are ticking over nicely, you get to relax, have some fun, watch Lola change with each passing day and be Riley's mentor.'

Cappy gives a dismissive laugh. 'He's a capable young man and I'd hate him to feel I'm looking over his shoulder.'

'Cappy, Riley isn't like that!' I blurt out. 'He's just a little outside of his comfort zone and still trying to work out his future role. Most couples when they marry buy a house together, but in our case, it's different. I've explained about the trust, and he was fine with that. However, because he's not putting any money in, I don't want that to change his perception of the fact that it will be *our* home.'

He lets out a 'Hmm,' as his eyes scan my face.

'And there's no nice way of saying this, Cappy, but Fiona seems to take pleasure in reminding Riley about his failures in the past. It takes two to make a marriage fail and yet she continually blames him for it falling apart. It's eroded his confidence. I didn't realise quite how much until recently. As hard as I try to keep impressing upon him what a difference he's made to the farm and where it's going, he thinks I'm saying it simply out of love.' I can see that Cappy is deep in thought and I sigh, gently.

'It's not a mentor he needs, Jess, but a friend,' he replies, firmly.

'Exactly! But someone who can gently steer him if needed… someone he respects.'

'Mum! Mum!' Lola calls to me, insistently, as she runs towards us. 'We're going to be late. Grandma Celia is waiting in the courtyard. Hey, Cappy. We're going to look at wedding dresses.'

Cappy bends so that their faces are level. 'And bridesmaids dresses, too, no doubt.'

Lola's face lights up as she grins back at him. 'I hope so! I've never had a posh frock before, not a floaty one.'

As she slips her hand in mine to encourage me to hurry, I turn to give Cappy a parting glance.

'Point taken, Jess. You can count on me to do whatever I can, discreetly, of course.'

The seed has been well and truly sown, and a warm feeling fills my heart.

Every seat in the cavernous village hall is taken. Luckily, as Vyvyan is one of the organisers, she managed to reserve us second-row seats and Lola is enthralled.

'Mum,' she whispers, leaning into me. 'It's a real fashion show, with real models.'

I try hard not to laugh and simply nod my head. Mum, who is sitting the other side of Lola, breaks out into a broad smile, as a hush falls over the audience.

'Introducing this summer's newest collection. To achieve that hourglass figure, here we have a glorious fit-and-flare dress. Hugging the body from the delicate lace bodice down to mid-thigh level, the flare comes just above the knee for ease of movement. Can we have a twirl, please?' The compere's silky voice has the model turning on her heels as effortlessly as if she were a ballerina.

Lola nudges my leg. 'It's so pretty, Mum,' she whispers.

And so white… and bridal. It's not what I see myself wearing, at all. I wonder what picture Riley has in his head for the moment he turns to see me walking towards him. I surreptitiously retrieve the phone from my handbag and begin texting. Everyone's eyes are on the stage, glued front and centre as the second model steps out onto the runway.

Help… the dresses are all so fussy. What do you see me wearing? x

Making sure the volume is turned off, I eagerly await his response. Lola nudges me again. 'Ooh… that's so romantic, Mum.'

The compere waits until the model stands perfectly posed in front of us. Her skin is flawless, her hair swept up on one side and fastened with a bejewelled clasp, a riot of curls softening the overall look.

'Here we have Monique,' he begins. 'She's modelling an off-the-shoulder, fitted gown with an illusion neckline and long sleeves. The sheer lace organza panel is embellished with delicate floral embroidery and a hint of sparkle.' As if on cue, she turns slowly on the spot. 'The illusion plunging V-back panel is highlighted only by a line of fabric-covered buttons, which creates a tall and sophisticated silhouette.'

The screen on my phone lights up.

You're in trouble if you're asking me for advice on wedding dresses. 😊

My fingers start texting. I take a quick snap of the next model as she negotiates the narrow runway in what must surely be the widest ball gown ever. The bodice is obviously corseted, because no one's waist is that small and from there, it's like an explosion of tulle.

> Don't complain if I end up with something like this, then. Lola's jaw just dropped and she's starry-eyed! 😊

I'd like to say the dresses get better but the more I see, the more downhearted I feel. They're all beautiful but whereas the first time around, it's probably true to say that I did turn into a bit of an obsessive bride, this time, I want a totally different vibe. How to achieve that, I have no idea, but I'm not going to be a vision in white dominating the whole thing.

'Mum... it's pink!'

I place a finger against my lips to remind Lola to keep her voice down and Mum turns her head to catch my eye. Oh no... she likes this one, too.

'And I'm sure you will agree that this is the very height of elegance,' our compere begins with great enthusiasm. 'In white lace over a blush-coloured taffeta, the illusion tulle on the back is encrusted with a row of pearly buttons. Gentle silver sparkles around the waist shine through the corset like a cascade of twinkling stars. The A-line silhouette is finished off with a modest train, creating the ultimate romantic, fairy-tale look.'

People around us start clapping and Lola joins in. Mum leans forward, putting one finger up as if to say *is that the one* before starting to laugh. I shake my head at her emphatically.

It isn't long before we're onto the bridesmaids' dresses and Lola is utterly captivated. A lot of girls like dressing up and dreaming about the day they'll get married. I don't want to spoil the illusion for her and if she wants a princess dress to wear on the day, why not?

When the show finishes, to my surprise, Riley appears, a huge smile on his face as he hurries towards us. And he's not wearing his work clothes. His hair is a little damp, so he's fresh from the shower, and wearing a white linen shirt with the cuffs folded back, teamed with a smart pair of navy-blue trousers.

'My goodness,' I remark as he draws to a halt, 'don't you look good.'

'Riley, you missed the show. It was awesome!' Lola declares.

He gives me a hopeful smile. 'The bridal wear shopping is done then?'

Lola pulls a long face. 'Mum didn't seem very impressed.'

Suddenly, all eyes are on me. 'Oh... I... um...'

'Lola,' Mum jumps in, 'shall we head over to the boutique area to look at the bridesmaids' dresses? They might let you try one on.'

My daughter turns to look at me. 'Can we, Mum?'

'Of course, you can. Riley and I will have a little wander around. If you do try on a dress, text me and we'll come straight over.'

Seconds later, Riley clasps my hand, looking down at me. 'Are you struggling with all this wedding stuff? Isn't it supposed to be a fun thing, planning a wedding?'

I lead him in the direction of the floristry stand, as we begin what is for me a delicate conversation.

'Riley, what are you expecting on the day?'

'I don't know... I just want you to be happy and I'll go with the flow.'

'No, you don't get to do that,' I reply, firmly.

'Do what?'

'Opt out. We've both been married before and I don't know about you, but I'm over the fairy-tale, white wedding thing.'

Is that a look of disappointment I see fleetingly etched on his face?

'What *do* you want?' he asks.

'I've told you what I don't want and now it's time for you to level with me.'

He flashes me a look tinged with anxiety, and he inhales sharply before he begins. 'The first time around, my stress levels were through the roof. It felt like if anything went wrong, it was going to be a bad omen. We blew our budget and some to make sure everything was perfect but look how that worked out.' As soon as he finishes speaking, Riley looks at me apologetically. 'Sorry, that sounds really jaded, doesn't it? I am so looking forward to *our* wedding day because somehow, I just know it will be different.'

'I understand exactly where you're coming from, Riley. But to make it happen requires a whole series of decisions to be made.'

We stop in our tracks, turning to face each other as people stream past us on both sides of the aisle. 'And when you think of our wedding, what do you imagine?' I prompt.

'This is going to sound a bit off-topic, but last year's end of summer party that we held in the grounds of Renweneth Manor was magical to me. Admittedly, a part of that was down to the fact that you told everyone we're together. I thought it was too soon, but you were right. When you know you've found the one, happiness comes from within. Even if we'd been drinking expensive Champagne instead of Prosecco, it wouldn't have made that night any more enchanting, would it? It was relaxed, informal, although everyone dressed up a little and, dare I say, it was more romantic because it wasn't organised to the nth degree.'

I throw my arms around his neck, hugging him tightly. 'You've put your finger on it, Riley. That's exactly what I want for our wedding day, and I think I know how to achieve it. Now, Mum needs a theme and a main colour for the buffet table, the invites and the decorations.'

'Oh no... you're taking me to look at flowers, aren't you?'

'I am. I'll tell Mum that we're going for a boho, country-style feel. No white frock for me; as for Lola, well, it's a special day for her too and she can have whatever she wants.'

'Does that mean I don't have to wear a suit and a tie?'

'You can come in something as simple as what you're wearing today. How about adding a waistcoat? Something fun, because that's what it's going to be – a day where it's not all eyes on the bride and groom, but one big party. But you will need a best man.'

Suddenly, all my concerns evaporate into thin air, just as my phone pings. Mum sends me a photo of Lola looking like an angel and I show it to Riley before calling her.

'We'll make our way over, Mum. Lola looks stunning. Has she fallen in love with it? What's the price?'

To my surprise, Mum interrupts me. 'No. She's just having a bit of fun and has already gone to change back into her own clothes. After doing the spinning around thing on the spot, Lola whispered to me that she'd be scared she might trip over in it.'

'Sensible girl! We're just off to look at flowers and then I think I can answer most of your questions.'

'Oh, that was quick. I knew this would inspire you and I'm glad Riley made the effort to join us.'

'Me, too. Mum. See you in a bit.'

13

One Headache After Another

Tuesday morning dawns and everyone at Renweneth Farm is feeling the effects of what has been an enormously successful, albeit tiring, Easter event. Mum and Dad left early this morning, but they were all smiles now that Mum has almost everything that she needs to finalise most of the wedding arrangements. There's still a question mark over the guest list, but I decided it's unfair to put pressure on Riley to make the call to his parents if he's not quite ready. I suggested she take the list Riley and I hadn't quite finished and cater for an additional ten people. It's better to have too much food rather than not enough.

Yesterday, I was doing relief cover, and did a bit of everything. From directing people into Ivy's cupcake- and cookie-making sessions, to helping at the animal pen that Clem from Pengali farm had set up in the courtyard. It was hands down a winner with everyone, no matter what their age. I mean, who doesn't want to watch a baby lamb being fed, or baby goats prancing around?

Riley volunteered to assist at the indoor pottery sessions, having no idea what he was letting himself in for. It mostly involved making sure people donned their aprons as it can be a bit of a messy pursuit, but he said he had fun.

Cappy, Keith and Lola ran the play area over in the first field. There was a giant game of noughts and crosses, two Easter egg hunts and a *hunt the rabbit* competition. Lola delighted in hiding ten stuffed rabbits around the site and Ivy made some small bags of bunny-shaped cookies as prizes for each child who spotted all ten.

This morning, Lola is at Daisy's house for a play date, and I make my way over to the bakery to see Ivy. It's market day and there are a lot of people coming and going.

Wenna directs me to the kitchen, where I find Ivy levelling a tray of sponge cake with a spatula, ready to pop it into the steam oven.

'Hey, how're you doing?'

She grins at me. 'Tired. I bet you are, too.'

'Being honest, it was the boost I needed. Just seeing people flocking here reassured me that our marketing strategy is working, and word is spreading further and further afield.'

'Well,' Ivy comments, swiping her forehead with the back of her hand, 'today, we seem to be just as busy again.'

'There's quite a queue downstairs, too. Those tall bistro tables in the courtyard with the umbrellas are popular.'

'Our polite notices asking customers to use the waste bins seem to work but I really do need to find another casual helper, maybe two, to see us through the summer. Especially if the concessions in The Courtyard Hub decide to go with Sunday opening.'

'We're having a meeting at six this evening to discuss it. I'll let you know how it goes. Don't feel you have to fall in line with their decision, though. For the individual retailers, it's a big step, but they're talking about pooling resources. They're thinking of organising a rota so not everyone would work every Sunday; some would cover more than one outlet. It makes sense to me.'

'That's a good idea but we're noticing the increased trade from the campsite now and I think it would be wrong for the bakery not to open seven days a week. I've already mentioned it to Alice at Rowse's bakery, we just haven't agreed a start date. By the way, Prudie popped in to say they sold three paintings over the weekend, and she was delighted.'

'Oh, I didn't see her,' I reply. 'Maybe she's avoiding me.'

'I doubt it. Prudie and Cappy spent half an hour in the café having coffee and cake together. She was in a good mood, so I think you can safely assume everything has settled down. Anyway, to what do I owe this pleasure?' She gives me a knowing grin.

'I want to ask you a favour.'

'Ha! You're so transparent, Jess. Ask away.'

'Our wedding plans are finally falling into place. Riley and I have decided that the ceremony is going to be an intimate affair. We're hoping that Riley's parents, his brother and his new wife, and Ollie will be there, but that's an unknown, probably until the last minute. That aside, Lola, my parents and Cappy will be there, but we'd like you and Adam to join us, too.'

'Oh, Jess… we'd love to be a part of it!'

She walks around the counter, keeping her sticky fingers in the air as she gives me a hug.

'It wouldn't be the same without you two. Just between us, Riley is going to ask Adam to be his best man. It's not going to be a formal affair, but the ceremony itself means a lot to me and Riley. The party afterwards is simply a celebration of everything in our lives that puts a smile on our faces and a warm glow in our hearts: the farm and our family and friends.'

'So,' she says, standing back, 'the cake… what are we doing?'

'Ah, right. I have been—' When my phone rings, I'm surprised to hear Riley's voice and his tone is dour.

'Jess, you'd better get over to the manor. We have a problem.'

'I'm on my way.' I let out a gentle sigh. 'Sorry, Ivy. I must go, Riley sounds stressed. I'm open to suggestions regarding the cake.'

As I step out into the courtyard, in the far corner to the right-hand side of The Farmhouse, someone has exposed the access point to the mains water isolation valve; it's surrounded by orange cones, which isn't a good sign. I hurry through the archway into the grounds of Renweneth Manor and I'm dismayed to see

Riley, and our two new plumbers – Rick and Nigel – deep in conversation. They're all bent over inspecting something.

'Hey, guys, what's up?' I approach them, realising that as I get closer, the ground beneath my feet is getting softer.

Riley straightens, his brow furrowed. 'It seems we have a serious leak. Better turn it off again at the other inspection point, Rick,' he says with a hint of urgency. The guy doesn't hang around and he sprints out into the courtyard. What we're staring down at appears to be little bubbles of water burbling up through the gravel path.

'How long has it been leaking?' As I glance around, it's obvious that a wide area is waterlogged. It extends into the orchard and the full length of the path to the side of the manor.

'It probably happened sometime over the weekend, but I'd say a couple of days, at least. We'll turn off the supply that cuts across the courtyard into the manor so it can start drying out. It's not the isolation valve at this end that's failed, so it's a breach in the pipe somewhere between here and the courtyard.'

Just when I thought we were done with ugly trenches around the manor and the paths were finally tidy again, this is one headache we didn't need. After a brief discussion, we stand around as Riley calls in a favour. While Steve's business has closed down, he has useful contacts in the trade.

'Sorry to bother you, mate, but we've got a major leak over at the farm. Rick is here finishing off inside and Nigel has now joined him, so I think between the three of us, we can fix it. But what we need is the use of an underground water leak detector, to allow us to pinpoint where to start digging. I don't suppose you know of one we could get our hands on urgently?'

Steve's guys not only lost their jobs, but their well-equipped vans too, and access to some of the more expensive tools they need to carry out their work.

'Really? Thanks, mate, it means a lot.' Riley turns to look at us, smiling broadly. 'I'm off to Polreweek. Steve has a detector kit in his garage. See you in a bit.'

He's so relieved that he simply turns on his heels and strides away, leaving the three of us staring down at the ground.

'Is it as bad as it looks?' I venture to ask.

They glance at each other, and Rick turns to face me. 'The ground will start drying out but old stone cottages like this don't have a damp course. If you touch the stonework, you can feel how high the water has travelled.'

He's right, if I stand further back, it's obvious that one massive section of the wall is a darker colour than the rest.

'You'll need some dehumidifiers inside as it will have gone right through the entire thickness of the wall. Until the central heating boiler is connected, it'll start drying out, but slowly, and the last thing you want is mould growing in the room behind this.'

Great… that's the main sitting room and the second biggest room on the ground floor. This is going to throw the schedule out yet again.

'Don't worry,' Nigel interjects. 'Once we know where the leak is, it'll take us no more than a day to dig the hole, cut the pipe, place a collar on it and do the backfill.'

My eyes travel across the garden, following the line of the pipe as the crow flies from the inspection point next to the manor, to the inspection point in the courtyard. Obviously, the high stone wall blocks my view, but it will probably mean digging up a patch of the beautiful lawn that is one of the main features of the landscaped gardens. With the wedding only four months away, I was banking on it looking pristine, even if half of the interior will still be a blank canvas.

The guys can sense how gutted I am, but it's just one of those things. 'I guess it'll mean a new flower border then,' I reply, pragmatically.

'We'll lay some boards around the hole, so we don't turn the grass into a mud pit. The grass itself will soon spring back up,' Nigel reassures me.

'Thanks, guys. How are you both doing?'

They glance at each other, fleetingly. 'It's been a lifesaver working here,' Rick admits. 'It's good to be back again and working on the second fix for you. Nigel and I have decided to set up on our own and are just sorting out our finances. If it's not a cheek... we were wondering whether you'd be happy for us to tell potential customers that we've done work for you here at Renweneth Farm.'

'Of course, you can! And if you get any business cards printed up, pop some into the bakery. Ivy is keen to promote local goods and services, and a lot of people within about a twenty-minute drive pop in regularly to buy their bread here.'

'We're going to set up a website and, at some point, we'd love to take a few photos of the main bathroom and the various en suites at the manor to start us off.' Nigel and I glance at each other and start chuckling. 'Oh, once it's all finished, naturally,' Rick confirms.

This time, the sigh I let out is a wearisome one. 'When the central heating has been commissioned and the kitchen is all plumbed in, if you guys can get the ground-floor cloakroom and the first-floor main bathroom finished in time for the wedding, I'll be ecstatic,' I admit. 'I was beginning to envisage sending our wedding guests over to the campsite to use the facilities there.'

'That,' Nigel states firmly, 'is not going to happen. I know some of the other trades are holding us up, but Riley is doing a great job of keeping everyone focused. A project this size, in such an old property, is never going to be straightforward. It's a privilege working on it, Jess. Everyone around here thought you'd end up selling the manor off to someone who would turn it into their weekend retreat. That would have been a shame, because when it was occupied, it was always a family home to people who provided much-needed jobs in the community. Just as you and Riley are doing now.'

I'm touched by his words.

'And we'll make sure your wedding guests have all the

facilities they need, even if it means working up to the wire,' Rick continues. 'Right, let's get back to work, Nigel, or Riley will think we've been slacking.'

I give them both a beaming smile and leave them to it. The guest list has just grown by four, and if I'm correct, Nigel's wife has recently had a baby and Rick has two little boys, so that's seven in total. But when people go the extra mile for you, they become a part of the journey and should be a part of the celebration. It's not just a wedding but also to mark the completion of phase one of turning Renweneth Manor into a home.

It's anyone's guess what we're going to be able to achieve in terms of the man hours required to do the work, and money is getting tight. It's time for me to go all in. Riley would be horrified if he knew I'm going to end up sinking every penny I have into this, but it'll be worth it. He's working so hard, and I know each setback takes a toll on him, but without Riley driving this project forward, it would have already fallen apart. It's time to throw some serious cash at it because he's had an uphill battle and that's not good for his morale.

'Hello? Jess... are you there?'

A lone voice filters up the stairs and I call out, 'Coming, Ivy!' Riley and Adam left for the gym about fifteen minutes ago. I was supposed to be locking up, but I ended up grabbing a paintbrush and the next thing I know I'm giving the windowsill in what will be the main bathroom, another coat. I manoeuvre my way around the boxes of sanitary ware stacked in the middle of the room and hurry downstairs.

'Sorry, I didn't know you were working,' Ivy apologises as soon as she sees me.

'It's time I quit. Erica rang to ask Lola over for a sleepover and Cappy is dining out again,' I smirk at her. 'He has more of a social life than me and Riley combined these days, but I'm so glad he and his old mates are meeting up again.'

Ivy is gazing around. Apart from contractors, me, Riley, and Cappy on a few occasions, no one else has been inside the manor since the work began.

'This is looking very different to that day you showed me around.' She seems impressed. 'It's not damp and dingy anymore.'

I roll my eyes. 'That's not quite true. We had a major leak over the weekend, and it's affected one of the outside walls. All work in the main sitting room has drawn to a halt and goodness knows how long it will take to dry it out. But would you like a quick tour?'

Her face lights up. 'Ooh… only if I'm not stopping you. I only came over to let you know that the guys texted to say they'll bring takeaway back with them. I suggested that we have it over at Smithy's Cottage. I bumped into Cappy on the way here and he mentioned that he was eating in town.'

'Hmm… I assumed he was going to The Trawlerman's Catch with Charlie and Clem.'

Ivy frowns. 'He was very smartly dressed, if that's the case,' she reflects. 'Anyway, I'd love a sneak peek.'

'I'm running out of steam anyway, to be honest with you. Let's start in the main sitting room.' We turn to our right and I lead her through the beautiful, reclaimed oak door into what will eventually be what Grandma would have called, in her youth, *the parlour*. A room used on Sundays and for special occasions when guests visited.

'Oh, Jess… I see what you mean.' We both gape at the side wall. 'Ugh… it's reminiscent of the café when Riley drilled into that pipe.'

'He's worried about the oak floorboards. He says they're suspended, so the damp won't soak up from the ground beneath, but until the wall dries out, it's filling the air with moisture, and we don't want a mould issue. He's hiring some industrial-sized dehumidifiers. If we also keep the windows open during the day, it will help speed up the process. The central heating should be fully up and working soon. However, Riley says it's best to let it dry out naturally at room temperature for a while to avoid the boards warping.'

'It's a large room,' Ivy comments, as she wanders around.

'Everything looks large when it's empty,' I point out. 'The walls, ceiling and cornice have only had a mist coat so far, but any further painting is now on hold. But you're right, it's going to be a lovely room for entertaining family and friends when we get together. Come and see the snug.'

I steer her back out into the hallway, and she trails her hands over the wood panelling.

'It's been a labour of love reclaiming this wood. There wasn't enough to do the hallway and the dining room, but I wanted the entrance to feel welcoming and countrified. The floor hasn't been done yet and there's still hours of painting to do, but the snug/family room is what's keeping me going.'

'Gosh, this is lovely!' Ivy exclaims as we step through the door.

'It's the only room that's nearly finished. Look how wonderful the old oak floorboards are after a good sanding and waxing.'

She walks around taking in every little detail. 'I love that smell when everything is new.'

The walls have been painted a soft sage green, which contrasts nicely against the white of the ornate coving and ceiling. 'The TV is going on this wall,' I explain, 'and over here, there will be a large desk to house the computer and two monitors for the gamers in our family. As long as the Wi-Fi is turned off overnight, they can have whatever they like in here. But I want some squidgy sofas to sink down into and hope that we'll spend many a winter's evening lounging in front of the log fire.'

Ivy is already standing in front of the fireplace, surveying the mantelpiece. 'What a beautiful finish on this.'

'It's cast iron and one of Riley's junkyard finds. It's graphite grey, but it's been polished, which gives it that shiny silver finish.'

'Have you chosen the furniture yet?' Ivy asks.

I shake my head. 'I'm waiting to see how the budget holds out first. Practical things like working bathrooms might have to take precedence over sumptuous sofas and elegant side tables, I'm afraid.'

She gives me a look of commiseration.

'All in good time.' I laugh. 'And I still have some lovely pieces of furniture I can upcycle. Right, follow me. These double doors open up into the kitchen/dining room.'

Now this is a jaw-dropping moment, even though it's yet another empty room. The only feature is the stop tap and the hot and cold-water pipes, indicating where the kitchen sink will be installed. Hopefully, very soon. But we immediately head over to the wall of bifold doors.

'What a total transformation! It's a massive space and those doors… it's gone from dank and dingy, to light an airy!'

We stand side by side, staring out. 'All the raised flower beds had to go. The whole area was dug up when they dismantled the old septic tank and installed a sewage treatment plant. Still, they did a good job and at least it's tidy. Eventually, we'll have a deck area so we can sit out at night and watch the sun going down. Riley is going to trim back some of the trees.' With the high stone wall, the sea isn't visible from the ground floor, but the sunrises and sunsets are awesome.

We walk on through to the boot room and pantry. 'Everything has been stripped out and the walls have a base coat but it's part of phase two.'

'Has much been done upstairs?' Ivy asks, curious.

'Just the stripping out and erecting the new partition walls. A lot of the supporting beams have been replaced and its mainly new wood throughout. You probably noticed that the staircase leading to the first floor is new, but there's just a ladder up to the second floor for the time being, so there's no access to the attic. The new layout means the claustrophobic backstairs will go and we're waiting for the new staircase to arrive.'

'They were steep, too. I mean you could only get half your foot on each step,' Ivy reflects, with a shiver. 'Imagine kids trying to run up and down those.'

I roll my eyes. 'I know. My worst fear. There's a long way to go,' I admit, 'but I'm hoping we can pick up the pace a bit.'

We walk back through to the front door.

'Extra manpower, you mean?'

'Yes, unfortunately, even though we're already running over budget. But Vyvyan and I have been looking at a couple of new initiatives to bring in some extra income over the summer months.'

Ivy glances at me, narrowing her eyes. 'If you find yourself struggling in the short term, our nest egg is just sitting in the bank. We're unlikely to even consider looking for a property until the babies are at least six months old, maybe even a year. I'll need to be close to work and home for quite a while.'

'Oh, Ivy.' Her offer catches me unawares and takes my breath away for a moment. 'That's so kind of you, but I have it under control. Just don't breathe a word to anyone about the overspend, as if Cappy hears about it, he will probably insist on dipping into his savings, or something daft like selling his house.'

Ivy chews her lip. 'But... you want him here permanently, anyway. Don't you?'

'Yes, I do, but he's already put Renweneth Farm in trust for Lola and me. He's given us enough; the next bit is down to me. I want him to enjoy the time he has left... buy a boat to tinker around with or draw up a bucket list and travel... whatever takes his fancy.'

'That's not how he'd see it.'

'I know, but the trust will eventually pay me back for the loans I've put in. That will be spread out over a few years. In the meantime, I need to ensure we get the basics done to allow us to use the manor as a family home within the level of funds I have left. And by then, fingers crossed the farm will have generated enough profit to finance the second phase of the work. Every new initiative Vyvyan and I can put into play will get us there quicker.'

As I open the door to step outside, Ivy puts her hand on my

arm. 'Remember, if you get stuck, you know where to come. We're happy at Smithy's Cottage and it'll do us just fine for a while to come. We're in no hurry to find a new home.'

We hug and the intensity of it tells me how concerned she is. 'I will, but please stop worrying. If it takes two years to complete Renweneth Manor, it's not the end of the world. But my aim is to have Ollie staying with us for our wedding on Sunday the sixth of August. By then, we'll have a family bathroom, a downstairs cloakroom, a snug, a kitchen/diner and three bedrooms.'

She stands back to look at me, her eyes sparkling. 'Is that all? Then everything's going to be just fine! And I'll do my best to make sure these little ones are here before the wedding so I can attend.'

Now that's a tall order. We both dissolve into fits of laughter as we make our way over to Smithy's Cottage for a well-earned coffee before our men arrive back from the gym.

'I'll show you the painting Prudie and her students so kindly chipped in to buy me as a thank-you present. Did I mention that it was Gryff, Wenna's husband, who painted it? And it was his first sale... I was so glad I chose it, but I had no idea he was the artist.'

'Wenna did mention it to me. That must have been a proud moment for him, Ivy.' I remember her pointing out one of the paintings and saying she'd love to have it in her sitting room.

'It's the view as you hit the beach at Penvennan Cove, after negotiating the steep walk down through the trees. It looks out across the bay, as far as the headland on the other side. It's such a romantic vista... I dare anyone not to fall in love with Cornwall if they do that walk.'

I remember sitting alongside Riley on an enormous rock, halfway down that steep descent, eating pasties and drinking beer while we gazed out over the bay. It's a memory imprinted in my mind forever and probably the day I realised this was a man to whom I could give my heart.

RILEY

14

You Can Run but You Can't Hide Forever

I thought that as Jess and Ivy will be at their candlelit yoga class tonight, I'd invite Adam around for a beer this evening and a chat. I text him mid-morning and he gives a thumbs-up. That's one mental tick off the list. My shoulders sag… asking Adam to be my best man is the least stressful task; he's a great guy and I value his friendship. The next two entries are more daunting, but work is calling.

By lunchtime, we've identified the location of the water leak and it's right bang slap in the middle of one of the beautiful lawns that you encounter to the right-hand side on entering Renweneth Manor from the courtyard. Jess will be upset about it, although Nigel, Rick and I are doing our best to limit the damage. Fortunately, by the time Jess has finished catching up with her paperwork, it will no longer be quite the ugly scar it is now.

'See you in an hour, Riley. We'll get this sorted by the end of the day, don't you worry,' Rick states, adamantly, before the two of them head off to the bakery.

I make my way through to the orchard to sit beneath the apple trees and spend a few minutes fighting with my conscience. How long can I put this off? The answer is that it's time to man up.

Seconds later, I dial my brother's number.

'Riley, it's nice to hear from you. How're you doing?'

'Good, thanks, Tom. Did you get our RSVP to the wedding invite?'

'We did, thank you. Helen can't wait to meet you and we're both excited to get to know Jess. With only five weeks to go, the nerves are really beginning to kick in at this end, I can tell you.'

I clear my throat, nervously. 'I bet.' This is awkward. 'I don't know if you're aware, but Fiona isn't talking to me. And, by the way, thanks for keeping it to yourself about Jess and me, as it took me a bit longer than anticipated to have the conversation with Fiona.'

'It was in confidence, Riley, and I never go back on my word. Fiona hasn't said anything to me but then our paths rarely cross.'

That means he's still in the loop, but Fiona only shares the things she wants him and Helen to know. I guess a part of that is my fault, as I've always struggled to open up, even to those close to me. I see and hear everything, though, and it's true to say that over the years, a lot of people have disappointed me.

My mum once said to me that I see everything in black and white; what I don't see is that most things in life are a variety of shades of grey. Everyone's perspective is different, coloured by their own life experiences. Maybe that's true, but when I'm in the wrong, at least I admit it and if I'm right, then I don't need to justify myself.

'Ollie came to stay for the weekend and we managed to grab some real bonding time. However, Fiona invited herself along too. I can't lie, it made things very awkward indeed. After the visit, she started texting back and forth about arranging another trip. As expected, when I broke the news, she didn't take it well and I received a barrage of nasty messages. Now she's ignoring me. I just wanted you to know what was going on in case you wanted to rethink the invite.'

Tom's reaction is instant. 'No, of course not. Fiona and Ollie will be there, naturally. As I said, we rarely see her, but we do visit Mum and Dad's to get to spend time with Ollie when they're looking after him. He's such a great lad and he couldn't wait to tell us about his trip to Cornwall. Mum was delighted, not least to hear you're doing so well.'

It's weird knowing they've been talking about me. I guess that's because it's only natural that Ollie would have wanted to tell them all about his trip to Cornwall. That's the other issue I need to address.

'It feels wrong to just turn up on your wedding day without talking to Mum and Dad beforehand. What do you think?' My breath catches in my throat; this is much harder than I thought it would be.

'Hmm.' Tom pauses for a moment. 'Do you want the truth?'

I steel myself. 'Always.'

'There are two sides to every story, bro, and I see them both. When the row with Will kicked off, you saw them rush to comfort Fiona and Ollie. That was only natural, as Fiona was in shock and Ollie didn't understand why everyone was so upset. When they turned to you a couple of hours later to discuss it, you were so angry about everything. They were horrified, not because they were blaming you for the fight, but because you were pushing them away.'

'But I remember Dad's words as I was trying to explain what happened… he said, "No son of mine would lash out in anger," and he meant it.'

'Yes. He did. Dad knew you weren't the one to throw the first punch. You were the one who cut yourself off, Riley; you turned your back on them and walked out. Mum and Dad were devastated.'

As Tom's words sink in, I can't believe how stupid I've been. Jess did try to warn me that I could be looking at it all wrong. 'But they never made any attempt to get in touch.'

'Neither did you. Remember, from that point on, they felt ostracised. They continued to be there for Fiona and Ollie, but as you can imagine, she was bitter. When Fiona told Mum and Dad that you'd stopped visiting Ollie, it hit them hard. Me, too, but I wasn't about to give up on you.'

I let out an involuntary gasp. 'It was Fiona who stopped the visits; she said it was distressing Ollie and insisted that I call him instead. Often when I rang, she'd say he didn't want to come to the phone and eventually, I gave up trying.'

Tom lets out a low groan. 'It happens, mate. Fiona had an axe to grind at the time, but I'm surprised she's cut you off again when the visit went so well.'

Do I tell him in case he hears another version? 'That weekend Fiona drove Ollie down... she, well... I wanted it to be a fun weekend, obviously. But it became clear on day two that Fiona was enjoying herself a bit too much and she started talking about *their* next visit. I didn't know how to handle it when she started to get overly friendly. Like it wasn't just about Ollie, but *us* as a family.'

'Ugh... that's all you needed. At least now she knows there's no chance of a reconciliation. She'll come to her senses, as Ollie does talk about you a lot. He said your cottage is amazing.'

'He did? He loved the moorland setting and I took them to Penvennan Cove. It was a stormy day and he said it was "epic", which made me laugh as he wanted to skim stones and the sea was so turbulent, they just disappeared without trace.'

'My advice, is to give Mum and Dad a call. Fiona won't make a fuss on the day; that's not her style. With Ollie there, he's just a chatty young lad who isn't interested in the past, and as far as I can tell, he really believes you're going to be a part of his life in the future.'

My chest constricts and my throat unexpectedly tightens. It takes me a few moments to shake it off.

'Are you still there?' Tom checks.

'Yes. And that's good to know, thanks. It's a bit of a relief, actually. One last thing: Jess and I are tying the knot. It's going to be a small family wedding, held at our local village hall. We'd love for you and Helen to be there at the ceremony. Afterwards, we're having a big party at the farm for the wider family and friends. It's Sunday the sixth of August, if you're free.'

'*If* we're free? Nothing could stop us from coming.'

It feels good; it's like a huge weight has been lifted from my shoulders. Tom has always been there for me in the background and, having finally repaid the money he loaned me with interest, he knows how much his support meant to me when I was at my lowest ebb.

'Great! Jess's mum is organising everything and will be in touch about accommodation. Most people are staying two nights, Saturday and Sunday, and she'll forward you the options. Everything is within a fifteen-minute drive of the farm.'

'Goodness, who would have thought. Two weddings in the family within three months of each other,' Tom begins laughing. 'Mum will go into panic mode as she and Helen spent weeks sorting her outfit. Now they're going to have to do it all over again.'

As we bid each other goodbye, I realise it will be good to see him again in the flesh. Now I have two phone calls left to make, but I'll save those for tomorrow evening. One to my parents and one to Jess's father to belatedly ask for her hand in marriage. I meant it when I told Jess I was old-fashioned. Now all I need to do is sort the ring. I'm doing a few jobs on the side to get some cash together. A couple of hours here and there, spent in my workshop of an evening, and it's surprising what I can knock up. By the time we attend Tom's wedding, Jess will be sporting an engagement ring. I just need to think of a romantic way of getting down on one knee for the belated proposal. With that, I burst out laughing. Everything about our wedding is unusual and that's why I'm so relaxed about it. It's not *the* big thing in our life; it's just a part of getting us to where we want to be as a family.

'You did an amazing job here, Riley,' Adam comments, as we walk around Wind Rush Cottage. 'And this was a shell of a place when you bought it, I gather?'

'It had four solid external walls but a roof you could see daylight through. Virtually everything inside was ruined. There was a little pond going on in the middle of what is now the sitting room, complete with a family of frogs. It had been abandoned and remained empty for well over a decade; that's why it was a bargain. No one else was fool enough to take it on.' I grin at him, and he chuckles. 'Let's head downstairs and I'll dig out the photos.'

'Only the fearless,' he replies as he follows me. 'Ivy would love this. Three bedrooms, everything so pristine… if we could pick this up and put it where Smithy's Cottage is, this would solve all our problems.'

I turn my head to give him a sympathetic glance. 'The downside is that there isn't another property within walking distance and it's about a twenty-five-minute drive to the farm.'

'Yeah. It's a real shame. Anyway, moving is a headache Ivy has convinced me we don't have to address for quite a while.'

I indicate for him to take a seat on the sofa and grab the photo album from the bookshelf, while he continues.

'The trouble is, I have no idea how quickly babies grow. Ivy has me reading all these books about child development, but it makes my head swim. At what age will it work for us to find somewhere bigger? I'm thinking we have a year. It will mean either getting them into a nursery for half-days or hiring a nanny. Once Ivy has established a routine, she thinks she can run the business working mornings, Monday to Friday. But what if the kids get sick? I'd prefer we employ someone to look after them. However, the costs start to mount up, as Ivy will also need to find someone to cover her afternoon shifts serving behind the counter on the staff's days off.'

'Business is doing well, though?' I check.

'Yes, it is. And if it continues like this, the peak season is going to be phenomenal. But you know what Ivy's like – she needs to be hands-on and when the babies are here, it's going to be tough on her. They'll be her number-one priority but it's all an unknown to us. I don't know if what she's planning to do is even possible.'

I shrug my shoulders. 'All I remember from the early years with Ollie is that we lost a lot of sleep. But I was working all the hours I could, so I'll freely admit that Fiona bore the brunt of it. I took my turn at night, walking him up and down to coax him back to sleep but when he was poorly, it wasn't easy for me to take time off work.'

Adam looks crestfallen. 'Chances are by then, I might not even be working so close that I can get home every night. Jess's mum has offered to come and stay for as long as we need, and my mum is equally keen to help. But with our spare guest bedroom being next door in the bakery, nights are going to be down to me and Ivy, and just Ivy when I'm not there.' He takes a sip of his beer. 'Anyway, at least we have help waiting in the wings. Ivy is already stressed over what she's going to wear to your wedding. The obstetrician told her that they won't let her go past about thirty-eight weeks, so our invite for two is probably going to turn into an invite for four. I told her she'll look beautiful, no matter what.'

'And she will,' I agree.

'Yes, but she simply rolled her eyes at me and told me I don't understand. Anyway, show me these photos.'

The *before* pictures make his jaw drop.

'You weren't joking, Riley.' As we leaf through, he stabs his finger at one shot in particular. 'Is that a tent in the middle of the room?'

'Yep. Me and the frogs shared a habitat for a while until I was able to replace the roof. They didn't like it when their pond dried up and I'd got rid of all the rubble and debris. It was a year before I had a room ready to install a proper bed, but my back was very grateful.'

'Wow. Now that's what I call roughing it. And you managed with just a camping stove for all that time?'

'It's why I'm so good at making omelettes. And beans on toast.'

He holds his beer bottle up and we chink. 'All credit to you, Riley. And during that phase, you worked driving the lorry and doing odd jobs to pay for materials as you went?'

'I did. That's when I really fell in love with Cornwall... well, what I really mean is the Cornish people. It's a beautiful part of the world so what's not to like? But no one questioned the fact that I was a loner living in an abandoned cottage on the moor. I always turned up on time, ready to give it my all and they respected that.'

Adam flicks through the last couple of pages and then leans back against the cushions. 'It must have been a lonely life at times,' he reflects.

'No worse than I deserved for the chaos I'd left behind me. I learnt a lot about myself during that period. At first, lots of my old mates came down to see what I was doing and lend a hand. It was a bit of novelty, you know, camping out. Throwing steaks on the barbecue and sitting around a campfire in the evenings to keep out the chill. But it didn't take long for them to drift away. The old Riley was a part of a growing business. He had a proper home, a wife and a young son. Here, I had a toilet at the end of the garden and a hosepipe in a shed, for a shower.' I give a little laugh.

He grins back at me. 'Having been there once, you're not about to let it happen again at Renweneth Manor, are you?'

'We'll have everything we need in time for the wedding. But that leads me onto the reason why I asked you here this evening.'

He stares at me, frowning. 'You have an ulterior motive?

'I do. Adam, I need a best man and while we're not doing the whole stag do thing and speeches... I do require someone I trust implicitly to stand next to me in the village hall to hand over the wedding rings. It will mean a lot to me if you'd take on that role.'

'Me? Wow. It would be my pleasure, Riley. I sort of assumed that as you're still in touch with your brother—'

'Tom's a great guy and I've a lot to thank him for, but Jess took a risk on me, and I think that was because you and Ivy didn't judge me. You welcomed me into Jess's inner circle and made me feel like I belonged there.'

Adam raises his eyebrows. 'But you did. You earned that right. Jess was floundering, unable to find the help she needed. From day one, you worked side by side and gave it your all.'

I smile to myself. 'Hmm… that's true. But going from odd job man to sleeping with the boss in what… less than two months? And with my history, I'd have understood if you were a little suspicious.'

'Mate, that's paranoia and you need to deal with it. You make Jess happy and, believe me, even Cappy could see the change in her once you were on the scene. What you and Jess have done has really put Renweneth Farm on the map; you should be proud, as that's quite an achievement.'

When Adam leaves, I'm still processing what he said. I'm used to thinking of myself as the guy who messed up. I live in fear, thinking I'm one step away from repeating it all over again if I get it wrong. Jess pushes me to make decisions and I'm happy to do that up to a point, but ultimately, she's the boss. Cappy senses my hesitation at times and I wonder whether he sees it as a weakness on my part.

At the end-of-summer party, when Jess announced that we were a couple, Cappy took me to one side and said that with the two of us at the helm, he knew the farm was in good hands. Maybe that's true, but Jess won't discuss her financial worries with me and it's as if it's a burden she feels is hers alone. I know the farm is a trust, and I'm glad about that, but it doesn't mean she can't talk to me about her troubles. Or that she should assume I can't help. And that's an issue I need to address. We're in this together, though thick and thin, as my mum used to say.

JESS

15

Loose Ends Everywhere I Turn

With The Courtyard Hub planning to open seven days a week in future, and Ivy staffing up to do the same, Cappy is jokingly referring to the farm as Renweneth Village. I will admit that it was good to strike that item off the list. It was a question I kept being asked but it required a vote among the concession holders. Ivy said she'd fall in line with them, even though I told her straight that the decision was hers entirely. Frankly, I feel she has enough to contend with right now but she's a businesswoman and financially, it makes sense.

However, these days it seems that for every item I delete, two replace it. I was so in need of last night's yoga session, as my shoulders and neck were full of knots after a long day spent poring over spreadsheets and updating budgets. Today, there's less tension but instead of working on the manor, sadly I'm still ploughing through my backlog of paperwork.

When the door knocker interrupts my chain of thought, I jump straight up and on swinging open the door, I'm surprised to see Vyvyan standing there with two takeaway coffees from the bakery in her hands.

'I know you're head down working, but I need a quick word,' she blurts out. 'This is by way of an apology for interrupting you.'

'Of course. Come in. I'm set up in the kitchen.'

When she sees the state of the kitchen table, she lets out a low whistle. 'That's quite a collection of piles you have going on there, Jess.' She hands me a cup and I give her a grateful smile, indicating for her to take a seat.

'Hmm... it is. The invoices are coming in thick and fast now. I've decided we need to step up the pace, as we're falling behind on the schedule. Anyway, how are you?'

Vyvyan looks pale. 'Personally, I'm fine but Kate Enys rang me about an hour ago and she's fuming.'

'Not again. You created an additional stall at the market just to accommodate her, so what does she want now?'

Vyvyan shifts uneasily in her seat. 'I'll simply repeat what she said. Allegedly, Prudie told her assistant, Karl, that if a bay becomes available in The Courtyard Hub, the painting classes might have a new home. Apparently, Kate was wandering around his little gallery in Polreweek, and they got chatting about the display in the bakery, when he mentioned his conversation with Prudie. He was quite excited about it. Kate must have gone straight home to call me, and she wanted to know what's going on. She thinks she's top of the list if one of the other retailers serve notice.'

'Oh no,' I groan out loud. 'Talk about half a story; this is like Chinese whispers. I feel badly, Vyvyan, as after the thing with Flo, I told you I wouldn't meddle again, and I meant it.'

We both take a slurp of coffee, and she gives me an acknowledging nod. 'I guessed someone had got their wires crossed, but I know Cappy's been involved and that puts you in a difficult position.'

An impossible one, in this instance.

'Prudie turned up at my door and I had no choice other than to invite her in and let her say her piece. Cappy was leaning on me, although he has backed off, but he made it clear he thought it was a mistake not to accommodate her. But I promise you I did *not* say she was next on the list. In fact, I told her straight that even if a bay became vacant, it wouldn't be large enough for her needs. It was an impassioned plea, and she brought my grandma's name into it, as she was one of her patrons. However, I told her she needs to look elsewhere to avoid disappointment as we simply can't give her what she wants.'

'And Cappy accepted that?' Vyvyan looks at me uneasily.

'I think he realised I wasn't being awkward, just practical. Is Kate next on the list if one of the bays in The Courtyard Hub becomes available?' I question.

Vyvyan shakes her head. 'No. There were three other applicants at the very beginning who didn't get a space. She's number four. All I said to her at the time she made the fuss was that I'd add her to the list.'

'And we both thought that giving her a market stall would be the end of it,' I reply, miserably.

We sit in silence for a few moments, savouring our drinks and wondering how on earth we're going to get around this.

'I can see why she's angry, Vyvyan,' I admit, begrudgingly. 'She thinks Prudie has jumped the queue, but Kate was wrong in the first place, and in hindsight, we shouldn't have bent over backwards to keep her happy. The fact she missed the advertising you did for the concessions wasn't our fault. The three people above her on the list... did we offer them a market stall?'

Her face brightens. 'We did! Do you remember Cappy and I drew up a revised layout, but he was concerned that with cars driving past, it restricted what he calls the walking corridor outside the barn.'

'I do. But in the end, none of them took up the offer anyway. And to keep the peace, Cappy simply moved a few stalls around to fit Kate in.'

'Yes.'

'Well, we haven't done anything wrong, but I need to talk to Cappy about Prudie again. Of course, this could be an old rumour resurfacing, but just in case she's still talking about it, one of us has to make it clear she's grasping at straws. I thought he'd spoken to her and explained that it simply wasn't doable.'

Vyvyan grimaces. 'I'm so sorry to pass this back to you, Jess. I can see from the state of this table that you have your hands full.'

'Hey, don't worry about it and thanks for being quick off the mark. I need to nip this in the bud, and I'll be having a word with Kate, too.'

'I could do that; it was just that I didn't have all the facts, so I didn't quite know how to answer her. I do now.'

She grins at me, as I drain the last dregs of my coffee. 'No, it's my mess and I'll handle it. That hit the spot, thank you!'

'By the way, your mum and I have teamed up to sort out your wedding guests' accommodation. The campsite is already fully booked, but Pengali Farm have offered to rent us one of their pasture fields for those with camper vans and caravans. And we've secured a block booking at Haynes Farm and Fitness centre.'

'Wedding?' I laugh. 'What wedding? Oh… I keep forgetting.'

Vyvyan shakes her head at me. 'Don't worry, we have your back. You sort this little lot, and we'll make sure everyone has a place to stay.'

We stand and hug. 'Thank you so much, Vyvyan. For everything you do… and Keith. We'd struggle without the two of you. If ever there's anything I can do for *you*, just say.'

Vyvyan stands back, giving me a rather hesitant glance. 'I don't know whether this is appropriate but, um, when Riley, you and Lola move into Renweneth Manor, will Riley be selling his cottage?'

'He hasn't decided yet.'

'When he does, can you let him know that Keith and I might be interested if it's within our price range?'

'You're thinking of moving?'

'It's closer to Renweneth Farm and it makes sense. We've been looking for something within a half-hour's drive for a while but, as you know, not a lot comes on the market.'

'That's the trouble with a rural location, isn't it? There isn't much to choose from. But I'll most certainly let him know. It will be a wrench for him and that's why he's dragging his feet, but August is fast approaching.' It's too far for Ivy and Adam but it could be perfect for Vyvyan and Keith.

'Right,' she replies as I walk her to the front door. 'Let me know how you get on with Kate and good luck. Oh, and with Cappy, too.'

The look we exchange is rather dour.

'I will.'

That's another two tasks to add to the list, so today is par for the course.

When I hear the front door open, I assume it's Cappy, although he said he was meeting up with Charlie. Something to do with the boat that Ivan is selling and they're hoping to take a closer look at it.

'Oh, Riley.' I glance up and see that he's wearing clean clothes. 'What's going on?'

'I have a little surprise for you, but first I thought I'd take you out to lunch.' He stands there grinning at me like a hapless fool.

'So, there's something going on that you don't want me to see?'

'Hmm... you could say that but trust me, you'll thank me later.'

I've made a lot of progress again this morning, even with the little interlude with Vyvyan and, to be honest, I'm more than ready for a break. 'Where are you taking me?'

'The Lark and Lantern, I think, don't you?'

'That suits me just fine. I'll grab my bag and I'll text Erica to let her know we'll be back by two. She's dropping both Lola and Daisy off as I'm taking them to the cinema at three this afternoon.'

Riley walks forward as I stand and he wraps his arms around me. 'You look like you need a hug, Jess,' he murmurs, softly.

'I do. I really do. You wait 'til I tell you what happened this morning and it's nothing to do with this little lot.' I wave my hand at the table.

'Let's talk about it on the way there. Come on, a hot meal and a glass of wine will soon put some colour back into those cheeks of yours!'

I love this pub. It's the sort of local visitors dream of having and it's only a ten-minute drive from Renweneth Farm. Our table in the conservatory has an amazing view out over the bay and the staff here are so friendly.

As we wait for our meal to arrive, it's Riley's turn to talk. Having told him all about the ongoing saga of Kate and Prudie, he commiserates with me having to sort it out.

'Come on, let's toast. Here's to…' the pause is ominous '…facing up to our fears.'

Well, that's rather worrying. 'And overcoming them,' I add rather quickly, as we toast.

'Of course!' Riley replies with a smile.

'Okay… it's your turn now. I can tell something is up.'

When Riley tells me it's official that Adam is going to be his best man, it puts a beaming smile on my face. I guessed there was a good reason for the fact that they skipped the gym last night. However, when he goes on to talk about the conversation he had with his brother, I'm surprised. For Riley, that must have been very difficult indeed.

'Well done you. It would have been wrong not to have told Tom about the situation with Fiona.'

He places his beer glass back down on the table, nervously moving it around on the placemat. 'I also rang my parents.'

My jaw drops. 'You did?'

'I wasn't going to, as it was just after nine when Adam left.'

The waitress arrives with our food, and I must admit I'm starving.

'Two haddock fillets with triple-cooked fries and mushy peas,' she announces, and the smell makes my stomach rumble.

Our conversation goes on hold for a few minutes. Everything looks better on a full stomach, and nothing beats the taste of freshly caught fish.

'This is good,' Riley states, stabbing his fork into a chip.

'Hmm. Just what I needed,' I confirm. 'Anyway, what were you saying?'

He smiles across at me. 'I've had a bit of a wake-up call, Jess.'

'You have?' I stop to take a sip from my wine glass, while my eyes search his.

'Tom made me see things from a slightly different perspective and Adam said something that made me stop and think.'

I continue eating, while watching him as he puts down his knife and fork to look at me.

'My parents didn't abandon me; I abandoned them. And Adam said that I'm paranoid.'

The fork is halfway to my mouth, and I stop mid-air. 'You're paranoid?'

He sighs. 'I didn't think I brought anything to the table, Jess. No money, just my muscle power and you pay me for that. Fiona never fails to remind me that I ruined her and Ollie's lives. She said I'd ruin yours, too, so I guess Adam's right.'

I put down my knife and fork with a clatter. 'That's utter rubbish, Riley. Without you in my life… mine and Lola's… we'd struggle. I was on my own trying to pretend I had it all under control when I didn't.' A sob catches in my throat.

Riley reaches out to clasp my hand in his. 'Oh, Jess… if you have a problem, then it's mine too. There's no need for you to pretend that everything is on track when I know it isn't. We're over budget and running behind. It's time you and I sat down and decided how we're going to make it work.'

I draw in a huge breath and give Riley a watery smile. 'I'd like that,' I confess.

'Are we done eating?'

I nod my head and Riley indicates to the waitress that she can clear our plates.

'Could we have two cappuccinos please and the bill when you're ready.'

She responds with a beaming smile. 'You got it!'

When she's out of earshot, he turns back to look at me in earnest. 'My parents were shocked to hear from me. They thought... well, you were right, from their point of view, I cut them off. It was an emotional conversation. Mum said that the reason they kept close with Fiona and Ollie was for my sake, as much as wanting to be close to their grandson. They hoped that one day I'd want to reconnect with my son. When I explained to them that it was Fiona who stopped the visits, they were speechless. She'd told them that my visits tailed off and, in effect, I abandoned them.'

It's crushing to see the look of pain reflected in his eyes. 'Having cleared the mortgage and handed over the family home to Fiona... that's not abandonment, Riley.'

He sucks in a sharp breath. 'They didn't know the terms of our divorce, or that I walked away with virtually nothing.'

'Or that she called you back from time to time if there was something that needed attending to,' I point out.

'I did it for my son, Jess. I guess in a way, it turned out to be a saving grace; if we'd lost all contact, he wouldn't have asked his mother to contact me when he had that awful asthma attack. I could have been a stranger to him, if it weren't for my odd trips back there to keep the house in good repair.'

That leaves one question unanswered. 'How do your parents feel about you and me going to Tom's wedding?'

'They've asked if we can meet up before the ceremony. Emotions were running high when we talked; I guess we're all sorry and, in hindsight, regretful for how things panned out. I said I'd run it past you and let them know. What do you think?'

'I think that's a great idea. After all, it's Tom and Helen's big day but what about Fiona?'

He shrugs his shoulders. 'I guess it's a case of hoping that sometime within the next five weeks, she decides to start talking to me again. I mean… knowing that we're all going to be together for the first time in just over five years now, even Fiona's got to be feeling nervous about it.'

'In case some of the things she's said about you come back to haunt her?' I offer and his eyes widen.

'Goodness, I hadn't thought about that.'

As our coffees arrive, Riley grows quiet, and we sit in a companionable silence for a while, staring out at the sea. Today, it's shimmering as the breeze whips across the surface, scattering the sun's rays as it gleams like liquid silver. How can life be filled with such abject opposites? I find myself wondering. We're looking out over nature's bounty and yet it feels like there's a cloud hovering over our heads. Like it or not, Fiona calls the shots and there's no way of predicting what's going to happen on the day.

16

It's the Little Gestures That Count… I Hope

Our journey back to The Farmhouse is a tad subdued but when we park up, Riley leads me in the direction of Renweneth Manor.

'I have something to show you that you need to sign off on,' he says, clasping my hand firmly in his.

People are coming and going as we traverse the courtyard and it's nice to see people outside the bakery sipping their drinks and enjoying Ivy's awesome cakes.

'Gaping holes are a sign of progress; I know that, because it means the water leak is fixed. While I appreciate the huge amount of work that's gone into it, you don't need my approval; it's your project.'

Riley pulls a long face. 'Rick and Nigel have been working flat-out to get this done and I think a few words from you would mean a lot.'

'All right.' I lower my voice as we walk through the archway. But when I see what they've done, I break out into a huge smile. 'Where's the hole?' I call out, and the two guys turn to look at me.

'Talk about timing – we're literally just tidying up.'

Riley and I stand, looking at the marvellous job they've done, and I can't stop grinning. 'I have a new bed of standard roses. You guys, this is amazing. No one would know that just yesterday, there was a massive hole here.'

They've even trimmed the edges of the lawn that butts up to

the freshly planted bed. And, yes, the grass around it is a little flat in places but it's not the ugly scar it could have been.

'I can't thank you enough. I know this wasn't an easy fix, but you've totally made my day. Come August, it will look like it's always been here.'

Now they're embarrassed and they start laughing. I look from one to the other and end up giving Riley a quizzical look.

'Honestly, Jess. It was like we were performing delicate surgery,' he declares.

Nigel joins in. 'Usually, we just start digging. It took longer laying out the boards and the tarpaulin to stack the soil on than it did to make the hole. Mind you, a digger would have been easier, but we didn't want to upset the boss, did we, guys?'

'Well, that deserves a reward. The cakes and coffee are on me. Go and sit yourselves down in the orchard and I'll be back shortly.' As I walk away, suddenly I'm humming to myself. And Grandma would have approved because roses were her absolute favourites.

Just as I'm about to exit the bakery, Ivy appears next to the counter. 'Here, let me help you with those. Where are you heading?'

'Thanks. Over to the orchard.' Ivy grabs the cardboard cup carrier as I gingerly carry the cake box in two hands. 'It's a little thank you to the guys. They've been doing some landscaping after our water leak.'

'Ah… the work inside is still on hold?'

I nod my head. 'Yep. Just until the side wall and the floor have dried out a little more. The dehumidifiers are still drawing out vast quantities of water, but Riley reckons come Monday, we can pick up where we left off.'

'That's something at least. Vyvyan was in this morning. Was she on her way over to see you?' Ivy asks.

'Yes. And I know, she looked a bit shell-shocked.'

'Ah, you thought so, too. I didn't like to say.'

'She had Kate on the phone complaining again.'

Ivy gives me a troubled glance. 'Really? I thought all that had died down.'

'Yet another misunderstanding caused, no doubt, by an off-the-cuff remark Prudie made about renting space in The Courtyard Hub. It's something I have to sort out with Cappy before it gets out of hand.'

'Oh… poor you. To be honest, Kate admitted to Wenna that she can't see herself ever having enough savings to launch her business properly. I don't know why she's still making a fuss, in that case. Unless she's just angry in general and lashing out.'

I glance at Ivy and notice that she's chewing her lower lip, a sure sign she's stressed.

'Ugh, I sort of wondered the same thing. Anyway,' I reply, narrowing my eyes. 'Something's troubling you. What's up?'

'To be honest, I was going to approach Kate to see whether she'd be interested in being a back-up for me.'

We both draw to a halt in the shadow of the manor's garden wall.

'It's a job that would suit her down to the ground, Ivy. I mean, she's both a baker and she's good at serving the customers.'

'I know, but if she's still going off on one about favouritism still, maybe it's best that I look elsewhere. At least time is on my side. Oh, by the way, Adam was chuffed Riley asked him to be his best man.'

'Ah, I thought he might be. It seems the wedding plans are finally getting somewhere.'

As we step through the archway and head into the orchard, Ivy reminds me that we still need to talk about the wedding cake. 'I'm not avoiding it; I just don't know what I want,' I declare as we approach the guys.

'A woman who doesn't know what she wants?' Rick suddenly pipes up. 'Riley, you're in serious trouble now.'

'I was talking about the wedding cake. As for the manor,

I know *exactly* what I want!' I inform him, as I ease the lid off the box of cakes and their eyes light up.

Now they're bantering between themselves, and Ivy and I leave them to it, wending our way back out to the courtyard.

'Don't give up on Kate just yet, Ivy. I'm going to drop by her cottage and see if I can catch her in. Just for a little chat to try to put this issue to bed once and for all. Wait and see what sort of reaction I get and maybe let the dust settle, then sound her out. I don't think she's happy working from a market stall just two days a week anyway. Unless she can afford to rent a commercial kitchen, she just won't be able to scale up even if she did get a place in The Courtyard Hub. Unfortunately, Prudie's careless words have incensed her though, and I can sort of understand that.'

'I think you're right. Let me know how it goes. Kate was fine helping me out when I first came here. The trouble with Prudie is that sometimes she's so focused, she can't see when she's put her foot in it.'

We say goodbye and go our separate ways, as I realise Erica will be here shortly to drop off Lola and Daisy. My working day is officially done, and the problems will have to wait until tomorrow.

The following morning, I drop by the manor to let Riley know I'm off to see Kate. He, Rick and Nigel are getting ready to commission the new central heating system, which is great news. We make arrangements to meet up at lunchtime and I tell him I have a few things we need to talk through, but he's only half-listening. His mind is otherwise occupied with the task they have ahead of them today.

It's only about a six-minute drive to Kate's cottage, one of a pair that is set back from the lane. She lives next door to Wenna and Gryff, and I think they've all been friends for a long time, well before they ended up moving to the village.

I am a little nervous as I rap the fox's head door knocker and stand back.

'Jess, I'm um... as you can see, I'm baking.' Kate stands there wiping her hands on a damp cloth.

'Oh, sorry... I won't stop you. Maybe we can catch up another time, Kate.'

Her forehead puckers up. 'Vyvyan said you'd be in touch; I just didn't think it would be this soon. Is it about a space in The Courtyard Hub?'

'Yes... and no.'

I can see she's in two minds about inviting me in, but she stands back and indicates for me to go inside. It's a charming, chocolate-box cottage: bijou and in some ways, it reminds me of Penti Growan, the little cottage we let out adjacent to The Farmhouse; it's quaint, with lots of character and is homely but up to date.

She follows me into the sitting room, and I turn to face her. 'There was a lot of chatter just before Christmas about people being hand-picked to fill the spaces at the market and in The Courtyard Hub. I can appreciate how you might think that, as you expressed an interest after all the spots had been taken. I'm here to explain the procedure and put you right on the latest rumour that seems to be circulating.'

'It's not down to *who* you know then,' she replies, almost dismissively.

'No Kate, it's not and I'd hate you to think that.'

'Hmm. You'd best come through to the kitchen and sit down.'

At least she's willing to listen to me, which is a good start.

'Right, I'm not tuning out, but these biscuits won't cook themselves. Take a seat.'

It can't be easy batch-baking in a small country kitchen, but she's made the most of the space she has. Instead of a kitchen table, there's a central island and I pull out one of the tall stools. Kate washes her hands at the sink and turns back to face me. She picks up a cookie cutter and starts lifting gingerbread men onto one of the greased trays in front of her.

'Vyvyan began advertising for small businesses interested in space at The Courtyard Hub a couple of months before the work began and the response was instant. I think in the end, only two ads went out and Vyvyan put a halt on it, because she had enough interest to fill all the bays with names to spare. The criteria was, and is, simple. First come, first served and the only caveat was that in fairness to our tenants, we wanted a wide range of products. We had two applications for stationery and cards, so the first one to apply got the slot and the second one went onto the reserve list if they pull out.'

Kate stops what she's doing to look at me. 'Okay, so I missed the ads, I get that. But now you're telling me I'm not next on the list?'

'Yes. You're fourth. The three people before you were among the original applicants and the waiting list is now closed for the time being.'

'But Prudie was only interested in the studio and Flo managed to snap that up.' This time, there's an edge to her voice.

'Prudie was sent a formal email offering her the space, but she didn't reply within the deadline set. We only had one other interested party and that was Flo.'

Kate narrows her eyes. 'Why is Prudie next on the list for a bay if she was only interested in the studio?'

'I can confirm that she isn't on the list. If Flo vacates the studio, then Vyvyan will approach Prudie, but a single bay wouldn't be big enough for her anyway. I thought I'd made that very clear but apparently not.'

'What about Ivy and the bakery?'

Kate's determined to find fault but I'm here to nip this in the bud.

'Again, it was advertised on our website and through our estate agent, but the only enquiries we received were from parties wanting to convert it into a convenience store and that isn't a part of the vision for Renweneth Farm.'

Kate sniffs the air, turning to grab some oven mitts and when she pulls out the tray a heavenly, chocolaty smell fills the air. She carries two trays over to cooling racks, lined up next to the sink unit.

'And yet, when I complained, Vyvyan found me a market stall just like that.' She turns and the eye contact is challenging.

'Look, Kate. I'll tell you exactly what I told Prudie. If we had the space, we'd be only too happy to welcome everyone who wants to join us. It could be argued that we bent the rules for you, not least because even with the market stalls, we try not to have too many similar products. It's not in the interest of the vendors. But Vyvyan spoke to the other bakery goods stallholder, and she felt your range was bespoke, whereas hers is more run of the mill.'

'Quantity, not quality,' Kate replies and my jaw drops. 'I'm only joking, Jess. The fact you've come to see me in person means a lot. I guess I've jumped to a few conclusions, and I am grateful you accommodated me. I just saw red when Karl was telling me that Prudie is hopeful of being able to set up her art school at the farm. I know she's an old friend of Cappy's and that must count for something.'

Kate doesn't miss a trick and here's where I need to be a little wary. 'She was also great friends with my grandma. And from the point of view of what Prudie is trying to achieve for the wider community of artists in Cornwall, Cappy truly believes it would be a great addition to Renweneth Farm. I agree with him, but we simply don't have enough space to accommodate her. I advised Prudie to look elsewhere to avoid disappointment. It would require half of the occupants of The Courtyard Hub to leave en masse, and the people on the reserve list to drop out, to give her what she wants. I simply can't see that happening and even if they did, it's not ideal anyway. There isn't enough natural light.'

'It's not that I don't like Prudie,' Kate reflects, her attitude softening. 'It's just that you know she's going to get her own way at some point, don't you? And I guess that's how you felt about me, going to such lengths to get me a stall.'

I give Kate a warm smile. 'No, it was distressing for both Vyvyan, and me, that you were upset, and you were kind enough to help Ivy out when she was struggling. You're a great baker, Kate, and you love what you do. Why wouldn't we want to support you?'

She turns, sliding a spatula under one of the freshly baked cookies and offers it to me.

'Chocolate orange. They melt in the mouth. Try one.'

Kate is right and my taste buds instantly react. 'Mmm... now that's a real treat.'

'I'm sorry for getting wound up, Jess. I think what you're doing at the farm is amazing. I know how hard it is to set up a business and how easy it is to fail. It hurts, and I let Prudie's anger about losing out to Flo fire me up because I, too, felt I was being excluded. I'll have a word with Vyvyan and apologise, as that was one long rant of a phone call.'

'How are you doing with the stall?' I ask, gently.

'It's keeping me baking and I'm getting telephone orders for my special occasions gift boxes. It's allowing me to keep going, just.'

'Well, the proof is in the eating, and you deserve success, Kate. I hope business picks up quickly.' As Kate sees me to the door, I have a sudden idea. 'Have you thought about maybe making up small cookie gift boxes and seeing if the stationery stall in The Courtyard Hub would sell them for you? It's a nice little gift to go with a card and would widen your exposure.'

'Ooh... now that's an idea. Thanks, I'll wander over there this afternoon. It can't hurt to ask, can it?'

'How was your morning?' Riley gives me an artful grin.

'Nerve-racking. I was straight with Kate and said the only person we broke our rules for was, in fact, her. I'm going to have a word with Ivy, because at the time, it looked like it was Kate stirring up trouble and gossiping. But it all leads back to Prudie. Even this latest incident is because she's... Oh, you can't blame the woman for having a passion. Honestly, when it comes to willpower and determination, Prudie is quite something. Now I'm beginning to wonder whether her plan is to wear me down.'

Riley is already halfway through his pastie, but as hungry as he is, he stops eating to look at me. 'And what... erect a studio for her in the middle of the courtyard? Ivy's customers need that space.'

I look at him, aghast. 'Do you think that's what Prudie is angling for? Don't even say that in jest. That is not happening. The courtyard is a communal area.'

'How about Cappy's idea of extending the mezzanine in the small barn? You could have two studios instead of one.'

That idea fleetingly passed through my mind, too. It wasn't a suitable solution for Ivy and Adam, but if it had solved all their problems, I would have gone with it. But an art studio needs a lot of natural daylight and there's nothing at all we can do to achieve that.

'Not you, too!'

He looks shamefaced. 'I'm just thinking outside the box, that's all. So, Kate now understands there's nothing dodgy going on, but you still have the little problem of Prudie to deal with.'

My shoulders sag at the very thought of it. 'Do you think it would be better coming from Cappy, or me?'

Riley's expression is one of concern. 'I don't know. The thing is Jess, in two and a half months, the lease on Cappy's house in Stroud will be up. I'm just throwing this out there, so don't shoot the messenger, but would it make a difference to his decision to stay if Prudie's art school were here?'

I'm rendered speechless. What is Riley trying to say? I stare at him questioningly.

'I only meant that they're friends and enjoy each other's company. Now that the Beer and Bait Club are meeting up again, wouldn't it be yet another reason for him to stay?'

'She's just an old friend of Grandma's, really. As far as I know, Cappy doesn't have any interest in art. Maybe this is something I need to deal with myself.'

However, I make a mental note to ring Mum for a chat. Cappy talks to her several times a week and perhaps she can give me an insight into what he's planning for the future.

'Oh, before I forget... Vyvyan and Keith are looking to move closer to Renweneth Farm. Vyvyan asked whether you were thinking of selling the cottage at some point.'

Riley's face pales. 'Oh... um...'

'Sorry, I only mentioned it because she asked. If you do decide to go down that route, could you have a chat with them before you do anything, given that they've shown an interest?'

It's no big deal and I don't want Riley to think I'm interfering, but I feel honour-bound to mention it.

'I will. Now, I'll clear the plates away while you sort out what it was you wanted to discuss, with regard to the work schedule on the manor.'

Today, the kitchen table is a lot clearer, and I switch on the laptop, plugging in the Ethernet cable while Riley makes us both a coffee.

'Oh, you've sent me an update.'

'Yes, sorry, I assumed you'd already picked it up. You asked me to ramp things up but, obviously, there will be a bit of a time lag. I can't talk to the various trades until you approve the corresponding increase in budget.'

As Riley saunters back to the table carrying two mugs of coffee, he gingerly steps over the trailing cable. 'You know, I'm going to get the electricians to pop in and hardwire this in. There's plenty of room for you to have a small computer table in the corner and it would avoid the trip hazard.'

'You're a real gem; do you know that, Riley?'

'Hey, if something is important to you, it's important to me, too. Anyway, have you calculated the impact of the delays on the bottom line?'

I let out an involuntary groan. 'Ugh... nothing comes cheap these days, does it?'

'Talk to me about money, Jess. The cost of materials keeps rising and I'm beginning to wonder whether the date we've set is too ambitious. There's no point in overextending yourself, is there? It'll just add additional pressure that you don't need right now.'

He's in earnest and it would be wrong of me to ignore Riley's concerns.

'You were probably right when you said I should double the budget, at least for phase one of the work. The good news is that the farm's income is growing and fast; the bad news is that what accompanies that is a big tax bill. Effectively, in the first year of any sudden jump, we get hammered, as I've got to set aside double the tax on the increase.'

'Ah... the payment on account. And the income is going to continue to grow, as you haven't yet had a full year's rental from The Courtyard Hub.'

'I know. That's why I've decided to make a loan to the business.'

Riley was just about to take a sip of coffee, but he immediately places the mug back down on the table. 'What?'

'It's just a loan,' I reiterate.

'Does Cappy know?'

I shake my head. 'There's no reason why he should.'

'Because you know he wouldn't be happy about it. And when will you get it back?'

I shrug my shoulders. 'I'm not in a rush; the idea is to continue to plough the profits into the manor until it's completed. After that, I'll receive staged payments after other capital investments at the farm are covered.'

I've never seen Riley looking so unsettled before, but as he sits there, I can see he's not happy about it. 'You're putting in your own money just so we can hit our target?'

'It's cash sitting in the bank doing nothing, Riley.'

'No, after ten years' of marriage and working, it's your nest egg. It's your safety net for the future if anything goes wrong.'

I stare at him pointedly and his eyes don't leave mine. 'No, having Lola, you and the farm is my safety net. This is our future and I'm done waiting.'

'Okay… what if I sell the cottage and you use that money instead? I'm not in a hurry to get it back, either.'

Now he's challenging me. 'That's daft, Riley, and you know it. For the time being, you need your own place, just until we sort things out with Fiona regarding Ollie. And whatever you decide about the cottage, that's your legacy to him.'

He wraps his hands around his coffee mug, looking dejected. 'True, but in the meantime, I could just move into The Farmhouse. Why would a loan from me be any different to a loan from you?'

'Because my money is readily available, and it takes time to sell a property.' I reach out to touch his hand. 'I know you mean well, but I know what I'm doing. Let's not make this about who's putting in what, because you're the driving factor to get the work done. We are doing this together, but it's slightly different because the farm is a trust.'

'But Renweneth Manor is going to be *our* home for the rest of our lives and that makes a huge difference to me.'

I tilt my head back and take a few seconds to gather my thoughts together.

'I love you, Jess,' Riley continues. 'If you have a problem, then I do too.'

'Money isn't the problem; it's the schedule. Let's put our heads together and find a way to make it work. We need to be in by the first of August, so that everything is ready for our wedding on the sixth. Can we get it done?' There's a catch in my voice before I fall silent.

'If that's what you want, that's what will happen.' Riley winks at me conspiratorially.

Somehow, whenever I succeed in tying myself up in knots, he has this knack of making everything seem so simple. I'm beginning to doubt that it's doable, but it won't be for lack of trying.

MAY

RILEY

17

The Proposal

The first half of May seems to have flown by. First thing tomorrow morning, Jess and I are setting off to York, ready for Tom and Helen's wedding the following day. Lola will be having a double sleepover at her dad's and she's mega excited about it.

I'm in the large shed behind the manor, scrabbling around for a piece of wood. I'm trying to repurpose an old armoire that has huge sentimental value for Jess. When my phone starts ringing, I'm surprised to see that it's Adam calling. 'Hey, mate. Is everything all right?'

'Yeah, all good. I need a favour.'

'Ask away.'

'Last night, Ivy asked me to look at one of the sliding rails on the stone art wall. I meant to pop into the café before I set off this morning, but I forgot. Karl mentioned it was sticking and it might need a plane to coax it. She won't like to bother you, but it'll probably only take a couple of minutes and I don't want Prudie getting on her case about it.'

'No sweat. I'll head over there now.'

'Thanks, mate. How are you feeling ahead of tomorrow?' Adam asks, hesitantly.

'Honestly? Conflicted. Obviously, it's a joyful occasion, but given the situation, my nerves are jangling. One moment I find myself breaking out in a cold sweat just thinking about it, the next I'm telling myself to man up.'

'Hey, that's only natural. But you're not doing this alone and with Jess by your side, you'll be fine.'

'I have no idea what sort of reaction we're going to get, Adam, but I'm simply going to hope for the best.'

'And are you all prepared for your romantic evening for two?' He begins chuckling to himself.

I make a small moan, glancing behind me to check that Jess isn't within earshot. 'As much as I can be. Ivy and Erica have the food all sorted and Cappy is charged with keeping Jess well away from the attic today. We're quitting work at five this afternoon so I can go home and change. Jess thinks we're going to The Lark and Lantern.'

'Well, you've certainly had your work cut out pulling this together. How did the video call go with Harry and Celia?'

'Jess's parents were surprised but pleasantly so. I said that things had moved so fast, and I felt bad that I hadn't asked for their approval to marry their daughter. It felt good and the look on their faces told me it was appreciated. They're old-school and I guess, in a way, I'm a bit of a traditionalist, too.'

'You know, I felt the same way when I asked Ivy's dad for his permission. Ironically, it was Jess's grandma who prodded me. She said that Ivy was getting impatient, and I should just get on with it, so I did.' He laughs softly to himself. 'Anyway, I hope it all goes smoothly tonight. Jess isn't one for making a big fuss and I think you've nailed it. Right, good luck for later, Riley, and thanks for the favour, mate.'

Late morning, Jess heads off for a meeting with Vyvyan and her accountant, Michael. Cappy gives me the nod when he sees her exit the car park and it's time to get things moving. There are several pieces of furniture to carry up two flights of stairs and when I call for a volunteer to lend a hand, I end up with three. Many hands make light work, as my dad would say, and when I let them in on the surprise, everyone is eager to do something to help.

Two hours later, I make my way over to The Courtyard Hub to see Anna. The jewellery stall is very popular and being able to watch her at work when she's making a new piece is fascinating.

'Riley! This is an exciting day for you.' She beams at me, pulling something from beneath the counter. She places a small, pale-blue box in front of me.

'I took the stone you chose and set it on a fourteen-carat, white-gold band, alongside three accent white diamonds either side.'

Gazing at it, it takes my breath away.

'You'll notice that the pear-drop-shaped aquamarine stone is flawless; I'm thrilled with how it's turned out.'

'So am I, Anna, and I can't thank you enough. Not only is it unique, but it's stunning. Jess is going to love it.' It might only have cost eleven hundred pounds, but I know that won't matter to the woman I love. This ring was designed for her, and it was worth working evenings to get the money together.

'Take it out and have a good look at it. Hold it up to the light. See how the stone throws soft blues from the faceted finish. It really is one of the loveliest aquamarine stones I've ever seen, and it was a real pleasure designing this for you.'

I very gingerly slip it back into the box, beaming from ear to ear as I do so. 'Let's just hope she says yes.'

Anna begins to laugh, and I join in. 'I think that's a given, Riley, as the wedding planning is in full swing, but every girl remembers the moment her guy popped the question, doesn't she?'

My stomach is in knots as I park the car and walk across to The Farmhouse. It's only the second time I've ever bought Jess flowers. I'm not even sure what's appropriate for a proposal, but the woman in the florist's shop suggested I wander around for inspiration. I kept going back to the roses, and as they were Jess's grandma's favourites, that's what I went with in the end. However, two dozen red roses and some frothy bits of greenery with tiny white flowers on them means the bouquet literally fills my arms.

As I stand here, wearing my best suit and waiting for the door to open, I glance around, conscious that I probably look like a bit of an idiot. But when Jess's face is staring back at me and she breaks out into one huge, beaming smile, I don't care.

'Jess Griffiths, would you be so good as to accompany me to dinner at Renweneth Manor?' I ask. Her eyes begin to sparkle. 'Oh, and these are for you.'

She puts out her hands to take the bouquet and before she has a chance to respond, I step forward to take her arm and lead her across the courtyard.

'This is... un... unexpected,' she stutters. 'And look at you! I didn't even know you had a suit.'

'I'm a man of many surprises,' I inform her, solemnly.

'Dinner... at the manor?'

'Yes, our first meal in our soon-to-be new home.'

When we step through the archway, her face lights up as she sees the flickering candles lined up along the half-height walls of the farmer's porch. I would have loved to have had a trail of tea lights to guide us up to the attic; however, as it's still a building site and I'm in charge of the project, I couldn't throw caution to the wind. We can't risk the place burning down, even in the pursuit of a romantic rendezvous.

'Riley, have you gone mad?' She giggles, but it exudes a happiness that warms my heart. 'This is crazy!'

'Just keep walking.'

With the new staircases now in situ, it's nice to be able to appreciate the progress that has been made. Yes, we've a long way to go, but I don't think either of us have really had time to take in what we've achieved so far.

As we step into the first of the attic rooms, nothing much has changed since we replaced the rotting woodwork, although all the damaged floorboards have now been replaced with reclaimed ones. It'll probably be another nine months before we start work up here in earnest, but I hope Jess isn't disappointed when she sees the pop-up restaurant. That thought makes me smile to myself as I grab her hand, leading her forward.

'And we're eating up here?' she queries, frowning.

The second room isn't any better. When I swing open the door to what will eventually become bedroom five, formerly known as the apple store, Jess sucks in a deep breath. She steps forward, to gaze in awe at her surroundings.

'This is magical, Riley, really magical!'

We managed to get the internal wall plaster-boarded and painted in half a day. The floor has been mopped and there isn't a speck of dirt or dust to be seen. The three stone walls set the ambience and a dozen scented pillar candles in large glass containers dotted around make it feel cosy.

In the centre of the room, with a breath-taking view out across the bay, the dining table is all laid up as it would be in a posh restaurant.

'This is... amazing, Riley,' Jess states, sounding slightly breathless. 'How did you...'

'The guys all pulled together while you were at your meeting. Do you recognise the table and the chairs? You aren't the only one who can upcycle.'

I offer to take the flowers from her so she can wander around and place them in a waiting vase half-full of water. 'My catering team thought of everything,' I add and laugh. 'Ivy and Erica did me proud.'

Jess is lightly skimming her fingertips over the painted and distressed table. 'I thought we put this in the skip. These two chairs, too.' She turns to look at me, as if she can't take it all in.

'The base of the table was broken but I managed to find something in a similar style. A bit of sanding and priming, and your favourite shabby chic finish was created by Cheryl, in The Courtyard Hub. She did the chairs too, once I replaced the dowels.'

Jess reaches out her hand to gently rock one of the chairbacks.

'They don't wobble anymore!' she exclaims. 'Oh, Riley... this is wonderful, truly wonderful. And our first meal here. Is that one of Erica's casseroles I can smell bubbling away in that hot pot on the dresser? Did Cheryl do the paint finish on that piece of furniture, too?'

'She did. Anyway, let me pull out a chair for you and I'll begin serving.'

But instead of turning away, I slip the ring box from my pocket and go down on one knee. Jess's face freezes. 'Jess Griffiths, I have your parents' approval to ask you for your hand in marriage. I promise to love you always and be the best husband, and stepdad to Lola, that I can.'

Tears seem to spring from everywhere and they're not all Jess's, as I open the box and hand it to her.

'I'm... I'm—'

I grab a napkin off the table and pass it to her.

'You've made me speechless, and I bet my make-up is a mess!' She sniffs. 'But you know the answer; it's a *yes* and looking back, I think deep down inside, I knew that from day one.'

When I slip the ring on her finger, it's a perfect fit and she looks at me quizzically. 'How did you... OMG! That day I went into The Courtyard Hub and Anna showed me some of the rings she was making. She encouraged me to try a couple on when I said how gorgeous they were.'

'I chose the stone; it's an aquamarine with a faceted finish and Anna said it's flawless. When you hold it up to the light, all you see are the soft blue tones reflected. It's special, just like you, Jess, and unique.'

As far as memories go, tonight couldn't be more perfect. If anything was going to spur us on to reach our goal, this is it. Not bad for a rough-and-ready builder-guy, eh? Jess's face is radiant and sitting here with the woman I love, I'm ready to face whatever life throws at us.

JESS

18

Happy Families

It's Saturday the twentieth of May; Riley grabs my hand, giving it a comforting squeeze, as he reaches out to ring the doorbell of his parents' home. It's a pretty bungalow on the edge of the village of Deighton, just a few miles from York. It certainly has kerb appeal and wonderful views to the rear across a swathe of fields and trees.

When the front door swings open, I can't believe the likeness between father and son, as we're ushered inside.

'Come in, come in,' a woman's voice in the background bids us.

There's an awkward moment as Riley hesitates for a second or two, unsure of how to greet his father, but it's fleeting. I grab Riley's hand and we follow his mother into a very cosy-looking sitting room.

'Oh my!' Her hands fly up to her face. 'I promised your father I wouldn't get upset, but I'm sorry. I... I was beginning to fear that this day would never come.'

I let go of Riley's hand and he rushes over to her. 'I'm sorry, Ma. I never meant to be a bad son.'

His mother throws her arms around him and out of the corner of my eye, I catch his father swiping his hand across his own eyes. The seconds tick by and I think we all need a moment to compose ourselves. The emotion in the room is tangible and I, too, feel tearful. I wasn't expecting to feel the full impact of what must have been an enormous sense of loss for them when Riley left. Now their son is back, they can hardly believe it. When his mum finally steps back, she takes a moment to wipe her eyes.

'I'll um... put the kettle on,' his dad pipes up. 'Tea, everyone?'

Riley and I nod our heads and his father quickly makes himself absent.

'Sorry, I haven't even done the introductions. Mum, this is Jess.'

Riley stands back and I stick out my hand feeling a tad awkward. 'It's lovely to meet you.'

'Please call me Phyllis. Eddie,' she calls out to her husband, 'leave that for a moment and come and say hello to Jess. Sorry, we're forgetting ourselves.'

When Eddie returns to the room, he immediately comes over to shake my hand and his smile is genuine. 'Welcome, Jess. I'm afraid I'm a bit all over the place this morning.'

It seems that he's just like Riley when it comes to handling emotional stuff.

'Take a seat both of you, please. Eddie, where's that tea?' Phyllis gives him a pointed look and he shakes his head at her, laughing.

'On its way, my dear. You'd best sit yourself down – you seem a bit wobbly.'

The look between them is poignant. It's as if they can't believe what's happening and they're beside themselves with joy.

Riley and I sit on the sofa next to the window, and his mum takes one of the single armchairs facing us.

'How was your journey?' she asks. 'It's such a long drive.'

'Just over six hours,' Riley confirms. 'We arrived about nine last night. We're staying in a little place close to the wedding venue.'

Eddie reappears carrying a well laid-out tray. I bet it's been the longest few hours of their lives waiting for the clock to strike ten.

Phyllis immediately takes over, as Eddie settles himself down in the seat next to her. It's a pretty room, not too fussy but the style is elegant and countrified. The drapes are cream with a scattering of wildflowers in various shades of blue and pale green.

'Help yourself to milk and sugar, Jess,' Phyllis says, placing two cups and saucers down on the coffee table in front of us.

'Thank you, that's very kind.'

'Oh, it's a pleasure, a total pleasure. To have a wedding is a joyful event, but to have Riley back in our lives and know that he's happy… well, it means everything to us, doesn't it, Eddie?'

'It does that, Phyllis.'

She hands her husband a cup and then settles herself back in her chair.

'It's—'

'It's—'

Both Riley and Eddie go to speak at the same time and his dad smiles at him, indicating for Riley to go ahead.

'It's good to be back and I'm sorry it took so long for me to reach out to you. I was a mess when I left, and it took me a long time to straighten myself out.' His honesty is touching.

'Look, my son, the past is the past. Your mum and I lived in the belief that one day, when you were ready, we'd all meet up again.' Riley's father looks across at his wife for support.

'Our biggest fear was that we weren't just losing you, but that we would end up losing Ollie, too. Fiona is a bitter woman, and she could so easily have cut us out of your son's life. She didn't do that, and to her credit, she's never said anything negative about you to us, but we heard some of the remarks she's made to other family members. Anyone who truly knew you could see what happened was out of character for you. But understandably, she was hurting and angry. The life she'd envisaged was falling apart. Fiona is a strong woman and a good mother; we have a lot of respect for her in that regard and Ollie is a pure joy to spend time with.'

I don't know what I was expecting, but this is not it. I thought they might be angry or want their son to explain himself, but they never doubted him, and Riley's expression is a pained one.

'I didn't abandon Ollie. Fiona made it more and more difficult for me to visit him. She wouldn't let me take him anywhere and she was always hovering. Then she told me that my visits were unsettling him and suggested I call him once a week instead. He was four years old, and I was no longer a part of his daily life; you can imagine how tough it was to engage with him in a meaningful way.' Riley looks haggard as the memories still haunt him.

'We guessed as much,' his mother replies, sounding weary. 'You must remember that Ollie became her entire world, Riley, and she clung on to him. He was so little; he didn't understand why you weren't there, and it must have been confusing. But we knew that one day, he'd want to know more about his dad. Even Fiona wouldn't deny him that right, no matter how bitter she feels about the past.'

Riley reaches out to clasp my hand. 'That weekend Fiona brought Ollie down to Cornwall, she invited herself to stay. It was awkward and that's when I knew I had to tell her about Jess and me. She was planning *their* next visit and now she won't speak to me.'

His father sighs. 'We know for a fact that Ollie is really looking forward to spending more time with you down in Cornwall, Riley. She'll come around – just give her time.'

'What we're concerned about,' I join in, 'is Fiona's reaction when she sees us together. We'd hate anything to spoil Tom and Helen's special day.'

Phyllis gives me a warm smile. 'Helen has made her aware that you're coming, so it won't come as a total shock. And we'll all be keeping an eye out. It isn't going to be easy for any of you, but life goes on. It's time for Fiona to let go of old hurts and this could be a turning point. In a good way. Well, that's what we're all hoping.'

We lapse into silence, and I reach down into my bag to pull out my iPad. 'We thought you might like to see some photos of Riley's cottage, and of Renweneth Farm and my daughter Lola.'

Phyllis's eyes sparkle. 'Oh, Jess, that's so very thoughtful of you!'

We while away a pleasant hour together and when we head back to our hotel to change for the wedding, Riley is like a different man. The part of him deep down inside that was broken is finally beginning to heal.

Thicket Priory, an elegant country house nestled in the heart of the Yorkshire countryside, is a dream location for a wedding. Although the grounds are extensive, with just thirty-five bedrooms, the house feels intimate as opposed to a corporate venue. The ceremony itself takes place under a beautiful hexagonal bandstand, with far-reaching views out over the Yorkshire countryside. As Tom slips the wedding ring on his bride's finger, the glittery lights in the domed ceiling above them lend a romantic feel to the occasion.

Riley tilts his head and leans into me, tightening his clasp on my hand. 'I wouldn't be here if it weren't for you, Jess.' He lifts my hand up to his mouth and kisses the back of it, his eyes full of love.

I glance around nervously, but the circle of chairs around the bandstand means that we can't see Fiona and Ollie from here. 'I'm so glad we did this. Tom and Helen look so happy, Riley, and a part of that is because you're here,' I reply, softly.

The day couldn't be more perfect. There's a beautiful blue sky with hardly a cloud in sight and all around us, the birds are singing their hearts out as they flit in and out of the trees. I can't even begin to imagine how long it took to plan this wedding, down to the tiniest little details. Just one look at the enormous smiles on the faces of the bride and groom is enough to show that it was worth it, and the photographs are going to be glorious.

'Did I tell you how stunning you look in that dress?' Riley whispers.

'Yes, and thank you. I didn't know whether it would be too much… but Ivy and Mum said it looked chic.' It's hard not to laugh. Me, looking chic? But I do feel rather elegant in a long, sleeveless, baby-blue, cowl-neck midi dress. The fabric has a little stretch to it and the side rouching on the bodice creates a flattering drape across the skirt, which has a modest slit. With some strappy heels, this bargain of a dress fit my budget and looks the business.

After spending over an hour piling my hair up on top and using curling tongs to create a mass of ringlets, when I eventually looked in the full-length mirror, I saw that the colour of the dress complemented my skin to perfection. Having spent the first two weeks of what has been a very hot May working with a landscape gardener to revitalise the borders in the grounds of Renweneth Manor, I feel both trim and bronzed.

As the groom finally gets to kiss his bride, everyone erupts, jumping to their feet and clapping their hands. It's a joyous moment and with somewhere around a hundred guests in attendance, it's the sort of fairy-tale wedding that dreams are made of.

Riley turns to face me. 'Does it make you want to rethink our cosy little wedding?'

I give him a beaming smile. 'No. And I'm a couple of inches too short to carry off a dreamy, princess-style gown. Helen wears it well; she simply sashays along as if her feet are barely touching the ground and looking at how radiant she is, maybe that's true.'

'That's all I wanted to know.' Riley throws his arms around me, planting a kiss on my lips. I have no idea if anyone is watching us, but he's oblivious anyway. I can't believe how relaxed he is, even though he's already had to introduce me to a constant stream of people from his past. The only people we haven't come face to face with yet are Fiona and Ollie.

The moment we walk into the awe-inspiring ballroom, stopping to check the seating plan, we hear an excited shriek. 'Dad! Dad!'

We both turn and I watch as an excited eight-year-old rushes into the arms of his father. 'Ollie... my little man! Don't you look smart for Uncle Tom and Auntie Helen's big day.'

I glance around nervously, expecting his mother to be a few paces behind him, but instead I see Phyllis walk towards us.

'Ollie and I have come to show you to your seats,' she explains.

'Thanks, Mum. Ollie, this is Jess.'

'Hi, Jess. It's this way. We aren't sitting at the same table, but you do have a cool view of the garden.'

Riley glances at me and what I see is a look of relief flash over his face as we follow our young guide. Ollie's as full of energy as Lola, and it's hard to keep up with him as he weaves in and out between people milling around trying to locate their seats.

'Here you are,' he shouts, beckoning with his hand. He even pulls out a chair for me.

'Thank you, Ollie. That's very gentlemanly of you.'

'Mum said you were coming, Dad. I didn't believe her!'

Riley ruffles his son's hair. 'I wouldn't have missed this for the world.'

Phyllis is standing behind me and she lowers her head. 'Tom and Helen put you on *the cousins* table,' she whispers. 'You'll be just fine. Fiona seems to be avoiding you both for now, but Ollie couldn't wait to come and greet you both.'

I give her a grateful smile as she turns to her grandson. 'Come on, my boy, let's get ourselves seated. I'm hungry.'

'Me too, Grandma. See you in a bit, Dad... and Jess.'

My goodness, talk about granddad, father and son lookalikes. They all have the same nose and chin; only the hair colouring differs. Ollie's hair is lighter, a sandy shade.

As the other guests take their seats at the table, Riley introduces me to everyone. It's not quite as awkward as I thought it would be. His cousins don't all live locally and when they ask where Riley is living now, and he says Cornwall, it explains his absence. It's funny, but often it really is only births, deaths and weddings when families gather en masse, and it seems the Warrens are no different to anyone else.

When I turn to look at Riley to give him an encouraging smile, his face is frozen, and I follow his gaze. So that's Fiona. She's tall and willowy, and Ollie has her hair colouring. There's a look of refinement about her that I wasn't expecting; I think it's the way she holds herself. She's a good-looking woman and she knows it. Having overheard her screaming down the phone at Riley, the image I conjured up bears no resemblance to the woman I see across the room. She carries herself with poise and confidence as she takes her seat next to Ollie. She smiles down at him with pride and love in her eyes. I know how much it hurts when you look at your child and are reminded of the person who is no longer at your side. My heart goes out to her, and I do hope we can get through this without incident.

'You run a farm in Cornwall, Jess. That must be hard work,' Riley's cousin, Simon – who is seated to my right – asks.

When I explain that it's not a working farm as such, but a family holiday destination, we end up having quite a drawn-out conversation. Thankfully, the person sitting alongside Riley is equally chatty and just like that, another potential problems melts away. It's funny, but one's imagination conjures up the very worst of scenarios. Today has turned out to be nothing at all like either of us feared.

As I'm making my way to the cloakroom, I hear a voice call out my name. 'Jess?' When I turn around, I'm dismayed to see that it's Fiona. She hurries towards me.

'Yes. You're Fiona, I presume.' I thrust out my hand. 'It's nice to meet you.'

My handshake is firm, and, to my horror, I almost end up crushing her hand. 'Sorry,' I apologise. 'I'm, um... used to a builder's grip.' Ugh. Did I really just say that?

I stand here feeling like I'm being vetted. Her eyes take in every little detail of my outfit and hair. For some reason, I suddenly feel awkward, clumsy even.

'It's about time we met. You didn't bring your daughter with you?' Her voice is totally devoid of any warmth.

'No. It... um... didn't seem appropriate.' What sort of question is that? She knows what a huge deal this is for Riley.

People are passing us in the corridor, but she makes no attempt to move, and I stand here, feeling like a rabbit caught in the headlights of an oncoming car.

'What makes you think that Riley won't do to you what he did to me?'

I look at her aghast. 'Sorry?'

'Run off when life doesn't go smoothly.'

Do I speak my truth and risk offending her, or do I mumble something and head into the cloakroom?

'Look, I know this is awkward, Fiona. I understand the hurt that comes with a failed marriage, when hopes and dreams are shattered. And how, as mothers, all we want to do is protect our offspring. We can either let anger and bitterness eat away at us, or we can show our children that life is what you make it. I ran away to Renweneth Farm to start over again. I guess it's something Riley and I have in common, but the truth is, everyone deals with it in their own way.'

'Ha, you make it sound easy.' The bitterness in her words is stinging.

'I didn't want to entrust my daughter with anyone, let alone a woman who was taking my place in her father's affections.

I had to suck it up and level with his new partner when I realised none of it was her fault. She was going to be a part of Lola's life whether I liked it or not. I chose to become friends with her and explain my concerns. I'm glad I did, because Lola enjoys the time she has with her dad and his new partner. It made a huge difference for everyone concerned.'

With that, I turn on my heels and hurry away from her. To my relief, she doesn't make any attempt to follow me.

19

The Pressure Is On

First thing Monday morning and as I'm walking across to the manor to start work, my phone kicks into life.

'How did Tom's wedding go?' Mum asks, hesitantly.

'It was lovely. Only one little incident when I bumped into Fiona, but aside from that, we got through it without a hitch. Ollie is a sweet lad, very polite and he so looks like his dad.'

'Ah, I've been thinking of you all weekend, Jess. I knew it was going to be a late night for you after the long drive yesterday, but I couldn't delay any longer. How's Riley... and how did it go with his parents?'

'It was a tearful reunion with Eddie and Phyllis. Oh, Mum... I thought my heart was going to shatter when I saw how much pain the time apart from their son had caused them. There were no recriminations; they're just two loving parents who never gave up on their son.'

'That's such a relief,' Mum says, letting out a deep breath. 'But as for Ollie and the future?'

'In the nicest possible way, I told Fiona she has two choices. Either make an enemy out of me, or a friend. It's precisely what Cappy said to me when Ben told me his girlfriend was moving in with him. I befriended Naomi because she wasn't a mum, but she was going to be a stand-in mum to Lola when she was with Ben. I wanted her to understand what made my daughter tick and let her know she could call me at any time if she had a problem while Lola is with them.'

'Let's hope Fiona comes to her senses. I do hope you don't have to go down the route of involving solicitors to gain access to Ollie. As parents, we all have a duty to put our children first.'

Mum's right but it's tough when your heart is breaking. Naomi was replacing me, and I'm replacing Fiona.

'I guess it's a case of waiting to see what happens next.'

'Changing the subject ever so slightly… what are we doing about the wedding invites?'

'Riley and I discussed this on the journey back. We're going to send one to Eddie, Phyllis and Ollie. It's not unreasonable for them to ask Fiona for her permission to take him to his dad's wedding. Up to now, she's allowed them to have him for sleepovers and they even took him away on holiday once, for an entire week.'

'Are we likely to be adding anyone else to the list?'

'You know what Riley's like. The more trades we pull in to meet our target on the manor, the more they become a part of our journey. But that's it for family. I'll send you snaps I took of the wedding. It was a fairy tale, Mum, a real fairy tale.'

She chuckles. 'Ah, that's wonderful to hear. It didn't give you second thoughts?'

'Goodness, no. But I did have this vision of what sort of dress I want to wear, but we'll need to find a dressmaker.'

'Ooh… at last! And I know just the person. I'll get her to give you a call.'

Riley waves as I step through the archway. 'Thanks, Mum. I must dash. The manor is a hive of activity, and the kitchen fitters are in today. I'm going to be here, there and everywhere making decisions. Wish me luck!'

'We need to cannibalise the sink unit. The supply pipe for the water comes up in the middle of the base board.'

I look at the carpenter, wondering why we're even having this conversation. 'You can't move the pipe, so go ahead. As long as I have a working sink by the end of the day, I'm happy.'

He gives me a thumbs-up and as I walk away, I smile to myself. What was he expecting, an argument? Little things like that I take in my stride.

'Jess,' Riley calls out and I hurry through to the hallway. 'Can you give the electrician access to The Farmhouse? He's hanging around in the courtyard. Aside from hardwiring that internet connection into the kitchen for your laptop, if there are any other small electrical jobs you want doing over there, now's the time to get it sorted.'

'Great. I'm on my way and I'll head straight back afterwards.'

Suddenly, the front door swings open and two burly guys block the doorway. 'Coming through, mind your backs!' one of them shouts and, with a lot of huffing and puffing, they manoeuvre what I assume is a larder unit between the door jambs.

I stand back and, as soon as it's clear, I hurry outside only to be confronted by a dour-faced Cappy. 'I was just coming to see you,' he states. 'Prudie was under the impression that you were going to find a solution for her. But this morning, Kate Enys told Karl that Prudie got the wrong end of the stick. She says she got that directly from you. What's going on?'

He's not happy, but this is not the place to have what is quite a sensitive conversation. 'I'm on my way to give the electrician access to The Farmhouse. Come with me and I'll tell you exactly what happened.'

Cappy looks at me, puzzled. 'An electrician?'

'Yes. I'm going to put a computer desk in the corner of the kitchen. Both you and I often work from there, and it will make life easier. It'll stop the Wi-Fi dropping out and it's safer, health-wise. You know... less EMF. Can you think of anything else he can look at while he's there? Any extra sockets, for instance?'

Cappy falls in alongside me. 'Why should it bother me? Give it a few weeks and I'll be back in Stroud,' he reminds me, sounding totally fed up.

If Prudie has been bending his ear, that's understandable I suppose. Talk about bad timing. Cappy won't want to stay if I can't smooth this over because Prudie isn't going to give up.

Having made us both a coffee, I sit myself down on the sofa facing Cappy.

'It's all a bit of a misunderstanding,' I explain. 'Prudie told me all about her plans for the art school. She needs a proper studio of her own and while I'm sympathetic to what she's trying to achieve, I told her straight that she should look elsewhere rather than risk being disappointed.'

'That's not what she heard, Jess,' he points out.

'But it's exactly what I said, Cappy. Unless half of the occupants of The Courtyard Hub suddenly up and leave in one go, we can't accommodate her. Even that would involve remodelling the whole ground floor. There's nothing I can do about it. However, it appears that Prudie heard what she wanted to hear. Somewhere in that explanation, she saw a glimmer of hope, but my parting words were clear. There is no solution to her problem.'

Cappy shakes his head sadly. 'I see.'

'She must have said something to Karl. Kate happened to drop into the gallery to browse and he mentioned it. Unfortunately, Kate was under the impression she was top of the list if one of the bays become vacant and poor Vyvyan got an ear blasting. I had to go to Kate's house to put her straight and tell her we don't treat people favourably. The only time we broke our own rules is when we added an additional market stall to appease her. And that was because she jumped in to serve in the bakery at short notice to help Ivy out. It seemed only fair at the time, but in hindsight, it probably wasn't a smart move.'

'Hmm.'

'I didn't for one moment think that Kate would repeat our conversation to Karl,' I admit, feeling gutted. 'I'm sure she wasn't being vindictive, just putting him straight. She did say he was quite excited about the idea of Prudie's art school being based here.'

Cappy sits back in his chair, linking his hands behind his head and letting out a deep, deep sigh.

'Who's going to put her right about this. You... or me?'

I gulp. 'So, you agree with me that accommodating her needs is out of the question?'

'Some problems can't be solved. We couldn't sort anything out for Ivy and Adam, and you're right, Prudie needs a bespoke, standalone studio. Even the mezzanine wouldn't be right. There's not enough daylight up there and Prudie's mentioned that to me several times when she's been teaching. Flo keeps the overhead lights on when she's running her daytime classes, too.'

I let out a silent breath of relief. At least he knows I'm not being obstructive.

'Leave it to me to let her down gently. Maybe I'll suggest I give her a hand looking for the right location. Could you spare me for the odd day here and there, if necessary?'

'Of course! Your project is done and although Riley and I appreciate everything you do at the manor, I told you – it's time for you to relax and catch up with your friends whenever you want. You're not on a schedule now, Cappy.'

'All right, point taken. It is fun now that the Beer and Bait Club are back together. With both Charlie and Clem keen to sink their cash into a boat, it would be nice if it were sorted before I head back to Stroud. Three heads are better than one when you're looking at rust buckets.' He gives a hearty laugh and, finally, I feel as if the Prudie saga is coming to an end.

'Sorry it's not doable for Prudie. I know it would have thrilled Grandma if we could have come up with a suitable option.'

I stand, gathering the mugs together in my hand. Cappy eases himself up out of the chair and walks over to put his arm around my shoulders, giving me a squeeze. 'It's no one's fault, Jess. Anyway, Riley will be wondering where we are. We'd best get back to work.'

After a day where I end up sitting at my dressing table in the bedroom, picking tiny flecks of paint out of my hair after having painted yet another ceiling, I can't wait for the bath to fill. My shoulders and neck are aching, and I can feel a layer of dust all over me. Even though it was only the sitting room floor that was being sanded today, the tiny particles of gritty dust get everywhere.

'Mum, it's just a very quick call as I'm about to jump into a bubble bath and wash off the grime.'

'Oh dear. Was it full-on?'

'Yep. It's unlikely my engagement ring will see the light of day for a while now. I was wondering whether Cappy has said anything about the lease on his house. It runs out at the end of June, I think.'

'No, he hasn't, and yes, it does. Lucas has been trying to sound out your dad to see if he knows what's happening. Cappy is required to give Lucas and Sienna a month's notice by all accounts, or the lease continues based on a mutual four weeks' notice by either party. Obviously, they're getting anxious as they want to know if he's coming back.'

'Oh! I didn't realise that. I thought it was for a set six-month period. I'm sure that's what Cappy said.'

Mum heaves a hefty sigh. 'You know what your grandad's like when it comes to paperwork, which is what he regards it as, Jess. And we both know he didn't settle here. The house wasn't right for him, and he's lost too many old friends. It's just a reminder of how old he's getting.'

Inwardly, I groan. 'I know. And he has so much more energy when he's here. Honestly, Mum, he works like a trouper, although I'm encouraging him to socialise more, and he is. The Beer and

Bait Club are meeting up regularly again. And he's uh… having lunches with Prudie.'

'He is? Gosh, that takes me back. I remember her having afternoon tea with your grandma. They would natter away for hours on end, according to Cappy.'

'And Charlie and Clem are thinking of buying a boat.'

Mum gasps. 'And Cappy doesn't want to be a part of that? It's his dream.'

'I'm so glad you said that, Mum. I think so, too. Is it wrong of me to try and encourage him to move back to The Farmhouse?'

'You know how I feel about it. Anything is better than thinking of Cappy sitting in his favourite local pub here in Stroud, in the corner they refer to as God's waiting room.'

'Precisely! Just thinking about it makes me feel depressed.'

'It's no wonder he started to go downhill. It's unnecessarily morbid and, to be honest, if they got up off their seats and went for a walk instead each lunchtime, they'd all last a heck of a lot longer!'

Ouch, that touched a raw nerve. 'I agree with you. But Cappy thinks Riley will only come into his own if he's the main man around here. He can't appreciate that Riley looks to him for advice because he doesn't always have the answer. Riley's a little unsure of himself, thanks to Fiona's efforts to make him feel like he's a total mess-up.' Argh, sometimes it's not good to say what you're thinking.

'Then see what you can do. Personally, I think it would be wonderful for Cappy to spend whatever years he has left at the farm. If he ends up back here, he'll just mope around again, and he was going downhill. Both physically and mentally. He's an active man for his age and he likes to be busy.'

Hmm. That means I need to clear up some loose ends. Namely Prudie. 'Well, I am working on it, Mum, and can you let Dad know that? He doesn't talk about it, but he's just as concerned as we are about Cappy. No one wants to see their parents fall into that negative mindset. I was horrified when he mentioned

God's waiting room. I mean, it's a dingy corner of a pub for goodness' sakes! I agree with you; why are they content to sit there watching the world go by, anyway? Every single day is precious. Eek… my bath could be about to overflow. I'm on it, and I'll let you know if there are any developments.'

'That's my girl! Sweet dreams.'

20

It's Time to Focus on Solutions, Not Problems

The following morning, my hair is still wet from the shower, when I swing open the front door to find Ivy standing there with a small box in her hands.

'Riley called into the bakery for a takeaway coffee and he said you'd popped back to The Farmhouse. I gather you had a little accident with a pot of paint.'

I roll my eyes. 'I'd just refilled the paint kettle and hung it on the ladder, one step above me, when I accidentally knocked it. That's one T-shirt and pair of jeans that are only fit for the bin. It was a tad embarrassing. Riley came to my rescue and wrapped a dust sheet around me so I could walk back without dripping on the cobbles.'

I stand back so she can step inside. With eleven weeks to go, I can't even imagine what it's like carrying two babies; I can still remember how uncomfortable I was at this stage and that was just having the one.

'I thought I'd bring you over a selection of cakes as a little *thank-you* present.'

My eyes widen. 'What have I done to deserve that?' I smile as I shut the door and follow her through into the kitchen.

'I waddle, don't I?' she moans.

'I'm not surprised. How big are the babies now?'

Ivy pulls out a chair and eases herself down onto it. 'About thirty-eight centimetres, apparently, and they weigh around a kilo each. It's really messing with my bladder at night. And my doctor warned me that the indigestion will only get worse.'

'Aww… How are you feeling in yourself?'

'Better prepared and less panicky now. It's just that standing for long periods gives me chronic backache, and if I sit still for too long, my sciatic nerve plays up. Oh, the joys! I'm beginning to sound like a real whinger, aren't I?'

'Hey, that's what best friends are for.' I grin at her.

'And this itching. I'm constantly having to put moisturising lotion on my tummy. That's only going to get worse too, isn't it?'

I nod my head. 'Sorry but the more you apply, the less likely you are to get stretch marks.' We both start laughing. 'Do you fancy a drink?'

'Thanks, but no. I've just had an herbal tea and I'm supposed to be heading back to the cottage to lie down for half an hour. The girls keep fussing over me and insist I take regular breaks. Anyway, you deserve a nice treat because I had a surprise visitor yesterday afternoon and it's all down to you.'

Hmm. 'Me?'

'Yep! Kate asked if she could have a chat. I don't know what exactly you said to her, but any grudge she was holding has totally disappeared. She said that if I needed any help either with the baking, or serving, she'd love to join the team.'

I pull out a chair and slump down into it, hardly able to believe what I'm hearing. 'She did?'

'Kate started to apologise, but I stopped her. In hindsight, it was only a few jaded comments from Prudie that riled her up. The timing was awful, and I think Kate got the wrong impression. That's all behind us now. She's agreed to cover for me given that I'm taking longer breaks. In the mornings, she'll relieve me for a couple of hours and work alongside Chelle in the kitchen. In the afternoons, she'll help fill in on Wenna's and Rose's days off.'

'Oh, Ivy, that's wonderful news. But it's not down to me. I just put her straight, that's all.'

'Well, it's a huge weight off my shoulders, Jess, it really is. Kate's going to give up the stall. Together, we're going to work on some healthy option recipes and start selling a range of biscuits and cookies. She simply loves baking, and all Kate wants is to be a part of something that has a future. You don't live to work, but we all need an income to keep going.'

Ivy slides the box across the table, and I take a peek inside.

'The smell... it makes my mouth water.'

'Some orange and vanilla slices with a hint of a chocolate drizzle and a few passion fruit and crumble bombs.'

'That sounds exciting. I can't wait to tuck in, but I'd better save them for after dinner or I might be tempted to scoff the lot.'

'You're entitled.' She beams at me. 'I heard the surprise dinner went well. Is there any chance I can see the ring?'

'Oh, of course! And thank you for what you did to help Riley make it so special. I must thank Erica, too. I'll go and grab it from my jewellery box. I daren't wear it while I'm working.'

As I race upstairs, a lot of thoughts are going around and around inside my head. Ivy and Adam's lives are about to be turned upside down yet again. When she no longer lives on site, I'm going to miss having my dear friend on the doorstep. And if Cappy returns to Stroud... nothing is going to seem quite the same going forward. But Ivy has solved a pressing issue, so that's a great result. It's time to put my thinking cap on and see what I can come up with while there's a vibe of positivity in the air, to convince him to stay.

'And we still need to talk about your wedding cake.' Ivy's voice drifts up to meet me as I clatter back down the stairs.

'I know.' I groan. 'It is on the list; if only I could put my hands on it, but it seems to have disappeared.'

'I think we should keep the heating ticking over on low for a while,' Riley informs me as we head through into the sitting room. It was supposed to be finished by now. 'The exterior stone wall still has a few damp patches in it, but I think we could start sanding the floor in here. What do you think?'

'I'm up for that task.'

'If you and I can do the snagging list on the kitchen first, it would be nice to get a second room totally completed. The kitchen fitter is planning on finishing tomorrow, as he has another job to go to.'

When Riley's working, he's in the zone, and it isn't until I stare at him unblinkingly for a few seconds that he breaks out into a smile. I know he's worried that we've only a little over ten weeks left. In that time, we have the sitting room, the main bathroom, the downstairs cloakroom and two bedrooms left to decorate. In fairness, all of the big jobs have taken a fair bit longer than anticipated.

'When are Rick and Nigel coming back to install the bathroom fixtures and fittings?'

'Once the painters have done the mist coat on the walls and ceilings. That probably won't happen until sometime next week. Rick said they have a couple of small jobs booked in, but as soon as they get the call, they'll head over here as quickly as they can.'

'That sounds optimistic. Shall we tackle this snagging list while the kitchen guys are at lunch?'

Riley steps forward to wrap his arms around my waist and give me a bear hug. 'Sorry, you distracted me for a moment. I was having a flashback to when you said *yes*. I would have felt pretty stupid if you'd changed your mind.'

'Well, I can't think of anything better than being married to a builder. Hmm... on second thoughts, maybe a hairdresser might also be a contender,' I muse, and he belly-laughs.

Riley reaches out to touch my hair. It's tied up in a scrunchie, sitting on top my head with bits flopping down because that's what it does.

'I like the messy look – it suits you. Very alluring. Unlike your idea this morning of wearing paint rather than putting it on the walls,' he teases me.

'Hey, I'm doing my best.' I elbow him in the ribs, and Riley releases me. 'While I have your attention, I need your help with Cappy.'

'Oh… this isn't to do with Prudie, is it?'

'No,' I state firmly as I follow him into the kitchen. 'Cappy has to let Lucas know whether or not he's returning to Stroud at the end of June. He's cutting it a bit fine to make his decision.'

'That's a good thing, isn't it? I mean, that he's not in a rush to return.'

'I think it's only this boat that Charlie and Clem are thinking of buying that is making him stick around. He's worried it could be a risky investment and he'd hate to see them lose their money. I just wondered if you could sow the seed.'

'About what?'

'Maybe to help with Lola's and Ollie's bedrooms? To cut costs, we need to think about built-in storage solutions. I was thinking we should buy some flat-pack units and then smarten them up. It would be right up his street, keep him busy until the wedding and he could get some fishing in when the weather's good.'

Riley gets the message loud and clear. 'I can handle that. I've still got to get my head around using this armoire in the master bedroom. You came up with a great idea, Jess, but it's going to take some figuring out.'

The idea is that while it looks like an armoire with a shabby-chic paint finish, it will actually be two doors that open up and lead into the en suite.

'Isn't there an old saying along the lines of *nothing worthwhile ever happens quickly*?'

'Yes, and it's just like you to remind me of that.' Riley picks up a clipboard lying on the countertop and clicks the end of the ballpoint pen. 'Right, boss. Cast your eagle eyes over the kitchen and tell me what needs remedying.'

As I turn full circle, a satisfied sigh escapes from my lips. The soft-grey, country-style units, the white and grey veined marble worktops and island, and the sleek-looking, brushed aluminium appliances look even better in situ than they did on the 5D kitchen planner. I don't know if it's the fact that the heating is taking off the chill that is making a difference, or simply that this is the heart of the manor. But suddenly, I can imagine us living here: Lola and Ollie having breakfast at the island, while Riley makes pancakes and I'm at the sink washing up.

'Jess?' Riley prompts me.

'Sorry. Some of the grouting on the tiles around the sink needs a little touching up. It looks like there might have been a few air bubbles and now that the heating is drawing out the moisture in the air, they've popped. Oh, those two doors on the base units beneath the island don't quite line up. And...'

Riley starts to grimace. 'They only have this afternoon to fix whatever's on the list.'

'Then we'd better speed this up, because I want everything to be perfect!'

When my phone rings and it's Mum, she has news that turns out to be a bit of a wake-up call for me.

'Jess, my friend wasn't available, but I've found another seamstress. Joyce is a friend of a friend, and she comes highly recommended. She doesn't usually take on last-minute orders, and certainly not when a client is so far away, but I managed to talk her into it. You'll need to have a video call with her tomorrow night to get the ball rolling. She says that with ordering the fabric and arranging at least two fittings, it's going to be tight, but it's doable.'

I let out a low whistle. 'Really?'

'I did warn you. Brides order their dresses a year in advance, and you've decided to have yours made. Joyce is doing this as a favour. You'll also need someone there with you with a tape measure, as she'll be wanting some very precise measurements taken.'

'Okay. If you can get her to email me with a time and a list of what exactly she needs from me, I'll see if Vyvyan's available.'

'But Ivy's a stone's throw away.'

I start laughing. 'I don't think Ivy is capable of getting close enough to me to take accurate measurements, Mum. She's like a barrel now.'

'Oh, the poor dear! Still, having two at once is a blessing and it means she doesn't have to go through it all again. Unless they decide to have three, of course.'

'Three? They're worried about finding a cottage big enough for two and she's already said the only other addition she'll be considering is possibly a cat, or a dog. Anyway, thanks for sorting that out and I'll spend this afternoon giving it some thought while I start work sanding the sitting-room floor.'

'That sounds like progress. How's the kitchen looking?'

'Soon to be perfect once the guys finish off a few fiddly little jobs. Are you and Dad okay?'

'We're out in the garden every minute we get. Oh, and talking gardens, have you ordered the flowers yet?'

Ah, I give myself a mental slap on the wrist. 'It's in hand.' Sort of, as soon as I can find where I put my wedding *to-do* list. At least I know what flowers I want, so it's just a case of making a phone call.

As I'm on the internet in search of a local florist's shop, my phone suddenly kicks into life.

'Hello?'

'Hi, Jess.'

'Oh, Cheryl. How can I help?'

'Sorry to bother you but... well, we were wondering if you could pop over to the hub. There are some rumours flying around and uh—'

We? Oh no! Just when I thought that was all behind us now that Kate is joining Ivy's team, something else crops up. 'I'll be right over.'

What I wasn't expecting was a sea of worried faces. All of the bay occupants are standing in a group at the back of the hub. There are only two customers browsing and Peter, who runs the book concession, is loitering in case they need assistance.

'What's going on?' I ask, feeling a tad daunted.

They all gather around me.

'Is it true that we won't be allowed to renew our leases because Prudie is going to turn this into an artist's studio?' Otis, who runs Healthy Happy Life selling organic nuts, grains and products, keeps his voice low but he's wearing a deep frown.

'Did Prudie tell you that?' I ask, trying not to sound angry.

'No,' Anna, takes over. 'The rumour has been going around for a while, Jess. I said there wasn't anything in it because you would have told us.' She gives me an apologetic glance.

'If folk outside of here are talking about it,' Jacob, who runs the pottery bay, gives me a dubious look, 'they must have heard it from somewhere.'

So, this didn't come directly from Kate, or Prudie. That's something, I suppose. As I'm about to respond, Otis steps a little closer.

'Look, Jess, it cost me a lot to set up here and if I'm going to be pushed out, I need to know.' His voice is low, but Peter is now talking to one of the customers and the other is flicking through a book, oblivious to our little gathering.

'Everyone, take a deep breath,' I state, firmly. 'There was a misunderstanding but I've sorted it.'

Jacob is still looking doubtful. 'What sort of misunderstanding?'

There's no point in me trying to gloss over this because they won't believe me. 'It's true that Prudie is looking to rent a large space to set up a school for artists, somewhere the public can see them at work. But look around you.' I wave my hand in the air. 'Fitting this place out with the bays cost a lot of money, time and effort. The whole point of the hub is to help small local businesses – you guys – not just to survive, but to grow. Why would I backtrack on that?'

Peter is ringing up a sale as three more customers step through the door, chattering away to each other, but no one makes a move. All eyes are fixed firmly on me.

'Prudie has a lot of clout in this area and even further afield,

Jess.' Tamsyn has the stationery and card stall. It's troubling to see a hint of doubt in her expression. 'And, rightly so. No one is begrudging her that, as she champions Cornish artists and it gets the word out there.'

'What's been particularly unsettling is that we all know how close Prudie is to Cappy and he's... sympathetic to her situation,' Cheryl explains, rather reluctantly.

The fact that even Cheryl thinks there might be some substance to this rumour astounds me; she sorted Riley out by painting some furniture for my big surprise. I can't believe she thinks I'm capable of doing such a thing.

'Hand on heart, guys, this is down to the rumour mill; people getting the wrong end of the stick and no one checking their facts. Prudie herself, and Cappy for that matter, will confirm that she's looking elsewhere to accommodate her studio.'

'What about Kate?' Jacob blurts out. 'She didn't get a bay, or a shot at running the bakery. Now she has to settle for working for Ivy.' The moment he finishes speaking, I can see he's mortified that came out sounding quite so accusatory. Under normal circumstances, he's a gentle man, usually very reserved.

It's clear that tensions are running high and even though I feel a little offended, if I were in their shoes, I'd probably be agitated, too. 'That wasn't an attempt to appease Kate. She didn't apply for one of the bays until after they were all allocated on a first-come, first-served basis.' I gaze from one to the other of them so they can see I have nothing at all to hide. 'Ivy isn't here because she's an old friend of mine; she's here because Alice and Jory Rowse changed their minds. And why wouldn't they, when out of the blue, they were given the option to take over the adjacent property, to extend their bakery in Polreweek?'

I stop for a few moments to let that sink in.

'It was a business decision on their part and I accepted that. But it left me with a huge problem. I had no option other than to find someone else to take it over. Aside from two people wanting to turn it into a convenience store, which would have spoilt the ambience here, Ivy's offer was the only one on the table.'

The silence is awkward.

'I said we had nothing to worry about.' Anna speaks up, and I could cheerfully hug her. 'Jess has invested a lot of time and money in the farm. The pressure must be immense. And, while I don't like talking ill of anybody, anyone who knows Kate as well as I do understands that sometimes she goes off on one of her tirades without getting her facts straight.'

I don't feel comfortable leaving it there, as this rumour probably came from Karl repeating what Prudie told him. It wasn't his fault that she decided to hear what she wanted, rather than to take in what I told her. Admittedly, Kate's earlier rants didn't help, but it's not fair her name should be brought into this now. That's all old news.

'It's a huge jump to go from working out of a home kitchen to taking over a commercial setup. The fact that she decided it wasn't an option for her is understandable. Kate is excited about working at the bakery and I'm sure she'd tell you that. As I said, this latest rumour came about because of a misunderstanding on Prudie's part. If I had empty space, I'd happily accommodate her but that isn't the case, I'm afraid. I'm just as disappointed as she is.'

Everyone turns to look at Jacob. 'My apologies, Jess. I wasn't trying to be contentious. I think I speak for us all when I say we love being a part of this little community and we're all very grateful to be here.'

'It's okay, Jacob. I understand. When you put your heart and soul into something, it's galling to think it might be snatched away from you. It's my job to make sure everything at Renweneth Farm runs smoothly and if you ever have any concerns, or questions, please don't hesitate to knock on my door. I'm here for you, always.'

It took me a while to calm my nerves after that little outpouring in the hub. One large mug of coffee later, I finally manage to get a grip of myself and pick back up where I left off.

'Is that The Greenhouse in Polreweek?'

'It is, how can we help?'

'I'm getting married on Sunday the sixth of August. I live at Renweneth Farm, up on the moor and I wondered if we're within your delivery area.'

'You are, but we don't open on Sundays, I'm afraid. We'd deliver your flowers on the fifth and you'd need somewhere cool to store them overnight. We can loan you buckets to stand the flowers in if that helps.'

For some reason, my heart is beginning to pound. I really don't know what I'm doing. 'That um… that sounds great.'

'We should make an appointment as soon as possible to sit down and go through your requirements. August is a popular month, and our order book is nearly full.'

'Oh, I see. Right.'

'Are you free any time tomorrow? We have a slot between ten and eleven in the morning and another late afternoon.'

'The morning appointment would be fine, thank you.'

'And the name is?'

'Jess, Jess Griffiths.'

'Right. That's in the diary. See you tomorrow, Jess.'

Suddenly, my head is starting to ache. Dresses, flowers… I don't know what to think about first. The minute I finish work, I will hunt down that list and get on with it. Mum can only do so much from a distance and after the effort Riley put into the surprise engagement dinner, I can't let him down.

My next call is to Vyvyan. Fingers crossed she's available if I can find a suitable tape measure. I'm pretty sure there's a canvas one in Grandma's sewing box that is stored away in the bottom of my wardrobe. I knew that one day it would come in handy.

21

There's Nothing Quite as Satisfying as a Tick List

'Mum, who's taking me to school today?' Lola checks as she pops a forkful of honey-drizzled pancake into her mouth.

Cappy, who seems to be in charge of the chauffeuring rota these days, responds immediately. 'Erica today, my sparkly girl, and I'm doing the Thursday and Friday runs.'

It's unusual for Misty not to be jumping around trying to get Lola to give her a few titbits, then I realise she's curled up next to Lola's feet. I think she was out hunting most of last night and now she's exhausted.

'What's on your agenda today, Jess?' Cappy enquires. 'I was wondering if we could catch up on a few things after breakfast, before you make a start.'

I glance at him, and he smiles nonchalantly back at me. 'I'm doing wedding prep first thing, then I'm off to the florists' shop in Polreweek. Then back home to change and sand some floorboards. It's all in a day's work.' I chuckle.

'Mum, is Ollie coming to the wedding?' Lola asks.

She catches me off guard. 'I'm not sure, lovely. It's a long drive...'

'But he came to stay at Riley's cottage, and it is a special day.'

There's the sound of a tooting car horn, and we all check the clock. 'Oh my, we're running late.'

'You go and tell Erica we won't be a moment, Jess,' Cappy says. 'Come on, Lola, let's get your things together.'

I rush outside and Erica winds down the window.

'Hi, Daisy.' I lean in, and she grins, giving me a wave.

'Long time, no see,' Erica bemoans. 'Our paths rarely cross these days, Jess. When is Cappy heading back to Stroud?'

'I know and um… I'm working on it,' I whisper. 'Hopefully, I can keep him here until the wedding, at least. How are things with you?'

Erica shakes her head from side to side. 'I'm fed up with all the boat talk. It looks like they might be going for a run out in it on Sunday. Cappy knows more than I do about it, though. They've always had a joke about *The Silver Wave* being a rust bucket and yet Charlie can't understand why I'm worried.'

'Cappy won't let them buy something that isn't seaworthy,' I reassure her.

'It's a lot of money and if they can't talk Ivan down on the price, they can't afford it anyway. They must have spent hours in the pub talking about it.'

Lola comes running out of the farmhouse, arms and legs flailing, throwing herself at me. I give her a hug and a kiss on the forehead. 'Be good. Have fun. Learn lots. Have a great day, everyone. Oh, and thank you, Erica, for your part in the little um… dinner surprise.'

The girls' ears prick up, but Erica gives me a conspiratorial smile and puts the car in gear as she starts to pull away. 'It was my pleasure,' she calls out. 'Ivy and I had a bit of fun. Hope your day is productive and we must catch up properly very soon!'

Cappy comes to stand alongside me and there's an exchange of waves.

'Imagine if Lola had a twin. Would we have coped?' I ask the question and turn to face him.

He scratches his chin. 'It would have been double the joy and double the trouble.' He roars with laughter. 'I guess Ivy and

Adam won't have anything to compare it to, so for them, it's going to be normal.'

'What's normal?' I question as we head back inside for a second cup of coffee. 'Anyway, what did you want to talk about?'

'A couple of things. Let me see…' He falls silent, while I make the coffee and carry the mugs over to the table. 'Ah, yes. Do you think Adam and Riley would enjoy a day out fishing on Sunday?'

I grin at him. 'Would they – heck, yes! Erica mentioned Charlie's on about it all the time. Is *The Silver Wave* safe to take out into deep water? Don't they refer to it as the rust bucket?'

Cappy laughs. 'It's a joke. Ivan moved to Cornwall and thought he'd buy a boat to while away his retirement. He was a marine mechanic and worked on all sorts of boat engines but, as far as I can tell, he's never been behind the wheel. The engine will be sound, as he says he's overhauled it, but it's still been sitting there in that falling-down hangar of a shed with a tarpaulin over it, for… I dunno… best part of ten years? Until they hitch up the trailer it's sitting on, and get it out into the open, who knows what they'll find. But Charlie and Clem are going to sort that out today. If everything looks okay, then Sunday is the day to test her out.'

'Are you going to be there for the unveiling?'

'I didn't commit myself, as I'm going to be a bit tied up at the manor.' My heart leaps in my chest as that probably means Riley has spoken to him.

'Oh. I see. The thing is… Erica would feel a lot better if she knew you were casting your eye over it, Cappy.'

'You think?'

'I know.'

'Okay, I'll give the guys a call. The other thing I wanted to mention, no… there are two things, now I come to think of it. Riley's up to his eyes in work, and I know you're getting pulled in all directions what with the bits and pieces for the wedding. I'm thinking of hanging around to give a hand, just until the big day is here. I think Lucas and his soon-to-be fiancée, Sienna, are quite settled. They haven't managed to find anything suitable to buy yet within their price range. Would it upset your plans if I stayed on a while?'

'Oh, Cappy, it would be a huge relief for me. Riley never complains, but I can tell when he's under pressure. And with Fiona still not having made any contact with him since our trip to York, I know he's stressing about it.'

Cappy nods his head in agreement. 'I'd feel bad leaving you to it, when I know that an extra pair of hands will be appreciated. And, hopefully, it won't be long before Charlie and Clem make up their minds about *The Silver Wave*. I'd rather like to be around for that. I don't know if it's common knowledge, but they have it in their minds to offer fishing trips at weekends. Don't repeat that to Erica in case I'm dropping Charlie in it.'

'I won't. You said there were two other things?'

Cappy's eyebrows go up. 'Oh, yes. Prudie. I've convinced her we should check out some of the outlying farms. I was thinking of the gym that Riley and Adam go to. They might have spare outbuildings. It's just a thought, but I'd like to get her sorted before I head back to Stroud.'

I'm flabbergasted. 'Prudie has accepted that there's nothing we can do to solve her dilemma?'

He nods his head. 'Yes. She's very happy with the arrangements at the bakery and the volume of traffic they get through there now means sales are going well. It is frustrating for her with the art classes, but she's mindful of not upsetting Flo. The smells of a proper artist's studio aren't exactly compatible with candlelit yoga classes, are they?'

We exchange an awkward look. 'I know, but it does make my heart sink. Grandma would have loved for Renweneth Farm to be a part of realising Prudie's dream. But everything happens for a reason, Cappy.'

'So, your grandma always said, Jess. Anyway, I'll be around a while longer and you never know, Prudie and I might just stumble across the perfect solution for her.'

'I do hope so and thank you for smoothing things over. I know how hard this has been for you. But I bet you're excited about the prospect of a day out fishing on Sunday. I'll keep my fingers crossed that *The Silver Wave* doesn't disappoint.'

'I've got a good feeling about her. Ivan might be a landlubber, but he knows his craft. He's no fool. But some prefer to work on boats, rather than take them out to sea. I think she's the love of his life and the problem is going to be letting her go. He's asking top dollar for her, so we'll see what happens.'

One thing I know for sure, Riley and Adam are going to be so excited if this trip on Sunday goes ahead. I can't wait to see their reaction.

Suddenly, everything in my little world seems a whole lot brighter than it was. Instead of the usual slump, when I realise that we're halfway through yet another week, it's turning out to be a wonderful Wednesday. I've found my wedding list; it was hidden away in the middle of a pile of invoices. By the end of the day, I'll be ticking off flowers and mine and Lola's dresses for the wedding.

And, thanks to Riley, my mental tick list scores too. Getting Cappy to stay on a couple of months longer might mean that, when the time comes, it'll be even harder for him to walk away. There's no denying that having time to reconnect with his old friends here has put a spring in his step and it's wonderful to see.

'Hi, Jess, I'm Joyce. It's lovely to meet you; just a shame it can't be in person. We have a bit of a challenge ahead of us.' The woman on the screen in front of me breaks out into a huge smile. 'Don't worry, it isn't the first rush job I've done, and it won't be the last.'

I like her *can-do* attitude. 'I can't thank you enough for taking it on, Joyce. This is my good friend Vyvyan, who is going to be in charge of the measuring tape, and my daughter will be joining us shortly.'

Joyce gives her an affirming nod. 'Hi, Vyvyan. We do have our work cut out but if we get it right at this stage, we might be able to manage having just one fitting.'

'That would be amazing, Joyce. I've got all the information in front of me that you listed in your email. It was really helpful, as it made me focus on the details instead of having this vision in my head that really wasn't very clear at all,' I admit.

Lola comes bowling into the kitchen with Misty close on her heels. 'Sorry I'm late!'

'Joyce, this is Lola.'

Lola gives her a sweet little wave, as she slips into the seat next to me. 'Welcome, Lola. This is exciting, isn't it? Have you settled on a style for your dress?'

Lola's eyes gleam. 'I want a princess dress, but shorter, with a swishy skirt.'

'That sounds wonderful. Jess, did you manage to get some photos to show me so I can see what we're aiming for?' Joyce is already making notes as we talk.

'Lola, can you hold up the one we found for your dress, while I talk Joyce through our ideas.'

Lola jumps up off her seat to grab one of the dozen or so printouts I have spread out over the table.

'We decided that we want the same fabric for both our dresses, don't we, Lola? We've chosen a sheer, summery, floral print. This is the shape that Lola chose.'

My daughter eagerly holds up the image to the screen.

'Good choice, Lola,' Joyce enthuses. 'We call that the *flower girl* style. So, it's a simple scoop neck, with a waisted bodice with capped sleeves. And you want some layers of soft netting beneath the skirt to make it swish. Did you want a zipped back, or buttons and loops?'

Lola frowns and glances straight at me. 'A zip would be quicker,' she points out and both Vyvyan and I give a little chuckle. 'You're right. A zip it is!' I confirm.

'Now, Lola, what length do you want? Ballerina style is mid-calf, or you can have it just below the knee.'

'Oh, just below the knee, please,' Lola immediately replies. 'We'll be chasing around the garden, and I don't want the skirt to get in the way. But I do want it to look pretty because it's Mum and Riley's special day.'

Aww… that's my girl, always practical. 'We didn't know whether a plain ribbon belt with a bow at the back might help set it off?' I add.

'Don't worry. When it comes to the final fitting, I'll be driving down with my car fully loaded and we can try a few little embellishments. It all depends on how busy the fabric is that you've chosen.'

This time, I hold up the image. 'I don't know how clear this is at your end, Joyce, but it's a soft blue background with quite a large, floral print.'

Joyce leans in closer to the screen. 'That's very pretty and unusual. I like that it's a bold print, but the colours are muted. The sprays of little white flowers behind the main blue clusters with the soft fern green leaves look like they might have a sheen to them?'

I nod my head. 'Yes, it's silvery white. It was on one of the websites you suggested, and I'll send you the link. Do you think it will work for both dresses? The style I've chosen is a basic sheath dress although I need some help adding a little something to make it a bit more…'

'Bridal?' Vyvyan interjects.

'I have a couple of ideas popping into my head already,' Joyce continues, sounding full of enthusiasm. 'That silvery hue elevates a beautiful, summery fabric into something a little bit special. I think it's going to work extremely well. Right. Vyvyan, if you have the tape measure to hand, let's start getting the basics down on paper now I know where we're heading.'

I thought it would take ten minutes. It takes well over an hour. In between, we have fits of the giggles, as Joyce directs Vyvyan with utmost precision. Lola and I are amazed at how many measurements it takes to go about making a custom dress.

There's a lot of banter and by the time we end the session, Lola and I are buzzing. Joyce knows what she's doing and we're in good hands.

That's another big fat tick off the list and a huge relief.

'Jess, can you do me a favour?' Adam's voice is low and it's obvious that something is up. 'Ivy's having those false labour pains, but it's been going on for most of the evening. I'm beginning to get a bit worried, and I want to get her checked out, but she won't listen to me.'

'I'm on my way!' I march straight into the sitting room and Cappy instantly looks up from his laptop. 'That was Adam. He's worried about Ivy. She's having a few pains. It's probably only Braxton Hicks contractions, but I remember how painful they can be. He asked if I'd pop over. Lola's sound asleep and I've already switched off her light.'

'He must be concerned to call you. Best not to take any risks at this stage. How far gone is she now?'

I grab my cardigan from the sofa. 'Nearly twenty-eight weeks.'

Cappy's face clouds over. 'Well, I'm not going anywhere and if you need anything, give me a call.'

'I will,' I call over my shoulder as I head out.

Across the way, all the lights inside Smithy's Cottage are on and the door is ajar. The sound of voices filters out from the sitting room as I step inside. 'It's only me,' I call out.

'…I'm fine,' Ivy states adamantly. 'I wish you'd stop fussing. Oh… hi, Jess. I'm sorry he called you over. It's just the usual.'

'No,' Adam replies. 'That's not quite true, is it? You don't usually get the other pain, you know, around the sides.'

Ivy looks tired and fed up; it's obvious that she's uncomfortable but with two babies gaining weight by the day, that's par for the course.

'You look a bit peaky, Ivy.' To my horror, her eyes fill with tears, and I walk over to sit beside her on the sofa.

'I've been timing the contractions and I swear they're getting closer and closer together, Jess,' Adam impresses upon me. 'Ivy won't have it, but they are.'

'Look, I'm no expert but if it were me, Ivy, I'd get it checked out. Especially if the pain is slightly different to normal.'

She presses her hands either side of her tummy. 'These shooting pains are new, and they just make the other pains even worse. I daren't move because one thing seems to trigger the other.'

'Braxton Hicks contractions should be irregular, Ivy – at random intervals from what I can remember. That's the only way to know whether it's the real thing, or not.'

Adam is pacing back and forth. 'I'm going to ring the midwife, Ivy. She gave you her number for a reason.' With that, he walks out of the room and Ivy looks shaken.

'It's silly. I'm just tired and feeling extra weary tonight. Everything hurts a bit more than usual, that's all.'

'I'm sure it's all fine, Ivy, but you want to be sure, don't you?'

She nods her head just as Adam returns. 'They said to go straight to the maternity unit for a quick check-over. And we should take an overnight bag in case they want to monitor you for a while.'

'Now I feel like we're making a big fuss over nothing,' Ivy retorts.

'No. That's not how they look at it. Prevention is better than cure. It'll just reassure you that everything is as it should be and then you'll know if you get another incident like this that it's a part of the norm for you. But clearly something is different because I can tell you're concerned.'

'Okay.' She holds out her hand and Adam helps her up off the sofa. 'There's a bag in the bottom of my wardrobe ready to go.'

Adam is clattering up the stairs, two at a time.

'Ivy, you're doing the right thing,' I half-whisper.

She looks at me, her eyes full of anxiety. 'I'm scared, Jess.'

'I know, which is even more reason to get checked out.' I put my arms around her very gingerly and give a gentle hug. 'Don't worry about the bakery. Give me the keys and I'll open up in the morning. I'll let everyone know what's happening. It's time to focus on you and those babies.'

Ivy isn't the only one who is feeling scared right now. If ever there was a time to ask the universe for some good karma, it's now.

22

A Roller Coaster of a Day

Chelle and Kate at the bakery are in shock this morning when I tell them that Ivy is in hospital. At least I'm able to give them an update, as Adam texted me late last night.

'They're monitoring the babies' heart rates and they're doing just fine. It seems that Ivy was dehydrated, so they've put her on a drip.'

'She's in the best place, but I bet both Ivy and Adam are beside themselves with worry.' Chelle and Kate both look troubled. No one was expecting this.

I leave the keys with them and tell them to give me a call if they need any help. They ask me to pass on their love and best wishes to Ivy, and reassure me that between the two of them, and Wenna and Rose, they'll make sure everything ticks over as normal.

My heart feels a little lighter as I make my way over to the manor. I'm conscious that Riley arrived about ten minutes ago but even so, I stop to sit down on one of the benches in the middle of the courtyard. I text Adam, so he can pass on the message from the girls to Ivy. As I glance over at The Farmhouse, I see that the light is on in Lola's bedroom. No doubt Cappy is downstairs sorting breakfast, as he's doing the school runs today. I'm about to stand when my phone springs into life and it's Adam.

'Good timing. I was just about to text you. Ivy and the babies are doing great this morning. Ivy's feeling much more like her old self now she's rehydrated. Apparently, the pains in her sides are *round ligament* pains. They connect the uterus to the pelvis and hold it in place. As they stretch, even laughing, sneezing or coughing, can cause a spasm. It sounds flipping awful, doesn't it?' He sighs wearily.

'I know, and with the babies growing bigger by the day, it's not going to go away. But you must both be feeling relieved. Just knowing what's going on is so important. Is there anything that can be done to help alleviate the pain?'

'They've advised Ivy to get more rest and yoga is good – apparently. And she should avoid sudden, sharp movements. Let's be honest, the latter isn't really a problem these days as Ivy can't do anything quickly, but she's going to book a few one-to-one sessions with Flo. There are specific stretching exercises that can help considerably.'

I let out a huge sigh of relief. 'What an awful night for you both, but it's great news.'

'The obstetrician confirmed that the plan is still on target for a normal birth, unless anything changes in the meantime, but they intend to induce her at thirty-eight weeks if she hasn't gone into labour by then.'

'I was under the impression that twins tend to come early anyway, so is it likely they'll need to do that?'

'Who knows? We're expecting them to let her home after the doctor's round, which is mid-morning,' he confirms. 'How are things at the bakery?'

'Everyone sends their love and best wishes. They wanted to reassure Ivy that she's not to worry about the bakery; between them, they have it under control. I'll pop back and give them an update in a bit.'

He lets out a deep breath. 'Thanks for coming to my rescue last night, Jess. I knew Ivy would listen to you. They've been wonderful at the hospital and told her straight that if anything happens that's out of the norm in future, we should just drive straight—' Suddenly, his emotions start to overwhelm him, and I wait patiently for the moment to pass. 'Sorry about that... it's just been a long night. I've arranged to take a couple of days off work, and I think it's time Ivy realised she's trying to do too much. With Kate on board, she has a strong team.'

'And they're all ready to step up, Adam. I can vouch for that. Ivy is well placed to slip into more of a supervisory role, as Chelle and Kate have everything under control in the kitchen.'

'I might suggest to Ivy that she invites her parents down for a couple of days. What do you think? If she has company, she can't be working.'

I give a little laugh. 'I think that's a brilliant idea. Once Ivy accepts the changes start now, she'll soon adjust.'

Adam goes silent for a few seconds. 'I do hope so, because you know what she's like. Ivy feels she always has to be the one in the driving seat, but she's put in the work, she's built her team, and it's time to delegate.'

'And how are *you* coping?' I ask gently.

'Truthfully, I'm trying not to panic. The nursery is all painted out now; it's time to start unpacking all those boxes and get the furniture assembled. If I can do that over the next couple of days, Ivy will feel we're getting somewhere. Anyway, I'm heading over to the hospital restaurant to get breakfast and a sausage sandwich to go for my darling wife, in case they do the toast and cereal thing. Honestly, she always hated sausages. Pregnancy is changing my wife in ways we could never have imagined.'

That makes me laugh. My go-to comfort food was peanut butter and jam sandwiches. Ben complained that even the smell of them made him feel nauseous, but I could eat them at any time of the night, or day. I haven't touched one ever since Lola was born. That's pregnancy for you. However, while time seems to be flying by for me personally, it can't go quickly enough in terms of just wanting to have the babies safely delivered and seeing Ivy cuddling them both in her arms.

It's mid-morning when Cappy waylays me. 'These storage cupboards in Lola's and Ollie's bedrooms…'

I was about to climb the stairs to see how Riley is doing on his secret project in the master bedroom; our paths haven't crossed all morning.

'I've started unpacking the boxes, but I need a diagram of what goes where.'

'Sorry, Cappy. I thought Riley had given you a copy. I'll head back to The Farmhouse and print one off.'

'How's Ivy doing?' he enquires.

'Good and the babies are just fine. She's going to need to take it a little easier from here on in and Adam is going to suggest her parents come down for a few days. I think that's to break her old routine, as it's time she took more of a back seat at the bakery. She's on the doorstep if they have any problems.'

'That's a relief. Is it okay to approach Adam about Sunday? Clem and Charlie are keen to do a trial run with *The Silver Wave*. If Ivy's parents are around, a day fishing might be a good way of relaxing Adam and I know Riley's up for it. He's got a big smile on his face this morning but it's not just about the fishing trip.'

I look at Cappy, askance.

'It's not my news to share. I just happened to be in the same room at the time he took the call, but you didn't hear that from me.' Cappy gives me a wink and I roll my eyes at him.

'Give me five minutes to get you that plan for the kids' bedrooms and I'll go in search of Riley.'

Still, if he's smiling then at least it's good news.

When Cappy offered to take Lola to Penvennan Cove after school for a stroll along the beach, I knew she'd be delighted. He suggested the two of them could pop into The Lark and Lantern for an early dinner afterwards. When I told Riley, he suggested we finish on the dot of five and he insisted on whisking me away for a cosy meal for two at his cottage. I wasn't going to refuse.

We talk as we eat, and it is nice having some alone time together when we're not actually working.

'I don't believe it!' I exclaim when he tells me his news. 'Your mother is amazing!'

'She's a miracle worker all right. Getting Fiona to agree to let her and Dad bring Ollie with them to our wedding is little short of a miracle. Your mum has been pressing me for a couple of weeks now to talk about what the guys are going to wear. Now that you have the colour sorted... it's... hmm...'

'Cornflower blue,' I remind him.

'She's keen to find some funky waistcoats to complement your and Lola's dresses. You don't mind if we don't do ties, do you?'

'No. Go with whatever makes you feel comfortable. Gosh... I'm trying to picture you, Ollie, Dad, Cappy, Eddie and Adam standing in a line. Now that's going to be one awesome photo! So, Eddie and Phyllis have Ollie for three days?'

'Yep. I don't know what was said, and Fiona still hasn't been in touch with me, but I'm over the moon.'

'Mum will be, too. With just over ten weeks to go to the big day, the only thing I need to tie up still is the wedding cake.'

'How did Ivy seem when you popped into Smithy's Cottage this afternoon?'

'Relieved and she said to say thank you for the flowers. She didn't want to make a fuss, but she knew something wasn't quite right and she realises things must change. Her parents are arriving tomorrow and will be staying until Monday. Adam told me on the quiet that her mum "will talk some sense into her" about not overdoing it.'

I think we're both relieved about that.

'And Adam texted me to say Ivy's delighted about the fishing trip Cappy, Clem and Charlie have planned for us all on Sunday. Apparently, her parents are going to take Ivy out for a slap-up Sunday lunch.'

'Personally, I think it'll do Adam good. Chelle, Kate, and Erica are going to insist that Ivy hand over the planning for our wedding buffet to them to take forward. I think it's for the best. She can still be in the background keeping an eye on things.'

Riley guffaws. 'Ivy, just *keeping an eye* on things? Good luck with that.'

'I don't think she has a choice. The doctor told her she must take it easy. I've told the girls that we aren't fussed about a big cake. A pyramid of cupcakes will be just fine and easier for them to bake in advance, as the guest list is creeping up. They can freeze them and do the icing drizzles the day before.'

'Are the numbers *creeping up*?'

'Well, we did say that we'd invite family, friends and everyone who worked on the manor or was involved in the farm. I wouldn't want to leave anyone out. I mean… look at Rick and Nigel. They have their own worries starting up a new business together and yet they drop everything for us when we need them. They both have wives and children. And Joyce has really come my rescue.'

'The seamstress?'

'Yes. Normally she does two fittings, but having given her a gazillion different measurements, we've agreed that she'll come to the farm on the Saturday for us to try the dresses on. She's bringing everything she needs to do the last-minute alterations on site, so the dresses will be perfect for the following day. How could I not invite her and her partner, who will be driving her down, to the party? Vyvyan is trying to find them two nights' accommodation somewhere. I think Mum has managed to sort everyone else.'

Riley clears his throat. 'They're welcome to stay here, Jess. After all, I'll have moved out by then and I'm sure my parents wouldn't mind; it's a big enough cottage.'

I'm just about to put a forkful of carefully wound pasta into my mouth when I pause to look at him. 'Does Fiona know that Ollie will be staying with us and not your parents?'

'I thought it was best not to quiz Mum about that. It's not like Fiona will be here to object, is it?'

I continue eating, but Riley can tell where my mind is going next.

'And no, I haven't made a decision yet about what I'm going

to do about this place,' he continues. 'It's too far from the farm for Ivy and Adam to consider, although it could be perfect for Vyvyan and Keith, if I sell up. But I'm warming to the idea of renting it out fully furnished. What do you think?'

I shrug my shoulders. 'That's a decision only you can make, Riley. You put your heart and soul into breathing life back into Wind Rush Cottage. I can totally understand why you might want to hang on to it.'

He falls silent and it suddenly hits me what a huge turning point our wedding represents for him. Not just the fact that we'll be a married couple. We'll also become a blended family and it'll finally draw a line under his past. I hope it will also free him from the sense of guilt he carries for what he sees as his past failures. It takes two to cause a rift, although he doesn't see it that way.

'This place saved my sanity,' he replies, his voice wavering a little. Then he looks me directly in the eye, as if he's made a decision. 'Maybe I'll get an estate agent in to give me a valuation. If it's in the right price range, it wouldn't hurt to let Vyvyan and Keith take a look around, would it?'

If I were going to sell a place I was attached to, which really meant something to me, I couldn't think of a nicer couple to hand the keys over to. A bit like when Ivy and Adam joined us at the farm. I knew they were right for the bakery, and it was only their unexpected news that made Smithy's Cottage too small for their needs. For Riley, it would be the perfect answer to sell the cottage to good friends, but I simply smile as I watch him resume eating. He's getting there, but it's one step at a time and that's fine by me.

We've a couple of hours before Riley has to drop me back home and I can't wait to be done eating. It feels like ages since we lay in each other's arms. It's a reminder that no matter what we're going through, we're doing it so we can be together forever. I thought I knew what it means to make a commitment to someone, but this time around, it's completely different. The one thing that I never question with Riley is our love for each other.

Back at The Farmhouse, my mind is buzzing, and I end up pulling out the master furniture plan for Renweneth Manor. The budget is tight now, as increased labour costs to get us back on schedule mean I've had to pare everything back. We've saved a little by earmarking pieces of furniture in the shed that I'm upcycling, and Grandma would approve of that. But even just focusing on the half of the house that will, fingers crossed, be finished in time for moving-in day, the list of items to buy is still quite lengthy. If I don't place the orders soon, we might not get everything in time, but it's hard to see a chunk of money like that disappear in one go.

I grab my phone and call Mum. 'Sorry it's a bit late but I'm going around in circles tonight.'

She gives a little laugh. 'I'm not surprised. I bet your head spins at times with all you have going on. That's good news about Ivy.'

'Yes. It was a wake-up call, for sure,' I reflect.

'I was going to give you a ring tomorrow. Thanks for sending over the details about the dresses. The fabric you've chosen is absolutely gorgeous and I'm so glad you got on so well with Joyce.'

'Now we've established the colour theme for the wedding, I hope it's going to be possible to get the guys sorted. It would be nice if their waistcoats could complement the dresses. Riley said he's not keen on ties, though, but I'll leave that for the two of you to talk through if that's okay?'

'I'm already on it, Jess!'

'Oh, and if I text you Phyllis's number, can you get Ollie's measurements to sort his trousers, shirt and waistcoat, too?'

Mum let's out a subtle shriek. 'He's really coming?'

'Yes. Phyllis and Eddie pulled off a little miracle there. Fiona still hasn't made contact directly with Riley, but it's a result.

Honestly, Mum, it would have been gutting all round if Ollie hadn't been there.'

'I know. It's been nail-biting, hasn't it? And how's the manor coming along?'

'That's part of the reason I'm calling. I'll be placing the order for the furniture shortly. Obviously, there are items in The Farmhouse I'd happily take with us, but if Cappy does stay, then I really don't want to pull it apart. He's so at ease there now and—'

Mum cuts in. 'Grief is a lengthy process, Jess. At first, it was difficult for him to face the memories. The changes you made bringing the place up to date helped him to see it in a different way. Yes, there are memories of your grandma at every turn, but now he's at a stage where they're a comfort. I think you're doing the right thing leaving it as it is. I know how important it is to you, your dad and me, that Cappy ends up somewhere he can be truly happy.'

It helps to hear Mum say that, as this isn't about what Lola or I want, even though if Cappy chooses Stroud, our lives won't be quite the same without him here. 'Then I'll plough forward on that basis. I don't suppose he's said anything since he told Lucas he's happy for the lease to roll on?'

'Not relating to the house, but he's like a different man these days. Cappy's been telling me all about this boat Charlie and Clem are thinking of buying. And he's mentioned Prudie a few times.'

'He has?'

'Yes. They're looking at options for this new art school of hers. He's trying to convince her to look a bit further afield.'

Now that's interesting. 'Anywhere in particular?'

'Falmouth was one of the places, but there were a couple of others.'

'But Prudie's assistant has a shop in Polreweek. I thought he was going to help her run the studio.'

'To be honest, I just let him talk and I don't like to ask

questions. But he seems a lot happier these days, more content; and from what I gathered, he's delighted to have a social life again. He said it's rather like the old days.'

I start laughing. 'He certainly has, and it's been good to see. Well, I do hope Prudie finds something suitable. Her daughter lives locally and it must be nice to have her family close. Another move will, no doubt, be quite an upheaval for her.'

'I'm sure she'll have plenty of help. Anyway, I'll have a chat with Riley and his mum, Phyllis, in the next day or two. Now I know what you and Lola are going to be wearing, I can jump online and see if I can find some waistcoats to show Riley. I'm sure he's up to his eyes in work and once I have everyone's sizes, I can order them. That was the last the big item on the list, so we got there in the end. Oh, I've ordered the invites you chose. They'll take about a week.'

Inwardly, I groan. Who has the time to write that little lot out?

'If you can give me a list of names and any addresses that I won't have in my little book, I'll get your dad to write them out. He has such stylish handwriting, and you know he loves his old-fashioned ink pen with that swanky gold nib.'

'Oh, Mum! That would be amazing. I'll give you a second list of invites that we can hand-deliver to people at this end. It really is coming together now, isn't it? But I will admit that's mainly down to you.'

She chuckles. 'That's what mums are for. And it's been my pleasure. No one could ever accuse you of being an obsessive bride but on the day, I think it'll turn out to be everything you wished for.'

'You know, Mum, I'm beginning to think so too.'

CAPPY

23

All Aboard

Sunday the twenty-eighth of May dawns and it couldn't be a more perfect day to head out to sea on a boat.

'Here we are then,' I announce to Riley and Adam, as I pull into the car park.

Riley cranes his neck. 'Where are we, exactly?'

'It's an old scrap yard owned by a friend of Charlie's. The Beer and Bait Club rent a lock-up here; it's where we store our fishing tackle, but it's been a fair old while since we had a proper day out.'

I wind down the window as I pull up alongside Clem's old Range Rover. 'Hope you brought the bait,' I call out to him, and he gives me a thumbs-up.

'Come on, lads,' I say to Riley and Adam, 'let's get ourselves sorted. Ivan should be here shortly.'

'It's good to see you,' Clem extends his hand to our two newest anglers.

'What a day we picked,' Charlie joins in, giving Riley and then Adam a high five.

'Just as well it's calm,' Adam jokes, 'as I've only ever had one trip on a ferry, and it was a monster boat. I'm not sure I have my sea legs when it comes to a smaller vessel.'

Riley pats him on the back. 'You're not alone there, mate. Guess there's a first time for everything.'

'*The Silver Wave* is a Cygnus CyFish. She's a 260 square footer and there'll be plenty of space to move around on deck,' Charlie explains. 'And, Cappy, you missed an unveiling. I think you're in for a bit of a shock.'

'Yes, sorry I couldn't make it. It's all *go* back at the farm as we're running behind. Are we wearing life vests today?' I chuckle.

Riley and Adam turn to look at me and I break out into a beaming smile. 'Don't worry. Clem and Charlie know enough to judge whether a boat is seaworthy, or not. Ah, here's the main man, Ivan. And there's plenty of vests to go round.'

After doing the introductions, we start loading the gear into the back of his minivan. 'You picked a good day for it,' he states. 'I know she'll be in good hands.'

'You could join us,' Clem offers.

'No. I might enjoy mending boats and eating fish but catching 'em is a different thing entirely. I've an engine to work on today for a friend. Right, she's anchored up just off Penvennan Cove, and a mate of mine will take you out to her. Let's get going, as you'll want to make the most of it. It's a lot of money, but she's worth every penny.'

Ah, the serious talk has already begun. Ivan is a canny old soul, but if he doesn't manage to get a buyer, his wife isn't going to let up. She's right, because if that shed does fall down around it, it won't do the boat much good.

'Wow! This is quite something,' Adam observes, turning his head so the gentle breeze doesn't whip the sound of his words out of his mouth.

The water is amazingly calm, with only gentle little peaks and troughs breaking on the surface. Clem is behind the wheel and he's cranking up the knots. It's time to test the engine.

'Penvennan Cove looks completely different from this angle,' Riley comments. 'We're just coming up to the cliffs below the moor and Renweneth Farm. Gosh, Jess would love this.' Both he and Adam seem enthralled by what they're seeing.

For me, it's like coming home. The sea is second nature to me. If I added up the hours I've spent on land and compared them to the time I spent away at sea, I don't think it would be an exaggeration to say it would be pretty even.

However, it's been several years since I've stepped off dry land for more than an hour here and there, and it feels so good to be back. As for *The Silver Wave*, my goodness this is way more boat than I was expecting, and Ivan is to be commended. It's in excellent condition but I'm shocked that Clem and Charlie are looking at something in this sort of price range. It's got to be well in excess of a hundred grand, maybe as much as a hundred and fifty.

Clem eases back on the throttle and it's time to get everyone sorted.

'What type of fish can you catch around here?' Riley asks.

'Pollock and mackerel for sure,' I reply. 'If we're lucky, now that the water is warming up, maybe some ling, conger, pouting and whiting. Maybe even some cod. The dolphins are out, I see!' I point to a spot about five metres away and both Riley and Adam are transfixed.

'They're very close. Do they always travel in numbers? I can see at least three of them.'

'Often.' I nod my head. 'Sometimes, they'll swim alongside the boat as if they're racing.'

Adam is in awe. 'That's something I never thought I'd see.'

'We tend to catch and release, guys. If we're not taking it home to eat, then we throw it back in. Is that okay with you?' Charlie checks.

We're all in agreement, as Clem weighs anchor and we start setting up the fishing lines.

'There are a few mackerel around. I'll show Riley and Adam what to do,' Charlie indicates for them to follow him.

I join Clem in the forward cabin.

'There you are. How did she handle?' I ask, wishing it were my hands on that wheel.

'Like a dream, Cappy. There's only one drawback.' He pulls a long face.

'The price?'

He inclines his head. 'We weren't expectin' this beauty. She was built in 2006 and Ivan hasn't cut any corners. She's been fully overhauled and all credit to him, it was love at first sight for Charlie and me. I mean... it's exactly what we want, as she'll make a perfect charter boat, but we're just gettin' our figures together and it isn't lookin' promisin'.'

Clem's disappointment is tangible.

'Have you tried bartering?'

'The lowest we can get Ivan down to is a hundred and thirty-five grand. It's at least fifteen under the proper askin' price and a bargain. Charlie is sinkin' in the lump sum he's gettin' from takin' early retirement, but I doubt he'll want to burden himself with a loan to help make up the shortfall. As for me, I'm usin' the best part of my savings, havin' handed the farm over to my son a few years ago. Our limit is our limit, and it looks like we're goin' to be forty-five grand short. This is lookin' more and more like a pipe dream, I'm afraid, Cappy. But Ivan is keen to sell now and we're wonderin' if we can do a deal. Pay him two-thirds up front and the rest in instalments once we set ourselves up to do deep-sea fishin' tours.'

I let out a low whistle. 'That's a big ask, Clem.'

'Yep, and if I were him, I'd probably refuse. But now 'ee has her back in the water, the pressure is on for him to get a buyer. It's a lot of money for anyone. For us two, we're only riskin' what we can afford to risk but if 'ee takes our offer, it will put the pressure on. I'm not sure whether me or Charlie feel comfortable with that, so it might mean walkin' away and lookin' for somethin' within our price range. It's a pity, though.'

He wanders off, leaving me to have a nosey around. The old rust bucket under the tarpaulin turned out to be a real diamond and none of us would have guessed that.

'I've got five! Five!' Adam shouts, sounding panicked. 'What do I do?'

Charlie rushes over to show him how to unhook the mackerel from the line. Riley looks on in amazement and I walk over to stand next to him, casting my line.

'It's not just about catching fish. There's something so cathartic about being out here. Do you feel it?' I ask.

Riley adjusts his sunglasses, then gazes around. 'I've been trying to put my finger on it. You know... how to describe the experience, as Jess is going to quiz me when I get back. All that pops into my head is that line "stop the world spinning, I want to get off". I don't know if it's from a film, or a song I heard, but it's just like that. Nothing seems real. It's as if the moment I stepped onto the boat, I was entering a different reality. That sounds crazy, doesn't it?' He bursts out laughing.

'No. It is a different existence. On a day like this it's heavenly. The water is so calm, the sky and the sea such an unbelievable shade of blue that it's hard to believe we're in the UK, and not anchored off some tropical island. It's as if reality is suspended for a while.'

'That's it, exactly! I feel that time has stopped and when I step back on land, the clock will start ticking again. It's crazy. How did you do this for so many years?'

'It's like having two homes: the sea and the land. Nature shows you her all and it teaches you a lesson. She gives and she takes away. A boat can be smashed to smithereens in a bad storm and it's by her grace – and fate, I suppose – that we make it back to dry land.'

'Do you ever get used to it... being stuck on land?'

I laugh. 'No. It's like a part of you is missing. There's a

yearning that never goes away. Out here, everything feels more real, because a simple mistake can cost lives. I've lain in my bunk and spent the early hours of the morning praying I'd live to see another daybreak. It's only then that you really appreciate what life means. It's like facing your maker and you promise you'll do better in future. No one likes to feel vulnerable; it's a truly humbling experience and I like to think that it made me a better man. What are Jess and Lola up to, today?'

'Online, placing orders for the furniture for Renweneth Manor. Lola is so excited we're at this stage. Jess has been dragging her feet, but if she leaves it any longer, there's a chance not all of the items will arrive in time.'

'It's a balancing act, managing a huge project like that. All credit to her—'

Riley's body jerks as the fishing rod in his hands gives a hefty tug and his eyes widen. 'I think it's a big one!'

'Then reel it in.' I laugh. 'Whatever it is, it's determined to wriggle off that hook.' I turn to our fellow anglers. 'If Riley can land this one, I think our barbecue back at the beach will be sorted, lads.' The line bends ominously, but the look of determination on his face tells me he's not about to give up without a fight.

The banter as we sip our beers, waiting for supper to cook on the grill, reflects the sort of day we've had. I saunter over to Adam, who has made his way down the beach to stand and watch the sun setting.

'It's mighty peaceful at this time of the day, isn't it?' I reflect.

Aside from a couple of dog walkers, there are only a few stragglers packing up their things ready to wend their way home.

'Yes. It's been a brilliant day, Cappy. I've had a *whale* of a time.' He half-turns to grin at me and I chuckle to myself. 'To be honest, I thought I'd be a bit… squeamish, you know… those poor fish.'

I nod my head, appreciative of his honesty. 'A healthy respect for the food chain is a good thing, Adam. That's why on days like this, we practise catch and release. We only bring back what we intend to eat and are grateful for it. Even the commercial fishermen thank our creator for their hauls. It puts food on people's tables and keeps a roof over their families' heads.'

His brow furrows. 'I guess I never looked at it in quite that way before.'

'It's the circle of life, but that doesn't mean any of us should take it for granted.'

'It's been a bit of an emotional roller coaster for me lately,' he admits. 'Today, I didn't have time to think about anything other than what I was doing, or simply marvelling at our surroundings. The dolphins were absolutely amazing. When I hauled in those mackerel, I was in panic mode. On the other hand, Riley's face when he landed that magnificent bass was one of incredulity and pride.'

'They'll all make for good eating. A dozen mackerel and that bass, which must be an eight-pounder at least, will give us a meal fit for kings. As for the other fish we caught, they get to live another day. Would you do it again?'

He shakes his head. 'No. But I'm grateful for the experience, Cappy. It was a distraction I needed to clear my head. I thought the pregnancy was going to be the fun bit, you know, getting everything ready, but instead, all I do is worry about what could go wrong. And this latest scare was a reality check. Ivy finally realises she must slow down.'

'It's nature's way of sending out a little signal. She's a tough cookie, is Ivy, but you're right, and her and the babies' well-being comes first. But with you by her side, you'll get through this, and the best is yet to come.'

Adam turns back to watch the sunset. 'I believe so too, Cappy. And then, hopefully, it won't be long until we get our home sorted and our happiness will be complete. Riley said you're staying until the wedding. Ivy's due a week later but we've been warned they won't let her go to her due date. You could be here to witness the excitement.'

'Five minutes to grub up, guys,' Clem calls to us, and I give him an acknowledging wave.

'Just between us, Adam, there's a chance I might not be heading back to Stroud after all.'

He turns to look at me, sporting a smile. 'That's great news, Cappy!'

'Hmm... maybe, maybe not.'

Adam looks puzzled. 'The farm wouldn't be quite the same without you there; Jess once joked that you're a part of the fixtures and fittings.' He laughs.

'Well, an opportunity has come up and I'm seriously considering it. Prudie might have found a place to house her art school, but it's in Falmouth. It's only about a forty-five-minute drive away but she's considering selling up; it makes sense for her to live close by. If it works out, I've offered to give her a hand doing any little jobs I can to keep the place ticking over; like a caretaker.'

'It would be a nice little run for you each day.'

No one, apart from Prudie and me, is aware of this, so I'm interested to see Adam's reaction. 'We're both on our own... and we enjoy each other's company. It makes sense that we find a little place... um... together.'

Adam's expression freezes for a second before he composes himself. 'Oh... I see.'

'It'll be a while until we know whether it's doable. It's a big step and it'll take some organising, that's for—'

Charlie suddenly appears at my side. 'It never gets old, does it, watching the sun go down? But the fish is ready. It's been a good day on *The Silver Wave*.' I can tell from his tone that reality is beginning to set in. It's probably a stretch too far for him and Clem, financially. But if Prudie and I settle down in Falmouth... maybe what they need is a third partner. It would be a nice little break for me lending a hand now and again with fishing trips.

'Come on, let's eat!' I declare, feeling a surge of optimism about the future. Maybe there's a lot more life left in this old dog than I thought.

JULY

JESS

24

I Hope Trouble Doesn't Come in Threes

We're halfway through July, and with only two weeks until moving-in day at Renweneth Manor – and three weeks until the wedding – this last month, we've had to pare down the use of the trades on site to a minimum. The budget is now running on fumes.

Riley, Cappy and I are all sick and tired of painting. The list of finishing-off jobs and snagging, like sanding out rough bits of skirting where the grit that still lingers in the air has settled on wet paint, seems to grow by the day.

'Morning, Mum, just a quick call. How's the budget going for the wedding? Is there enough money in the pot to cover everything?' I ask, keeping my fingers on one hand crossed.

'Oh… um…' That moment of hesitation in her voice sets my nerves on edge. 'The savings that resulted from getting Joyce to make your wedding dress, and Lola's princess frock, helped to offset the extra catering costs from the revised guest list. The flowers came in a little over budget… but I got a good deal on the invitations.'

That's not the question I asked.

'By the way,' Mum continues, changing the subject ever so slightly. 'We've now had all the RSVPs back and it's a good job the grounds of the manor allow us to spread out. It's going to be one big party!'

It was a blessing passing everything over to Mum and Dad to

handle, but if we're going to end up with a deficit, I know what they're like. I don't want them to feel it's their responsibility to make it up.

The problem is, Michael sent me an email first thing to say there's a shortfall in the farm's main bank account. He's popping in this morning to discuss it. I'm just about to transfer the last of my savings into the account to cover the outstanding invoices on the manor. It would be unwelcome news indeed if we have an overspend on the wedding account. 'I just thought I'd check whether the account needs topping up as I'm um... working on the budgets today.'

'Is it all going well at your end?' she quizzes me, sounding concerned – which is exactly what I didn't want.

'Yes. Same old... we're running behind, but we'll get there,' I reply, breezily. 'Cappy has been tied up a bit lately, but he's around every day now until it's all done.'

'Ah, this thing with the boat. Is he really going to get involved with it?'

'The truth is, after mentioning it once after the fishing trip, he hasn't said anything about it since. Charlie's official retirement date isn't until the last day of August, so I don't think they can do anything until he's received his lump sum. Erica is talking about throwing him a party at the bakery to celebrate it.'

'Oh, that explains it then. No doubt they'll be on edge in case another buyer steps in.'

'I hadn't thought of that. Cappy has been a little quiet lately; coming and going, but not saying a lot.' It's not like I can question where he's been and what he's doing, but usually he's quite forthcoming. 'Are you and Dad okay?'

'We are. Constantly on the go as usual. What with the wedding planning and we've had a bumper crop of just about everything in the garden this year. I've been kept busy making jams, jellies and chutneys. I'll be bringing down a box-full for that new pantry of yours.'

'Aww... I'll look forward to that. It'll probably be the only home-made stuff on the shelves.' I laugh. 'Anyway, I hate to love you and leave you, but I have a meeting in half an hour with my *accountant*,' I labour the word. 'Then I have a unit Cappy made for Ollie's bedroom to paint.'

'It sounds like you have your hands full as usual, Jess. But the end is in sight. Well, until you start the second phase of the work on the manor, but you've all earned a rest. And a honeymoon.'

I give a gentle sigh. 'Hmm... at some point early next year.' If funds allow, that is. Riley and I each contributed half to the wedding budget, but I know that after repaying his brother and buying my engagement ring, it'll take him a while to build his savings back up again.

There's a slight pause.

'I don't know if your dad and I did the right thing,' Mum continues, sounding a tad uneasy. 'Ever since we sent out the invites, people have been calling about a wedding present list. I know you glibly told me that when two households combine, there isn't much you need by way of toasters and china.' Mum's tinkling laughter echoes down the line because that's exactly what I said. 'The enquiries were about vouchers, or asking if it was okay to gift cash. Most people are aware that you have some big items of furniture to buy, but you've been so busy, we didn't want to bother you. So, when anyone asks, we simply give them the account number and the sort code and ask them to put their name in the description when they do the transfer. Together with a little bit of an underspend, the balance is growing by the day.'

'Oh, I see.' Well, that's unexpected.

'That way, we can print out a list so you and Riley can thank everyone. Even Riley's parents have made a transfer.'

'They have?'

'Yes. I had a lovely chat with Phyllis when we made contact to sort out Ollie's outfit. She said they felt a bit awkward talking to Riley about money, but they wanted to give the same amount to you and Riley as they did to Tom and Helen. Anyway, money is still coming in. I think pretty much everyone I'm in contact with down there has already contributed.'

I gulp. 'I'll leave that in your hands then, Mum. Thank you.'

The whole idea was that the party was a celebration not just of our union, but it was meant to be a heartfelt thank you to everyone who either supported us here on site, or emotionally at a distance. It was our gift to them.

'Anyway, you can book that honeymoon without worrying. And don't concern yourself about Cappy; whatever he's doing, he's happy. He hasn't mentioned coming back to Stroud and if he intended to do that, I'm sure he'd been making noises about it by now.'

'We couldn't have pulled off this wedding without you and Dad taking control. I'd have floundered. Let Dad know that Riley and I really, really appreciate the time and effort you've both put in.'

'It's been our pleasure, Jess. As Cappy says, it's nice to feel needed.'

I'm touched by her words and if ever I needed my parents, it's been over the last couple of months.

As I sit across the table from Michael, he isn't smiling. 'That last income and expenditure account you sent over, Jess... well, doing a quick tally against the most recent bank statement for the farm's main account, there's just over a twenty-four-thousand-pound shortfall. I know you're still moving funds around, and you might have further transfers to do, so I could be panicking over nothing. But I was under the impression that you were keeping the tax money in there, rather than the secondary account... unless I'm getting confused.'

'That's right. I've one further amount to transfer into the secondary account, which is ring-fenced to cover the renovation costs only. I intend to do that today, and it'll be my final loan. All the invoices should be in by the end of next week,' I reply, trying my best not to sound as thrown as I feel.

'And, aside from the loans you've been making to the business, you only transfer over the net profit each month into that account ready for phase two of the work, is that correct?'

'Yes. Based on the calculation we agreed. Are you saying I've got it wrong?'

'No, I checked the transfers. As you know, I suggested we err on the cautious side, so the percentage to cover tax and outgoings is well within the margins. That's not the problem.'

He slides a printout of the latest bank statement across the table, and suddenly I feel as if someone has turned on the heating in The Farmhouse kitchen. A sensation of panic starts to mount in my chest.

'We paid the second half of the prior year's tax at the end of July.' He leans over to point to the figure on the statement. 'We've had the final tax bill through now for last year. We can cover the payment due at the end of next January, but not the one due next July. That's working on the basis that you want to keep three month's overheads at a bare minimum, in addition to the tax.'

'I... I... thought that was what I was doing,' I stutter. 'I don't know what's gone wrong, Michael. I'm going to have to do a reconciliation between my budget spreadsheets and the bank statement.'

His frown deepens. 'Are we in trouble, Jess?'

'I don't know.'

'It's an odd amount to be adrift by.' Michael pulls a wad of sheets from his briefcase. 'I was obviously thrown when I did the calculation, so I printed off the last three months' transactions and highlighted expenditure that isn't a part of the usual running costs. If they're all to do with the work on the campsite, then it ended up costing you significantly more than the figure you originally forecast. I hope there's another explanation as I hate to be the bringer of bad news at this stage.'

He's diligent and I appreciate that. 'Leave it with me and I'll get back to you as soon as I can.'

I can tell he feels awkward and, as I see him out, he very politely asks if we're on target to move into the manor at the beginning of August.

'That's still the plan and we're getting there. It's just going to be an exhausting couple of weeks to do the finishing touches in time for moving day.'

He turns on his heels. 'Look, why not let me investigate the problem, Jess? You don't have the time.'

'That's really kind of you, Michael, but I've signed off every invoice that has gone through and I should be able to get to the bottom of it quite quickly.'

'This is the last thing I wanted to drop on your desk right now. Seriously, if you change your mind, just give me a call.'

As we say goodbye and I close the door, I slump up against it. The transfer I'm making today will virtually empty my savings account. I was prepared for that, even though for a while, the prospect of selling Smithy's Cottage to Ivy and Adam seemed like the answer to all my problems.

The question I couldn't bring myself to ask Michael is whether our current level of income will be enough to foot the shortfall by the time we get to next July. I've clearly messed up, but how? Aside from the manor, where the only question was going to be the size of the overspend, none of the other budgets I've been managing are overspent. The expenditure on the Courtyard Hub was more or less spot on, so I'm reeling.

Riley was right about the renovation work on Renweneth Manor, though; he said to take my original budget and double it. He wasn't joking and, in fact, once I've added up the final total, he was probably not far off for the first phase. Even so, I've monitored every single penny as I knew what the absolute cut-off point was. I've never raided one budget to shore up another. A part of me wants to start looking into it straight away but if I do, Riley will know something is wrong. I'm going to have to work on it at night, after Cappy has gone to bed, as it's time to get back to painting.

It's going to be tough to hide my concern; I can't just conjure up that sort of shortfall out of thin air. And even though our profits are increasing, that's what I'm reliant upon to complete the work on the manor. I literally feel sick to my stomach.

Towards the end of the afternoon, as I walk across the courtyard, I spot Adam.

'Hi, Jess,' he calls out and I'm surprised when he hurries towards me.

'You're a little early arriving home today.'

'Yes. Ivy hasn't had the best day. She's spent most of it lying on the bed as her ankles are swollen. I think she needs a bit of cheering up. I'm planning on keeping her mind occupied this evening binge-watching a new series I've downloaded.' He gives me a hopeful grin. With four weeks to go, I seriously doubt Ivy can find any position in which she's truly comfortable.

'Poor Ivy. Tell her I'll pop in to see her sometime tomorrow. Enjoy your evening.'

I'm about to continue on towards The Farmhouse when Adam clears his throat noisily. When I turn back to look at him, he seems ill at ease.

'Jess, um, how are things with Cappy? There's been no mention of him returning to Stroud.'

'No, there hasn't,' I reply, my voice full of optimism.

He stares at me, and I can tell there's something he wants to say but he isn't sure whether it's the right thing to do, or not.

'Is there somewhere private we can go?' he asks, making me frown.

'Of course. How about the orchard?'

'Perfect.'

We turn in the direction of the Manor House. It isn't until we've settled ourselves down on the wooden chairs beneath one of the old apple trees that I question him.

'What's up?' I enquire, cagily.

'I'm not sure I should be mentioning this. When someone says something is *between you and me* but doesn't go on to say not to tell anyone... it's just, if you're not already aware of it by now, then I feel bad not speaking up. It's been on my mind for a while, but I'll be honest, I do feel conflicted. In hindsight, I'm even wondering whether I was supposed to say something to you but I can't be sure.' His face is solemn.

Gosh, this sounds ominous. 'Look, Adam, if you're that uneasy about whatever it is, I promise that I won't pass a single word of it on.'

He sighs. 'That day we all went fishing, Cappy and I ended up having a bit of a chat as we watched the sun go down.' He pauses and I wait patiently until he's ready to continue. A little chill starts to run up and down my spine. 'Cappy said he might not be returning to Stroud but that he would be staying in Cornwall.'

He gives me a pointed look. I'm taking it that Adam wants me to question him.

'In *Cornwall*, as opposed to Renweneth Farm?'

He nods his head.

'Cappy is thinking of moving to another location?' It's impossible to hide my surprise.

Another nod of his head.

Why would Cappy do that? Adam is obviously waiting for me to ask another question, but I don't know where to go next. I can see that he's getting frustrated.

'It's to do with Prudie,' he blurts out.

My mind goes into overdrive as I try to piece this together. 'She's found a home for her art studio, and it isn't local? I know they've been looking further afield.'

Another nod of his head.

But what has that got to do with Cappy? Why would it affect him where Prudie ends up? Then another thought hits me and as I glance at Adam, his eyes widen. The penny has literally just dropped, and the realization of what it implies is clearly etched on my face.

'That's all I can say. I'm sorry,' he apologises. 'If I was meant to pass it on, I have. Sort of. And I wasn't… well, my conscience has been troubling me. Forewarned is forearmed. I must go.'

He stands and I lean in to give him a hug. 'Of course. Ivy's waiting. Thank you, Adam. I won't breathe a word of this, I promise you. But if it was some sort of message for me, it might not be too late to do something about it.'

The look of relief I see reflected in his eyes is like a burden has suddenly been lifted from his shoulders. 'I know you want what's best for Cappy; we all do. He's such a grand old chap and the farm means so much to him. Right, ugh… life, eh?'

As he walks away from me, I sit back down in my seat as I let it sink in. I knew Cappy and Prudie were good friends, but this is a shock and some. I'm stunned.

Two bolts out the blue in one day is rather overwhelming. Let's hope what little there is left of today passes quietly. I now have two problems to work through and I don't really know which one to tackle first, because it feels like my world is starting to implode.

25

Panic Stations

'Mum, Mum!' Lola comes rushing into my bedroom and as my eyes spring open, I glance at the clock and see it's just before midnight.

'What is it, my darling girl? Did you have a bad dream?' I vault out of bed, wrapping my arms around her as I can see how shaken she is.

'No. There's an ambulance in the courtyard. It's Ivy.' Her chin wobbles.

Lola yanks on my hand, literally pulling me across the landing and into her bedroom. We peek out of the window and it's obvious that it's the garish flashing light that woke her.

'Mum, can you check if Ivy's okay?'

I turn to plant a kiss on her forehead. 'Of course, I will. Now you hop into bed, and I'll be back in a couple of minutes.'

Cappy suddenly appears on the landing, looking concerned. 'What's up?'

'It's Ivy. There's an ambulance in the courtyard. I'll pop over and see if there's anything I can do.'

'Oh, right. I'll um… put the kettle on.'

Stopping only to grab a thin, knitted jacket to throw over my pjs, I swing open the front door and hurry across the courtyard. The door to Smithy's Cottage is open and I gingerly step inside. There's some frantic activity going on in the sitting room and I hover by the doorway. I can't see Ivy, but I can see Adam. He's standing on the opposite side of the room and his face is ashen. The moment he spots me, he strides out into the hallway.

'Ivy was fine all evening, Jess,' he half-whispers. 'All of a sudden, she said she felt dizzy and light-headed. She started sweating and felt nauseous. They're checking a few things before they get her into the ambulance.'

'No pains?'

'No,' he replies, letting out a long slow breath.

'Will you go with them?'

'They said to follow in the car.'

'Let me drive you, instead.'

'That's kind of you, but I'll be fine. Once I know she's in safe hands, I'll feel a lot better. I intend to stay with her, and it might be useful to have the car there in case I have to come back to fetch anything. Thanks for popping over to check. I'll text you as soon as we know what's happening.'

'Give Ivy our love. And if you need anything from here, just call me, no matter what time it is, and I'll bring it straight over to the hospital, do you hear me? You've enough to worry about. You're all in our thoughts, Adam.'

This time, he hugs me with a fierceness that tells me how concerned he is.

'Stay strong and think positively,' I whisper into his ear, before I disappear out through the door.

When I walk back into The Farmhouse kitchen, Lola is sitting at the table sipping a cup of hot chocolate.

'I couldn't get back to sleep, Mum. How is Ivy?'

I glance nervously at Cappy, as I kneel next to Lola.

'The paramedics are taking very good care of her, Lola. They'll be whisking her off to the maternity hospital shortly and Adam is going to follow the ambulance.'

'But her and the babies... they will be fine, won't they?' Lola's brow is furrowed.

Miaow. Miaow.

Goodness, now Misty is wide awake, too.

'That's what hospitals are for, Lola. The doctors know what they're doing, and she'll be in good hands. Adam will let us know what's happening as soon as he's able. In the meantime, finish your drink and how about you and Misty snuggle down together in the tepee?'

'Oh, Mum, that's a great idea. Isn't it, Misty?' She reaches out her hand and Misty comes trotting forward, always eager to receive a stroke.

'I'll just settle these two down,' I inform Cappy and he gives me a supportive smile.

By the time I return to the kitchen, he's sitting at the table, looking a little anxious.

'Hopefully, it won't take long for the two of them to fall asleep,' I sigh as I slump down onto the chair opposite him.

Cappy raises his eyebrows. 'And how is Ivy really doing?'

'It's hard to say. Adam said she hasn't had any pains. Apparently, her ankles swelled up earlier in the day. She suddenly complained of feeling unwell and that's why they ended up calling the ambulance. I didn't see her; I just spoke briefly to Adam.'

Cappy looks as dejected as I feel. 'It's not labour then?'

'No, it seems not. I just told him to think positively and ring if he needs anything. He promised to text as soon as they know what's happening.'

'Come on, drink up. There's no point worrying until we know there's something to worry about.' Cappy points at the mug in front of me and I take a sip, then another.

'This is hitting the spot. Thanks, Cappy.'

'The number of times I've sat around this table late at night with your grandma sipping hot chocolate doesn't bear thinking about.' He chuckles. 'She said it was a pick-me-up and better than a cup of strong tea when it comes to having a shock. I remember the night we got the phone call that you'd gone into labour with Lola. My, that takes me back.'

Cappy's in a reflective mood and suddenly I realise after what

Adam said, I might have cause to worry. If ever I'm going to raise the topic, it's probably now or never, given tonight's unusual events.

'You do like what I've done to The Farmhouse, Cappy, don't you?'

He looks at me askance. 'Of course. You've made a grand job of it.'

'You… didn't prefer it as it was?'

He hitches up his left eyebrow. 'No. I hated that old, dark furniture. Your grandma didn't agree with me but if she could see it now, she'd fall in love with this place all over again.'

My stomach begins to flutter nervously. 'In two weeks and one day, I'll be moving out. It'll be the end of another era.'

'I know. But life moves on, Jess.' He raises an eyebrow, sounding prosaic.

And just like that, I realise he has no intention of moving back into The Farmhouse permanently. My mind goes into overdrive. I need to think fast.

'I have a bit of problem, Cappy. I haven't got to the bottom of it yet, but I've messed up and… well, I'm looking to boost our income. If Prudie is still searching for a home for her art studio, I think I've come up with a solution to accommodate her here at the farm.'

This time both of his eyebrows shoot up. 'You have?'

'I reckon there's room to erect a reasonably sized studio the other side of Penti Growan's courtyard garden and parking space. One of those kit-form, prefabricated buildings they use for garden offices and that sort of thing. What do you think?'

He looks genuinely surprised. My stomach dips, hoping it isn't too late to sort something out.

'If it weren't so dark,' he laughs, 'I'd go straight out with the measuring tape to check there's enough space.'

I know precisely what he's thinking. 'None of us drive into the courtyard now since the bakery extended the outside seating areas and we have the new extended car park. There's no reason the parking for Penti Growan can't be an allocate space in the main parking area, too. That would free up an even larger area.'

'That's true,' he muses. 'Even Fred, from Rowse's bakery, parks on the pavement out on the road when he's delivering the bread.'

I watch as Cappy sits there, mulling it over.

'Instead of the huge, five-bar gate, we could have two bespoke, wrought-iron gates made for the entrance to the courtyard. Opening them would take up a lot less room.' I stop for a moment to let that sink in. 'Anyway,' I go on, trying to make my words sound casual, 'it's just a thought in case she's still looking.'

Cappy remains quiet.

'I'm off to bed,' I conclude. 'Thank you for the hot chocolate, Cappy.'

I stand, and on my way over to the sink with the mug, I stop to plant a kiss on his cheek.

'If Adam texts, Jess, knock my door and let me know how Ivy and the babies are doing. It's going to be a long night.'

'I know... and I will.'

The seed is sown, and I can only hope that it isn't too late. What a fool I've been. Loneliness is an awful thing at any age; for Prudie and Cappy, finding someone you can spend your remaining years with is a lifeline. It's a reason to go on. Grandma wouldn't want Cappy to simply fade away when there's plenty of life left in him. As she told me once, shortly before any of us realised she was ill, 'I want Renweneth Farm to be a comfort for Cappy and for you all.'

I truly believe that now it's my job to make that happen and I can't thank Adam enough. There is no such thing as a coincidence. The fact that he opened up to me and then – out of the blue – tonight's unfortunate incident created the perfect opportunity to broach the subject, bears all the hallmarks of fate working its magic to me.

Then I think of Ivy and her two babies. Please, please, please let everything be okay; I send a silent prayer out into the universe.

What we need now is some good news, because no matter what problems any of us have, that's the one sure thing that will be guaranteed to turn our frowns into beaming smiles. Everything else... well, all things pass in the fullness of time and looking back, a stumbling block often becomes just another little blip on life's path. One we either side-step, sail over once we find a solution, or we take a detour, and it becomes a lesson learnt.

I've been drifting in and out of sleep for a couple of hours and happy to do so, because all my worries seem to have wound themselves up into a tight ball. When sleep finally comes, I find myself desperately trying to unravel everything to see what's salvageable. It's exhausting, and I actually prefer the gaps in between when I surface for a short while and realise that I'm having a nightmare. What is chilling, is that even in the wee hours of the morning – just before dawn – the reality of what Ivy and Adam are going through, coupled with the thought of Cappy moving away and my financial woes, seem like a living nightmare.

A sudden sensation that sweeps through my body makes me sit up and I realise the phone next to me is buzzing. It's a text and as my fingers click away, I find myself holding my breath. It's three-forty-two in the morning.

> Jess, the babies are here. We've named them Eli and Phoebe! Ivy is exhausted but the doctor says they're all doing fine. I'll call you in the morning... heck it is morning. What a night!

And with that, tears of joy begin to trickle down my face. Nothing signals hope and happiness for the future like a new arrival, and this is double the joy!

None of us slept very well last night and when I tapped on

Cappy's door, I wasn't really surprised that he, too, had been drifting in and out of sleep. Even though we were quiet, seconds later, Lola padded across the landing and from that point on, none of us got any more sleep.

This morning, our sparkly girl isn't quite so bright, even though she's excited talking about the babies now that Eli and Phoebe have arrived. Lola asks when they're coming home, but I warn her they might have to stay in hospital for a few days. She's so tired that by eight o'clock, I suggest she goes back to bed to snuggle up with Misty and a book.

'What are your plans today, Cappy?' I ask, thinking he'll want to take it easy.

'Oh, I'm off out shortly. There are a few things I need to attend to, but I'll be back at work on the manor by ten, ten-thirty, latest. How about you?'

'I'm still waiting on an update from Ivy. She texted earlier to say that Phoebe has a touch of jaundice. They're waiting for the results of a blood test, to find out whether she'll need phototherapy treatment. Ivy said she'll call me later to let me know what's happening.' I bet both Ivy and Adam are shattered but thrilled to finally be able to hold their son and their daughter in their arms. As for me... it's much less exciting.

'In the meantime, I might tackle some paperwork. Riley is getting a valuation on Wind Rush Cottage first thing this morning, so he probably won't get here until about the same time as you. By then, after a bit of a caffeine hit, I'll be ready to join you both.'

I'm hoping that a few uninterrupted hours will allow me to get to the bottom of what's gone wrong with my budgeting.

He smiles at me. 'If you're tired, don't push yourself too hard, Jess. Everyone needs a day off every now and again.' Cappy stands and as he walks past my chair, he gives my shoulder a reassuring squeeze.

'When I think of what Ivy's been through, one bad night's sleep is a doddle.' I laugh, and he joins in.

'It is a rather wonderful thing to happen, isn't it?' he responds. I nod my head in agreement. It most certainly is.

I can't find one item of expenditure on the bank statement that isn't on my spreadsheets. It doesn't make any sense. Whether it's because my mind feels a little foggy, I don't know, but it isn't until I begin sipping my third coffee that a horrible thought pops into my head.

As I begin ticking off the transfers into the main account, it doesn't take me long to identify the error and I'm totally gutted. I immediately call Michael.

The moment he answers, I break the bad news. 'I found the problem and you're right. The balance looks healthy, but within it, the amount set aside for the next two tax payments is short by twenty-six-thousand and eighty pounds.'

'That's pretty close to the quick figure I cobbled together. And you can explain it?' He sounds almost disbelieving.

'Yes. Cappy was forecasting a spend of thirty thousand pounds on his project. That covered the new car park and entrance, building the new shower block on the campsite and converting the old shower block alongside the old hay barn into a bespoke toilet facility for market days. He came in under budget by nearly four thousand pounds. The problem is, I never transferred the funds across from my savings account. That money was swallowed up in the overspend for the manor.'

A sudden chill runs down my spine as I hear Michael draw in a long, slow breath. 'Oh, Jess. That's totally understandable given everything you've been juggling. And you've done well, given that Renweneth Manor is a bit of a money pit. You didn't let it get totally out of control; you reined it in at the right times, so don't be too hard on yourself. Let me run some updated cash projections for the next six months. Hand on heart, I'll be surprised if we can't make some, if not all, of the money up.'

I can't help sighing. 'I've never robbed one budget to shore up another, Michael. That's a dangerous way to operate and just knowing there's a deficit is a huge knock to my confidence.'

'I know, I know,' he replies, firmly. 'But overall, the cash position in the main account is good and, let's be honest, personally you've put in every penny you have. The business owes you and it will take time to pay that back. If I can demonstrate to you beyond a shadow of a doubt that by the time we have to make that tax payment in July, there will be more than enough to pay it, will you stop panicking?'

It's not how I operate, and he knows it, but I don't have a choice. 'Thanks, Michael, for having my back. I feel… foolish.'

'Jess, this is just between us. No one needs to know. The farm isn't about to go broke; it's in a really good position. Vyvyan was telling me some of her plans for this Christmas and now that she's tapped into using the village hall to host various fayres, she already has three bookings during the farm's quiet season next spring. Has she told you about the book worm festival? She's a real dynamo.'

'I know she is, and she had to explain that one to me, but she's already signed up five authors to come along to do talks, sign books and take part in various group readings. We couldn't manage without her and Keith, we really couldn't.'

When I tell him Ivy and Adam's news, he gives an uncharacteristic 'Whoop!' To which I burst out laughing. The once incredibly staid and rather serious Michael is as invested in the team and what we're doing as everyone else. I can't wait to meet his wife for the first time at the wedding party.

'I'm so grateful to you, Michael, and I'm relieved to have identified the problem; it's a lesson learnt, for sure.'

He gives a modest little laugh. 'It's what you pay me to do. I doubt I'll ever have another client like you, one who isn't just in it for the money, if you know what I mean. It's not about getting rich; it's about creating something bigger… something that benefits a wide circle of people.'

'The more, the merrier. If I hadn't started over again at

Renweneth Farm, I wouldn't have crossed paths with Riley. This was meant to be, Michael.'

I truly believe that.

'I popped into The Farmhouse Bakery the other day for cake and coffee, and I sat for a while looking at the paintings. As I was leaving, a guy came in to remove two of them and put up two new ones. I started chatting to him, as I've decided to buy one of the small ones for Wendy's birthday.' He pauses for a moment, and I quickly scribble down her name. On the invite, we simply put Mr and Mrs Thorncroft. 'It just... well, I thought of all those local artists and how wonderful it is that Ivy offered them the use of the wall space for free. Karl said it was doing better business than his own gallery in Polreweek. Now's that community spirit, and it's all because of you, Cappy and your late grandma.'

Suddenly, I feel a tad tearful. 'Oh, Michael. What a lovely thing to say.' In truth, it's the boost I need before I start my real working day.

'Don't worry. If all my clients were as proactive as you, I wouldn't have a single grey hair.'

We both begin to laugh; his hair is almost totally grey and probably has been for the last ten years.

AUGUST

JESS

26

Hopes, Dreams and Expectations

It's Saturday the fifth of August and tomorrow, Riley and I exchange our wedding vows. The last three weeks have been exhausting, both mentally and physically, but we got through it. As I step through the archway of Renweneth Manor into the courtyard, I hear two babies crying and I find myself grinning. Little Eli and Phoebe are a welcome addition and as I glance at The Farmhouse, I can imagine Ivy cooing to them softly, as they both demand their feed at the same time.

Over at the bakery, Cappy is holding the door open for Prudie and she steps over the threshold. I wave to them. They hurry towards me, and Prudie gives me a fierce hug.

'How are you both settling into Smithy's Cottage?' I ask and she smiles at me.

'It's perfect, Jess.'

I glance at Cappy. 'It's like a new start,' he confirms, turning to clasp Prudie's hand in his.

It's good to see them both looking so happy. 'Any… um… news about the boat?' I enquire, tentatively.

Cappy's smile expands. 'We told Ivan straight, either he accepts a deposit, with the balance payable as soon as Charlie's funds come through, or we walk away. We knew he didn't have any other serious interest. Lots of men dream about owning a fishing boat, but few realise their dream.'

'It means a lot to Clem and Charlie that Cappy's able to join them, doesn't it, my love?' Prudie interjects. 'They're not messin' about, and Ivan knew that. Anyway, it's a done deal. Honestly, Jess, you should see the three of them together plannin' their new company.'

'Are you tempted to step on board once *The Silver Wave* is theirs?'

She looks at me and her face falls. 'Absolutely not!' she states, emphatically. 'Besides, we've just had the delivery date for the studio. Four weeks and counting down the days.'

My left hand flies up to my mouth. 'Seriously?'

'Yes. And then I'll really feel a part of the Renweneth community.'

I try not to burst out laughing. She's living in Smithy's Cottage with Cappy; I think it's a given she's one of us now and I'm so happy for them.

'How are Ivy and Adam settlin' into The Farmhouse with the babies? They're so tiny, and so cute, but they certainly have their hands full,' Prudie reflects.

'It's going well, and the babies are gaining weight. Ivy's parents travelled down a couple of days ago to give them a hand with the unpacking. Adam's parents are due to arrive later today. They'll be here for two weeks, as they have a caravan pitch on the campsite. Isn't it wonderful though, hearing those cries? And then it all goes silent, and I imagine Ivy and Adam walking around, each cradling a baby in their arms.'

It's funny how things work out when you least expect it. Adam took a brave stance that day he opened up to me, and the next morning, even though Cappy had hardly had any sleep because of the developments with Ivy, he couldn't get out of The Farmhouse quickly enough. I had no idea that Prudie was about to sign the lease for her new art school later that morning. They already had their eyes on a small cottage close by. In an instant, everything flipped over and the pieces of the jigsaw that is Renweneth Farm began to miraculously fall into place.

The look of disbelief on Adam's and Ivy's faces when I offered them the chance to rent The Farmhouse until they were ready to buy it, was a truly magical moment for me. I don't think it will be too long, given the success of the bakery, before they finally have their foot on the property ladder and their future is assured. Ivy wept with joy, knowing that the bakery was just across the way and her best friend was on call.

'And how are you feelin', Jess? Are the nerves kickin' in on the eve of your weddin' day?' Prudie reaches out to touch my arm. 'If there's anythin' I can do, you only have to say. I'd dearly love to get involved.'

I can see that she means it and I want to make her feel needed, not just for Cappy's sake.

'The flowers are being delivered today and they have to be stored in a cool place. If you and Cappy could sort that out for me, I'd be very grateful. Plus, any help you can give me tomorrow, Prudie, when it comes to setting them out, would be truly appreciated. Both at the village hall and for the party afterwards.' After all, she does have an artist's eye.

'That's not a problem, is it, Prudie? I'll make space in the old brick coal outhouse, next to the shed behind the manor.' I glance at Cappy as he gives Prudie a tender smile.

I can't remember the last time I saw him looking so at ease. I genuinely believe he felt his life was winding down. Being one of a declining club of old guys sitting in *God's waiting room* at his local pub in Stroud didn't help matters. Now he has a new lease of life *and* a companion whose company he enjoys.

Men like Cappy need someone to look after, but they also appreciate having things done for them. Now I have Riley, Cappy has found someone else to focus on and I know that Grandma would approve.

Prudie and I got off to a bad start, but her heart is in the right place. What she's doing isn't simply pursuing her own dream, but creating a legacy that will help and support new artists to keep going. It's the very personification of what we're trying to do here at the farm, and this is the perfect home for her.

On my way to do a walkaround of the market stalls and check everyone is happy, I don't even reach the gate before my phone rings. As I put it to my ear, I'm feeling optimistic.

Today, we have Keith, Len, and a new guy lending a hand, directing traffic to make sure things run smoothly. I hope he fits in, because it won't be long before Cappy will be spending his weekends doing other things. Like setting sail whenever the weather is good or assisting Prudie in her smart new studio.

'Hello?'

'Jess, where are you?' It's Riley and he sounds on edge. He's back at Wind Rush Cottage waiting for his parents and my seamstress, Joyce, and her husband, Frank, to arrive.

'Just heading into the car park to do the rounds. Is Joyce there already? She must have set off early.'

'No. I'm still on my own. I just had a call from Mum and Dad. They dropped by Fiona's place to pick up Ollie, but no one is home. They've had a bit of a phone-around but have drawn a blank. They don't know what to do.' He sounds distraught. 'Oh, hang on a second... I have an incoming call; it's Dad. I'll let you know what's happening.'

Keith spots me and waves to attract my attention.

'Okay,' I reply. 'Stay calm. I love you.'

I hurry across the car park, replacing my frown with a smile. 'Hi, Keith, how's it going?'

'Good. Another great turnout. The florist's van is parked up in Clem's field opposite. Where do you want 'em to take the flowers?'

'Could you let Cappy know? He and Prudie are going to sort that out for me. How's the new guy doing?'

'Great. He's mannin' the overspill car park and doin' a grand job of it.'

'Ah. I just wanted to check everything was okay. Sorry to rush off, but I have lots of last-minute things to do. It never ends.'

'I'm surprised you're so calm. This time tomorrow, you'll be floatin' on air, though, after all the plannin' you've done.'

I give him my brightest smile, wondering why Riley hasn't rung back yet. 'I'm sure I will,' I reply, cheerily. Then I turn and retrace my steps to Renweneth Manor.

I'm about to unlock the door when my phone finally kicks into life again. 'Riley?'

'The next-door neighbour just told Dad that Fiona and Ollie drove off early yesterday evening and they saw her put a suitcase in the back. She never intended to let him come to our wedding, Jess. My parents are so upset; they feel they've let us down, but I told them it's not their fault and they should jump in the car and just get here.'

Suddenly, I feel like I'm in a daze. None of us expected that. 'Oh, Riley...' My words peter out, as what can I say? This weekend was about us as a family of four and without Ollie here, a part of *us* is missing. It was supposed to be the start of our new life and now this will cast a shadow over everything. I try to gulp down the huge lump that has risen in my throat. I know that shedding tears is only going to make things worse but it's hard to suck it up.

'It's mean, Jess. I... didn't... th... think Fiona would sink that low j... just to hurt me.' Riley stumbles over his words, sounding just as choked as I am.

In the background, I hear the loud rap of a door knocker and Lola's high-pitched voice. 'Riley, Riley, tell Mum that Joyce is here! I'll get the door.'

'Does Lola know?' I ask.

'No.'

'I'm on my way, Riley. We'll get through this... somehow.'

The ringing sound in my ear is a good sign; my number isn't in Fiona's contact list and will simply come up as unknown. That's the only thing going in my favour right now, as she seems to be avoiding family contact.

'Hello?'

I close my eyes for the briefest of moments, thinking *this is it*. This is my one chance and I need to speak from the heart.

'Fiona, it's Jess, please don't hang up.'

Seconds tick by. 'How did you get my number?' Her voice is cold.

'From Riley's mum. That day we went to see his parents, they both impressed upon me what a high regard they have for you. The fact that you're a good mother to their grandson and how hard you've fought to give him as normal a life as possible—'

She scoffs. 'It was their son who messed up. Why wouldn't they acknowledge what I've been through? What Riley put both me and his son through?'

No, no, no... this is going in totally the wrong direction. 'Look, Fiona, ruining what should be the happiest day of my life, my family's life, won't get him back. Will it?'

She breathes out noisily and I fear she's going to cut me off.

'Do you really want that on your conscience for the rest of your life? And what if Ollie doesn't forgive you?'

The silence is deafening and I wait, unsure about what will happen next.

'Should I feel guilty at trying to grab at least one last chance to mend the rift before it breaks Ollie's heart?' she replies angrily.

I gasp as her words feels like a physical blow to my chest; it knocks the air out of me. In my head, I remember feeling as desperate as that after Ben left. I thought if he came back, it would all be different and I could convince him to stay. The difference between Fiona and me is that I realised there was no going back. Love either thrives or it withers. Then suddenly, a thought creeps into my head.

'Fiona... is this about Riley and me, or is it about *you*? If there's someone new in your life, you mustn't feel guilty. Maybe it's time to move on.'

'And have Ollie confront me at some point in the future and ask why I didn't try harder to keep his Dad with us?'

Do I answer truthfully, or do I quit before all hope is lost... Where is that inner voice when I need it?

'Fiona, I get it. But what if Ollie doesn't see it that way? What if he blames you for missing out... What if he feels you excluded him from taking part in a family celebration? Split families work best when everyone puts the children first. Don't you think that Riley and I could have just gone off to a registry office well before now to tie the knot? We didn't because—'

'And what if I'm right? Did that even occur to you? What if Riley ends up walking out on you somewhere down the line?'

The lines goes dead. I went too far.

She's wrong and it hurts her to know it, so in retaliation, she wants to hurt me. Sometimes the truth is too painful to hear. Now what do I do? If I tell Riley about this call, he'll know that I killed any chance of Fiona having a last-minute change of mind. It's my fault now, not Fiona's, that Ollie won't be attending our wedding.

I thought I could talk to her, woman to woman, mother to mother. Ex-wife to ex-wife. *Jess*, that annoying inner voice rebukes me, *with the best will in the world, you can't heal everyone whose path you cross.* 'But it's never been quite as important as this,' I reply, my voice reverberating around the cloakroom. 'Our future happiness relied on this and I've not just let Riley down, but Lola and Ollie, too.'

Joyce and Frank are a lovely couple. After numerous trips back and forth to their car, Riley's dining room has become Joyce's temporary sewing area.

Lola can hardly contain herself. 'Did you bring a sash just in case my dress needs a little something extra?' She questions Joyce, who beams back at her.

'Of course, I did! A choice of several, actually. You'll have to be a little patient, though. First things, first.' Joyce takes the two garment bags Frank is holding aloft. 'Thank you, darling. Now, Lola, shall we go upstairs so you can try on your dress? You'll need your shoes, oh and Frank, have you seen that box with the underskirt?'

'It's already on the bed upstairs in the spare room. That's right, isn't it, Riley?'

'Yes. You're sleeping in the room to the front with the en suite, and my parents will be using the room next to the bathroom. Lola will show you the way, Joyce, and I'll pop the kettle on.'

'Ooh…' Frank sighs. 'I could murder a cup of tea!'

I take Frank into the sitting room and then in the guise of helping Riley, head straight for the kitchen. The first thing we do when he sees me is to hug each other.

'I'm so, so sorry that Fiona has done this to you… to us… Riley. I can't even imagine what's going through Ollie's mind.'

'He was so full of it when I spoke to him three nights' ago. He's never worn a waistcoat before, and he was saying it made him feel very grown up. How can she do this to him, let alone us?'

I take over making the drinks, laying up a tray. 'Your parents have left now, haven't they?' I check.

'Yes. They didn't know what to do. Mum was in tears and Dad was frantically reaching out to anyone who might know where they are. Tom and Helen had already left. He offered to turn back, but Dad said there wasn't any point. Fiona could have taken Ollie anywhere and if she doesn't want to be found, it won't be somewhere obvious.'

Our little bubble of happiness has suddenly burst and all we're left with is the sad, deflated remains. 'I wish we could cancel the wedding,' I mutter, tearfully.

If Riley were to find out what I've done, it might change things between us. I know that if he wanted to try again with Fiona, he would have left Renweneth Farm a long time ago, but she can't see that. Nothing is going to wreck what we have because it's me he loves and I must never forget that.

'Neither of us want that, Jess.' His tone is desolate. 'But I don't know how we're going to pick ourselves up from this and continue on as if nothing untoward has happened. I can't even imagine how Lola is going to react.'

I stop what I'm doing and take a deep breath. What is that inner voice telling me? 'If we let Fiona ruin our day, then she will have achieved what she set out to do. Even though it won't be the same, we're going to have to put on a brave face. Leave Lola to me; once I'm feeling calmer, I'll think of something to say. But what about Ollie?'

Riley closes his eyes for the briefest of moments. It's not anger that is welling up inside of him, but a tangle of emotion. 'Maybe Fiona needs him more than us, right now. What he'll make of that in the future, I don't know, but it's her call.'

Disappointment is an awful thing to deal with but, through no fault of our own, that's what we're left with. Maybe that phone call wasn't a mistake after all. Telling the truth is a good thing; how it's received is another. In my heart, I know that Riley will forgive me because I meant well. But is that simply hope on my part, believing that?

The moment Lola walks into the sitting room and stops to do a twirl, my heart begins to pound in my chest, and I burst into tears.

'You... look... totally adorable!' I sniff, swiping my eyes on the sleeve of my top.

'Oh, Lola. You wait until Cappy sees you in that princess dress. You really will be his sparkly girl. Do that twirl again!' Bless Riley, he's pushing his pain to one side and doesn't intend to let anything spoil Lola's excitement.

'Did you notice that my shoes have little heels, Riley?' She's glowing.

Joyce has let her have her moment, but now she's fussing over some little tweaks to the bodice as the neckline doesn't quite lie flat. 'What do you feel about the length, Lola? And is the netting poufy enough?'

Lola does yet another twirl. 'I love it just as it is, Joyce.' She claps her hands together in front of her face, unable to contain herself. 'It doesn't even need a sash, does it?'

I have to agree with her.

'No. It doesn't,' Joyce confirms.

'If I'm careful,' Lola looks at me in all seriousness, 'I'll be able to get up into the tree house. I promise I'll make sure I don't catch the skirt, Mum. What do you think?'

'I think you look beautiful, Lola, and it's going to be a day to have fun swishing around and doing whatever you want to do.'

'Is Riley going to see your dress, Mum?'

I turn to look at him. 'Of course not. It's back luck.'

'Let me just put a couple of pins in, Lola, and then the three of us can head upstairs so your Mum can slip into her wedding dress.'

My wedding dress. Tomorrow is almost here and no one knows what I've done. Or that it's always going to be tinged with sadness, and – for me, bitter regret – for ruining any chance of Fiona having a last-minute crisis of conscience. That's karma teaching me a lesson. How big is my ego, that I really believed baring my soul to Fiona would work? Her pain isn't any less than mine. It's humbling. The only thing I know for sure is that every single day I have with Riley in my life is a blessing.

By the time I drive Lola back to Renweneth Farm, leaving Riley to await the arrival of his parents, and Joyce to do a few tiny adjustments to the dresses, my parents are busy watering the plants in the manor's gardens.

'Here they are, then!' Dad calls out, as Lola runs up to him.

'Pops! I can help you do that!'

I give Dad a quick hug and leave him and Lola to it, heading over to Mum. As I throw my arms around her, despite my smile, she can tell something isn't quite right.

'How did the dress fitting go?' Her eyes eagerly search mine.

'Joyce has done an incredible job; she's a total star. Just a couple of little adjustments and Riley will bring the dresses back to the farm after Phyllis and Eddie arrive.'

Mum frowns. 'I thought they were setting off early?'

I'm too distraught to say anything right now, so instead I turn to look at Lola and Mum's gaze follows mine.

In the background, Dad is busy talking to his granddaughter. 'We're only giving the plants in the shade a little drink for now. We'll do the others later, when the sun goes down, Lola. Can you give me a hand with the deadheading, too?'

'I'm on it, Pops. I know what to do as Mum is always out here doing that. She either pulls up her top, or the bottom of her skirt a little, to gather the bits.'

'Oh.' He laughs at that. 'I think we can find a little bucket, don't you?'

As they saunter off, chattering away, Mum and I head inside. It's time to let go and accept that what will be, will be. It's out of my hands now.

'Cappy let us in,' Mum chatters away, oblivious to the thoughts whirling around inside my head. 'It's looking absolutely fabulous, Jess. You must all be exhausted.'

You can do this, Jess, my inner voice tells me in no uncertain terms, *don't give up now.*

'Come upstairs and take a look at the master bedroom. Riley has done an amazing job of it.'

When Mum spots the armoire, she does a double take. 'Is that the one Cappy bought your grandma for their twenty-fifth wedding anniversary? It looks a little... different. It must be the paint. I love that chalk finish and the slightly distressed look.'

'Ah, but it's not a cupboard anymore,' I reply, tugging ever so slightly on the ornately carved wooden knobs and swinging open the doors.

Mum gasps. 'Oh, Jess, that's stunning.'

The thing with rambling old houses is that you have space to bring a vision to life. Mum saunters over to the slipper bath, running her hand along the roll top as she gazes around.

'What a little sanctuary! Well, it's not *little* by any means but you know what I mean. It's more like being in a spa. All these cupboards and the wooden panelling. It all blends in so nicely. Oh... his and hers sinks. Bliss!'

Mum is in bathroom heaven and the truth is that I am, too. It can't all be for nothing. Too many people have been involved to get us to this stage and they did that because they believed in me and Riley.

'You got there. Your dad and I thought you were being a little overly optimistic, but you and Riley pulled it off.'

I raise my eyebrows to the heavens. 'Yes, with a lot of help. And just when we were starting to relax and get ready to enjoy what promised to be an amazing weekend, Fiona has spoilt everything, Mum.' I can't believe I just said that.

Sometimes a good sob is necessary, and I can't contain my tears of disappointment any longer. Mum simply puts her arms around my shoulders and waits patiently until I'm able to pull myself together.

She grabs a tissue from the shelf and as I compose myself, she gently asks the question. 'Ollie isn't coming?'

Does knowing only half the truth turn it into a lie? I don't have the heart to tell her about my desperate plea to Fiona.

'No. The next-door neighbour said Fiona took him off somewhere in the car late yesterday afternoon. We're both totally devastated, and we haven't even broken the news to Lola, yet. I don't quite know how to broach the subject.'

Mum shakes her head, letting out an anguished sigh. 'Argh. That's unbelievable. I really don't know how anyone could be that... selfish. Poor Ollie. What must he be thinking?'

'It depends on what Fiona has said to him. I know what it's like to be hurting when the man you love, loves someone else.

Maybe she came up with a valid excuse, who knows? I doubt she'll tell him the truth; how can she? Let's face it, he's old enough to argue back and stand his ground. I mean... his dad is getting married, and we've taken pains to make it clear we regard him as a part of our family. Maybe she'll tell him that the wedding has been postponed, or something. That way, she can face the fallout later and he'll go along with whatever she has planned. She thinks she's protecting him, Mum.'

'Really? Well, as a mother, I'm disgusted, Jess. You don't put yourself first, ever. And when it's vengeful, as this is, you don't use your child as a pawn to get back at someone.'

The silence around us just seems to make everything else feel a little worse.

'Come on, Cappy said the flowers are in the old brick building. Let's go and take a peek. He said you haven't seen them yet.'

That's what we do best in times of trouble, isn't it? Push our shoulders back, raise our heads high and soldier on. It's a pretty good ethos to live by, because what choice do we have, anyway? Giving up is not an option. Tomorrow, if that's what life has planned for me, I marry Riley. That inner voice was right: it's not my job to save the world. I hope I've succeeded in giving out enough good karma, to warrant having my dreams come true.

27

And Finally...

Renweneth Village Hall is an old stone-built building that sits on a parcel of land backing onto open moorland. Apparently, it was once a private church belonging to a wealthy landowner whose grand home nearby, parts of which dated back to the thirteenth-century, was destroyed in a fire decades ago. It's a solitary landmark, with only the overgrown ruins of a country house in view as a reminder of the past. It's a pretty building and the isolation lends an air of tranquillity to it.

It's run by independent trustees for the benefit of the local community. Vyvyan told me that when they gained a licence to hold civil ceremonies there, it guaranteed the future upkeep of what has, over the years, become a core meeting place for the community.

'We're running a little late,' Dad informs me, as he extends his hand to help me out of the classic, dark-grey Bentley. It was one of my parents' presents to us. It's a similar car to the one that took Mum to the church on her wedding day.

'I thought that was the custom,' I reply, nervously. My legs are feeling a little wobbly and it isn't because I'm wearing heels. However, I will be glad to slip on some flat shoes once we've back home again. That sounds so good... back home.

Adam strides towards us. 'At last! Riley was getting worried, and he sent me out to see if there was a problem. You look amazing, Jess, totally amazing.'

He simply looks handsome, and tired, as any new dad would be but beneath that, what I see is the happiness at his core. His wife and babies are thriving, and each day brings yet another new experience.

'Thank you, Adam.'

Mum appears in the open archway that shelters a pair of old oak doors, which lead into the village hall. Dad links his arm in mine, and as Mum hurries towards us, we speed up a little.

'I adore that dress on you, Jess. And that floaty shawl around your shoulders... that's a surprise. You look every inch a bride, my darling daughter.'

It's just a cleverly constructed swathe of tulle that matches the lining of the dress. 'Joyce said it added that bridal touch. It simply lifts over my head and sits atop each shoulder; after the service, I'll take it off.'

Mum was at the dress fitting, but Joyce surprised me this morning with this added little touch. The simple floral, knee-length sheath dress with capped sleeves, fits like a glove. The semi-transparent, floral print pattern isn't fussy. The faded, cornflower blues are diffused by an array of clusters of tiny white flowers, which have a silvery sparkle to them. The soft green leaves complete the overall effect; from a couple of inches below the scooped neckline, Joyce lined the fabric with a slightly paler blue, as she did with Lola's dress. She exceeded my expectations and then some.

Adam clears his throat rather circumspectly and Dad gets the hint.

'Right, Jess, are you ready?'

I glance at him and nod my head.

Adam links arms with my mum and with a parting smile, they hurry back inside the village hall. Being a traditionalist, Riley slept in the spare bedroom at the bakery last night, so our paths haven't crossed since yesterday evening. It felt like the longest night of my life without him by my side, after a week of bliss living together at the manor. And now the moment has arrived.

As the doors open, a string quartet – another present from Mum and Dad – begin playing Pachelbel's 'Canon in D'.

As the delicate music reaches our ears, Dad turns to look at me. 'I'm so proud to be escorting you in to stand next to the man you were destined to be with, Jess.'

His words take my breath away because I know he's right.

As we step through into the spacious, open-plan hall, I feel calm. The huge, wooden beams overhead are decked in places with garlands of fresh greenery to augment the floral displays. The team who prepare the hall for the ceremonies has done a fabulous job. Vyvyan's growing links with the organisers, now that Renweneth Farm has joined forces to attract off-season events, means she's been instrumental in turning this into my dream venue. I'm touched by the amount of effort that has been put in to add not just a hint of romance, but a real sense of occasion that you normally only experience in a church.

The floor comprises a mix of small quarried, terracotta and dark-grey tiles; a series of diamond-shaped insets break up the plainness of it. The sun is streaming in through the arched, leadlight windows. In places, the diamond-shaped, hammered glass creates shards of rainbow light like ribbons fluttering in the air; the setting is peaceful and tranquil. Time for reflection, as we head towards the group of family and friends clustered together in the centre of the hall.

Lola rushes forward, catching my free hand as she steers us towards Riley. It's a special moment and Dad disengages his arm from mine, planting a fleeting kiss on my cheek before I turn towards my groom. Riley's eyes start to tear up and when I spot Ollie standing next to Adam, my breath instantly catches in my throat. I can't stop myself; I rush around to give him a hug, a solitary tear rolling down my cheek.

'My goodness, what a handsome young man you look!'

I half-whisper. My voice echoes and everyone smiles, as the background music begins to fade away quite gently.

I have no idea what has happened, but all that matters is that our nearest and dearest are all gathered here today. I give everyone an acknowledging smile and note the double buggy parked in the shade on the far side of the room. Ivy grins at me, putting one thumb up and crossing her fingers with the other. The twins are asleep and peace reigns. She's standing next to Riley's brother Tom and his wife Helen, who both give me a beaming smile.

When I turn back around, Riley slips his hand into mine and squeezes it. The look on his face is one of pure happiness. It seems that miracles do, actually, happen.

The majestic Bentley slowly pulls away from the village hall and I turn to face Riley. 'I nearly fainted with joy and relief when I saw Ollie. How did you manage that?'

Riley, too, seems in shock. 'I got a call from Mum and Dad just before nine this morning. Out of the blue, Fiona dropped him off at Wind Rush Cottage.'

'What did she say?'

'Well, they only spoke very briefly at the door, as Fiona wouldn't go inside. Ollie was all smiles, apparently, and he kissed his mum goodbye as if nothing were awry. Maybe she told him the arrangements had changed and she'd agreed to drive him down, who knows? He doesn't seem to be aware that we were all panicking about him. All Fiona said was that she was going away for a few days and could I take Ollie back home on Friday.'

'Friday!' My jaw drops. 'That's awesome news, Riley.'

I can see he wants to give me a hug, but I'm covered in this frothy profusion of tulle. I slip it up over my head and cuddle into him as he wraps his arm around me.

'Fiona may never forgive and forget, but she loves her son.

And Ollie loves his father. She did the right thing, Riley. It's what a mother does.' And I will always be grateful to her.

The driver slides back the glass partition and calls over his shoulder. 'Are you comfortable in the back, Mr and Mrs Warren?'

'We're absolutely fine, thank you, and what a wonderfully smooth drive.'

'I thought we'd take the scenic route, as you don't want to be the first ones to arrive back at the farm. Just relax and enjoy a little quiet time together.'

What a perfectly lovely thing to say, and so thoughtful. It's true that a little kindness goes a long way and coming from a total stranger, it's touching.

Riley and I are taking our first steps together on a new and exciting journey. Even though the events leading up to today have been fraught, I wouldn't change a thing. The enforced time we've spent apart has only served to make what's happening seem even more special. Having Ollie here, though, is the crowning glory, because if he'd been absent, it would have spoilt our memories of this special occasion. And soon it will be time to party. Life doesn't get any better than this!

Walking through that wonderful old archway into the grounds of Renweneth Manor, we're treated to a huge round of applause and good wishes.

Kate, Wenna, Rose and Erica have been acting as our stand-in hosts while the ceremony took place. They hurry across to give us a hug and extend their congratulations.

I glance around and everyone has a glass in their hands; people are happily standing around in groups chatting and laughing.

'Thank you for doing the meet and greet, ladies, and for getting everything all set up. There's quite a buzz going on.' Riley and I didn't want anyone hanging around waiting, as is the norm for weddings. A dozen photos at the village hall was enough and we've asked our photographer not to do posed shots at the reception, but to simply snap away to capture the ambience without spoiling the fun and relaxed atmosphere.

'Everyone loves the boho country theme,' Wenna informs us. 'And didn't Prudie and your mum do a brilliant job of the floral displays? Wait until you see the buffet table. It all looks so natural, but nature is opulent in its own way. It's simply beautiful.'

Lola and Ollie have already disappeared, making a beeline for Daisy and a small group of children running around the orchard. I think the tree house is going to be very popular today, I muse, as we enter the wedding marquee on the front lawn.

Riley and I stand hand in hand, as we take it all in. The beautiful old glass vases and jugs that Lola and I bought at the wedding fayre are equally spaced along the entire length of the L-shaped table. Stuffed full of pale-blue, mop-head hydrangeas, with clusters of gypsophila and stems of white freesias with their distinctive citrusy fragrance, it all looks stunning against the crisp white cotton table covering. Three waiting staff are laying out the buffet as it's being ferried across from The Farmhouse Bakery kitchen. It's more chic than shabby, but it's not fussy looking.

'We can't thank you ladies enough for what you've done,' Riley comments, sounding a little overwhelmed.

My eyes travel over him. He's every inch the handsome groom, in his open-necked, white linen shirt with the cuffs turned back, the waistcoat with its delicate, brocade, floral pattern, and his navy, slim-fit trousers. The photo of Riley, Cappy, Dad, Eddie, Adam and Ollie is one to treasure, for sure. And Lola standing next to me, holding my simple bouquet as if she were scared she was going to drop it. She gazed up at me, and the moment our eyes locked, the photographer took the snap. The smile on her face was wonderful to see. It was full of unbridled joy and happiness.

'Your shoes are under the table, Jess.' Kate grins at me.

'Oh, thank goodness. Heels are not my thing. I keep sinking

into the grass.' Two seconds later, my feet are very happy indeed. I pick up the wedding shoes, ready to put them away.

'That's better,' Riley remarks, laughing. 'I'm used to peering down at you a little; being eye to eye made me feel like I was in trouble.'

Everyone around us gives a little laugh.

'We're nearly ready to announce the buffet is open. Cappy said he'd do the honours. Do you want me to go and find him?'

'Yes, please. Riley and I are just going to pop into the manor. Tell him not to wait, just go ahead. Everyone is going to be hungry. Little nibbles are fine but it's time for something more filling.'

Riley is still, rather gingerly, carrying my flouncy tulle accessory over his arm and he's as eager as I am to head inside. When we get to the door, he places his hand on my arm to stop me. 'It's tradition for the groom to carry the bride over the threshold,' he states, firmly, holding the bundle of tulle out to me.

In the background, people start clapping as he scoops me up in his arms. I give a wave and there's a chorus of hoots and 'congratulations'. Once inside, it's cool and blissfully quiet when the door swings shut.

'Mr and Mrs Warren are home,' Riley half-whispers, as if to himself.

'We are. And, thanks to so many people, everything has fallen into place rather nicely, hasn't it?'

He gently lowers me to the floor. 'Are you happy with how things have turned out, Mrs Warren?'

I lean into him, shoes in one hand, tulle in the other, and he wraps his arms around me. 'Ecstatic. The party is in full swing, everyone is smiling, and the sky is blue. I didn't want us to be in the spotlight all the time. This is a celebration, a thank you, to everyone who is a part of our lives.'

'I know. I feel the exact same way. But if we don't reappear in a timely fashion, you know what everyone will be thinking.' Riley looks at me suggestively.

'There's plenty of time for that later,' I muse. 'I don't know about you, but I'm starving.'

'Good. Me, too! And then we need to circulate.'

In a sea of familiar faces, Riley and I go our separate ways, stopping to talk to people as we wander around, most of whom have plates in their hands. The buffet has been well received.

I turn, and Riley's parents are suddenly standing next to me. 'Phyllis and Eddie!'

'Congratulations, Jess.' His mum homes in for a hug. 'What a wonderful ceremony it was at Renweneth Village Hall; it brought tears to our eyes to see the two of you standing together, looking so happy. And to have Ollie there, too, allowed us to breathe a huge sigh of relief.'

'I know,' I reply, lowering my voice. 'I could have sobbed my heart out when I saw him! After thirty-minutes of having my make-up applied, I had to be really firm with myself.'

His mum gives a little giggle. 'I did notice.'

'We heard a tap on the door,' his dad takes over. 'And there they were. Fiona didn't make any attempt to explain, she just said that she was going away and asked that Riley take him back on Friday. We're happy to drive down and pick Ollie up to save Riley the trip.'

I give them a grateful smile. 'That's very kind, but I think it will do the two of them good to have a few hours in the car alone together. Neither Riley, nor I, made it known what had happened, so even Lola doesn't know why he arrived at the last minute. I simply told her Ollie's travel plans had changed. I decided that until we knew for sure what was happening, it was best to think positive.'

'Well, it definitely worked. And what a lovely reception, Jess. We've been talking to some of the guys who did work on the manor to get it this far. And people who have stalls in The

Courtyard Hub. Everyone is so engaged with what's going on here. For us, this has been quite an experience.'

'Ask Riley to give you a tour. He's worked tirelessly since the first day he arrived on site. Without him, we wouldn't be where we are today.'

I can see they are both delighted to hear that.

'It's amazing what two people can achieve when they pull together. In our hearts, we felt that one day, he'd find the right person. We just never thought it would be in Cornwall,' Phyllis admits. 'But it's good to see him so happy and relaxed.'

'We wanted the ceremony to be our inner circle, and the reception to be a party for wider family and everyone who has been involved in turning the farm into a thriving community.' I glance around me. 'Have you met Alice and Jory Rowse? They supply the bread to The Farmhouse Bakery. Their son is over in the orchard, playing with Lola and Ollie.'

'No, we haven't spoken to them.'

'Then let me introduce you. They're such a lovely couple.'

I leave them all chatting away quite happily and scan around for Prudie. She and Cappy are on their way back to the marquee with empty plates in their hands. I increase my pace to catch up with them.

'Hey, guys. What do you think of the buffet?'

'Champion,' Cappy instantly replies. 'Ivy and her team have done us proud.'

'I've been looking around for her,' I admit, 'but she's nowhere to be seen.'

'The two of them headed back to The Farmhouse to feed the babies,' Prudie informs me.

'Great. I'll just pop in to see how they're doing. I'll catch up with you both in a bit. If you can keep an eye out for Phyllis and Eddie. I've left them with Alice and Jory for now.'

'Will do.' Cappy gives me a wink as I turn and hurry away.

Instead of using the door knocker, I tap gently on the glass and wait. A couple of minutes pass and I'm about to turn away when the door swings open.

'Jess! Come in, come in.' Adam is juggling a baby in his left arm and a feeding bottle in his right hand. When I step inside, he pushes the door shut with his foot.

'We're upstairs in the nursery.'

In a way, very little has changed inside. Cappy and Riley simply moved the sofas across the way, while Adam and Phil the plumber did the same with the furniture from Smithy's Cottage. Everything in the nursery, which used to be Lola's room, is new.

'Ahh... I don't want to interrupt. I just wanted to pop in to thank you both for your part in making today go so smoothly. You did wonders keeping Riley calm this morning, Adam, despite the last-minute drama – and the buffet is going down a storm, Ivy.'

She's sitting in one of the two nursing chairs, breastfeeding baby Eli.

'Come, sit next to me. I'm sure Adam's arm is aching. Phoebe likes to take her time when it's her turn to get the bottle.'

My eyes light up as I settle myself down into the chair next to Ivy and Adam gently lowers Phoebe into my arms. Oh, it's such a wonderful feeling as this tiny bundle looks up at me and her mouth opens as if to say, *I'm waiting?* It makes me smile to myself as Adam passes me the bottle and seconds later, that cute little mouth is sucking away.

'I'll make some coffee.' Bless him, Adam makes a discreet exit so the two of us can talk.

'The twins were so good during the ceremony,' I exclaim. 'I thought the music might upset them.'

'No, we fed them and then literally headed over to the hall about ten minutes before you arrived. They were both flat-out. It's a guaranteed hour, minimum, of peace and quiet, until the first one stirs and wakes the other one up.'

I knew Ivy would take it in her stride, even though she worried herself to the nth degree reading all those parenting books. The thing is… theory doesn't always reflect real life. Babies tell you what they want and when they want it.

'And how are you settling in?' I ask.

'Oh… Jess. It's beyond our wildest hopes and aspirations. The bakery is just across the way, and we have all this extra space. But how could you possibly let go of your beautiful old pine kitchen table?'

My expression alone should give her the answer. 'Because it belongs here; I know you love it and while you've already made the place yours in other ways, my grandma would be delighted to think of you and your little family sitting around it.'

'My accountant feels quite confident that based on my first nine months' turnover, some of my income could count towards getting the mortgage. Our deposit is ready to go, so fingers crossed, we can get this deal done.' The look she gives me is meaningful. 'This time, it's really happening. You've made our dream come true and, hopefully, it means the same for you and Riley. The manor looks lovely, but it needs to be finished sooner rather than later. And what was with Ollie suddenly appearing just like that?'

I tell Ivy the saga and now she's a mum herself, she can see why I kept hoping it would turn out all right in the end. In the cold light of day, Fiona wouldn't hurt Ollie just to get back at Riley. She realises it's time to move on, for all our sakes.

My walk back through the gardens to find Cappy and Prudie takes longer than expected. How can I not linger to talk to Michael and be introduced to his wife, Wendy? Or spend a few minutes talking to Vyvyan and Keith, who are so excited to be buying Wind Rush Cottage from Riley?

'Cappy!' I wave, as I spot him talking to Lola and Ollie in the orchard. He waves back and indicates that he'll make his way over to me.

I turn and head back out into the courtyard to wait. It's gone six and everything is quiet, although the lights are still on in the bakery. Following a delightful afternoon tea service in the marquee, with dainty sandwiches and the best selection of cupcakes anyone has ever seen. And Ivy, bless her, went that extra mile in designing a magnificent, alternative wedding cake. The enormous sponge cake was hardly visible, hidden by a mountain of glorious summer fruits, glistening with one of her special glazes. And next to it, bowls of clotted Cornish cream because it's good to be both naughty and nice.

Now her team is prepping for this evening's barbecue. Fortunately, we managed to hire a company to come on site and roast a whole hog, which we sourced from a local farm. It's been cooking for hours now, and all Ivy's team have to tackle is a mountain of rolls to be sliced and a variety of cold salad dishes to grace the buffet table.

It's satisfying listening to the general buzz emanating from behind me. Wedding parties are often a bit of a divide. Lots of people are coming together for the first time, and friends can feel as if they're on the outer edge of two different family circles that don't always gel. We don't have that problem in quite the same way, as the moment people get talking, they find the link and realise they're all here because they're a part of the bigger picture. I like that thought.

'Jess!' Cappy walks towards me carrying two champagne flutes in his hands, closely followed by Prudie, who is also carrying a glass.

'I can feel a toast coming on,' I chuckle, as he hands me one of the glasses.

He turns to gaze at Prudie.

'We were just chattin' with your parents and sayin' that everythin' has happened so quickly, that neither of us has had time to let it sink in. You've done a wonderful thing for this community, Jess, and it's widely appreciated.'

Cappy nods his head in agreement but remains silent.

Instinctively, we gravitate towards the space that will, in just a few weeks' time, house The Carne School of Painting.

'When you suggested this, Jess, I was rather taken aback.' Cappy looks a tad embarrassed. 'Now, with the new double gates into the complex already installed, what a difference it makes. The studio is going to sit quite nicely abutting the courtyard and Penti Growan.'

We stare across at what is quite a sizeable footprint and I try to imagine the art studio, with its floor-to-ceiling wall of glass frontage, in situ. Michael was delighted, as Prudie is renting the space from us, but it was her responsibility to raise the funds to buy the rather impressive cedar-clad building. It will arrive on the back of a lorry, ready to assemble.

'This is really goin' to happen.' There's a sense of something akin to disbelief in Prudie's voice as she raises her glass. 'Cappy and Jess... here's to the start of a new era for us all. There are so many talented, but strugglin' artists out there, who will find this a lifeline: a reason to keep goin' even when their passion doesn't earn them enough to cover the cost of the paint and the canvases. What this represents is hope. Rubbin' shoulders with their fellow artists and talkin' to people who are genuinely interested, and inspired, by their work will make all the difference.'

Prudie's words are moving. As we chink, someone calls her name.

'Prudie, can I borrow you for a moment?' Adam strides towards us in earnest. 'There's someone interested in buying one of the paintings in the bakery.'

Prudie's face breaks out into a smile. 'Please excuse me, Cappy and Jess. Business calls!' She hands her glass to Cappy and the glance they exchange is rather touching.

As I watch her hurry away, I let out a happy sigh. 'I'm glad we made it work. You were right, Cappy, it will be good for Renweneth Farm to have the art studio here.' And to know that he isn't going anywhere is an even bigger bonus.

'I'm well aware that you had your heart set on me moving

back into The Farmhouse, Jess, but it wouldn't have worked. Life moves on and there is no going back, because it will never be the same again. And I wouldn't want it to be. The memories I have of living there are dear to me, but I'll be honest, that first time I came to stay at Smithy's Cottage, it felt right.'

'Oh, Cappy, how I wish you'd have shared that with me, back then.'

He looks a little embarrassed, as he tilts his head to one side. 'I didn't know how you would feel about Prudie and me. It wasn't something either of us planned; it just happened. We've got quite a lot in common, but we're also two very different people. At our age, we accept our differences, whether that's in our opinions, or the things we like to do. But knowing we aren't wasting what time we have left is important to us both. And, at night when we close the front door, just knowing someone is there to listen, sympathise, talk through the day is a great comfort. We're good company for each other and it's a blessing.'

'If life has taught me one thing, Cappy, it's to grab whatever happiness you can, when you can.'

His smile is one of acceptance and contentment.

'I think Grandma would be proud of us. She always said that you can only live your life one day at a time, because you never know what tomorrow will bring. We're going to continue making a lot of good memories here, aren't we?'

'We certainly are, Jess.'

'And Riley, Ollie, Lola and I can't wait to have a day out on *The Silver Wave*. We want to be your first paying customers.'

Cappy gives me one of his characteristic winks. 'I think that you, Lola and Ollie will probably spend most of the time dolphin spotting, but we might have a shot at turning Riley into an angler,' he jests. 'But it'll be an unforgettable day, no matter what. You'll get to view Renweneth Farm from the sea. Your grandma and I bought the place after she encouraged me to hire a small boat for the day; we set a steady pace and followed the coastline. When she saw Renweneth Manor, she was totally enthralled. It was love at first sight; she said it called to her.'

I think back to what Grandma said to me after I told her Ben had fallen out of love with me. The words are etched in my mind. She said she wanted Renweneth Farm to be a comfort to Cappy, and to us all. It didn't make any sense at the time, but then no one knew she was ill. But she also said that when the work was done, she wanted Cappy to buy a boat. 'Once a captain, always a captain,' she'd said, with a faraway look in her eyes. Instinctively, she knew that day would come.

Instead of speeches, we have dancing and a catalogue of songs that turn into a bit of an extended karaoke session. Even after darkness descends, the candlelit garden is aglow with lights but eventually, we all begin to wane. It's been a truly wonderful day and our happy, but tired, guests start to make their way back to their accommodation.

After Ollie and Lola are safely tucked up for the night in their rooms, Riley and I end up sitting beneath the apple trees in the orchard to unwind. As tired as we are physically, it's hard to switch off.

'I hear Prudie sold that big painting on the main wall in the café.'

'Yes. Jory bought it for Alice as an anniversary present when he saw how drawn she was to it. The artist is quite popular, so it came with a hefty price tag, but Prudie said he's one to watch and it's a sound investment. I think it was a rather lovely thing for Jory to do.'

Riley smiles to himself.

'What?'

'I bet you have your eye on a painting, too.'

I chuckle softly to myself. 'There's an artist whose work I like; I'm just waiting for him to paint the view from the cliff walk. One day, he will.'

'Did you know that there's a wedding present kitty? Your dad was telling me about it just now.'

'Mum did mention it, although I thought we'd made it clear we weren't expecting presents, as the party was to thank friends and family for the part they played leading up to today.'

Riley pulls a wry face. 'He said that it's topped thirty thousand pounds.'

'What?' I gasp, astounded.

'My parents gave us the same as they gave Tom and Helen. It's quite a chunk of cash apparently, and your parents put in a lump sum too, even though they paid for the hire of the Bentley and the quartet at the village hall. With all the other smaller amounts from family and friends, we're going to have a lot of thank-you notes to write.'

My head is reeling. 'Oh... that was so not necessary.'

'Look, Jess, you can't refuse a gift because it's rude. If people want to give, you simply have to say, "thank you" and get over it. I know you're not about receiving, it's all about giving, but one's wedding day is sort of an exception.'

As some of the candles begin to flutter and then go out, I glance around, grateful that today was everything I'd hoped for and so much more.

'You know when your dad asked what we had planned, and I said that we were taking a break before we start work on the manor again,' I begin.

'Yes...' Riley replies, hesitantly.

'Like everything else, breaks require planning, and we've sort of fallen short there.'

He starts laughing. 'I was thinking the same thing. Postponing the family honeymoon until after New Year is a good idea, as we'll all appreciate a little sunshine by then.'

'We certainly will.'

He nods his head in agreement. 'And in the meantime?'

I tilt my head back a little, gazing into nothingness as I consider my answer. 'Walks along the beach at Penvennan Cove, hiring *The Silver Wave*, of course, for a fun day out. Chillaxing in the grounds of the manor…'

He runs his hand along his chin. 'Is that all?'

'While Ollie's here, we need to pack in as many family moments together as we can. Fun things… like having a midnight picnic in the tree house maybe and building a crazy golf course in the garden. How about buying wet suits and taking a few surfing lessons together?'

His eyes widen. 'Really?'

I nod my head. 'I'm sure Lola and Ollie will come up with their own ideas. After that, what if we get back to work? Lola enjoys getting hands-on and for the last couple of weeks of the school holidays, she and Daisy can have sleepovers. They love playing in the tree house; it's like having their own domain and who knows… Fiona might even let us have Ollie for a long weekend before term starts again.'

Riley reaches out to grab my hand. 'I know where this is going.' He chuckles. 'You're on countdown to Christmas already, aren't you?'

My eyes light up. 'Imagine it, Riley. The biggest Christmas party the farm will have ever seen.'

'Bigger than last year?' he queries.

'Yes, because everyone will be here. Ollie, your parents, your brother and his wife. If the weather is awful, how many people do you think we can comfortably invite along to Renweneth Manor?'

'Fifty… sixty?'

'Just imagine it. Log fires burning in the grates, Christmas carols in the background. The kids playing board games and charades. We'd need everything on the ground floor completed and if the guest bedrooms were, too, that would be a bonus. It's been such a happy, glorious day. One that made us all count our blessings. But more than that, it's validation. Every single moment, all the sweat and tears have culminated into this. One big push and the end is in sight.'

A flashback to earlier this evening, when I scanned around taking in the smiling faces, the bursts of laughter, and the wonderful camaraderie, fills me with elation.

'Love is actually all around, isn't it?' Riley murmurs leaning into me and sounding a little overcome.

'It is, my darling man. My rock. My everything.'

He raises the mug of coffee in his hands, and we chink. 'Here's to an old-fashioned family Christmas. I love you, Mrs Warren. You make me a better man.'

No, Riley, even I can't improve upon perfection. Together, we inspire each other to be the best that we can be. That's how you know you've found the one.

★ ★ ★

About the Author

LINN B. HALTON is a #1 bestselling author of contemporary romantic fiction. In 2013 she won the UK Festival of Romance: Innovation in Romantic Fiction Award.

For Linn, life is all about family, friends, and writing. She is a self-confessed hopeless romantic and an eternal optimist. When Linn is not writing, she spends time in the garden weeding or practising Tai Chi. And she is often found with a paintbrush in her hand indulging her passion for upcycling furniture.

Her novels have been translated into Italian, Czech and Croatian. She also writes as Lucy Coleman.

Acknowledgements

Writing the third and final book in this series gave lucky me yet another excuse to go back to Cornwall in the name of research. It's always good to visit my Cornish friends and to spend a delightful afternoon chatting with the members of the Tregolls Lodge Book Club.

Cornwall has always been an enchanting destination for me, and whenever I visit, I return home feeling renewed and uplifted. The coastline is enchanting but the landscape, too, holds a powerful draw. And how I wish Renweneth Farm really existed, because it's a place I'd love to call home. One day, maybe my husband and I will find our own perfect Cornish retreat...

I would like to give a virtual hug to my inspirational commissioning editor, Martina Arzu – it's a sheer delight working with you.

A special shout out goes to the talented Meg Shepherd, who created the stunning covers for this series. And a heartfelt thank you to the diligent eyes of the copy and line editors who polish the manuscript so expertly – without you, this series wouldn't sparkle.

Grateful thanks also go to my agent, Sara Keane, for her sterling advice, professionalism, and friendship. It means so much to me.

The wider Aria team and Head of Zeus are a truly awesome

group of people, and I can't thank you enough for your amazing support and encouragement.

To my wonderful husband, Lawrence – you truly are my rock!

There are so many family members and long-term friends who understand that my passion to write is all-consuming. They forgive me for the long silences and when we next catch up, it's as if I haven't been absent at all.

Publishing a new book means that there is an even longer list of people to thank for publicising it. The amazing kindness of my lovely author friends, readers and reviewers is truly humbling. You continue to delight, amaze, and astound me with your generosity and support.

Wishing everyone peace, love, and happiness.

Linn x